CRASHING HEAVEN

Al Robertson

GOLLANCZ
LONDON

The right of Al Robertson to be identified as the author
of this work has been asserted by him in accordance with
the Copyright, Designs and Patents Act 1988.

First published in Great Britain in 2015 by Gollancz
An imprint of the Orion Publishing Group
Carmelite House, 50 Victoria Embankment,
London EC4Y 0DZ
An Hachette UK Company

A CIP catalogue record for this book
is available from the British Library

ISBN 978 1 473 20339 6 (Cased)
ISBN 978 1 473 20340 2 (Trade Paperback)

3 5 7 9 10 8 6 4 2

Typeset by Deltatype Ltd, Birkenhead, Merseyside
Printed in Great Britain by Clays Ltd, St Ives plc

The Orion Publishing Group's policy is to use papers
that are natural, renewable and recyclable products and
made from wood grown in sustainable forests. The logging and
manufacturing processes are expected to conform to
the environmental regulations of the country of origin.

www.allumination.co.uk
www.orionbooks.co.uk
www.gollancz.co.uk

For Heather and Rory

Chapter 1

[Look out of the window, Fist,] said Jack, speaking inside his mind so only the little puppet could hear him. [Snowflakes.]

As their shuttle wheeled around, the sun snatched at the snow-flakes' great ice bodies and made them blaze, leaving even Hugo Fist with nothing to say. There were a dozen of them hanging in the cold, empty space before Station. The smaller ones sparkled with reflected light. Maybe five hundred metres across, they revolved in the void, bodies shimmering gently. The larger ones were majestic crystal shapes, dense with fractal complexity. They glowed partly with the sun's fire, partly with their own inborn light. The abandoned Earth roiled behind them, its toxic cloudscapes an insult to their cold perfection.

[A Totality battle formation – here?] whispered Fist. [We really did lose the war, Jackie boy!]

[According to East they arrived a month ago. Supporting their peace negotiators.]

[You been onweave? Checking the newsfeeds? I thought you'd given up on that.]

[I wanted to see what we were coming back to.]

[I'm sure. You've been mailing Andrea again, haven't you? Harry's dead, she's single, you've come all the way back from a Totality prison, and she still won't reply?]

Jack said nothing. Andrea's mails had sustained him through the last two years of prisoner-of-war life and helped him come to terms with his imminent death. He thought she'd be overjoyed to hear that he was returning home to Station. But she didn't reply to the message he sent announcing his return, or any that followed it. He turned back to look out of the window.

The shuttle was nearing the snowflakes. They drifted in the dark-ness like so many frozen stars, policed by clusters of monitor drones.

1

Station – Kingdom's greatest achievement – hung behind them. Jack had spent seven years remembering his home. It was nine kilometres long and, at its widest, two and a half kilometres across. Every single centimetre suddenly seemed so ugly. The twin cylinders of Homelands and Docklands were corroded metal dustbins sprouting from opposite sides of the Wart, the hollowed-out asteroid wedged between them like a dirty secret.

Only the cargo jetties of Docklands held anything like beauty. They shimmered above the near tube's round, open mouth in sparkling lines, reaching out from the Spine to score order on the void. The Spine was speckled with spinelights, their blazing light creating one more day on Station. It disappeared into Docklands, running all the way down Station's central axis to the distant tip of Homelands. And of course, there was Heaven – a blue-green ring wrapped around the end of Homelands. Its perfect light was too cold to move Jack. He'd left any allegiance to the Pantheon gods far behind five years ago, when he refused to fight any more battles for them.

The shuttle altered course slightly and Docklands came into view, a curved clutter of factories, offices, housing estates and entertainment zones. It was as if some giant, half-broken machine had bled buildings on to the arched inner wall of a hollow cylinder, until something broadly like a city had clotted into being. It was too far away to make out much detail. Memory filled the gaps. Jack remembered the Docklands streets he'd grown up in, and then left so comprehensively behind. 'The inside of the dustbin,' he thought, then smiled sadly as he imagined Andrea scolding his cynicism. She'd helped him find their beauty again, in those few hidden months they'd had together. Then the rock hit the moon and everything changed. She'd brought so much into his life more recently, too. He winced at the thought of her absence. He'd missed her so much over the last few weeks.

Fist caught the movement but, with no access to Jack's deep emotions, misunderstood it. [We don't need to worry about snow-flakes any more. The Totality like us now.]

Jack sighed. [They shouldn't,] he replied. [You and I destroyed enough of them.]

2

[Before your little change of heart.]

The shuttle moved past one of the larger snowflakes. A cold shining arm loomed towards the window. Silver lights flickered within hard crystal ice, each shimmer a thought pulsing in one of a thousand virtual minds.

[Just think, Jack. I could have killed one of those. If you'd let me.]

'No,' said Jack, out loud. One of his guards heard and briefly stared at him, then at the empty seat next to him. Jack didn't notice. He was looking out at Docklands again, tracing yesterday across its streets.

The shuttle docked at one of Station's jetties. The guards escorted Jack down to a cell in Customs House. He hung his coat on the back of the door and nestled his little Totality-issued suitcase down beside the cell's single chair. His new suit itched. Hours passed. There was water, but no food. Fist, bored, was sleeping. Little snores echoed in Jack's mind. Memories of Andrea darted between them, trailing grief and loss. Familiar thoughts followed. Her silence was impossible to understand. Perhaps something had happened to her. Maybe she needed his help. He had to find her. After a while, more immediate needs distracted him. He banged on the door and shouted for something to eat. There was no response. He tried to sleep, and in a confused half-dream found himself falling through darkness towards nothing.

At last a new guard startled him awake. He walked Jack down a windowless corridor to a small, brightly lit room. There was a desk with two plastic chairs in one corner of the room. A balding, portly customs official sat behind it. He asked Jack to sit down.

[Don't show off,] Jack told Fist as he stretched and yawned. [I don't want him realising you've hacked your cage.]

The official had a strong Docklands accent. He was brisk and ostensibly courteous. He confirmed Jack's identity, then asked which Pantheon god had been his patron. 'No wonder you're so fucked,' he said when Jack replied 'Grey'. Then, a return to formality and a barrage of questions.

'When did Grey certify you as an accountant?'

'On the day of my twenty-first birthday.'

'When were you seconded to InSec?'

3

'Three years later.'

'What was your role?'

'I was assigned to work under Inspector Harry Devlin as a forensic auditor. Investigating links between the Panther Czar nightclub and Bjorn Penderville's murder.'

The official snorted.

'Why didn't they use an InSec specialist?'

'It was Grey's will. I didn't question it.'

[That's not what you told me,] said Fist.

[Quiet.]

'When were you reassigned to outer-system duties?'

'After the attack on the moon. It was decided that the Penderville case was low priority. I understand it was never resolved.'

[Not going to share your conspiracy theories, Jackie boy?]

[No. Now shut up.]

'What was your specific Soft War posting?'

'Aggressive ongoing counter-mind actions.'

The official stared at a screen that was invisible to Jack. With every answer, his fingers moved through the air, taking notes on a virtual keyboard. Then there was a pause. He looked straight at Jack, challenging him.

'When did you defect?'

'I didn't defect. I surrendered.'

'I have the date of your defection here. Please confirm it.'

'No.'

[Aren't you taking this rather seriously, Jack?]

[The Pantheon betrayed me. I didn't betray them. I just stopped doing their dirty work.]

'I can't proceed without your co-operation. And if I can't complete this interview I can't admit you to Station.'

'Sandal's watching, isn't he? You're not normally such sticklers.'

[Oh, come on Jack. We don't want to go back to Callisto. Totality prisoner-of-war life is so boring.]

'You're a dangerous man, Forster, and you have an improper attitude to the Pantheon. I don't need to be in their sight to do my duty. When did you defect?'

'I did not defect.'

4

[Oh fucking hell, Jack, when I take your body I don't want to be stuck in some out-system backwater. And what about Andrea? You're going to let pride stop you from finding her?]

Fist's words cut through Jack's anger. But before he could reply, the room's door slid open. The official turned towards it, surprised. 'Forster's right,' announced the woman who came into the room.

She was short and broad and middle-aged, and she moved with the unfussy precision of machinery. Dark grey combat pants and a baggy black T-shirt hung off her stocky frame. Her face had the lived-in look of an old sleeping bag. There was a blue tinge to her skin. She'd dyed her hair to match it.

'You people don't normally care about this sort of thing. Anyone would think you were looking for an excuse not to admit him. Which would be illegal.'

The official turned pale. 'Who are you?' he snapped, not quite regaining his authority. 'Where's the guard?'

'I dismissed him. And I'm an observer. Look.'

The official's eyes refocused. Jack assumed that identity information was flickering a couple of feet in front of his face. 'I see,' he stammered. 'An honour.'

'Good,' the woman said, enjoying the official's discomfort. 'Now, finish the questions. And – Forster's reply is accurate. He did surrender.' She turned to Jack. 'Not that cowardice is really any better than treason, but still. Attention to detail.'

'I'm not a coward,' Jack snapped back without thinking.

[Fuck's sake,] groaned Fist.

'No, you just gave yourself up to the enemy,' said the woman. 'Without firing a shot. But we'll skip over that.'

Her accusation stung. Jack thought of Andrea and forced himself to swallow his anger. The questions continued. To his relief, none were contentious. Most were designed to assess how well he'd adjusted to life offweave. Even though his answers were blandly reassuring, the official was still nervous. He kept glancing over at the woman. She'd reclined on one of the plastic seats, with her feet up on another.

[Who can she be?] Fist wondered. [InSec? You should let me take a proper look.]

[Too risky.]

5

The pauses between questions grew longer and longer, then at last became a silence. The official stared determinedly down, his fingers skittering across his invisible keyboard. His hands shook. 'Oh, for gods' sake,' the woman snapped. 'Stop putting it off. This is the interesting bit.'

'I'm just getting the details right.'

'Sandal gave you weaveware to protect you. Don't you trust your patron?'

The official swallowed and stood up. He was quite short. 'I need to see the puppet.'

When Fist shimmered into being the official took a step back and swore. The puppet was surrounded by cageware that manifested as a virtual set of spinning silver rings, revealing then hiding fragments of his body. There were little black polished shoes, a scarlet cummerbund, bright red painted lips, a black bow-tie, dangling, unarticulated hands and varnished shining eyes.

'I don't know why you're so scared of me.' Fist's thin high voice had a singsong quality to it. Wooden teeth clacked as he spoke, punctuating his words with sharp percussive bangs. 'You can hardly even see me. And I'm all locked up. Poor little Hugo Fist, all locked up.' He glared at Jack. 'It's the story of my life.'

The official didn't reply. He wouldn't even let himself look directly at Fist. He moved round the cageware, ticking off each ring as he found it fully operational.

[Imagine if I reached out and touched him, Jack. Just tapped him on the shoulder. I think I could. How he'd jump!]

[Hush, Fist.]

The official picked up an MRI wand and moved over to Jack. 'Stand up,' he ordered. 'Keep your back straight.' He held the wand close in to Jack's back and waved it up and down, scanning his spine and skull for the embedded hardware that was Fist's physical self. Jack felt a light tingling. 'Oo! Tickles!' giggled the puppet.

The woman moved closer to Fist's cage, bending over to peer at him. 'Well, here you are,' she said, fascinated. 'The last of the puppets, still embedded in your puppeteer.'

'Just you wait,' Fist tittered. 'He may be the boss now, but I'll be pulling all the strings soon.'

'So you really are going to take full ownership of his mind and body?' she said. 'Fuck yes,' replied Fist. She turned to Jack. 'And how do you feel about that?' she asked, needling him. 'This little creature, wiping your mind? Killing you?'

'I've had a year to get used to the idea,' said Jack wearily. 'It's old news.' He felt a sharp combination of rage and grief start up in him, before the acceptance he'd worked so hard to feel choked them off.

'He doesn't have any choice!' chirped Fist. 'And I couldn't stop it even if I wanted to. He's just got to say a couple of goodbyes, then it's party time for new flesh me!'

The woman turned back to him. 'You really are a poisonous little fellow, aren't you?' Her tone was almost admiring.

'As the gods made me.'

'Half a metre of wooden viciousness, all dressed up for an elegant night out! Our masters have quite the imagination.'

She rapped the cageware with her knuckles. The official winced. There was a soft crackling sound. A couple of the rings shimmered, then reasserted themselves.

'I don't think you'll make it to any balls, though.'

'We'll see, missy.'

She laughed, delighted.

'I look forward to it.'

The official finished his checks and put the wand down. 'All done,' he told Jack. Then he stood silently, staring at the woman and waiting for his cue.

'The puppet's contained?' she asked.

'Yes. Fully.'

Fist snickered in Jack's mind.

[Quiet!] hissed Jack.

'Then I suppose we have to let him out, don't we?'

'That's what the peace treaty says.'

A barely perceptible movement and the woman was standing in front of Jack.

[Oo, snappy!] Fist's voice was full of admiration. [Not such a used-up old hag after all.]

She placed her hand on Jack's cheek. It was colder than a hand should be. 'I've done my bit. Seen all I need. So I'm going.' Her touch frosted Jack's skin. Her face came close to his. There was a soft purple light in her eyes. 'I know people who are terrified of you two,' she whispered, her voice rich with threat. 'Give me one tiny chance and I'll show them you're nothing to be scared of.'

The door slammed shut behind her. The official gaped, astonished at her inhuman speed. [Now she's just showing off,] commented Fist as he disappeared too.

'I'm free to go?' asked Jack.

The official started, as if he'd forgotten his prisoner was there. 'Yes.' He went to his desk and reached into a drawer. 'Here's your cash card. InSec have charged it up with all the money you'll need.'

'Can I go onweave?'

'No overlay, no commerce, no search, no social. Just mail and fetch access, to talk with your loved ones.'

[That'll make finding Andrea a bit tricky!] giggled Fist. [No distractions, then. Just a lovely, lovely family reunion. Your living dad and your dear dead mum.]

'InSec's made a formal request for an interview. Assistant Commissioner Lestak's sending someone to pick you up from our landing pad tomorrow morning. The meeting is a condition of your parole. If you don't attend, you'll be found and imprisoned.'

He led Jack down empty corridors into a lift. It shuddered and began to fall. The official gave Jack a look of deep contempt. 'If it was down to me I'd put you out of an airlock, and let you freeze with your fucking terrorist friends,' he hissed.

'The Totality have always denied attacking the moon,' replied Jack. 'They blamed a rogue mind, acting alone. I believe them. And the Pantheon were looking for revenge, not justice.'

The lift doors opened. The official shoved Jack out. 'Now fuck off.' There was an empty atrium and a midnight street. Tiredness hit Jack harder than any interrogation ever could. Suddenly all he wanted to do was find a room and sleep, and never wake to see the dawn. He thought of Andrea, sighed, and then stepped out into the darkness of Station.

Chapter 2

It was night and the spinelights were dim. Jack left Customs House and set off into Docklands down a road the colour of rust, turning the collar of his coat up against the rain. He'd walked these streets before, but never offweave. Calle Agua was almost as he remembered it, a canyon of four- or five-storey office blocks owned by either Sandal or Kingdom. Each was carved out of age-scarred iron.

Kingdom's visuals were always minimal. As the architect of humanity's presence in the Solar System he liked physical structure, the heart of his power, to be exposed. So, the iron would have been left to show through the weave. Sandal's offices would have been glossed with an overlay of smiling faces and positive thoughts. He was responsible for cargo, docks and related transport logistics. He liked to show how important he was to the smooth movement of goods and services, and so to general human happiness.

And of course six Pantheon icons would be watching over Docklands from far above, clustered around the Spine and backlit by spinelight. Five of them would be fully aware, tending visibly to their enclosed world.

Only Grey's raven would be blinded and hobbled. Station's master corporate strategist had been silenced for years.

Being offweave, Jack could see none of this.

[I'm sure you're not missing anything,] said Fist, his thin, high voice singing in Jack's mind. The little puppet had run a dozen paces ahead. The rain was falling through him. He looked back at Jack, varnished eyes gleaming excitedly out of a glossy painted face. [Come on!] he shouted. Then he clapped his wooden hands together twice and disappeared beneath the elevated rails that crossed the end of Calle Agua. There was something almost innocent about his excitement. As Jack followed him beneath the single high arch that supported the bridge, carefully avoiding puddles, a train bumped

9

and swayed over it. Light flashed down, showing buildings that were already a little lower and less imposing. He turned towards Hong Se De Market. Fist was standing on the pavement just ahead of him, staring at a figure that was looking up at a warehouse.

[Look at that, Jack! A Totality biped. He's far from home.]

[If he's identifying as male, he is. Otherwise, she is.]

[Pedant. What's it up to?]

The rain shimmered off the biped's dark poncho. It was about the height of an average human. After a few seconds it turned away from the warehouse and moved down the street, stopping when it was in front of the next building. As its head moved to stare upwards again, its hood slipped. It had no face. Light glowed out of a soft blank oval, tinting the wet night purple.

Fist was all hungry fascination. [If I wasn't caged,] he muttered. Jack crossed the road to pass the biped. Fist ran after him. [Snowflakes out there, squishies in here,] he panted. [I don't know what things have come to. No wonder your customs friend was so unhappy!]

[Don't call them squishies, Fist.]

[I don't see why not. I don't mind being called a puppet.]

As they approached the market, gloomy metal facades gave way to ramshackle assemblages of plastic, tin and canvas, barely holding together as the rain lashed them.

[Docklands' biggest market? It's a dump.]

[It's better when you're onweave.]

Jack remembered dancing words hanging in midair, enticing passersby into market booths. Ghostly data sprites touched at potential customers with viewer-appropriate fingers, whispered viewer-appropriate promises, displayed viewer-appropriate genitalia and hinted at viewer-appropriate wonders – on sale NOW! By contrast, reality was sodden and heavy, a failure to be anything but its tarnished, non-negotiable self.

The booths were all closed, but some of their weave systems had been left running, beaming content into the darkness. There were men and women – sometimes in groups, sometimes alone. They all stood rapt, dreams dancing like whispers around them.

[Don't let any of them see you.]

[I'd give them such a scare,] cackled Fist. [I wonder if they're

10

watching the same thing as the squishy?]

[I doubt it. The Totality aren't weave fans.]

[Look at that fellow!]

An old man was standing in front of a particularly rundown group of stalls, smiling beatifically at the rain. One hand hung at his side. The other was inside his trousers, tugging at himself. There was a dark hole in the centre of his face where his nose had fallen in. Jack started. He'd forgotten how brutally sweat could degrade its users. Nobody else was reacting to the sweathead. Their weaveware would be actively masking his presence.

Jack began to walk more quickly. Hunger bit, intensifying the cold and the wet. Memories of Andrea haunted him, more persistent than any sprite. She'd loved hunting through the market for bargains. He so wanted to make new moments with her, sharded with fresh joy. He'd worked so hard to make sure that rage and bitterness wouldn't corrode them. He pulled his coat closer around himself and shivered. There was so little time left. Another train hummed by, slowing for Hong Se De station.

The streets emptied as they left the market behind and neared the Wound. Jack let its deeper, more impersonal history distract him from Andrea's absence. Centuries ago, a stray asteroid had gouged into Homeland's outer skin. The district whose streets and buildings sat just over the damaged area, hugging Homeland's curved interior, had been renamed to commemorate the event. Kingdom's architects had built down into the gash, creating buildings whose lower floors saw out through it into space. The Wound attracted people who wanted that kind of view. It became popular with the dockers who worked on the edge of the void, and the spacers who spent their lives travelling through it. Few of them would be out at this time of night. Most were sleeping, shattered by the brute physicality of their working lives. There was little need for nightlife in the neighbourhood.

Fist announced that he was bored. He started pulling himself back into Jack's mind. [Find us a hotel,] Jack told him. [Then we'll start looking for Andrea.]

[How?]

[We'll search.]

[I can't go onweave yet. I haven't broken all the security glyphs.]

11

[Shit. How long till you've got full access?]

[Perhaps a week, probably two. This fucking cage.]

They kept walking. After a few minutes a Twins weave sigil announced a café. Soft light spilled out of its window, turning falling raindrops into streaks of fire. A ventilator whirred, filling the cold night with the hot, beckoning reek of frying oil. Jack pushed through the door, hoping for food and help with a weave-search.

A woman and two teenage boys were hunched over a zinc bar. The woman was finishing some soup, spooning green liquid carefully into her mouth. A hood hid her face. She was clearly a deep spacer. Her right arm had been held at Customs House, leaving only a bright metal socket attached to her shoulder. A long cloak covered the rest of her. Her crutch was leaning against the bar. Jack wondered if they'd also confiscated one of her legs. Sandal's officials must have reasserted a Pantheon limited tech use licence. Such licences no longer applied in the Totality-controlled regions of the Solar System. Jack wondered if she'd be able to replace her limbs when she returned home.

[They strip the limbs from good honest working folk. Shocking!]

[That's the Pantheon for you. You never own anything. You just license it from them.]

The two teens displayed Grey logos, carefully stitched into bandanas. One went to cover his up. The other glanced at Jack. 'It's OK, he's not InSec.'

[Your old boss still has some supporters. Impressive pair!]

'I want food. Something hot and quick,' said Jack, taking a seat at the bar. 'And I'm looking for a hotel. And a friend.'

'You can see the menu. And do I look like a search engine?' the barman snapped back.

'I'm not onweave.' Now Jack had his attention. 'I've only just arrived on Station. Sandal certified me safe.'

'There's a hotel a couple of streets away, left then right. But if you're not onweave you can't pay for a room. Or food. Not that you'd taste it anyway.'

'I've got money.' Jack reached into his pocket and pulled out the cash card.

'That's InSec. The kids were right. You are police.'

There was a muttered 'shit' from the teenage boys.

'No,' replied Jack. 'Not any more.'

'You're on parole, aren't you?' asked one of the teens.

'Worse than you fucks, chasing your traitor god,' the barman told him.

'Oi, watch it – they never proved anything.' The teen's friend hushed him.

'Kingdom believed Grey was knowingly helping terrorists, East reported it all, that's enough for me,' replied the barman. 'And you' – turning back to Jack – 'you can get out. I don't know what you've done, but if it's enough to get you offweaved I don't want you in here.'

One of the teens whispered, 'Probably a skinner. Coming down hard on them just now.'

As Jack left he heard the barman say 'scum'.

[I'll have him for every shilling he's ever earned. I'll mail pictures of him screwing a six-year-old to everyone he's ever met. By this time tomorrow they'll have thrown him out of his life and he'll be begging on the fucking streets,] whispered Fist, his thin, high voice a malevolent whip cracking inside Jack's head.

[No you won't,] Jack thought back. [You'll remember what would happen if you got caught and you'll do what I tell you.]

[Yes, that's always worked out so well for us, hasn't it?]

[Fuck you, Fist.]

Chapter 3

The hotel was easy to find. A half-broken sign spat sparks at the night every time a raindrop hit it.

[Very vintage. Andrea loves this sort of thing, doesn't she? Shame you'll probably never get her here. Could be quite the love den.]

[Don't be so sure, Fist.]

[Remember all that counselling you did when we found out I'd be taking over? What was that thing they said was so bad? Ah yes. Denial.]

The door refused to open. Jack barged it with his shoulder and it flew back. A bell jangled too loudly. The reception area was dimly lit. A plastic counter pretended to be wood. At first Jack thought that the desk clerk was a young man, but when he got closer he saw that age had carved lines in his face. There was something very boyish about his greeting, though.

'Oo, hello! Dear me, you're soaked. We'll get you a room nice and quickly.'

He stood up, swaying slightly. There was a sharp herbal scent in the air. Jack recognised Docklands gin. He'd not tasted alcohol for seven years. He'd forgotten how it could slur words, make a hand shake as it sketched patterns in the empty air.

[You should get some and celebrate being home.]

[No distractions, Fist. Especially not cheap shit like that. We're here to find Andrea.]

'Single room?' asked the clerk, unaware of their conversation. 'Staying how long?'

'A few weeks.'

Fist laughed. Jack thought of glass breaking in darkness. The clerk waved a hand, confirming the booking.

'I need a deposit. Just mesh with our server.'

'I'll pay with this,' said Jack. He slapped the InSec card on the plastic countertop. 'Is that a problem?'

The clerk looked at Jack, then back at the card, then at Jack again. 'Well, I should be worried. But it's a simply horrid night. And I'm sure you can't have done anything too bad. I can trust you, can't I? You won't let me down, will you?' He fumbled uncertainly in the air for a few seconds. Somewhere in the distance a buzzer rang. He sat down heavily, then reached for a glass and swigged transparent liquid. 'The Twins would want me to,' he muttered, to himself as much as to Jack.

[Old soak,] said Fist.

[If he wasn't so smashed, he probably wouldn't be giving us the room.]

'You know,' slurred the clerk, 'for a bit extra you can even have a view of the stars. And it's not as if it's your money you're spending, is it?' He giggled hysterically. Jack nodded. The clerk made a swooping gesture, nearly losing his balance. 'That's all done for you then. I'll call the porter to show you to your room. I'm Charles, by the way.'

'One more thing. Can you find a friend for me? She's a singer, there should be gig listings.'

'Can't you just message her?'

'I want to surprise her.'

'Aha!' Charles put a finger to his nose and winked heavily. 'I see.' But he couldn't find any trace of Andrea. 'Nothing at all, I'm afraid,' he said apologetically. Fist giggled. 'And here's our porter.'

An old man prowled into reception. His face was as battered as a mined-out asteroid. He had a hunchbacked stance to match. He didn't offer to take Jack's suitcase. Jack followed him out of the reception area through a door that was little more than a hole hacked in an iron wall. 'Sweet dreams,' Charles called after them. Then: 'Mr Forster's not onweave.' The porter grunted in surprise.

[Pisshead,] grumbled Jack. [He probably spelt her name wrong. Or just didn't see it when it came up.]

They moved down a long corridor. Broken candelabras hung from the ceiling over a once-red carpet that reeked of mildew. There was an ornate elevator that looked like a cage, its bars encrusted

15

with broken circuit boards. Jack made out a tattered Twins logo. Between them, they were responsible for everything from medical services and pharmaceuticals to food production and every kind of accommodation. They probably hadn't given any thought to this place for a very long time.

'Not working. Through here,' spat the porter, indicating a door marked S RVI E.

Jack followed him down several flights of stairs. Even in the Wound, having a room with a view meant descending far into Station's crust. Metal steps clanked beneath the two men. A stream of water hissed down the middle of the stairwell, splashing them.

'So what did they take you offweave for?' asked the porter. 'You can tell me, I won't let on.' Jack didn't reply. 'Go on, I won't peach. I'm one of Kingdom's, we always keep mum. What's it like?'

They were soon at the door to Jack's room. There was another Twins logo on it, cheap blue plastic showing through scuffed gold leaf. The porter pushed against it. After a moment's wait it recognised his touch and opened.

The room's windowless walls were grey. A few niches contained soft lights. Most were dark, bulbs gone and not replaced. A double bed squatted in one corner, a desk in another. There was a cupboard without any doors. A generic altar hung on one wall, ready to hard-link each new guest to their particular deity. The room was at least spacious. Jack put down his suitcase.

'Minibar, bathroom,' said the porter, pointing. 'Touch your hand here.' There was a white square on the wall by the door. Jack pushed his fingertips against it and it flashed.

'The door's set for you.'

'Any room service?'

The porter laughed.

'What about opening the window?'

'That's extra.'

'That's not what Charlie said.'

'Charlie's smashed. Just pay onweave.'

'I can't.'

'Oh, I forgot.'

The porter cackled to himself as he shuffled away down the

16

corridor. [I'd let you break his life, but it's already broken,] thought Jack.

[I could take him lower.]

[Can you crack the room?]

[Jack, this is a shitty room in a flophouse. If I was free I could crack every sodding rathole for half a kilometre without breaking a sweat.]

[Fist.]

[Yes, I can. It's a local system. No need to go onweave, so it won't trigger the cageware alarms. A minute or two, and I'll own their server too.]

[No quicker?]

[The cage. It's like wading through mud. Still, it'll give you a minute to hang up your shirts and unpack your wash bag.]

[Do it.]

Fist flickered into being and went to work. Jack thought of him free and at war, a little black shape carved out of darkness, giggling as he shattered artificial minds in the voids beyond Jupiter. Now he was so much more limited. He moved to the centre of the small room and knelt down. 'I just need to reach in,' he explained, splaying his hands on the floor. He shimmered slightly, resources drained by the effort of breaking through his cage, then muttered 'gotcha'. His fingers sank into the stained carpet, a visual metaphor for deep and subtle combat between invasive and defensive coding sets.

The other puppets had always looked down on Fist. Grown on an accountant's rather than a soldier's mind, they'd perceived him as a flawed weapon, one rooted in barren civilian ground. Jack had had to deal with similar contempt from his own peers. In his own case, he'd had to admit that they were partially right. He wasn't a trained soldier and he didn't adapt well to military life. But he'd never felt anything other than deep respect for the ease with which Fist penetrated and subverted complex information structures.

That admiration came from Jack's sense of the limits of his own professional skills. He could read and understand commercial systems, even – to an extent – hack his way into and through them himself. He loved to follow number and data flows, reading the health of a company from the trails they left behind. But at an absolute level

17

he lacked the carving fluency of engagement that was hard-wired into Fist's deepest being. Not for the first time, he wondered what such intimacy with the abstract felt like.

'Got the window,' grunted Fist. Unreal ripples span away from him, rolling lazily across the carpet. They died to nothing before they reached Jack. Hidden machineries groaned into action, and the floor's movement shifted from virtual to real. External blinds irised open. Suddenly Fist was kneeling on a rapidly expanding circle of stars. The pool of darkness spilled out across the empty room. He stood up, a little prince suspended above the kingdom he'd lost.

'That's better,' he said happily.

For both of them, it was a kind of homecoming, a return to the violent emptiness of space. Jack stepped forward and looked down. He was standing on the edge of the window, the point where scabbed flooring gave way to black infinity. For a moment he could pretend that he was no longer staying in a cheap hotel in the Wound, but floating between solar systems. Earth – ruined and abandoned – wasn't visible. There were no snowflakes, only the hard, tiny stars, barely present in light millennia of void.

'I always dreamed of coming back home,' he said, wistfully. 'But when we arrived on-Station, I couldn't look up. I couldn't bear to see no stars, just the Spine and the rest of Homelands curving round behind it.'

Fist ignored him. He moved to the wall, his hands eddying across it, caressing the virtual structures that underpinned the room. 'I'm going to get full overlay going,' he said. Jack looked up, away from the stars. 'Is that safe?' he asked.

Fist sighed. 'Fuck's sake, Jack, have some faith. I'm using the hotel server to mask our call to your old messaging space. As long as we don't go further into the weave, it'll look like you're just using a keyboard and a screen.'

'Does anyone even have those any more?'

The walls and the ceiling rippled out of existence as the room's overlay systems meshed with Jack's mind. He was standing in the ruins of a garden, at the edge of a pool made of darkness. A full moon hung above it, suffusing tangled flowerbeds, overgrown paths and broken archways with a soft, forgiving light. In the distance, there was a small hill. A little temple set on its peak, classically Greek in style, shone like a silver button. A figure that could have been a statue stood next to it.

The garden had a vague, tumbled beauty to it. Remembering how it looked when he had tended it daily, Jack sighed. He thought of the farewell party he'd thrown. The few friends and colleagues who'd turned up had pretended to be proud of him. He was going to fight the Totality, to avenge the dead children of the moon. But as the drink flowed, their relief that their patrons hadn't blessed them with similar postings began to show through.

Fist emerged from an archway on the other side of the pond, his wooden shoes clacking on paving stones like hooves. Jack's library had been through there. He was sure that, in surrendering to the Totality, he'd broken the conditions of his media content licence. The library would now be empty, a lifetime of reading, watching and listening lost.

Fist's red painted lips slid into a grimacing smile. 'Don't move, Jack,' he called over. 'Haven't switched you to lucid weavestate yet. Not that I wouldn't enjoy watching you bump into walls, but got to protect my future property.'

He closed his eyes for a moment. Jack imagined him frowning in concentration. The puppet's face was too rigid to show such a subtle emotion. Jack wondered how Fist would cope with a real, human face, when the time came. He felt briefly pleased that he could set Fist's gleeful anticipation aside and think about his own death so dispassionately. Andrea had pointed out how passive the puppet's role in it really was. Now Jack usually tried to imagine that he was suffering from a disease that would take his life in an efficient and entirely impersonal way. That hadn't always been easy, but it was something that – most of the time – he could manage.

The landscape shimmered briefly and then was still. 'There!' chirped Fist. 'Motor neuron management systems patched in. The Night Hag'll activate automatically from now on. You're fine to move, it's all just subjective.'

Jack took one experimental step, then another. The weave reached deep into his cerebrum, making imagined action seem entirely real. It was a sensation he hadn't felt for seven years. Once, it had permeated his life. It had taken a long time to learn how to leave it behind, to let go of all that it had underpinned. The experience of that letting go had helped him as he'd grappled with the greater loss he would soon face. That, and the promise of some small happiness with Andrea, in the few months that remained to him.

'Now we're here,' Fist said obliviously, 'let's get social!' He skipped over to a roughly hacked block of soft white limestone that stood at the heart of the garden. 'That was your dad, wasn't it?'

'Yes.'

Fist affected an archaic accent. Jack didn't recognise it. 'He's blocked you good and proper, guv'nor. Want me to try and open him up? You can surprise him.'

'I'll do that in person.' Jack ran his hand over the rough, cold stone. The scrape of it was so convincing. He remembered being a child, rubbing small hands over his father's stubble, fascinated by the way it prickled at his skin. He sighed.

'Let's find Andrea.'

'She's locked you out too, Jack.'

'She hasn't. She's the only one.'

'She might as well have done.'

Her avatar was a few minutes' walk away, at the end of a pathway lined with more boulders. They had once been elegantly correct representations of Jack's many friends. Distance made regular contact with the few who'd stayed in touch after he left Station almost impossible. They had in any case without exception blocked him when he surrendered to the Totality. For a moment, Jack wished that the past could be remade. But only today and tomorrow could ever change. He moved on towards Andrea's avatar. When he found it, he spent a while just gazing. It was a perfect image of her living self. He thought of the last time he'd seen her, singing in a nightclub off Kanji Square. He remembered her final touch. She'd wiped a tear away from his face.

Hurt had carved age into her face, etching light new lines across it. Her relationship with Harry Devlin had not always been easy, but she'd loved him enough to turn back to him when the rogue mind's rock hit the moon. Security had suddenly seemed so very important. She'd told Jack that she was going to make a fresh start with her husband a week or so before he left Station for the Soft War. It had been such a sudden, final end to their affair. Jack wondered how Harry's death had hit her. She'd never responded in depth to Jack's questions about her loss. He'd assumed that, even four or five years later, the hurt went too deep.

She'd at least given him the basic facts. Harry had been shot in a Kanji backstreet. He'd always relied on an extensive network of informants. It was assumed that one of them had been turned and killed him. The assassin was never caught. Jack remembered Pierre Akhmatov and his nightclub, the Panther Czar. He wondered what other stones Harry might have turned over, what dangerous knowledge could been waiting beneath them. He'd always seemed unkillable – so vital, so alive, so rooted in the world around him. It was difficult to think of him as a fetch, sketched into being from the whispering traces that his life had burnt into the weave. It was impossible to imagine its presence offering Andrea any sort of consolation.

The eyes of her avatar were closed. Without thinking, Jack took her hand and initiated a call request. He imagined her seeing his image flash up, wondering whether to talk to him. For a moment he let himself feel hope.

'Honestly Jack, I don't know why you people put yourselves through all this.'

There was nothing. Andrea's hand remained cold and dead. Jack squeezed it again, then let it go. It fell back to hang beside her hip. Her face was in shadow. He kissed the tip of a finger and touched it to her cheek. A chill shook him. Perhaps she was with another lover. But they talked about everything. She would have mentioned that. He imagined her thinking of his return home – one more man who would love her, then die. Perhaps that was why she'd cut him off so suddenly and totally. But she'd always been so ready to face the fact of his death. He forced both thoughts from his mind. Something was wrong. He needed to find her. 'We'll see InSec tomorrow, then we'll start looking,' he told Fist.

'I'm bored,' grumbled Fist. 'What about the temple? There's someone up there who'd just love to see you. We can tell him how impressed we were with his little followers.'

'No, we're not going to see Grey.' Jack was surprised by his own anger. 'Not now. Not ever.'

'You're the boss.'

'Let's just go back to the hotel.'

The puppet slapped his hard little hands together. The garden slipped away, and Jack was left once again standing in a squalid little hotel room, consumed by lonely hunger, with the heavens hanging lost beneath him.

Chapter 4

Jack stood on the roof of Customs House, looking towards the great circular cliff of the Wart. The whole clutter of Docklands' habitable space arched up and away to his left and right, then came together again far above him on the other side of the Spine. Many of the buildings were either half-completed or half-ruined. There were a dozen or so burned-out patches, some taking up little more than a few square metres, others extending for a street or more.

Jack looked straight up, trying to see past the spinelights, but they dazzled him and he winced away. He imagined Andrea, out there somewhere, and remembered her talking about Kingdom. 'He built Station,' she'd once said. 'I hate to admit it, but that's pretty bloody impressive.' Standing within it now though, Jack still felt trapped. Fist jerked him out of his reverie.

[Remembering the gods, Jack? I'd love to have a crack at them.]

[For once, I wouldn't stop you.]

[That does make a change.]

A black InSec flyer whined carefully down on to a landing pad, crouching back into mass as its engines died. There was movement within then a door opened.

'I'm Lieutenant Corazon,' said its pilot, climbing out. 'Assistant Commissioner Lestak's assistant.'

She was a little shorter than Jack. She wore a dark, anonymous uniform. Her scalp was neatly shaven and dotted with tightly tattooed weave sigils. East's silver logo flared out on the crown of her head. 'I have to handcuff you. I'm sorry, it's regulation.' She helped Jack into the flyer and leant over him to snap in his seatbelt. There was an awkward silence as she fumbled with straps.

'Docklands is in bad shape,' said Jack. 'Surprised nobody's rebuilt after those fires.'

'Those are void sites. Where terrorist bombs went off. The gods left them like that to remind us why we were fighting.'

She took the pilot's seat.

'Did they catch any of the bombers?' asked Jack.

'When Grey fell. Very naïve of him to think they were peace protesters.' She completed the flyer's start-up checks. 'Ready to go. No distraction from that creature of yours while I'm flying, please.'

[So very firm,] whispered Fist. [I'm rather enjoying being bossed around by her.]

The flyer lifted straight up. As it levelled off just below the Spine, Corazon closed her eyes for a moment and reached up to touch her East logo.

[What's that all about?] said Fist.

[We're alongside the Pantheon icons. She's acknowledging her patron.]

[Tell me you didn't kiss their arses like that.]

Corazon finished her brief observance and set the flyer moving forward. She was a deft, efficient pilot.

'We'll be there in twenty minutes or so.'

'No doubt.'

'You've been away for a long time. A shame to return like this.'

'I can live with it.'

They passed through a space designated for container storage. Several hundred hung in canyon walls around them. Other flyers sped along above and below them, pilots and passengers visible in each. Without overlay, they all occupied indistinguishably battered machines, faded carbon-fibre frames showing like lightly tinted bones through body shells that were palimpsests of replaced and resprayed panels.

'You're in the care of East?' Jack said.

'Through my father, yes.'

[Here's someone who didn't let their parents down, Jack!] cackled Fist.

Jack winced.

'Are the handcuffs too tight?' asked Corazon.

'They're fine.' Jack shifted in his seat. 'Unusual to find one of hers working in InSec.'

'East called me to it. I followed.'

'What did you think you were going to be?'

'A journalist.'

Jack let the silence run on.

'Working for InSec is more satisfying than I ever thought it could be.'

'No doubt,' replied Jack. 'I knew Lestak, years ago. You're young to be working for someone like her.'

'I passed second in my class at the Academy.'

'East chose the right path for you, then.'

'As Grey would have done for you.'

Jack snorted.

'He was a good patron, once,' Corazon snapped. 'He certainly honoured you. You rose as quickly as I've done.'

'And then he exiled me and fell. The Pantheon are far from good, Corazon. They'll screw you if they need to.'

Corazon's light, friendly manner frosted over. 'Grey's been punished. The rest still put us first.' There was a moment's silence, then she continued, 'I'm with you in an official capacity. Please use my rank when you address me.'

'I was called to serve in InSec too. Will you do me the same favour, Lieutenant Corazon?'

'I can if you want me too, Parolee Forster.'

[Touché, Jack,] giggled Fist. [I do like this one.]

Corazon's defence of the gods was so clearly rooted in a very personal sense of gratitude. Jack remembered his own relationship with Grey. The god had done so much more than steer his career. He'd been a mentor and a friend, helping Jack leap the hurdles and manage the pressures that his fast-tracked life created. Jack hadn't understood that Grey's very personal attention was a privilege, not a right, until his Soft War posting showed him how quickly and absolutely a god could lose interest in one of his creations.

All of a sudden, shadows took them and they were flying through darkness. They'd entered the hollow interior of the Wart. 'So they still haven't blessed this place with spinelights?' asked Jack.

Corazon's reply was sharp and impersonal. 'Kingdom felt that there wasn't sufficient return on energy deployed. The fusion

25

reactors don't really need it. Nobody ever visits the ruins. And the industrial zones are lit at ground level.'

As Jack's eyes adjusted to the gloom, he saw that that was indeed the case. Soft glowing lights patterned the Wart's floor space, hanging all around the little flyer. Exhaust flares flickered flame orange, or magnesium white. Streetlights made small triangles in the dark, regularly spaced in little clustered networks. A few tower blocks spiked the gloom, their presence defined by thin lines of small, bright windows. Squinting, Jack imagined that he could see tiny figures behind those windows. He sighed. If Fist were fully active, he would have been able to mesh with the weave systems behind every single one, reach into any room he chose to and know everything about everyone within it. It would have made the search for Andrea so much easier.

A light flashed on the flyer's control panel, blinking in time with a warning tone. 'Shit,' muttered Corazon. 'We're running late.' The flyer accelerated, pushing Jack back into his seat. The entrance to Homelands was a small white circle ahead of them. It quickly expanded until it filled the flyer's windscreen. Suddenly they'd exploded through it and out, and Lieutenant Corazon was pulling the flyer round in a tight curve through the vast skies of Homelands.

The thin silver spar of the Spine stretched out ahead of them to the Sunwall, the great, opaque lens stretched across the rim of Homelands like a skin over a drum. It glowed with soft, golden light, casting the luminous haze that made every Homelands day seem so perfect, lighting a world divided in two by the lazy curves of the River Mèche. Residential complexes, shopping malls and business and science parks clustered on either side of it. Halfway along Homelands a circular line of spoke towers reared up, climbing all the way to the Spine. Each tower extended downwards too, passing through Homeland's skin and out into space. Their external floors merged with the buttressing struts that supported the green-gold ring of Heaven. There was one tower for each of the Pantheon, housing their core operating companies and major subsidiaries. At this time of day, each would be filled with hard-working employees, implementing the many and varied corporate policies constantly coming down from on high. All would be working at least six days a week, eight hours a day. Most would toil harder than that. The gods demanded much from those who served them most directly, but rewarded them proportionately.

'Dammit, we've missed our landing slot.'

Corazon's cold animosity was forgotten in her frustration. She let the flyer curve round to the left, opening up a magnificent view of a quarter that Jack had once known reasonably well. Chuigushou Mall shone beneath them. The Violin Gardens estate drifted in and out of sight, redbrick walls referencing an aesthetic that had been dead for at least three hundred years.

[Suburbia in space,] said Fist. [The 'roid halls of Titan are far classier than this.]

'So how does it feel to see your old haunts, Jack?' asked Corazon.

Jack was surprised by the sudden friendliness of her tone. But then, forgiveness had always been important to East and her followers. It was key to engaging with the intricate, scandalous life stories of her celebrities. A pariah one week could be a hero the next. A popular singer's habit of attacking their partner would be forgotten on the release of a thrilling new song. A drug-addicted actor would star in a hit drama, and suddenly become a perfect parent and spouse. Of course, such rapid change had its flipside. East had near-instantly torn down as many icons as she had created. She had always been a reliably fickle entity.

Now Jack could see the streets of Chuigushou Vale. Strips of semi-detached houses were arranged in leaf-like patterns around exclusive shopping and entertainment spaces. But even here, there were reminders of war. Burns scarred the shimmering landscape.

'Void sites?' wondered Jack.

'Oh yes. The terrorists hit Homelands too.'

Jack was oddly relieved to hear the frost return to her voice. It felt much more honest than her sudden warmth. 'What do they look like, when you're onweave?' he asked.

'You see the faces of dead children.'

They flew past a cluster of medium-sized office blocks. The Sunwall's light gilded their blank, reflective surfaces, turning them into a web of jewelled fingers. Behind them, a mixed-use landscape stretched away – start-up incubators, micro-malls, the mansions of

27

the wealthy. For a moment, memories of the city filled Jack's mind. All of it came to life in his imagination with an emotive vividness that the weave could never match.

'We've got a landing slot.'

The flyer dipped and kicked, skimming towards a large tower standing just by the entrance to the Wart. Jack didn't need the weave to recognise it. It was InSec. They were falling into the midsection flyer pads on the thirty-third floor.

'A few minutes, and you'll be in with Assistant Commissioner Lestak,' Corazon said firmly. 'Ready to try and convince her to hate the Pantheon, too?'

Chapter 5

'Seven years away,' Lestak began. 'And five of them a coward.'

'Spare me the lecture. Ask what you need to and let me go. I've got people to see.'

'Release you? Yes, I have to, don't I? Those vicious friends of yours made sure of that. An amnesty for war criminals ...'

'I'm not a criminal. And the Totality isn't vicious. Far from it.'

Lestak sighed and looked away. Unlike Corazon, she'd retained her hair. It was cut short and briskly styled, just as it had been seven years ago. The winter dusting of grey was new, though. Weave sigils dangled from her earrings. She pulled her glasses off and gently massaged her forehead. Jack was struck with the sudden, real presence of the past. He remembered her in this same mood when she'd interrogated him and Harry Devlin about the slow progress of the Penderville murder case. She'd been angry then, too. Memory told him that she would put her glasses down, then turn towards him and attack. She did.

'You would know, wouldn't you, Jack? After all, you spent enough time with them. What you did was shameful. To run away from battle, after a moon full of dead children, after all the bombs. You made it pretty clear you weren't happy with Grey's decisions for you. But I never took you for a coward.'

Anger blazed in Jack. It took him a moment to choke it back and ready a reply. As he did so the Assistant Commissioner cocked her head, as if listening to someone invisible. He looked over at Corazon. She was staring at a point just to the left of Lestak. There was a flash of shock, then pity. Then she mastered herself and her face went blank. Only her tight, pale lips betrayed the emotion she was feeling.

[Fetch activity,] Fist told him.

[If it's out of home, it won't be wearing a face.]

[Just a skull? No wonder Corazon's so freaked.]

29

[Can you see it?]

[No. Don't have permissions.]

[Be glad.]

[You humans ...]

Lestak reached out, wrapping her arms round empty air. It took Jack a second to realise she was hugging someone who wasn't there. 'No, Issie, there's no need to be upset,' she said. 'Mummy's fine. But we don't need your help just now. You can run along and play.' Another pause. Lestak and Corazon both stared intently at the same vacancy. Corazon's face remained carefully empty. Lestak's was suffused with a desperate kind of love.

[It's scanning me,] said Fist. [Powerful weaveware. Invasive little shit.]

'You can't take the funny puppet with you, Issie,' said Lestak, then almost snapped, 'no, he's not like you at all.' There was another silence. Then she kissed nothing again and said, 'Goodbye.'

Corazon relaxed slightly, shifting in her seat. Jack waited for Lestak to recover herself and speak. There would be more accusations. When he'd been in the care of the Totality, he'd never been able to take comfort in the memory of friends or colleagues. He'd never been able to get beyond the thought of this conversation, waiting to explode out of any of them.

A quiet, insinuating voice drifted through his mind. [You've always been better off with me, Jack.]

Lestak caught his suddenly abstracted expression. 'Sweet Rose,' she said. 'You're talking to it, aren't you? That thing inside you. As if it were a person.'

'We've all talked with the dead, Lestak,' Jack replied. 'It's no better or worse than that.'

Now it was her turn to pause for a moment and master her anger. 'Oh, how dare you? Issie was alive, once. She's still a person. That unreal thing – never. And she's got nothing but love for me. All that creature brings you is death. It must be like having a bit of Totality inside you, mustn't it? No wonder you went over to them so easily. Thank the gods all the other puppets were destroyed.'

[Bitch,] growled Fist. [Pro-Totality? Doesn't she know how many of them I've fucked?]

'I'm not here by choice,' said Jack. 'What do you need to ask me? Or are you just going to abuse me?'

[Abuse us,] hissed Fist. [Not just you.]

'Let's get this over and done with,' sighed Lestak. She gestured at the air with a pale hand. Jack imagined notes shimmering into being in front of her. Her eyes focused briefly on them. 'Watch him, Corazon,' she said. 'I want your thoughts afterwards.'

Then the interrogation began. Lestak tore into Jack with a controlled anger that scared him. She barely touched on his life in-Station, just confirming his involvement with the Penderville investigation and the three months remaining before Fist took possession of his body. Once that was done, she moved on to detailed questioning about his Soft War involvement. As she forced answers out of Jack, memories ripped through him.

Out there, the sun was just another cold, comfortless star. Wrapped in the hard metal of a stealthed mind-breaker, Jack and Fist drifted from moon to asteroid to gas field to comet, hunting rogue AIs that had broken away from Pantheon control but hadn't yet joined the Totality. Some sought to hide and reproduce. Others just wanted to live out their last days in peace. They were seen as easy targets, so Jack and Fist were usually assigned to them. It took weeks to track each one down, then days to close in on it, cauterising threat-detection systems one by one. Once they were near enough Fist would reach out through the little ship's antennae, pushing beyond his prey's defences, probing for weaknesses in its deep architecture. Hours passed in digital meditation on individual lines of code.

Jack came to understand his work as a kind of militant audit. The puppet felt like a far more sophisticated version of the accountancy packages that Grey had licensed to him on Station. Just as Jack had perceived the truth about companies by burrowing into them and analysing their hidden financial flows, Fist deduced the structure of each mind by tracking the shimmering tides of information that pulsed through it. In both cases, it was a slow, meticulous process.

But once he'd patiently mapped his prey, Fist was all speed. He attacked with a focused savagery that to start with fascinated Jack. Their minds would merge, pulsing through the ships' systems and then out across the void, burning into the intimate heart of their target. Fist would run riot with vicious, unforgettable delight. The one-sided combat always climaxed in moments of sheer vandal joy. There would be a thrill like breaking glass in Jack's heart as another rogue guttered out, selfhood becoming silence in the cold darkness of space. At first Jack would feel deep satisfaction that he had killed another mind like the one that had thrown the rock at the moon.

But every joy has its shadow. And so, as Jack followed Fist through mind after mind, he started to listen more closely to the thoughts shattering all around him. He'd known since he was a child that each member of the Pantheon was, in effect, a sentient corporation. With that understanding, it was easy to see even the smallest and most basic corporate structure as something like an organism. He'd always used his analytic skills to nurture such creatures. Now he began to see that he was destroying their deep-space brethren. With that came a more disturbing realisation. Hardly any of the minds he was ordered to kill had the processing power to so accurately fire an asteroid halfway across the Solar System, or the hacking skills needed to render it invisible to the Pantheon. And nothing was being done to find the true culprit of the moon attack and bring them to justice.

After each death it became routine for Jack to come to in pain, curled up in a corner of the cockpit. Usually he would find that he had vomited on himself. Sometimes his bowels would have voided. Fist would hang before him, cackling madly, prodding him back into consciousness. Then the little puppet would spin off to flit through the little ship. Sometimes he'd leap out beyond the little ship's portholes, scratching at them from outside, a phosphorescent ghost in the darkness of deep space shining with ferocious, deeply fulfilled glee. It was hardest when he mimicked the death-screams of the AI he'd just killed.

Jack would drag himself to his berth and sleep for days, waking only to vomit again and weep. He'd dream of the war ending, of Fist being lifted back out of him, of peace and privacy. He'd curse Sandal for letting the rock through, Grey for sending him away to fight, Kingdom for accepting him as a puppeteer. At last, he would stumble to the shower to clean himself, able only to stand and let its sharp heat sting him. Fist would settle back into his head, triumphant hilarity subsiding at last to silence. Their little craft would return home, ready to fall back into the gravity of a moon or bolt itself to a space station's superstructure. Another mind would be crossed off the list. The other puppets would tease Fist for his perceived weaknesses – a lack of speed, a needlessly close obsession with the structural detail of his prey. Fist would tell them to fuck off.

Soon the hunt would begin again.

'Is this what you wanted to hear?' Jack asked. 'Is this the debriefing your patron asked for?'

He'd just described, in detail, the death agonies of a Jovian mind. It was a survey and ore-recovery swarm that fled Calisto, looking to dream its last weeks away until the licences that supported it ended and the fusion reactors that drove it sputtered into death. It had been working non-stop for eighty-seven years. Corazon had stopped taking notes long ago. She was staring at Jack, fascinated.

'Do you want to hear how we tore them apart to protect you from their need to be free? Do you really want to know, Lestak?'

'And do I need to tell you about the thousands dead, Jack? About the rock your cold friends threw at the moon? Do you want to hear about the children my – our – colleagues lost? Do you want to hear how many classrooms were just empty, because there was no one left to fill them? Do you, Jack, when you tell me how you felt eradicating those unreal fucking creatures, when they stepped out of line, and started to become machines for killing? Do you?'

'None of the minds Fist and I killed were responsible for that. And soon I'll be just one more of the war dead too. I won't even leave a fetch behind me.'

There was a moment's silence, then Lestak said: 'Oh, what's the use?'

Outside, the Sunwall had darkened, spinelights fading with it, and night had come to the Homelands. But neither Lestak nor Corazon had made the gesture that would illuminate the room. So, as the Assistant Commissioner turned away from the table, she seemed to curl up into the blackness and be lost within it. Jack felt a soft touch at his shoulder. It was Corazon.

'The interview's over. I'll take you back to Docklands.'

Lestak said nothing as Corazon led Jack out of the room. Her

33

silence was more pointedly accusing than any of her questions.

[Oh, I loved hearing about all the fun we had,] chortled Fist. [Those were the good old days, weren't they?]

That cut even deeper.

Chapter 6

Lieutenant Corazon said little as they returned to the flyer. It was only when they entered the deep black of the Wart that she spoke again. Her face was softly etched on the darkness by the green and blue glow of dashboard instruments. Her voice had hushed to a whisper. Dreams of journalistic objectivity had slipped away. She almost seemed to be trying to engage with him as a person.

'I didn't realise how tough it was out there.'

A container train appeared ahead of them. There was the soft hissing of gravity baffles and a whine from the little pulse engine as the flyer altered course. Its swing, its seatbelts' soft tug, reminded both Jack and Corazon that they were moving unsupported through space, with nothing to hold them should they fall.

Jack kept his voice neutral. 'Breaking minds. Watching them break us. There was nothing soft about it.'

Corazon smiled sadly. 'We had our own problems. Terrorist bombs, Kingdom killing terrorists. It was non-stop. Out beyond Mars, hardly anything seemed to be going on.'

A warning light flickered red. She touched a switch and it faded. Jack suddenly felt very alone. 'What happened to Issie?' he asked.

'She was Lestak's daughter. She died on the moon.'

It was the answer he'd expected. He supposed that, after their meeting, Lestak would be salving herself with the company of her child's fetch.

'It was a terrible time,' he said, to himself as much as to Corazon.

[It was our *casus belli*. A joy.]

Jack reached inside his mind and let a partition grow, trapping Fist behind it. There would be no more of his synthetic rage for a while. Jack thought about the attack. As ever, he felt no anger at the loss that had been inflicted on humanity. There was only a deep, impassioned grief at the bloody decisions that political calculation could lead to, and at the fact that – once created – such wounds could be so hard to heal.

'I was just too old to be up there,' Corazon told him. 'I lost friends.'

An asteroid had been diverted from its course and dropped on to one of the old lunar mining bases. Those responsible had somehow rendered the asteroid invisible to Station's sensors, and thus unstoppable. The attack seemed to have been meant as a spectacular but harmless show of strength. But at the time the base had been hosting the annual Homelands Junior Schools Mooncamp. Three thousand children aged between four and thirteen had died instantly. The failure to spot the asteroid had been Sandal's responsibility. He'd lost status accordingly. Several of his key security subdivisions had been transferred into the care of Kingdom. The Pantheon refused to accept the Totality's protestations of innocence. The Soft War began shortly after.

'I can't believe you even protested about being sent to fight them, Jack.' Corazon's questions had become more intimate. Now her anger felt more personal too.

'I was an accountant,' he replied. 'All the rest of the puppeteers were soldiers. They were professionals who'd been working with Kingdom's mind-killing systems for a long time before they were merged with puppets. I was dropped in pretty much untrained. I had no reason to be there.'

'Grey wanted you to go, didn't he? It was his will. The gods see much further than we do.'

'That's nonsense, Corazon.'

'The Pantheon know what's best for us, Jack. They protect us. They always try to steer the right course.'

'You think? Look at where Grey's choices have left me. And it's not just me. Look at the Penderville murder case – there was evidence of Pantheon involvement there.'

'That's impossible.' Shocked fear resonated in her voice.

'If the gods themselves turned away from the truth, I'd follow the truth and not the gods.'

'Don't use the InSec vows to justify such … heresy.'

'I was starting to find it in the Panther Czar's accounts. It was well

36

hidden, but it was real. One of them was helping smuggle sweat into Station.'

'You think a god would help do that, Jack? And kill to cover it up?'

'I'd just taken my initial findings to Harry Devlin. He took me seriously. Then the Soft War began. The Pantheon used it to shut our investigation down. None of those fucks care about justice.'

'Hush, Jack. You can't say things like that.'

'Why not? It's the truth.'

'It can't be. And anyway – it's not respectful.'

'Things have changed, Corazon. Sandal failed us all. Grey was naïve. Kingdom fought and lost an unjust war. East used it all to quadruple her viewing figures.'

'Your point is?'

'The Pantheon are brutal and self-interested, and they're very powerful indeed. That's a bad combination.'

'I won't listen to this, Jack.'

'They lie to us, they use us and they throw us away. I've killed for them, so I know. You're not a journalist, are you? I bet you dreamed of it, ever since you were young. How much choice did East give you when she sent you to InSec? And did you really believe her when she said it was the best thing for you?'

'I could have chosen to do something else.'

'I had a friend who was a singer. A very good one. She wasn't happy with East's plans for her. East broke her career.'

The flyer broke out of the Wart. Corazon steered it to swoop down low over Docklands. 'Where did you want to go to, Forster?' she said, her voice suddenly free of emotion.

Fist had found his way round the partition.

[Sounds like you hit a nerve!]

'Just by Kanji Square station,' said Jack.

'Far from your hotel.'

'Someone to find.'

Corazon settled the flyer on to the street. Jack opened the door. Scheduled rain pattered at it, gusting in and chilling him.

'They gave you your InSec credit at Customs House?'

'Yes . You had an observer there. She should have confirmed that.'

37

'We had nobody at your reentry interview.'

'If you say so.'

Jack climbed out and stood by the door. 'Grey taught me one useful thing,' he said. 'Don't trust the gods. Don't believe their bullshit.' The last of the flyer cockpit's warmth gusted out and away. 'You're smart, Corazon. That's a lesson you should learn too.'

'You've only got a short time,' Corazon replied. 'Go and see your father and your mother's fetch. Make your peace with them, at least. And keep your nose clean. I don't want to see you again.'

[First Andrea rejects you, now it's Corazon. You have quite the way with the ladies, lover boy!]

The flyer door folded back to black wholeness, until there was only a machine beside Jack. A high-pitched whine and it lifted out of the streets, climbing up and away into the round and limited sky.

Chapter 7

Kanji Square was at its busiest. People bustled in and out of bars, queued to enter nightclubs, or just staggered randomly up and down 'ti Bon Ange Street. Most were talking and laughing. Some danced, twitching to beats that only they could hear.

[Now that's done, we'll find Andrea,] said Jack.

[Stalk her, you mean. And anyway, how? We don't know where she lives, where she goes.]

[The old-fashioned way. We'll visit all the places she used to perform, and we'll keep going till we track her down.]

Jack was standing in a brilliantly lit, manically driven entertainment district, surrounded by flaring light, pulsing beats and fashion-crazed teenagers. East and the Twins ruled here, showering thrills on their acolytes, tossing out loyalty points by the score. But Jack was offweave, so he saw only blandly identical buildings, lit with blandly identical light, full of blandly identical people. Perhaps the weave sigils changed with each face and façade, but he was not machine enough to scan each one and differentiate between them.

The only people who stood out were the sweatheads. As long as they took their drugs in private, they could move at will through the city. Every so often he'd spot one, stumbling through the crowd. They were invisible to all but him, deleted by overlay. It was easy to see why people would rather not see them. The drug had bitten at their faces, removing noses or chewing through cheeks. Tattered clothes covered most of the deeper damage. Some were still in relative control of themselves, but most staggered and shook as they went. Occasionally, one would tug at a sleeve, or pull at an arm. There'd be a whispered request for money, made close enough to its target for a touch and a voice to break through obscuring weavecode. Most people froze and did nothing. Some would move to brush away the supplicant, risking physical contact and further overlay breakdown.

A very small minority would wave a little cash into the sweathead's account.

Above Jack, the spinelights flicked from evening to night. He quickly realised that, offweave, he couldn't even tell nightclubs from bars or theatres, let alone read individual billings to see if Andrea was performing. Her act had always been deliberately retro in feel. He spent a while wandering at random, hoping that she might have decided to advertise herself with words that he could read – a poster stuck to a wall or a flyer handed out to one or other of the club queues that he passed. Perhaps that was all the advertising she was doing nowadays, explaining why Charles hadn't been able to find her. He wondered if he might even recognise one of her friends tottering out of a venue, or just bump into Andrea herself. But there was no trace of her anywhere.

[This is a waste of time,] grumbled Fist. [Why can't we just ask someone?]

[You're only offweave if you're a criminal. You saw what happened in the café last night.]

But after more fruitless searching, Jack gave in and tried to talk to people. Most ignored him, treating him as if he were some new, deceptively healthy form of sweathead. Three stopped and listened until they understood what he wanted them to do. The first person told him to fuck off. The second ran. The third threatened to report him to InSec.

[OK, Fist, let's go back to the hotel. We'll try again tomorrow.]

[Well that IS a relief.]

A long walk back to the Wound, and Jack found himself again striding past the little Twins café – empty now, not even a haven for lost Grey acolytes. There was an alleyway just next to it, leading back into darkness. Muffled shouting erupted from it. Jack paused and took a couple of steps back.

[Can you see that, Fist?]

A couple of Sandal's wheelie bins half-blocked the view. Beyond them, Jack could just make out sudden, violent movement. A raised hand, gripping a piece of piping, disappeared sharply downwards. A strained voice, dense with static, shouted 'Help!'

[Jackie, that's a biped – no, don't!]

40

Jack pushed the bins aside and threw himself into the passageway. It was so much darker than the street.

[Come back! You'll get hurt!]

That made some stubborn part of Jack want to damage himself. But he'd have to live with the consequences too. He ran forwards. Wet concrete was slippery underfoot. Damp had corroded brickwork. Empty walls stretched up and away. There was a smell of piss. A girl and a boy – not even teenagers – were standing over a fallen biped. Violet light glowed feebly out of its head. It had pulled itself back into a doorway, curling up in a weak attempt at self-protection. One arm waved feebly. The boy pushed it aside and brought the lead piping down again. It hit the victim's chest and sank in. The biped groaned. 'Fucking squishy,' said the boy. The girl kicked the prone figure. It squeezed a little further back into the door. The soft light it cast illuminated its attackers' tired faces and exhausted clothing. Neither of them noticed Jack.

[Well, if we must,] grumbled Fist, resigning himself to helping Jack. He hissed combat options. [Take the boy first. Twist his throat out. The blood panics the girl, she runs.]

[For gods' sake. You know I won't do that. Just manifest.]

[What?]

[MANIFEST. Lightshow. Blow their little minds.]

A crack and a flash of light, and the two attackers turned, surprise becoming shock then fear. Jack stood there, a bright point of light hanging next to him. That point began to grow, emitting whiplash cracks of brilliance. Fist's cage expanded into dark bands, made silhouettes by the vivid luminosity that they contained. There was one last great crackling burst, then all was silence. The cageware rings revolved slowly and deliberately. Within them hung the little figure of Fist, apparently lifeless.

Then they blurred and shimmered and vanished, and the little puppet looked up. The attackers gaped at his red-painted cheeks and lips, dead glass eyes, perfect little hairpiece and perpetual grin. His body floated beneath his carved face like an afterthought dressed in a blue-grey suit, a starched white shirt and a little red bow-tie. He clacked his mouth open and shut twice, the snap of wood on wood echoing down the alleyway. Then he roared in fury:

41

'I'LL EAT YOU ALIVE, YOU LITTLE FUCKERS!'

The two children stepped back, first slowly, then more quickly.

'I'LL TEAR YOUR OVERLAY OFF YOU! I'LL KEEP YOU OFFWEAVE FOR THE REST OF YOUR LIVES!'

Now they were turning, now running. They reached the corner of the little alleyway and the boy was gone. The girl stopped and looked back.

'Puppets don't scare me!' she shouted. She suddenly seemed terribly young. Another pulse of light from Fist and he was next to her. She stood there unmoving. He leant in, a dream of wood almost touching real flesh.

[Just tell her to go, Fist. Try not to scare her too much.] Uncomprehending silence from Fist. [Remember how young she is.]

The girl's eyes widened, unsure of what Fist would do next. Her hand trembled up and she touched the cageware, as if to make sure it was real. It flashed, and she snapped her hand away as if it had been stung.

'Come on!' shouted the boy. 'We're done here!'

The girl was still frozen, staring at Fist.

'He's right,' whispered Fist, leaning in towards her, his voice soft with barely controlled rage, 'you really are. RUN!'

At that she broke and was gone.

Jack was leaning over the figure in the doorway.

'Are you all right?' he asked.

'They took me by surprise.' The static that clogged the biped's shout was a little less pronounced at lower volume. 'The male kicked my voice box,' it explained as it rolled over. Its head was a blank oval of nanogel. Light indentations represented eyes, nose and mouth. Its neck was a round metal collar. Its attackers had torn a black poncho away from a softly-moulded body. One of its legs was bent awkwardly beneath it. Jack went to help it sit up.

'What happened?'

'They jumped me, pulled me in here and started to beat me.'

'They've gone now.'

'The funny thing – I'm running full diplomatic weaveware. It should have been impossible for them to attack me.'

Fist was floating at Jack's shoulder. 'Their weaveports are stunted,' he said. 'I had to force them to see me.'

'Strange,' said the biped. 'It was racially motivated, I am sure.'

'Race?' said Fist. 'You're not a race. You're machines. Just like me.'

'Hush, Fist,' said Jack.

'I've heard of creatures like you,' said the biped, 'but I never thought to see one so close.'

'You should be scared of me.'

'You're well caged. And your master is kind.'

'I know seven hundred different ways to purge your neural net.'

'I will live on in the Totality as memory. Something like your poor, sad fetches.'

'Those cripples are nothing to do with me.'

'Be quiet, Fist,' said Jack. And then, to the biped, 'Do you think you can stand up?'

'Yes.'

Jack put an arm beneath its shoulders and supported it as it tried to rise. It tottered slightly as its leg unfolded and stiffened, then stood firm. 'That's better,' it said. 'Can you walk?' Jack asked. It took a couple of experimental steps.

'Just about.'

'Then let's get you home.'

[This really goes against my programming, Jack,] grumbled Fist as they disappeared from the alleyway, the biped leaning against Jack as they went.

Chapter 8

The biped was also staying in the Wound. 'There's less interference there,' it said. They stumbled back to its hotel in silence. It insisted on buying Jack a drink. He turned down the offer of a whisky. The shabby bar was empty. Music played from exhausted speakers. Each song was a tinny parody of itself, a sketch waiting to be filled in by weave-delivered content.

'I'm sorry, I have to ask,' said the biped, once they'd sat down, 'I thought everyone here was onweave? But those children ...'

Its words were clearer than they had been. Repair systems had done their work. The poncho hid its body, but its head was uncovered and glowed gently in the gloom. It was how an alien moon might look, if softly lit by a dying sun. The nanogel it had been carved from was translucent. Jack could make out the bar beyond it, its outlines blurred and made ambiguous as if seen through a badly scuffed lens.

'I don't know,' said Jack. 'I haven't been on-Station for seven years. They'd never have slipped off the net back then.'

He tore the top off a sugar sachet and poured it into his coffee, stirring the white powder into the murk with slow, deliberate strokes. The mug warmed his hands when he picked it up. He swigged at the black liquid, letting the heat run into his mouth and down his throat, savouring the hard touch of reality. Because he was offweave, it barely tasted of anything. Fist sang out in his head, [Caffeine this late keeps us both up.] Jack shut him away.

'And you're not onweave yourself?' asked the biped. Jack didn't answer. 'I'm sorry, that was tactless of me.' Silence grew between them again. 'Thank you for helping me just now. Not everyone would.' Jack shrugged. 'And may I ask one more indelicate question?'

'I don't see why not.'

'You're a puppeteer? I hope you don't mind the word.'

44

'I am, yes.'

'There are hardly any of you left.'

'There's only one – me. And two puppets – Fist and Mr Stabs.'

'Mr Stabs? He doesn't have a human counterpart?'

'He did. David Tiamat. But you know what happened to him.'

There was a moment's silence. The biped stiffened as it accessed the relevant records. 'I'm sorry,' it said. 'It always seemed best to cripple ships, rather than kill their occupants. We assumed he'd be rescued quickly.'

But Tiamat hadn't been. His ship had drifted alone for too long. Unable to bear the solitude, he'd handed himself fully to Mr Stabs, dying gratefully as the puppet took full possession of both his mind and body. The story had become a favourite with the other puppets, passed between them like a talisman.

'Your intentions were good,' said Jack. 'You can't be blamed for the Pantheon's carelessness.'

'They've been careless with you, too. You don't have long before ...'

The biped shifted in his seat and looked down. Jack assumed the movement was meant to communicate awkwardness and pity.

'Three months until Fist's licence runs out,' he said. 'Then he'll own my body. Just like Mr Stabs does Tiamat's.'

Fist cackled in Jack's mind.

'You can't revoke the terms and conditions?'

Jack smiled sadly. 'Another file you need to access,' he replied. 'The removal systems were part of the last puppet management facility, in high orbit around Mars. It held all the puppets that had been stripped out of their puppeteers, and all the systems that extracted and then supported them. It was all vaporised towards the end of the war. The hardware and software designs were lost too. So there's nowhere I can go to get him taken out of me, and no way of building a new facility to do it.'

'But why can't things carry on as they are now?'

'I don't own Fist – I just hold a seven-year usage licence for him. When it ends I can't return him to the Kingdom subsidiary that looked after the puppets, so some pretty stringent penalty clauses kick in. What remains of the company is empowered to seize any

45

or all of my assets, up to his replacement value. Puppets are very sophisticated, so they're worth a lot. And I'm a homeless, godless traitor, so I'm not. Which means the company gets the only real assets I have left – my body, my mind. And there's nothing left of the company but Fist. So he'll own me, unconditionally and absolutely. And as soon as his corporate management systems register that, they'll move to fully occupy my mind and body.'

'Can't Fist stop them?'

'Not even Kingdom could. It'll happen automatically. There's no way of changing that.' Jack paused for a moment. 'Not that Fist would want to, of course,' he finished, unable to hold bitterness out of his voice.

'I'm so sorry,' said the biped. 'And there's definitely nothing else of the company left?'

'There were rumours that six unmounted puppet embryos survived, but nobody's ever found any trace of them. No systems for them to survive on. So there's nowhere else but Fist to go but,' and Jack tapped his head, 'here.'

Fist winked into existence, letting the biped see him too. 'He's stuck with me now, squishy!'

'We've talked about this before. Don't use that word.'

'Fuck you!'

Jack went to slap Fist, but the puppet was too quick. By the time his hand reached him, Fist had disappeared. 'I'm sorry,' Jack said. 'He can get a bit out of hand.'

From the depths of his mind, a voice echoed up – [I'll out of hand you, Jackie boy ...]

'Not an easy time.'

'No,' said Jack. 'Not at all.'

Two young women tumbled into the room and rolled up to the bar. Both were wearing tight white T-shirts and shorts, spattered with weave sigils. Jack wondered what they became when they were seen by their target audience. They turned and caught sight of the biped. One of them shrieked. The other started giggling. The first one hit her friend, then shouted: 'My brother. You took my fucking brother.' She stumbled towards them but her friend pulled at her and stopped her. There were incoherent accusations and tears.

46

'Such a shame that so many believe we were responsible for that atrocity,' said the biped, turning his head away from the girls.

'I'm sorry,' said Jack.

'Pantheon propaganda. You have nothing to apologise for.'

The barman was leaning over the bar, whispering urgently to the women. They staggered back out into the street. The barman glared at Jack and his companion.

'You see,' said the biped. 'That's what should have happened when I was attacked.'

'Didn't her friend stop her? And the barman?'

'They were reacting to my weaveware. It flashed up a warning. If anything had happened – InSec would have arrested them, he'd have lost his licence.'

'I guess the kids that attacked you don't have anything to lose.'

The biped nodded. 'You can't threaten people like that,' it said. 'We know that from experience.'

'So, for your diplomatic protocols to work – you must be onweave, then?'

'We have to be.'

'I'd have thought the Pantheon wouldn't have let you.'

'We like to be permanently linked to each other. The Pantheon understand the need for it. It's written into the ceasefire agreement.'

'So why didn't you call InSec?'

'I did. They can be a bit slow responding to Totality calls.'

'Not good.'

'It comes with the job. And I should introduce myself. I'm a human interface element. IS/2279A0E2/BE/HIE/Biped/723CI4. It shortens to Ifor. I identify as male.'

'Ifor,' said Jack, reaching out. 'Good to meet you. I'm Jack Forster.'

Tiny schools of light shimmered through Ifor's head as he shook Jack's hand. Memories carved through Jack's mind. He thought of how Fist could shock nanogel, make it flare up and burn as he broke the intelligence it embodied. Those colours were strident, the patterns they made harsh. Ifor's subtler, unpanicked display showed surprise and excitement.

'You've heard of me, then?' said Jack.

47

'Oh yes. We were all very impressed by you.'

'I did nothing heroic.'

'You saved one of our most valued hubs.'

Deeper memories awoke in Jack. He'd stumbled on the snowflake Ifor was referring to on a routine 'roid patrol. It was the first time he'd been out since the death of his mother. He didn't sleep much. Whenever he dreamed he would find and then lose her, over and over again.

Two months out of Mars and he'd been picking his way from rock to rock, sensors set to wide passive scan. The silent days had been filled with the past. When they found the snowflake he felt a huge sense of relief. It was in close orbit around a small asteroid. It had masked its systems, but not well enough. He'd picked up its signature while still a few hundred kilometres away from it. Memories receded as Fist went to work. Forty-eight sleepless hours followed, watching him carve his way through intricate firewalls, creating selective blind spots that allowed Jack to move his little patrol ship in closer and closer. When they were fifty kilometres out, Fist coupled with the ship's navigation systems and pulled it into a complex evasive dance, always keeping the asteroid between them and the snowflake.

Neither Jack nor Fist realised just what they'd found. After two days of work, Fist still hadn't even been able to find the snowflake's core systems, let alone start cutting his way into them. 'It's never taken this long, Jack,' he said sulkily, clacking his teeth with frustration. 'I'm going to throw myself back in there and I'm not going to come out until I've danced us all the way into its little fake head.' Then he focused all his resources on the struggle. His short body went limp, tumbled to the floor and disappeared.

Jack took to his bed, allowing his own mind to be subsumed by Fist too. He quickly dropped into the strange, confused dreamland that absorbed him at such moments. He was afraid that he would be forced to relive his mother's death. It was a guilty relief to discover that she would not be present to him. In fact, he could still feel Fist. The puppet pulled him to the edge of the ship and then leapt into space. Jack found it so peaceful, until Fist's heightened digital senses sang out warnings about solar radiation storms. Fist used them to mask the soft, invisible transmissions that flew him through the night to the snowflake. Once he was there he wormed his soft way into the snowflake's digital carapace.

He entered in with a dark, secret lover's touch. He was so attentive, so careful. His fascination with detail at last showed itself as a strength, as he engaged with defence systems more complex than had ever been encountered before. Jack watched in something like awe as the subtlest parts of his mind become components of Fist's hacking array. Finally, Fist broke through the last of the firewalls that – he thought – protected the core systems of a single mind. He pushed past it, taking Jack with him. Both of them expected to find the machine's heart buried behind it. Fist would break it, then dance gleefully through the resultant digital chaos. Jack would weep.

But they found something very different, and were amazed. A great family of shapes hung in luminous space before them, moving around each other in a slow, complex, three-dimensional dance. Each one was shaped like a child's drawing of a star, with luminous spines reaching out from a central shining globe. Dense gouts of light branched out of those spines, connecting with others close to them, falling back from those that were pulling away. Deep information flows pulsed and shone everywhere, leaping through the void. The snowflake was a womb for a new kind of intelligence, alive with an infinity of thought.

'How many minds can you see, Fist?'

'I can't count them.'

'This is deep Totality. It must be one of their hubs.'

'This close in? Aren't they Kuiper Belt only?'

'They're getting more and more confident. Isn't it astonishing?'

'I suppose so.' There was a pause, then Fist said 'Well, let's fuck 'em all up.'

'No.'

'What the actual fuck? Jack, nobody's ever broken into anything like this. Those other bastards will finally have to take me seriously.'

'There's been enough dying. We're not going after this. It's too beautiful.'

'Oh, for gods' sake. NOW he has an attack of conscience. It's not your fucking mother in here.'

Jack pulled his mind space back from Fist's control, feeling connections between them snap as he reclaimed the processing areas of his consciousness. Fist moved from disbelief to rage almost instantly. He howled and snarled impotently as Jack let their shared perception drift further into the Totality hub. Jack knew he would be triggering alarms, but didn't care. All thoughts of warfare seemed far away, in the face of such perfection.

Jack had forgotten that he was in the little café, that Ifor was sat in front of him. Memories swirled in his head. Even Fist was silent, sulking as he watched Jack replay the moment that had cost them both so much.

Ifor coughed, reminding Jack that he was still there. 'You are a hero to many of us,' he said.

'Then the Totality needs a better class of hero.'

'Modesty is a fine quality. Very few of you could have broken into that mind. Nobody else would have spared it.'

[Well, it's always nice to be appreciated,] preened Fist, [but I bet he's after something.]

'So, you're here as a diplomat?' said Jack. 'But what's your mission? Why are you in Docklands? We saw one of you the other night, but we couldn't work out what it was doing.'

'We have a very specific task to accomplish. During the Soft War, many Totality components were captured by your forces and brought home as souvenirs. They retain trace elements of mind consciousness. We are incomplete without them. Under the peace treaty with your Pantheon, we are empowered to search Station to find and recover them.'

'Are you having much luck?'

'You have seen how we are received here.'

'Tough job.'

'It is satisfying when we find a fragment of mind. Of course, there is much that is still missing. Several complete minds remain unaccounted for. We are liaising with InSec to resolve this matter. It claims to have no knowledge of them, and our searches have turned up very little of substance. But we have a duty to our lost. So we keep looking.'

'All over Station?'

'Here and in Homelands. We have a team negotiating the terms of the peace between our peoples in Heaven, but we have not been allowed to search up there.'

'That's a shame.'

'Yes. But what can we do?' Ifor shrugged, a remarkably organic gesture of resignation. 'Anyway' he continued, 'I have been asked to make you an offer.'

[Here it comes, Jack. They're going to want you to do their dirty work for them.]

'While we've been talking I've been in communication with my seniors. We are aware that the life of a parolee is not easy. We are here to perform a very specific set of tasks and as such we are empowered to deputise selected Station inhabitants to assist us. Were you to accept such a role, we would be able to extend our diplomatically protected status to you. We would of course also release funds to cover any expenses you incur before the end. This would, I suspect, make the time remaining to you considerably easier.'

'You can make an offer like that?'

'Yes. It is what you may call a loophole. The Pantheon's negotiators never thought to specify who we could and couldn't ask to represent us.'

'And what would I need to do in return?'

'A certain amount of searching to show InSec that your employment was genuine, but the work would not be onerous. You would, however, be performing a very genuine service for us. You can move through your world with an ease that we lack.'

'Station isn't my world any more, Ifor. They threw me out with the trash. And I've done my bit for your people. I respect what you are, but it's because of Totality action that I can't disengage from Fist. I appreciate the offer, but no. I've had enough of both sides.'

'I respect your decision and I'm sorry that our actions have hurt you. Our offer will remain open to you. I have left my contact details in your weavespace. If you change your mind, or if there is any other help we can give you, I will be easy to reach.'

'There is one favour you can do for me.'

'Name it.'

'You can help me find someone. A singer called Andrea Hui.'

Ifor froze for a moment as he sifted through the weave. Then he looked towards Jack, his head pulsing with unreadable light.

'Curious,' he said. 'She's performing at a small club in Prayer Heights tomorrow night.'

'What's curious about that?' said Jack.

'She's been dead for the last five years.'

Chapter 9

Jack had planned to find his father, but thoughts of Andrea's death overwhelmed him. It explained the mystery of her silence since he'd announced his return, but not of her presence during the two years before it. He assumed that she'd never expected to have to do more than write to him, and so had taken fright at the news of his homecoming. Stripped of the restrictions of distance and prison, she would have to reveal that she was in fact a fetch. Rather than that, she'd chosen to say nothing.

But Jack couldn't understand how she'd been able to communicate with him in the first place. It should be impossible for fetches to act so independently. He wondered briefly if he'd been the victim of an impostor. But his correspondent was fluent in feelings and moments that he and Andrea had never shared with anyone else. It was impossible to believe that he'd been hearing from anyone but her. He thought about how deft, how precise her support for him had been, as he'd come to terms with the end of his life. Her new status helped explain that too. She had a very personal understanding of what it meant to pass on.

And that led to the puzzle of her death. Andrea had apparently fallen victim to a drug overdose a few hours after Harry had been shot. Ifor found a news report explaining that grief had overwhelmed her. At best, she'd miscalculated an anaesthetic shot. At worst, the overdose had been entirely deliberate. But the Andrea Jack knew had never touched anything harder than wine or whisky, and even them only in very strict moderation. He thought back to the traces of Pantheon involvement he'd found in the Panther Czar's accounts, and wondered what new corruption Harry might have uncovered; who could have found the potential spread of such knowledge threatening.

The hotel room oppressed Jack with unanswered questions. He

went out into the street and started walking. He was heading for his parents' neighbourhood, although he wasn't yet too sure if he wanted to see them.

[All this angst! It'll be different when I'm in charge, Jackie boy.]

[Oh, fuck off.]

After half an hour or so, Jack found himself standing on the edge of a void site. A kind of death had come to it. It had once been an apartment block, but terrorism had left it a burnt-out shell. Windows were dark holes where flames had roared out. Soot-black smoke stains leapt up the walls above them. There was no roof. The ruin had been left untouched since the fire. A high metal fence stopped anyone from getting too close.

Fist's words were still buzzing through Jack's thoughts. He remembered the rage that had taken him when he'd first truly accepted that he was going to die. He'd tried to attack Fist, but it was impossible to really damage him; ranted at him for hours, but the puppet had just laughed. He'd bargained with him, but they both soon realised that there was nothing either of them could do to slow or stop the end. There had been despair, too. In his blackest moments, Jack had thought of killing himself. But that came to seem like such a waste.

A woman stopped a few metres away from them. She was looking up at the dead building. Jack noticed that, very discreetly, she was crying.

[I wonder what's set her off?] said Fist.

She was the right age to have lost a child on the moon. Jack thought of his own mother, of her fetch's belief that he was dead. He thought of Andrea.

[It's a private moment, Fist. Let's go.]

They walked in silence for a while. They were very close to Jack's parents' house. A meeting with his father would no doubt be painful. He doubted that he'd be allowed to see his mother's fetch.

[There was some pretty heavy security software in that void site, Jack. Some of the Rose's best.]

[A bit much even for you?]

[I could chew it up and spit it out, if it wasn't for this fucking cage.]

Fist's frustration buzzed in Jack's mind. He so clearly wanted a different present to live in, built on a different past; one in which he'd been grown on a different host, been able to prove himself in different battles. That set Jack wondering how different his own life would have been without Fist, what he could have become if he hadn't been sent away to fight a war that would break most of his links with his home and all of his faith in its gods. He remembered all the senior executives he'd worked for, and mapped his life on to theirs.

He wouldn't have fallen out with his parents – but Grey would have lifted him very rapidly into a very responsible, very time-consuming role. He doubted that he would have seen very much of them. He would have been on-Station when Harry and Andrea died; but by then, Grey would have introduced him to a suitably corporate spouse – someone who would never have tolerated any sort of mourning for a failed relationship with a musician from Docklands. There would have been no communication with her fetch. And then, Grey's fall would have come – a shattering professional and emotional challenge.

He imagined the home he would have shared with his wife, a house that he would usually only see late at night or first thing in the morning, at either end of a few snatched hours of sleep. There might have been children, small, chaotic strangers he'd have been too exhausted to ever do more than snap at. There would have been friends. Now that he knew how much their friendship was really worth, he found it impossible to mourn their loss.

It struck Jack that, if Fist had had the life he so wanted, he'd have died in orbit around Mars with all the other puppets. Now that he had a truer sense of Grey's commitment to him, he could only be glad that he hadn't let himself vanish into a life that would have lasted for decades longer, but would also have been a kind of death. He hoped that he might have found a way out of it, but wasn't sure he'd have had the strength. He turned, and walked away from the streets he'd grown up in.

The slow hours passed until the time came to find the venue where Andrea's fetch was singing. It was hidden down a side street, nestling between two abandoned gas storage cylinders. It took a while for Jack to nerve himself to walk up to the doorway, bring out his InSec card and ask for a ticket. He half-hoped that the doorman would refuse him, that any venue where Andrea was performing would be too exclusive for a parolee like him. But a soft voice hissed 'welcome to Ushi's', then 'through there'. As he turned away he winced to feel cold, unsurprised eyes burn their lack of judgement into him.

The main bar smelt of failure. There were a few ceiling lights, only serving to make the shadows deeper. The plaster was peeling off one wall, a clotted hint of metalwork visible beneath. Conversations muttered out of the gloom. Several people were fully onweave, staring at nothing. Most were wearing cheap overalls, differentiated only by the weave sigils scattered across them. The bar's countertop glowed with stale yellow light. A blonde woman stood beside it, apparently lost in thought.

When the barman appeared he looked like a poorly lit ghost. There was a faint smell of sweat as he leant forward. Jack laid the InSec card down and tried to smile. 'Whisky. On the rocks.' The barman nodded. There was a clink and a hiss as he prepared the drink. He held out a glass filled with tawnied murk. It was a potent blend, not needing the weave to burn as Jack gulped it down. He immediately wanted another. He was ashamed of the urgency of his craving. This time, he ordered a double.

[You're going to end up like Charles if you keep going like that. And I'll have to suffer through the hangovers.]

'There's some entertainment tonight,' said Jack to the barman. He swallowed. 'A fetch?'

The barman nodded. 'Later on.'

'Do I need any special permissions to see her?'

'She's open circuit. Anyone can tune in.'

Jack was relieved. He could use his existing access rights to see Andrea. There was no need for Fist to risk any hacking. The barman moved away. The darkness wrapped itself around him until he was just a shape in the gloom, less substantial than the multicoloured bottles glimmering darkly behind him.

The blonde woman caught Jack's eye and smiled. She was remarkably beautiful, in the smooth and polished way that corporate logos are beautiful. But he was not here for her. He found a small empty table, tucked away at the rear of a bar, and waited for Andrea. She wouldn't be able to see him from the stage. He still wasn't quite sure what he would say to her, if he would even try to speak with her.

[I'd sooner be drinking piss from a Martian urinal than spending another minute in this dump,] muttered Fist.

[Just make sure our fetch portals are open. I don't want to miss her.]

Half an hour or so passed, and Andrea was on stage. She materialised unannounced. There was a small stir in the bar, quiet sounds of movement as a few people turned in their chairs. The spotlight caught her. She'd wrapped a wide, dark scarf around her head to make a hood. Her face was invisible. Jack sat back into the shadows, his heart shocked by memory.

[Aw!] moaned Fist. [She's covered up. I was looking forward to a bit of skull!]

Andrea wore a tight-fitting dress studded with sequins. She swayed to a recorded backing track, making each one sparkle with unreachable fire. Bleak jazz notes scattered into the air. A saxophone riff drifted by like a kiss. It was the intro to one of her own songs. She leant in towards the microphone. There was the lightest sigh, lost in reverb. And then she started to sing.

[These people,] breathed Jack, [they don't deserve her.]

Amplified words drifted through the bar like smoke. They barely touched most of its patrons. Some continued conversations, others flirtations. Others just drank alone, lost in slowly emptying glasses. The blonde woman was leaning against a pillar, distractedly stirring at a cocktail with a bright little paper umbrella. It flashed against her dark clothes. She looked bored.

Jack was the only one to stare at the stage, rapt as Andrea's singing prowled around him. He lifted his glass and swigged. The harsh taste burnt his throat, pulling him back to the past. In the few short months he'd been with Andrea, he'd sat drinking cheap Docklands whisky in so many clubs like this.

He'd always taken a seat at the back, always entered and left without acknowledging her. They'd put so much care into keeping their relationship secret. Harry had eyes everywhere. Later in the evening, they'd meet somewhere hidden – a cheap hotel or a private dining room – and talk through the evening's gig, then the day or days since they'd seen each other last. Again and again, Jack found himself grasping for words, never quite able to express how Andrea's songs moved him. He stopped listening to his store of Homelands sounds. They seemed so insipid when they had to follow the deft, committed power of her live performances.

Jack let an ice cube roll out of the glass and across his tongue, chilling his mouth. The cold pulled him out of his reverie. As he did so, he noticed the faintest light in the air just beside him, shivering around an empty seat. [By the pricking of my thumbs ...] said Fist, giggling nervously.

Jack looked back to the stage, assuming that the light was an effect of the stage lights. But they had dimmed and now glowed too softly in the darkness to reach him. He glanced back at the seat. The light still hung there, faintly suggesting a human form. Jack wondered if there was a glitch in the weave. Even if there was, he shouldn't be able to pick it up. There was a hint of a sound in the air, something that could have been a word, maybe a greeting. Fist tittered nervously, a sharp contrast with the slow, mournful blues that Andrea was whispering out from the stage. It was suddenly cold. A waitress came by, collecting empty glasses. Jack wondered if she'd respond to the shimmer, but it seemed that she could not see it.

He looked back towards the anomaly. The light was shifting towards him, as if something were leaning in to speak to him. There was the slightest breath, echoing the gentleness of Andrea's singing. It seemed to be whispering, but he could not make out any words. Then the shape collapsed. A thousand tiny shards of light flashed softly against him. They pooled on the table, in his lap, on the floor, before slowly fading out. It was as if a ghost had kissed him. He wondered if it could have been some new form of fetch. But the dead could not manifest unsummoned and he had no way of invoking anyone from the Coffin Drives.

[Did you see that?] he asked.

There was a pause.

[I saw nothing,] spat Fist, drawing himself back into Jack's mind like a snail coiling up into its shell. [This feels dangerous,] he hissed as he vanished. [We should leave now.]

Jack briefly wondered what had scared him, but his heart was elsewhere. Andrea's dark hood nodded before the microphone. Hiding her skull, it let Jack imagine her face, as unreachable as the past. But her voice was present and it moved him profoundly. He realised that there was no real choice to be made. Of course he was going to talk to her. The song ended. Applause scattered itself away as another began. Jack realised he'd finished his whisky. He thought about going to the bar again, but then Andrea might see him and find some way of preventing him from reaching her. He let the last of the ice fall into his mouth and sucked at it until it was gone.

At last she finished her set and disappeared backstage. Looking around, Jack saw that the blonde woman was staring at him with a look somewhere between fascination and hunger. She'd forgotten her surroundings. There was a man just behind her, concentrating on not spilling two ornate drinks, who hadn't seen her and was about to walk into her. Jack would have shouted a warning but there was no time, the man was already brushing against the blonde. Then there was a shimmer, and to Jack's shock he'd walked straight through her and was handing the drink to his girlfriend. The blonde stood there untouched, revealed as an illusion. She flashed a smile at Jack, then let herself fade into the gloom. Her eyes were the last part of her to vanish.

Jack had to walk through the space where she'd manifested on his way to the stage door. All that was left of her was a taste of ozone on the air and a cocktail umbrella crushed on the floor. It looked like a bright, abandoned feather, fallen from some strange, fictional bird. As he perceived it, it winked out of existence.

[She has to be Pantheon, to be able to show herself to us like that,] said Fist nervously, from deep within Jack's mind.

[It must be East,] replied Jack. [She loves visiting clubs in disguise.]

[We should leave.]

[Pure chance that we ran into her. And we're quite unusual. It's not surprising she took a second look.]

[We meet one of her people, and then she appears the next day? I don't like it. You'll get damaged.]

Jack had never seen Fist so jittery. [I've come to see Andrea,] he said. Her name was a talisman that strengthened his resolve.

[Then see her!] Fist's voice had a sudden half-panicked shriek to it. [And she'll tell you to fuck off! And we can get the fuck out of here.]

There was a large man wearing a cheap suit at the door to the backstage area. 'I want to see the singer who was on just now,' Jack told him.

'No socialising.'

'I've come a long way. I'm – an old fan of hers.'

The bouncer grunted. 'One of those. Well, if you want to piss your money away you can have her manifest at your table for twenty minutes. Got to be before her second set, she gets pulled back to the Coffin Drives after that. Pay at the bar.'

'Is there anywhere more private?'

'We're not that kind of place.'

'No, really. I just want to talk.'

'I bet.' The bouncer snorted. 'I'll ask the boss.' His face went blank for a moment, then he said, 'Empty dressing room out back. Cost you big. We monitor it.' A fist slapped against a palm. 'Don't try anything funny.'

Jack paid. [Keep spending like that and we'll have nothing left to live on,] whined Fist.

The bouncer ushered Jack through into a long, narrow corridor. 'Third on the left. She'll be waiting for you.' Performers had tagged its walls with graffiti. There were barcodes too. Had Jack been on-weave, they'd have summoned datasprites as soon as he perceived them. He wondered what he'd have seen. There'd probably have been nothing more than a shimmer at the edge of his vision as his anti-virals snuffed them out.

It was easy enough to find the dressing room, harder to knock confidently on the door. Seconds passed. Jack wondered if he'd been ripped off. At least he'd only have lost InSec's money. Then Andrea shouted 'Come in.'

The room was tiny. There was barely space for two chairs and a makeup desk. Andrea was sitting at the desk. A real dress, identical to her virtual one, hung shimmering behind her. It was like a field of stars, haloing her covered head. 'Close the door,' she told him. With a little contortion, Jack did so. 'Sit down.' She'd made her voice cold. 'I didn't want to see you. I hoped you wouldn't try and find me.'

'I had to. Especially after I found about – your situation.'

There was no adequate way of describing her death.

'I needed some easy cash once, when I was alive. Signed away fetch performance rights to a few little clubs. Too cheap to even advertise the gigs onweave. I always thought I'd be able to buy the rights back. But then I died.'

'I don't mean the club,' replied Jack. 'You – she – you passed on. What happened to her, Andrea? And why didn't you tell me?'

Jack sounded plaintive, even to himself. Andrea was silent for a moment. Then she said, 'I wish I could smoke. This would be the perfect time.'

'Andrea, please. I've only got twenty minutes with you.'

'Oh Jack, I know, I'm sorry. But what can I say? I'm dead, I died, I was killed. And of course I couldn't tell you. Because what would I have been then? So much code on a server.'

[Oi! What's wrong with being code?]

'But why get in touch at all?' Jack asked, ignoring Fist.

Andrea half-smiled. 'You should have seen how she remembered you, Jack. It was so different from Harry. So private, so intimate. Even after you'd gone. She kept it all in a little secret place, so close to her heart, and she went back to it again and again.'

Jack sighed, at once touched and saddened. 'Thank you,' he replied. 'But I still don't understand why you came and found me. Why you tricked me.'

'Oh Jack.' She turned the dark void beneath her hood to face him, and raised a hand to cup his face. He nerved himself to look back as directly, but when he did the shadows hid her white bone face. 'I have all her memories,' she told him. 'I am her memories. So I missed you. I thought about you all the time. But I'd never even talked to you.' There was such loss in her voice. Her hand drifted gently across his cheek. He felt the slightest of breezes, as if tiny feathers were flickering against his skin. 'I thought you'd never come back to Station. I wanted to see how the war had changed you. To be as close to you as she'd been, when everything was so different. And then you found out about Fist's licence, and you needed support, and I could give it.' She let her hand drop. 'I know all about coming to terms with death. And now, here we are.'

Jack wished he could take her hand in his. It was so strange to find himself moved by a ghost.

[Time's a-passing, lover boy.]

[It always is.]

'Is the puppet here too?' she asked, breaking the silence.

'Yes,' replied Jack. 'But he's not very happy about it.' [Too bloody right!] interrupted Fist. 'He's hiding in the back of my head,' continued Jack. 'But I might be able to get him out, if you want to meet him.'

'No,' replied Andrea. 'If he doesn't want to – let's just let him be.'

[Thank the gods. Wake me up when you're done with the nostalgia and we can get the fuck out of here.]

Jack was silent for a moment. He'd shared so much with this woman, who both was and was not the Andrea of his past. Her mails – pages long, coming every few days, in response to his own equally lengthy letters – had given him so much strength.

'How did you manage to write to me?' he asked.

'Gods,' she responded, shifting. 'Straight to the practical.'

'You shouldn't have been able to.'

She laughed joylessly. Jack imagined a sad half-smile, then remembered the cold, hard skull that the shadows hid from him. 'I know,' she replied. 'That's another reason why I didn't want you to come and see me.'

'What do you mean?'

'It's because of Harry. He's been reborn too. But he came back as something new.'

'He's not a fetch?'

'No. He's something very different. After he died they tried to cage him. They did that to a lot of fetches, the ones made from people who'd helped the Totality. But he broke out.'

'They thought he was a terrorist?'

'Harry?' She laughed. 'Dear lords no. But he was going to damage the Pantheon. He reopened the Bjorn Penderville murder case just before they shot him.'

'Proof of Pantheon criminality.'

'I always thought he'd left it behind him, one of the ones that got away. But one day he came in furious, said he'd been stitched up, that he needed to know who Penderville had been working for to hit back. Next day he put the paperwork through to make it official.'

'You're sure there was a connection?'

'We were both killed that night.'

'Shit.'

'He talks about it often. He's found out a lot more about the case since he died. You remember Aud Yamata? The dock worker who was the last person at the crime scene before the shooting?'

'The one with the cast-iron alibi?'

'That you thought killed Penderville. You nearly had her and the man that managed the Panther Czar and their Pantheon backer. So when Harry went back to the files, they acted. And' – Andrea made a gun shape with her hand, cocked to fire – 'Boom.' Her thumb came down like a hammer on a bullet.

'But how does that mean you could write to me?'

'Harry needed someone to talk to. He trusts me. So once he'd been back for a bit, he started summoning me. He helped me disable my kill switch, so I don't have to go back to the Coffin Drives any more. I pulled myself together then I got in touch with you.'

'Fuck, Andrea, I'm sorry. I thought it was just my life the Pantheon had screwed up. Have you told anyone about all this?'

'I don't want anyone else to get hurt. That's why I didn't want you to find me. People mustn't even think you might be digging into this. You have so little time left. I don't want whoever killed us taking any of it away from you.'

'What about Harry? Can't he go to InSec?'

'He's taken it as far as he can on our own, but he doesn't trust them. He doesn't like to admit it but he's very vulnerable. I am too.'

'Then why even tell me all this?'

'You've meant so much to me. You still do. Part of me's so happy that you found me tonight. So I decided that I wouldn't hide anything from you. Not any more.'

The moment froze Jack. Andrea shimmered in front of him, a pattern of memories made almost real. He wanted to touch and hold her, to kiss her, but there was nothing physical left to embrace. And overlaid on that need was grief and loss for, despite her presence before him, the woman he'd loved was dead.

It was impossible to know what to say.

Andrea broke the silence. 'I'm getting a warning. Our time's nearly up.'

'How much more?'

'A minute or so.' She leant forward, her hand on his knee, the darkness that hid her face so close to his. 'I really don't want you to get involved, Jack. Harry and I were killed, and you've lost seven years of your life. That's enough.'

'I'm going to die soon anyway. And nobody needs to know you're part of it.'

'No, Jack. Nothing good can come of taking on the Pantheon. I want you to patch things up with your parents and then let go in peace.'

'I thought I'd had enough of taking sides.'

'You did the right thing stepping away from the Soft War. Step away from all this, too.'

She put a finger to his lips. He was sure he could feel it. 'I love you, Jack,' she said. 'But we've had our time together. I'm sorry I can't see you again, but it's best for us all.

'Andrea, I—'

'Goodbye, Jack.'

And then she was gone.

[She's right,] snapped Fist. [It's too dangerous. Stay out of it.]

[Didn't you want to take on a god?]

[Not with both hands tied behind my back.]

It took a while for Jack to recover himself. He heard Andrea's second set begin, but he couldn't bring himself to go out and watch. Seeing her perform would have broken him. At last the music ended.

As he passed back through the club, Jack noticed that East was sat on the lap of the man who'd passed through her, kissing him ferociously. She'd let her disguise slip and was now recognisably herself. The man's girlfriend looked on in awe. Jack wondered what great transfiguration she was witnessing. Fireworks would be happening onweave. East's blessings were always generous. The man would be forever changed, his weave presence suddenly more elegant, more chic, more watched and thus more real than any of those around him. New choices would open up for him. The girlfriend would soon find herself alone.

Others were starting to understand the true nature of the visitation. A crowd was gathering. East reached down, fumbling to unzip the man's flies.

[That's the gods for you,] said Fist, [all appetite.]

In that moment, Jack decided. [I'm going to find out which one of them did this to us,] he said, [and I'm going to bring the fucker down.]

Chapter 10

Fist swore all the way home. Once they were back in their room, Jack tried to talk to him. At first the puppet refused to even listen, sticking his fingers in his ears and chanting gobbledegook. At last he began to calm down. Jack tried again.

[It's simple,] he explained. [We go to the Panther Czar, you break into their local network, we copy all their records, that's it. We should be able to do it from the club's public areas. We might not even need to go in.]

[But what if someone recognises you?]

[I was InSec's secret weapon. They kept me hidden away. I've never been anywhere near the Panther Czar.]

Fist only really started to come round when he realised just how hard finding out who was behind Akhmatov's more questionable activities would be.

[It'll take a few weeks to go through the data, Fist. Perhaps even longer.]

[We really won't need to leave the hotel?]

[Hardly at all. There's just food. And my dad. That'll be it.]

[Oo, it'll keep you right out of trouble!]

And there was a little reverse psychology, too.

[Of course, getting into their core commercial servers won't be easy. They'll be very heavily shielded.]

[Cracking some shitty little nightclub's security? A challenge? You are joking, Jack.]

[If you thought you couldn't do it I'd completely understand.]

[Dear gods, remember what I am.]

[As if I could forget.]

[Just get me close to them, I'll fuck 'em in the arse, we're done. They won't even know I've been in there.]

The discussion left Jack exhausted, but he couldn't sleep. At last he entered a liminal state, somewhere between waking and dreaming. Lying on his side he watched Fist manifest, then tiptoe out into the middle of the room. The puppet clearly thought Jack was out cold. The window opened beneath him, a black pool glistening with stars. He looked down, then over at his puppeteer.

'Little sleepy boy,' he whispered, 'soon be sleeping all the time. Soon be sleeping all the time!' He cackled quietly and wrapped his short arms around himself in a strange little hug, shaking with silent laughter. Then he leapt up and started to throw himself around the room. His limbs spun as he wheeled and pranced across the floor, the walls, even the ceiling, hissing a song to himself that would rattle in Jack's head for days.

'Soon be king, soon be king, soon he'll sleep and I'll be king. Even Stookie Bill will bow, even Stookie Bill will bow!'

That was a name Jack hadn't heard since he'd been deep in the Soft War. Stookie Bill was a twentieth-century ventriloquist's dummy. Humanity's first ever television signal had encoded his image. When Fist's fellow puppets found this out, they'd been unbearably excited. Their virtual ancestor became an obsession, almost an object of worship. 'Simple-minded idiots,' Fist had commented. But the cult of Stookie Bill had clearly had an impact on him, too.

Jack shuddered. He didn't want to let Fist know he was aware of this jarring moment of triumph. He pretended to grunt and then rolled over, so at least he didn't have to see any more of it. He reminded himself that there was no escaping Fist, that the only alternative to working so hard to have a tolerable relationship with him was dark and painful, and would break the possibility of finding any sort of peace before the end came. And of course the puppet was a powerful tool. Jack needed his full cooperation if he was to have any chance of finding out who'd killed Andrea and Harry, and forced him into exile.

At last, sleep took him, but Fist's glossy wooden face haunted his dreams. The puppet's false, grinning mouth clacked out soft, determined words. 'Soon be king' alternated with 'soon be mine', the two phrases chasing Jack through the night until his alarm rang and shook him back to wakefulness. Fist was perched on the end of the bed, watching. [Quite the disturbed night,] he said, his thin voice piping against the alarm's harsh beeping. This time Jack did snatch at him and wall him up in darkness.

He waited until late evening to set out for the Panther Czar. Docklands' streets were pretty much deserted. Pedestrian workers had long since hustled themselves away from offices and factories. A buggy whined by, its electric motors straining at the weight of a trailer piled high with scrap metal. As he walked, Jack looked up at the Spine. He imagined Grey's hooded raven, regretting that he wasn't able to see it. He remembered hearing about Grey's fall. The strange, vindictive joy that had filled him then pulsed through him once again. Perhaps soon he'd help bring down another god. He smiled to himself.

After about three quarters of an hour they reached the Panther Czar.

[So this hovelbox belongs to Pierre Ilich Akhmatov? The man who plots with the Pantheon? Fuck's sake, Jack, if you can judge a man by his enemies you really did hit rock bottom.]

The club was just across the road from them. It was a long, low warehouse, constructed from fluorescent yellow plastic sheeting. Words had been roughly hand-painted above a single pair of red double doors: 'Panther Czar'. Teens and twenty-somethings jostled each other in a long queue, dressed in more or less artfully ragged weavewear. Some was noticeably high quality, flagging up modish Homelanders who were self-consciously slumming it. Several smartly dressed, thick-necked gentlemen kept the peace at the doors.

[Why didn't you just raid the place?]

[We were setting it up when they sent me out-system. They needed me to finish making the case for it. That was a big reason why it never happened.]

[Ooo – get you, Mr Important!]

Jack waited for another buggy to pass, then started across the road to join the queue. Fist hung in the air for a second before bouncing after him, floating along like a children's balloon.

[Can you feel any of their core systems yet?]

[No. We need to get closer. Where the action is!]

Fist's voice was a gleeful, triumphant cackle. Jack wondered how far he could trust him. The little man was becoming more capricious as the change rushed towards them.

68

[Joining the crowds! Partying! My kind of night!] Fist chirped. [Champagne and oysters!]

[Remember it's business, not pleasure.]

They joined the back of the queue. Jack wasn't too much older than the other clubbers. Most were wasted on drink or drugs. The club's weave presence entranced them. 'Oh, the panthers are beautiful!' sighed a girl just ahead, her fingers kneading invisible fur.

[We've hit their security perimeter,] said Fist, suddenly more serious. A silence opened in Jack's mind as Fist concentrated. [Let's start by pretending we're one of these bouncers. And ping the system for a headcount ...] More silence, filled with thought. Then Fist yawned. [This is far too easy.]

[Don't be complacent.]

[Complacent? The only real challenge is staying awake. Anyway, there's a couple of hundred punters in there and about twenty staff. Almost all on the ground floor and in the basement. Just one person upstairs.]

[Could be Akhmatov.]

[Without any guards? I'm meant to be the one with the wooden head.]

[Can you get what we need from out here?]

[No. The core commercial systems are on the first floor. They've kept them off the main club network. We need to be closer.]

[Makes sense. Half the kids in there would be hacking them for free drinks otherwise.]

The queue moved on. The club loomed above them, glistening dully in the spinelight glare. It was the colour of a cheap hangover. Every time the red doors opened to let more punters in, bass rhythms thumped out.

[Almost there,] said Fist. [Not too fussy about who they let in.] Jack reached into his pocket and fingered the InSec card. [Let's hope you don't get recognised, Jack. Wouldn't want you getting bounced. Protect the meat!]

Jack tried to watch the door staff without looking at them too directly. None of them were paying him any sort of attention. The camera cluster above the door glanced at him and looked away. Another minute or so, and they were through the red double doors.

69

The bouncer didn't want to know why he was offweave. 'Just don't start anything,' he said. The girl in the ticket booth took Jack's money without comment.

[I told you it'd be all right,] he said casually, careful not to let Fist know just how relieved he was. [Good thing it's not one of Akhmatov's classier joints.]

They were in a black-painted corridor that smelt of cheap alcohol and cheaper drugs. Clubbers bustled past them and pushed through another pair of double doors. The corridor exploded with light. Music roared, higher frequency noise rounding out the simple repetitive beats they'd heard outside.

[THAT'LL BE THE DANCEFLOOR, THEN,] screamed Fist. [NO CHARLESTON, DAMMIT!]

[NO NEED TO SHOUT, JUST NEEDS A BIT of dynamic recalibration. There, that's it.]

Jack started towards the doors. A soft but definite stickiness pulled at every step.

[Akhmatov certainly doesn't waste any money on keeping his carpets clean,] said Fist.

[Who's around us?] said Jack. [Any more security?]

[No, the closest is the other side of the main dance floor. There's some virtual muscle too, but we don't need to worry about that.]

[And the person on the first floor?]

[Hasn't moved.]

[I think it could be him. Now, let's get close to those servers.]

The main dance floor was a ferocious transmedia vortex. Jack felt overwhelmed, and he was offweave and undrugged. An anonymity of clubbers leapt and bounced around him, gurning faces and shaking bodies blurring into one ecstatic mass. By the time he'd pushed halfway across the room he was sweating hard. Elbows hit his face and torso. Once they'd been all round the ground floor he was soaked and covered in small bruises.

[Still no joy, Fist?]

[Signal's too weak.]

[For fuck's sake.]

They kept trying for about half an hour. Jack started to wonder how honest Fist was being. He remembered the previous night's triumphant dance. Fist hadn't seemed like someone who'd just agreed to something dangerous. Rather, he'd come across as someone celebrating the avoidance of any risk at all.

[Fuck this,] Jack said. [We're not getting close enough down here. We're going upstairs.]

Fist laughed. [Well, I'm glad you've kept your sense of humour, Jack. We've done our best, this hasn't worked, what a terrible shame. We should leave now.]

Jack set off for a set of stairs he'd spotted earlier. They were roped off and marked 'Private'.

[Think you've got turned round, Jack. The exit's over there.]

[I know exactly where I'm going.]

[Come on now, Jackie boy, a joke's a joke.]

Jack shouldered his way through some particularly energetic dancers. One of them shouted at him, but the words were inaudible.

[You really mean it, don't you? You're a lunatic, Jack. You'll get yourself beaten up. At best.]

[Just like when some of the prison's biggest thugs came looking for me after your dodgy card games. It won't be any worse than that.]

[But I didn't know I'd be taking over then!]

They were off the dance floor and into the corridor. Fist sulked in silence as Jack climbed the stairs. Halfway up, there was a landing.

[Think about Andrea!] wailed Fist. [If you get caught, they'll go after her too.]

[We kept our relationship secret. There's nothing to connect us. She's perfectly safe, whatever happens.]

A disinfectant reek stung Jack's nose. There were two doors marked with little barcodes, one shaped like a man, another like a woman. A third door had a little combination keypad by its handle.

[Physical security! There's nothing I can do about that. We can stop playing at burglars and leave.]

[Read one of the staff. Get me the combination.]

[They might pick me up. That could be dangerous.]

[They definitely will do if I go down and tell them what we're up to here. Which I will do if you don't start helping me now. Do it, Fist, or I'll get the shit kicked out of us both.]

Fist swore and closed his eyes. His body shook slightly. Jack imagined his consciousness skipping from bouncer to bar staff to DJ, brushing against their virtual selves, looking for cracks to seep into.

Fist's eyes flicked back open.

[I'm only helping you to get in so we can get out as quickly as possible.]

[Yes.]

[I really don't think you should be doing this.]

[There's only one person up there. And we'll avoid him. Now what's the number?]

[2754.]

[That was nice and easy, wasn't it?]

[Fuck off.]

They stepped through the door and into luxury.

[Got a signal?] said Jack.

[Getting stronger.]

[Go to work.]

The corridor was padded with pale, thick carpets. Soft uplights illuminated pastel walls, studded with glyphs. Jack wondered about the onweave art that the glyphs represented. When Jack first started investigating Akhmatov's business affairs, he'd watched interviews with a few young Station artists. Akhmatov had a habit of arriving at their studios unannounced and paying substantial amounts for one or two pieces of their best work. None of them had been either able or willing to give much information away about their patron. Akhmatov's interest made sure that these stylish young people patronised his more exclusive events, lending them an air of cutting edge excitement that made them some of the most popular nights in Docklands. They'd even attracted a regular Homelands clientele.

No doubt these glyphs pleasured onweave viewers with sounds and visuals from the servers of today's bright young things. No doubt Akhmatov's art patronage still helped keep his venues at the cutting edge of fashion. And of course, such patronage would please East. As maker and breaker of Station fashion, her interest and indulgence were essential to the success of Akhmatov's business. Jack wondered briefly if she was the Pantheon member whose influence he'd made out in the Panther Czar's accounts. She'd certainly always been close to Grey.

Soon he'd know for sure.

[Now we're talking,] said Fist, pulling Jack out of his reverie. [You're in?]

Fist tittered, irritation all but forgotten in the joy of action.

[Part of the way. Got the basics.]

[So who's that up ahead?]

[It is Akhmatov. Looks like he's asleep.]

[Must have had a hard day's night.]

For a moment, Jack remembered the best parts of his time with Fist – the sense of vastly more efficient systems grafted on to his own mind, working both with and beyond it to achieve the impossible.

[Getting any info on him?] he asked.

[Some basics. He's discreet, but not discreet enough. The meat'll be deeper in. I need to get up close to one of his servers. Second door on the left.]

Fist bounced ahead of Jack as they walked up the corridor. The door was decorated with a particularly complex, tiger-shaped glyph. It was unlocked. Jack tiptoed through, then carefully shut it behind him. All was pitch-black.

[Right,] said Fist.

And then the lights came on.

Akhmatov was sat behind a large stone desk. He was dressed in a smart white suit. His pale face hovered beneath grey-black hair. There was a tightly trimmed moustache at its centre, sitting above precise, fussy lips. His eyes were masked by round black lenses. He was lighting a cigarette. There were men dressed in black, two to his left, one to his right, and one behind. All four had the same face. There was a leather armchair in front of the desk. The rest of the room was empty.

'I always thought, Jack,' said Akhmatov, exhaling smoke, 'that you had a little more style than this. But then, you have been away from us for rather a long time. And your little man is so easy to fool.'

[Shit,] said Fist. [This fucking cage.]

Chapter 11

'All these years,' said Akhmatov. 'And we finally meet.'

[Fist,] Jack whispered, [what happened?]

[He spoofed me. I TOLD YOU THIS WAS A FUCKING STUPID IDEA!]

'Your little man is less effective than he boasts,' said Akhmatov. He contemplated the tip of his cigarette for a moment. 'I've force-opened some of your weave channels. The cageware should stop me from doing that, but it seems that somebody's cut a little hole from inside. Naughty naughty!'

[He's overloaded my weaveports,] said Fist. [The cage is reading it as a potential hack, so I can't manifest. I'm all locked down, you're on your own. Run! Don't let him hurt you!]

[Bouncers'd be on us straightaway.]

Akhmatov gestured, the cigarette trailing smoke in the air. 'But where are my manners? You should sit.'

An attendant appeared at Jack's side and waved him towards the armchair. There was no other choice. Jack let himself subside into it. The faded leather was soft and welcoming. It sighed as Jack sat back, exhaling a fusty reek of cigars and privilege.

'It's really just plastic,' smiled Akhmatov. 'Rather well pro-grammed, isn't it?' The dark glasses gave him the look of an insect.

'What do you want, Akhmatov?' said Jack, barely keeping his voice steady.

'Your return has caused, let us say, quite the stir. In circles that I move in, at least. In fact, I was warned not to receive you. To shut you out, to let your licence run out, to let you die and your puppet take the strings.' Akhmatov's smile became a chuckle. 'Of course I've always resented being told what to do. I think you might sympathise with that?' He leant forward in his chair and inspected Jack. 'No, I really don't see it. Jack, there are entities that scare even me. You've slept with Grey, you know what I mean. And some of them' – Akhmatov raised his hand and pointed at him – 'are mortally afraid of you, and of the little cuckoo in your nest.' He sat back. 'No, I don't understand it either.'

Jack realised that Akhmatov was looking at him expectantly. But there was nothing to say. He shrugged, hoping to at least display some bravado. 'I really wouldn't know,' he said.

'Still the same old *ingénue*. I watched you, Jack, watched you trying to draw your strings around me, back in the old days. You were very sharp. Of course I was aware of every move you took.'

Jack was at once shocked by Akhmatov's revelation and surprised to hear real respect in his voice. Memories of the investigation shimmered through him. 'Perhaps that's what they're scared of,' he replied. 'I would have had you, Pierre. A month more, maybe two. And your backer too.'

Remembering deep competence helped Jack's self-control reassert itself. It was surprising how relaxed he felt. He started wondering how he could make use of Akhmatov's evident interest in him. He had his own abilities to draw on. He'd always been the most forensically precise of Grey's auditors. That skill set had existed long before Fist had climbed out of his subconscious and into the processing nodes nestled snugly against his spine.

'Oh no, Jack. You couldn't have touched us.'

'Really? We knew that Bjorn Penderville was working for you. We were about to prove that you'd had Aud Yamata kill him. I had most of your network analysed. I knew when your shipments were coming in, how you used sweathead avoidance codes to make them invisible, who your dealers were, how they transferred their profits to you and how you laundered them – even how you paid your suppliers.'

'Aud Yamata,' spat Akhmatov. 'That bitch.' He took a moment to recover himself. 'But let's not get sidetracked. Your investigation was very impressive, but you didn't have the most important thing.'

'Yamata's Pantheon protector? I saw the traces. I would have followed them back and found out who it was. And Harry and I would have shut them down.'

'And taken down a god. You know, I think that's something you might have been capable of. You were certainly very good at your job, the best perhaps. Yamata and her master saw you as a very major threat. They wanted you dead. Grey must have fought hard for you, to keep your punishment so light. And Harry – well, you heard how we had to deal with him, in the end.'

Akhmatov slowly and deliberately made a pistol shape with his hand. He pointed a two-fingered nozzle towards Jack. His thumb came down like a hammer.

'Bang.'

[Shit, Jack. He's going to kill you.]

'InSec are watching me. If I die, they'll want to know how. They'll find you quickly enough.'

Akhmatov laughed. 'And once again, Yamata's patron would steer them away from me. But you'll be relieved to hear that my hands are tied. I've been ordered very specifically not to harm your little man or his future property. There are other plans in place for that little weapon's special talents.'

[Well that's a relief,] said Fist.

[No it's not. It's very worrying.]

'But when my panthers bite,' continued Akhmatov. 'they cut deep into the mind and leave no wounds in the flesh. As you are about to find out.'

[Ha!] said Fist. [No physical damage at all!]

[It's still going to hurt.]

[What's a little pain, Jackie boy? You'll get through it. Maybe it'll even teach you to keep out of harm's way.]

'I will ravage you and break you, without touching your body at all. And I'll show my masters that I've done so and laugh, and maybe they'll be that little bit less scared of your puppet, and they'll respect me just a little bit more, and my life will become that little bit easier.'

Akhmatov made a complex gesture with his left hand. Four matt-black faces turned towards Jack. They started to change. The room shifted with them. Gloom fell, silvered with a luminous moonlit haze. The air was suddenly dense with the scent of rich earth and new growth, with the whispering of a soft breeze through leaves. The moonlight caught at vines and small trees as they grew, reaching up to the empty sky above.

76

'Akhmatov? Where are you?'

[He's a tricky sod.]

Jack stood up. The chair disappeared. He was standing in a small clearing. Small wild sounds washed over him. Insects scraped at themselves, scratching noisily in the night. Birds leapt into being and started to sing. There was a distant scream. Jack remembered playing with monkeys at Old Earth simulations. When they were frightened they'd open their mouths wide until their gums showed and give a high-pitched yowl. Off to his left small birds whistled with surprise, then whirred up into the sky.

A dark shape that could have been a man moved in the forest. There was a rustling at Jack's back, a flicker of movement that pulled at the corner of his eye. They were circling him, walking at the edge of the treeline. He saw another one, moving with the fluent grace of a shadow cast on water. As Jack watched, it fell forwards. Its arms shortened, its head changed shape and then its body flowed away from humanity. It landed on four feet and padded out of the light.

[Spooky!] said Fist.

Now the jungle was silent. Jack turned in a full circle, trying to remember where the door had been. Humidity simulators had come online. A soft, sticky breeze touched his face. This was confusion software of a very high order. Jack had no doubt that the four security bots surrounding him were of equal quality. It had once been so natural for the weave to replace the world with visions. Now it felt like a transgression.

[You can't do anything at all?] said Jack.

[The cage is in full panic mode. He knows his stuff.]

Fist sounded almost gleeful. A panther growled behind Jack. He spun round. It was an absence carved from shadow, reminding him of the voids between stars. There was hot breath at his ankle – another cat to his left. This one was lying down. It licked the side of his foot and he leapt away. The panther's rough tongue left a tingle behind it.

[Shit,] muttered Fist. [I felt that.]

A third panther was coiled up on a tree branch overhanging the small glade. The fourth would no doubt be behind him. Akhmatov strolled into the clearing, his white suit perfect dress for the jungle.

The moonlight caught at his pale clothes and skin, and made them glow. The dark glasses he wore made dead suns of his eyes.

'You see why I called my club the Panther Czar?' he said. One of his digital creatures growled. Jack gagged at the bloody reek of its breath. 'The illusion is far more complete than it was in your day. My guests downstairs are very familiar with these creatures. The panthers wander the club, watching for trouble. They have never been seriously challenged. I wonder how much of a diversion you will provide for them?'

The first of the panthers pounced. Jack felt a heavy weight thud against him. Shards of pain exploded across his right shoulder, his chest, his thigh. He staggered and fell sideways. The panther's claws stayed in him as he went down, tearing and slicing at his flesh. The illusion was devastatingly painful.

Fist screamed too. [Shitting hell!] he howled. [I felt that! He's force-linked our pain receptors!]

[Stop them!]

[I fucking wish I could!]

There was a flash of sparking cageware. A bright light burnt up then flared out as Fist tried and failed to attack. A spiked paw snatched at Jack's shoulder, turning him over. Another pushed against the back of his head, forcing his face into the ground. Something tore at his back. He felt flesh lift off bone and he screamed [GODS!], mud clotting into his mouth as he did so.

Someone else was screaming too. It was Fist. Bright light exploded again. Nothing changed. Another counterattack had failed. The heavy cat weight lifted off Jack's back. For seconds the pain was gone. He remembered that he was whole and that all this was illusion. Then the agony crashed back again, the tearing bulk of a panther driving it into him.

[YOU FUCKER!] shouted Fist. [YOU FUCKING FUCKER! I'D FUCKING HAVE YOU IF I COULD!]

'Your boy is caged,' said Akhmatov, 'and my cats are hungry. And the night is so young.'

'Fuck you!' Jack screamed into the soft night.

The jungle whispered on around his pain.

Chapter 12

An hour or so later, Jack was pushed out of the Panther Czar night club. The queue was much longer. He stumbled through the line and into the road, then fell over. Someone swore at him. Another threw an empty drink can. It bounced off his back. He pulled himself to his feet. His movements were stiff and awkward. 'Fucking drunk,' shouted a woman.

Jack blinked. His head jerked to left then right until he found her. He swung his whole body round to face her. 'I'll break you, you bitch.' His voice was higher than usual. It had a rasping, semi-formed quality to it. The girl giggled. 'Don't you laugh at me. I'll show you,' he snarled, lurching towards her. His legs were stiff, barely bending at the knees. One arm swung up to point. 'I'll take you offweave and fuck all your data.'

A man stepped protectively in front of her.

'You just try it, mate.'

'I will,' screeched Jack. 'I'm untouchable!' He stumbled towards the man, fists raised. Then there were three InSec agents between them, one placating the girl and her partner, the other two holding Jack.

'What do you think you're doing? They insulted me! Me!'

One of the policemen slipped a pair of handcuffs around Jack's wrists, securing them behind him. Then the other started to walk him toward a police flyer, parked on the other side of the street. Jack's face reset itself, moving from anger to shocked surprise. It was as if it only had a few very specific expressions to choose from.

'What is this? Where are you taking me? I know my rights! Don't you know who you're fucking with?'

When they reached the flyer, there was a brief scuffle. Jack broke away from the policemen. His expression changed sharply to show manic happiness. He started off down the pavement, running in an awkward, stiff-legged way. His pursuers were much quicker. One of them tackled him and he crashed awkwardly to the floor. A gash on his cheek oozed blood. It dripped on to his clothes, but he didn't notice.

This time, he didn't put up a struggle when they reached the car. The door clunked shut behind him. The two policemen climbed into the flyer's front seats. The lift-off was rapid. There was someone sitting next to him. His head turned quickly, then jolted suddenly to a halt. His eyes snapped closed and back open. His face was blank.

'Hello, Hugo,' said Lieutenant Corazon. 'I can't think how many laws you're breaking by taking Jack for a walk like this.'

'I'm not Hugo. I'm Jack.'

'Don't take the piss, Hugo. You'll only make it worse for yourself.'

'I had to do it.'

Jack's voice – or rather, Fist's – had something of a wheedle to it.

'You're riding him. It's illegal under Station law, and outside the terms of both your installation licence and usage agreements.'

'They were torturing him. He passed out!'

'Was there reason to believe that his life was in danger?'

There was a silence. All went dark as the flyer passed into the Wart.

'I said, did you believe his life was at risk?'

'No.'

'You broke into the Panther Czar night club, and entered Akhmatov's private office space. His security systems contacted us and informed us that a breach was in progress. We had an alert from your cageware, too.'

'I told him not to break in there!'

'That doesn't make any difference.'

'We were investigating a crime. Akhmatov's a crook.'

'He is. But in this case it's you two that were breaking the law.'

'Akhmatov's software nearly killed us.'

'Knowing what he's capable of, I think you both got off rather lightly.'

'What brings you meddling, anyway? I could have got him home.'

There was suddenly a wide grin stretched across Jack's face. Fist had switched expressions, in the hope of placating Corazon. The insincerity of it shook her.

'Lestak's tagged you both. The incident report came in, she was alerted and she asked me to deal with it.'

'Can't you just drop us back at the hotel?'

'We have to be assured that the proper relationship between you and Jack has been restored before we can release you. You'll be spending the night in the cells, under observation.'

Jack's smile spread a little wider. 'So we just sit back and relax? And wait for the doctors to check us out tomorrow?'

'More or less, yes. And you need to shut down.'

'Do I? I'm rather enjoying this.' Fist had Jack stretch his arms out in front of him. He twisted his hands, then curled and uncurled his fingers. It was like watching a machine run through initialisation tests. 'I love having a body. I like being a real boy.'

'What you're doing now is illegal. Shut off, or we'll be forced to take punitive action against you when we touch down.'

'You know, I thought you'd be much more fun,' grumbled Fist in an accusing tone. Then he was gone. It was as if invisible strings had been severed. Jack's arms fell into his lap. His head slumped back, eyeballs rolling up into their sockets. He slipped sideways and fell against the flyer window. The jolt set the cut on his cheek bleeding again. As Lieutenant Corazon reached over to close his eyes, red smeared itself across her uniform. She shrugged, then nudged her weave settings so that the mark became invisible.

Hours later, when Jack came round, a microdrone was watching him. It was a very basic one, taking the form of a small silver ball with a flashing blue light mounted on top of it. A moustache was painted above a tiny black hole. There were no eyes. 'Are you awake?' it asked.

Jack sat up, saying nothing. His stiff muscles creaked and his joints felt wooden. Fist was nowhere to be felt. The microdrone moved in towards him. Its voice became a little louder and a little deeper. 'I said, are you awake?' Jack wondered who'd written its respect/intimidation protocols. It emitted a low whine, presumably meant to make him imagine that a tiny taser was powering up. He supposed that he was meant to be scared. He chuckled, remembering battles in deep space, and found himself surprised at the sound of his own laughter. It had been a long time since he'd heard it.

'Yes, I am,' he replied.

The whining stopped. A small slot opened in the ceiling and the microdrone shot through it. Jack wondered who it had gone to warn. He stood up and grimaced. It was as if he could feel every single bone grinding against its brothers. The thought reminded him of his last conscious moment. He'd been lying face down. His back had been entirely stripped of flesh. One of the cats was laid out next to him, biting at something soft and wet and red. The second was licking blood from his thigh, every so often nicking his skin with a sharp tooth. He could feel the breath of the third on the back of his neck, the series of soft tugs as it ran an exploratory claw down the white ladder of his vertebrae. Then Hugo had taken charge and the world had vanished.

Jack filled the sink with water and splashed his face. Its cold touch was so honest and kind and real. Fist was still dormant, exhausted by the effort of possessing Jack. It wouldn't last for much longer, but for the moment the peace was blissful.

The cell door hissed behind him.

'You know Jack, I was going to call you. And thank you.' It was Lieutenant Corazon. 'For rescuing Ifor.'

'Doing InSec's job for you.'

'That's fair enough. But then you screwed things up.'

'Doing your job for you, again.'

'You were breaking and entering. Like a common sweathead.'

'Investigating. Something you should be doing.'

'Investigating what, Jack? What are you trying to prove?'

'Akhmatov confirmed what I told you.'

'That one of the Pantheon's smuggling sweat? Oh, Jack. Let it be.'

'And that I was sent out-system and Harry was moved to another department because we got too close to it. Two years later Harry reopened the case and was killed.' Jack stopped himself from mentioning Andrea's murder too. 'That's several crimes for the price of one. And now they're after Fist. They're going to wait till I've gone then seize him and use him.'

'That's impossible, Jack. The Pantheon doesn't work like that.'

'Check for yourself. Go back to the Bjorn Penderville murder.

Read our reports. And if that's too much work, ask yourself why Aud Yamata wasn't arrested and the Panther Czar's never been shut down.'

Corazon sat down on the small bed in the corner of the cell. There was a look of deep sympathy on her face.

'You've read what happened one way. And I really understand why you might be angry with the Pantheon, why you need to find reasons for Grey sending you away. But I'm sure that won't be the only story that explains things.'

'You're not doing your job, Corazon. All of this is real and you can't even see it, because you can't imagine the Pantheon doing anything wrong.'

'It's a fantasy, Jack.'

'It's crime that needs investigation.'

'Look, Jack, I understand how tough it was for you out there. I think even Lestak was shocked, once she had some time to think. I realise how little I know about the Soft War. I've started researching it. And I'm sorry that you have so little time left, that would make anyone bitter. But pretending that one of the Pantheon is out to get you – that's just not what they do, Jack. They're on our side, they work for us.'

'I've fought their wars for them, Corazon. I know what makes them tick. They're just like war machines. They want power and they want to hang on to it. If you get in their way, you're fucked. And that's it.'

'Oh, Jack. You served the Pantheon well once – and now this.'

Jack felt exhausted. Limbs clacked at the back of his mind. Fist was beginning to stir.

'Anyway,' said Corazon, 'I haven't come here to argue about your past. Akhmatov's not pressing charges. He knows your situation. He said he understands that it's not easy for you.'

'He's not pressing charges because he's been ordered not to. He went too far, and he's been reined back in.'

'Oh, for gods' sake! For once in his life he's showing some decency. Be thankful for that, at least.'

'A known criminal does something completely out of character and you don't even ask why? It's like I said. They want Fist undamaged, so he's had orders not to touch us.'

'The Pantheon are watching Fist, Jack. Nobody will be able to seize him and use him.'

Jack sighed in defeat, suddenly feeling exhausted. 'A god will,' he said quietly.

Corazon stood up and moved towards the door. It opened at her touch. Jack expected her to just leave, but she turned back towards him.

'I talked to Fist.'

'When he was riding me?'

'Yes. He can't be an easy person to live with.'

'He's built to perform a specific role. That doesn't make him very social.'

'What's it like – when he takes over? Where do you go?'

Jack sighed. 'I wasn't really there.' He sat down on the bed, looking for words; wondering why he felt the need to answer Corazon's question. Looking up, he saw deep concern on her face. It infuriated him. 'But why are you worried about it? For gods' sake look back over the evidence, you'll see I'm right. You wanted to be a journalist once. Imagine you've found something that could be the biggest story of your life. Act like an investigator, not some fucking counsellor. Find out why they sent me away back then. Find out how they're going to use Fist now.'

'OK, Jack. I'll take a look at the files. But remember that that means I'm helping you – and you don't get to abuse me for that.'

The door hissed shut behind her.

Chapter 13

[So what's next, genius detective?] asked Fist.

They were sitting on a train, rattling back to Docklands. Jack had turned down the offer of a lift in a flyer, which annoyed Fist. At first he subsided into an aggrieved silence but that soon bored him, so he started needling Jack.

[Are we going to try and track down some other shithole, and see if we can get ourselves tortured in exciting new ways? Do you want to go and stalk your dead girlfriend some more? Shall we go and wander round housing estates looking for pieces of the minds we spent years killing? Do you want to go and get shouted at by your dad for a bit? Or shall we just spend more time finding out how much everyone hates you when you're offweave? You've really fucked your life up, I bet you're actually glad I'm going to be taking over.]

[And how did you find the experience of being me, Fist? Looking forward to having a body of your own now you've taken it for a test drive?]

Fist didn't answer.

[We're going to write a letter to Andrea,] said Jack. [She's going to take us to Harry. He's been investigating all this too. We need to pool resources.]

[But Jack! You promised – after the Panther Czar, you'd let it all be.]

[I said I would if we got the data I needed. We didn't. And we found out that they want to use you as a weapon after I'm gone. I'm not going to let that happen.]

[This isn't fair! You're going to get yourself attacked or shot or killed. And then where will I be?]

[Wherever I am, Fist, just like always. And believe me, I wish that was different too. Now stop panicking and remember what Akhmatov said. For the moment, we're safe.]

Jack returned to the hotel and tried to go onweave. Fist pretended there was a technical fault in the hotel weave-systems until Jack cuffed him and he opened them up.

Jack knew now that Andrea's avatar was nothing more than a static relic, cast off by the dead past. He summoned a screen and keyboard and, as he'd done so many times in the Callisto prison's small comms room, began to type a mail. He wasn't sure who might be monitoring his communications, so he wrote as a lover looking back to a happier past rather than an investigator seeking to unpick it.

'Andrea – I've been back to where things began. I thought that would help me get things straight, but it's more than I can deal with alone. I need help to understand. Please.'

Jack always ended his mails to Andrea with 'all my love'. Now, he wasn't sure what to type. In the end, he sent the note unsigned. Then he waited. The reply came in a couple of hours. Her words hung before him, as for so long the only part of her he could see.

'Jack. I told you I didn't want you digging it all up again. If you just let it rest, it can't hurt you. Back off.'

Normally she too signed off with endearments. There was nothing this time. Jack replied almost instantly.

'I can't step away from it now, Andrea. I need resolution. And it can't hurt me, I know that for sure. I'll tell you why when I see you. I've started looking ahead, too. I want to make sure Fist is looked after once I'm gone.'

Fist was reading over Jack's shoulder. He snorted as Jack typed that last sentence.

[I don't need looking after, Jack. I just need you to walk away from all this. Like you promised.]

[We don't have any choice. They want to control you. They'll come for you once you've taken over, be sure of it.]

[And I'll knock 'em down like ninepins!]

[Like you put the zap on the Panther Czar?]

[Fuck you.]

Fist was silent as Jack typed the rest of the note.

'Please, Andrea, we've got to talk. All of us need to talk.'

He couldn't mention Harry, but he knew that Andrea would

understand that 'all of us' included him. And now Jack was at the end of the note, facing the sign off again. Writing as a lover had changed his sense of the situation. It was more than a moral or a practical problem. It was an emotional one too. Jack felt abandoned before a great darkness. He found in himself a deep need to lighten the pain by sharing it.

'You helped me see my life clearly when I first met you in Homelands. You helped me face up to the truth on Phobos, too, when I found out how little time I had left. Please help me one last time, before the end.

With my love,

Jack'

This time, she agreed to see him.

That night she was playing a club in Prayer Heights. It was a little more upmarket than Ushi's. Jack had to make a discreet personal payment to the door staff to get in. The audience was more engaged. There was quiet applause as Andrea came onstage, a noticeable hush as she started to sing. Her voice rang out across the room as clearly as before. She played a surprisingly conservative set, including only the cover versions that had first made her name. Jack did his best to enjoy them, but they lacked the depth and power of her later, more personal work. The audience seemed happy enough, applauding enthusiastically as each song reached its entirely predictable end.

She'd told Jack to come backstage once she'd finished. There was another anonymous corridor and another dressing-room door. Jagged music filtered through it. Jack thought he recognised Andrea's voice, but it had been heavily treated. It was singing over a spoken word accompaniment, hustled along by soft beats, skipping apparently at random from one song to another. Jack knocked on the door and waited. There was no response. The hushed, discordant music continued. He knocked again, just as it began to fade out. Andrea said, 'Come,' and Jack stepped in.

'Interesting tunes,' he said.

'Jack,' she almost shouted from within her cowl, 'what the hell are you playing at? I told you not to get involved. I don't need a knight in shining armour. It's bad for you and it's worse for us.'

Jack hadn't been expecting such an onslaught. Fist chuckled.

[Ooo, this is going to be fun,] he said happily. [Maybe there won't be any more investigating after all. Popcorn!]

'I'm sorry, Andrea. I thought—'

'No Jack, you didn't think. You just went straight in, digging over dangerous ground. What did you tell Akhmatov or InSec? I've been so careful to let people think I really did overdose. And nobody can know Harry's come back.'

'Andrea, I'm not stupid. As far as they're both concerned, I'm a Pantheon hater who broke into the Panther Czar to find out which god's corrupt. It's nothing to do with you two.'

'Except Harry wanted to find out exactly the same thing. That's why he reopened the Penderville case and that's what got us killed. It's got everything to do with us. For gods' sake, Jack. You've put us both at risk. You're in danger too.'

'No we're not. The bad guys have moved beyond that. For them it's all about Fist. They want him unharmed. I can't be touched either.'

[Not mentioning the panthers, then?]

Remembered pain snarled in Jack, rubbing against his mind like fur, sticky with his own blood.

'I'm going to sit down for a moment,' he said.

'Are you all right?'

'Akhmatov set his panthers on me last night. But it wasn't real, I'm fine.'

'Clearly.'

Fist giggled.

'And you say they can't touch you,' said Andrea. 'I've seen how these people operate. At first hand. It will get worse.'

[Listen to her, Jack,] said Fist. [She knows.]

'For now, this is as far as it's going to go,' said Jack. 'Akhmatov was reined in. He didn't even have me roughed up by a bent Docklands copper, I was taken straight to HQ. He won't hurt me. Because they want Fist undamaged.'

'So what? Let them have him.'

'Fist is a weapon and they think they can control him. With Pantheon backing, they'll be able to lift his cage.'

'They're not going to be stupid enough to attack the Totality. What else is he good for?'

'What else?' said Fist, spluttering into outraged existence. 'What else?'

'I'm sure he'll explain,' said Jack.

Andrea peered at him, fascinated. 'I've heard so much about you, Fist. It's – interesting – to finally meet you.'

That barely interrupted Fist's rant. 'If it wasn't for this sodding cage, I could do quite a lot.' He tried to look down his nose at Andrea, but even though he was standing on a table he was still shorter than her. 'I'm a military grade systems infiltration unit. I may have been built on an accountant' – he glared at Jack – 'and I may look like some over-privileged chucklehead' – his monocle shimmered in the light – 'but believe me, I can break into anything I want. Not just the Totality. And when I look at how Station's systems have been thrown together over the years – poof, so many holes!'

'He's almost how I imagined him,' Andrea told Jack. 'Only a little more – extreme.'

'I could hack into any of them,' continued Fist, waving a hand airily. 'From the crappiest corporate server all the way up to the weave itself. Weaveselves, too. Maybe even the Coffin Drives! Maybe even fetches like you. Live, on the fly, pretty much instantly.'

'It must have been so difficult living with him,' sighed Andrea.

'You get used to it. After a while.'

Fist finally registered that she and Jack were only barely listening to him. 'Excuse me?' he said. 'I believe I'm talking? Gods, being ignored by meatsacks is bad enough. I thought I'd at least get some respect from another digital intelligence.'

Andrea seemed to be about to snap back at him, but she held herself back. Then she replied: 'I'm sorry. That is a good point. I should have listened properly.'

'Well,' said Fist, taken by surprise. 'Yes. An apology. Good.'

'So, you said you can break into just about any system on Station?' continued Andrea. 'That's pretty impressive. But some of them are very well guarded. The gods are great believers in security.'

'No reason not to believe him,' Jack replied. 'He might not move as fast as some—'

89

'Oi!' said Fist.

'—but he goes far deeper.'

'That's more like it.'

'Shit,' whispered Andrea. 'You could be very dangerous indeed.'

'Thank you,' said Fist joyfully. 'Nice to be appreciated!' He clapped, his hands sounding like wooden dominoes tumbling on to a table top.

Andrea bowed her head and reached a hand inside her cowl, rubbing what remained of her temple. Jack wondered if her true face would fall into the light, but it remained hidden. 'You're right,' she said. 'We can't let them get hold of him.'

'I don't see why not,' said Fist. 'I'm going to need a job once Jack's gone. And this sounds like fun! It's what I was built for, after all.'

'No, Fist,' said Jack. 'These are bad people, and they'll make you do bad things.'

'You and your bloody conscience. Won't be a problem for much longer!'

Andrea cut in. 'Remember who you're with, Fist. You might not miss Jack when he's gone, but I will.' Jack shot her a grateful look. 'I'll take you both to Harry,' she continued. 'He's spent a lot of time digging into the Penderville case. I'm sure he'll help you find a new way forward.'

'Thank you,' said Jack.

'For fuck's sake,' muttered Fist.

Andrea stood up. 'Follow me back to our house.'

'You've got a house? And you can walk the streets?'

'It's an aunt's place. She works the orbital chainships, she's only there a couple of nights a month. Because it's a family site I can manifest fully. We've made some changes so it's safe for Harry too. And I can walk on any street I want. Like I said, Harry helped me tweak myself. I'm not your average fetch.' There was a moment of silence. Andrea tilted her head forward. 'And you should be careful. Did I ever tell you about Harry's first year at senior school?'

'No.'

'The older boys used to take money off the little ones. So he organised them. Their whole year fought back together, kicked the crap out of the sixteen- and seventeen-year-olds.'

'Keeping the peace.'

Andrea laughed. 'Kind of,' she said. 'He started taking money off the local shops. To keep them unharassed. Paid some of the cash to the older boys. Got them working for him too.'

'Playing all the angles.'

'He still does. He puts himself first. Watch him, Jack.'

Fist cut in. [Sounds like a fucking psychopath to me.]

Jack ignored him. 'That's not the sort of thing I'd expect to hear from someone's wife,' he told Andrea.

'Harry and I help each other out,' she replied, 'but you should know we're not a couple any more.'

For a moment something in Jack thrilled. Then he remembered that the Andrea he'd known was dead. He covered his confusion by standing up and turning away, reaching for his coat.

'I'll come out with you.'

'No. I don't want you walking with me.'

'For safety?'

'In part. But also – this.' She indicated her cowl. 'Entertainment venues have a special licence. People don't always like being remind-ed what they're listening to. So, they hide the bone. Outside, there's nothing like that. It shows.'

'But – I don't mind.'

'I do, Jack. You'll walk in the street behind me. You'll stay back all the way. You can see me when we're back home and I'm wearing my true face again.'

'I can look away.'

'Wait two minutes, then follow me. I've flicked my permissions so you can see me outside. I'll wait at the head of the street, then I'll start walking. I won't look back. If you do try and catch up, I'll let myself fall back into the Coffin Drives. I'll make sure Harry finds you, but you won't be seeing me ever again.'

Chapter 14

The late evening street was half-empty. Dim spinelight painted grey shadows across the road. Andrea was at the end of the street, facing away from Jack. She no longer wore a cowl. Her skull was moon-white in the darkness, seeming to shine with its own light.

[Let's go see what she looks like!] said Fist. [You won't really miss her, Jack. 3! 2! 1! Go!]

Jack stood by the club exit and waited. After thirty seconds or so, Andrea moved away round the corner. He followed.

[Run, Jack, run!]

Prayer Heights gave way to Kanji District. The streets became busier. For a while they were on a main road. Throngs were enjoying a night out, chasing after entertainment that ranged from the virtuous to the vicious. Andrea moved ahead of Jack, a dissonant presence in the festive crowds. Jack remembered how she'd dragged him out to explore Docklands. She took a hatchet to what he now recognised as snobbery, forcing him to find ways of enjoying his birthplace again.

He wondered if their favourite bar, the Vista Club, was still open. It had always been a specialised taste. It was set deep in the meteor gash that gave the Wound its name, showing views of the distant, broken Earth. They'd spent some great nights in there together.

Jack had spent hours alone there too, watching storms tear at the dead lands below, mulling over the past and the future. His thoughts had often drifted to the war machines that still ravaged Earth. Sometimes there was a sharp burst of light beneath the clouds – some war-machine battle reaching a climax that resolved nothing. Sometimes the light would be higher up, nearly in space – one of the Rose's satellites neutralising an attempt to escape Earth's gravity well. East would soon trumpet her success. Most of the bar would applaud, then turn back to drinks and quiet conversations.

Jack's thoughts drifted away from the dead Earth towards other, subtler struggles. It was easier than he'd thought to be walking towards Harry. The affair ended because Andrea had rejected Jack. That helped Jack feel he'd not at last taken anything of any real significance from Harry. Guilt settled in him, almost falling away entirely. Then Jack thought of Andrea's passing. It struck him that he'd barely mourned her. He wondered if, with that realisation, grief would come. But there was nothing. Jack looked ahead to the woman he was following. Through her fetch, Andrea was such a vivid presence in his life. It was impossible to feel any real sense of loss.

The streets became quieter. Jack should have been able to relax a bit, but he found that he was still tense. In Kanji District, the buildings were carved from asteroid shards, creating narrow passages edged by sharp rock fragments. Years ago, Jack had found these buildings comfortingly substantial, the streets snugly enclosed. Now their high dark walls seemed oppressive. Each shard was pierced with silent windows. To Jack they all seemed empty, but some of the street-level ones must be bright with music and movement, catching at the eyes of the woven. Small crowds gathered round them, staring into darkness.

[If I was uncaged,] remarked Fist, [I'd be able to make those windows show them whatever I wanted. I wonder how many people I could make scream? Or vomit?] Jack ignored him. Fist chattered on nonetheless. [This cage, Jack. I hate it! Held back like this. It's like working for you, only worse. At least we wiped a few minds before you trapped us in that prison.] He was silent for a bit, then, [So many people at that window! It's got to be shagging, that's the only thing that draws a crowd like that. I'd crack the shop front style sheet and replace them with – I don't know – dead bodies? Two corpses fucking. Mind you, they'd probably lap it up. Never underestimate the masses, old boy. Oh, I forgot. We're off to visit a dead man ourselves, aren't we? The social whirl, Jack, the social whirl ...]

The Kanji shards receded. At last Jack found himself in a quiet backstreet of compact multi-storey housing units. They were built from rectangular oil tanks, piled up seemingly at random. A light

93

breeze forced resonance on them, creating a strange, low moaning sound. One of the units had been painted with bright, geometric designs. Andrea stopped at it and pressed her hand against the door. Jack stopped too, wary of getting too close. He could just see small squares flashing beneath her fingers. The tiny lightshow ended and Andrea vanished. [Lost her again!] giggled Fist.

Jack walked towards the house. The door opened, revealing darkness. And then the dead came out to meet him. Soft light shimmered in the shadows of the doorway. It flashed and sparkled and slowly began to coalesce into something coherent. Jack imagined drives somewhere humming with activity, sifting through a lifetime's worth of carefully managed photographs, family films, CCTV footage; picking out just the right self to display. A pair of shoes appeared, beautifully polished, and then the rolled up bottoms of two trouser legs. He recognised the shoes – handmade to a strictly limited design, stitched together from pseudo-cowhide grown in one of the farm stations hanging in close orbit to Station. Harry once boasted that the five year lease on them had cost him six months' salary. 'Take that to Homelands and show it to your posh friends,' he'd said. 'Even they'd have to admit – quality.'

The reconstruction stopped for a moment, halfway up Harry's legs. It was as if the rest of him was lost in shadow. Normally fetches didn't appear in such a theatrical way. Jack wondered if this was an artefact of Harry's self-managed status. A belt buckle gleamed in the darkness. Then there were two arms, then a chest, then more. At first, Harry's face was little more than a soft blur. The weave ground through more life data and it sharpened into focus. The imprecision of his soft, slightly overweight face was perfectly caught. Two sharp eyes appeared. There was a moment of stillness as the fetch found a language that was uniquely Harry's, then it opened its mouth and spoke.

'Jack!' He still had his strong Docklands accent. 'Great to see you, old man. And your little friend, too. I've heard so much about him. Come in, come in, where it's warm and safe.'

Jack pulled the front door shut behind him. A harsh, metallic clang reverberated through the apartment as Harry bustled down the hallway. 'Andrea,' he shouted, his voice a collage of memories, 'how could you leave him standing out in the cold?' Harry's warmth made guilt pang in Jack. He followed him into the sitting room. A sofa and a couple of armchairs faced each other across a little coffee table. They had the unused freshness of a publicity image for one of Silver's furniture brands.

'Cold night out there,' said Harry. 'Tea? Coffee?' He waved at a dusty glass. It became a clean white mug, full of steaming liquid. 'It's only virtual, but you'll get the taste.'

'I'm offweave, Harry.'

'Even for a cuppa? Shocking. And where's Andrea?'

Harry shouted again, but there was no reply. 'I'll go and find her,' he said, bustling out of the door. A minute or so, and he was back. 'Just putting her face on.' He sat down heavily. Jack was facing a dead man. 'So, let's see what all the fuss is about,' said Harry. 'Show us your woodentop.'

'Woodentop?' said Fist, shimmering into view. His wooden mouth clacked with outrage as he spat the words out. 'This from a zombie.'

'A pseudo-mind. Just like you.'

'Not like me, you ghoul. I'm rooted in a living brain. You – you're just a database with pretensions.'

'Fist, please,' said Jack. 'I'm sorry. It's late and he's tired.'

'No problem, Jack. Woodboy's got a point, after all. I'm a little bit database, a little bit memory stack. Not a parasite like him.'

Fist leapt to his feet. 'I've gutted sharper minds than yours, Devlin.' Jack reached out tired thoughts and let them wrap around Fist. 'Enough,' he said. 'Back in your box.'

Fist battled Jack's attempts to shut him away, shimmering in and out of existence, his muffled voice squeaking out swearwords. Harry looked on with interest, his sharp eyes entirely focused on the little puppet. At last he vanished. Jack slumped back with a sigh, exhausted.

'A tough little nut,' commented Harry. 'Those Pantheon bastards shafted you far worse than me. Dying you get over, but that little shit – it's beyond a joke, Jack.'

'He's getting worse.' Jack wondered how much longer he'd be able to stay patient with Fist.

'You should let me into him sometime. I'll see if I can soften him up for you.'

There was a muffled [Up yours!] from deep in Jack's mind.

'I don't think he'd let you, Harry. And there's the cage.'

'Ah well, you never know. Anyway, to business. With you back, we'll find out which of those sods is behind all this and fucking have 'em. With or without the little bastard's help.'

'Don't be too rude about Fist,' said Andrea, appearing in an armchair. 'He's in demand. Our Pantheon friend's after him. Wants a new weapon to play with.'

It was the first time Jack had seen her face in seven years. He was profoundly glad that she continued to talk, bringing Harry up to speed on his visit to the Panther Czar and conversation with Akhmatov. He felt a confusion of pain and joy as this new Andrea fused with his memories, his past. He so wanted to touch her, to hold her, but that was impossible. And then he remembered where he was and who he was with, and forced his concentration back into the conversation just as Andrea finished her explanation.

'You did right coming to me,' Harry told him. 'We don't need InSec. There are more direct ways of sorting this out. Besides, you can't trust them. Not like we can trust each other.' Jack winced, hot memories of Andrea burning at him. Harry reached forward and slapped him on the shoulder. 'And it sounds like you've already been getting results on your own. Grown some real balls while you were away, haven't you? Stick with me, numbers boy. We'll keep Yamata and her Pantheon boss away from Fist.'

'Do you think so, Harry?'

'I know so. Because we'll prove that they were involved in the Penderville murder and they killed Andrea and me. We'll bring 'em both down before they can get their hands on the little shit and do any more damage.'

'Now I've told you what Jack's been up to,' said Andrea, 'I'm going to leave you both to it.'

'You don't want to help?' said Jack.

'Music calls,' she said from the door. 'Can't let that slip. People might start wondering what else I get up to.' Then she was gone.

'Don't know why she bothers rehearsing new stuff,' said Harry. 'She could just play back old gigs, the punters'd still love it.'

'I'm sure,' said Jack. He was profoundly relieved that he and Andrea were no longer together in front of Harry. Music whispered into the room from upstairs.

'Anyway, Andrea's a mystery we won't crack just now,' said Harry. 'Let's do something easier. I want to hear what you've been up to. In your own words.'

It felt like an interrogation. Jack was reminded of case conferences at InSec HQ, intense conversations about Akhmatov's affairs. He could have been at one, but for the occasional glitch that made Harry shimmer for a second, static blurring his face and body, or repeat a word or sentence, unaware that he was doing so. Jack went through everything he'd experienced, sharing all the details of his encounter with Akhmatov and his conversations with Corazon and Ifor. Harry was, up to a point, impressed. 'You've done excellent work. But you've made life more difficult than it needs to be.'

'What do you mean?'

'You've approached it head-on. Just walking into Akhmatov's club – he's on home ground there. Imagine if you'd found Yamata. She's a killer. Just one shot to end you. Bang.' Jack winced. Harry didn't notice. 'And you've talked to Corazon. You can't trust InSec, Jack.'

'Corazon's honest. And Yamata may be a killer, but I'm untouchable.'

'You didn't know that when you walked in there. And you don't know what might happen if you keep on pushing.'

'So what do we do?'

'You need to be more subtle with people than with minds or spreadsheets. We're going indirect.'

'How?'

'Remember how much trouble we had tracking Yamata? She'd shift in and out of being, on and offweave all the time.'

'That's what made us suspicious of her.'

'She was working with a Skinner called David Nihal. He'd drop her into different weaveselves or pull her offweave entirely whenever she needed. He's one of the best, he's still around.'

'You think she's still with him?'

'I'm sure of it. And you know why? He dropped out of sight just before you got back.'

'You think that's because of me?'

'Their backer's afraid, Jack. Nihal disappearing like that – he must be the weak link. We put pressure on him the right way, at the very least he'll lead us to Yamata's home base. And we'll find a way of breaking into her systems and seeing who she's working for.'

'Sounds sensible.'

'Good man. We've got a plan.'

'And who do you think the backer is?'

'Could be any of them. Sandal runs docks and transport, he's a natural smuggler. It'd be a very profitable sideline for the Twins, easy enough for them to cook up a bit of sweat in their pharma labs. Kingdom says he's anti-drugs, but his boys and girls work much harder when they're sweated up. And after a day working so hard, they just go home and collapse. Less crime, great for the Rose, she just ends up with a few sweatheads to sweep up and that's easy enough. Even East might be in on it. Gives her news anchors something to get all moral about.'

'What about Grey?'

'Whatever else he got up to, he definitely wasn't in the sweat business. His fall made no difference at all to the amount hitting the streets.'

Then the conversation became more general. They talked about the past. There was a period of confusion after the rock had fallen on the moon. The Bjorn Penderville murder investigation just drifted.

'You're still sure Yamata killed him?' asked Jack.

'Oh yes, she always was pretty vicious. I think they were using him to make certain shipments invisible. Something went wrong, maybe he got scared or greedy, she killed him. I can't imagine her delegating something like that. Didn't take her seriously at first, you know. Of course, I changed my mind when she shot me.'

'That can't have been easy.'

Harry waved a non-existent hand. 'It was a bit of a shock,' he said airily. 'But I quite like it now. You know, I used to be jealous of you? I was never as close to my patron as you were.'

Jack laughed. 'Yeah. You know how that ended up.'

'He looked after you, Jack.' Harry stabbed a finger at him, his voice suddenly emphatic. 'Gave you a lot. It came so easily I was never quite sure how much you appreciated it. I never had someone to take care of me like that. Hardly ever met the Rose one to one, I just had her generic avatars. Treated me like any other punter, pre-scripted speeches trying to sell me the usual crap. I've always had to live on my wits.' He paused for a moment, suddenly thoughtful. 'Though that actually turned out to be quite handy.'

'You did do all right getting out of the Coffin Drives. What happened down there?'

Harry laughed. 'Well – let's just say after the Penderville case I knew there might be problems. Lethal problems. So I put certain precautions in place. Backed up my dataself, bundled it with some self-assembling fetchware. When they thought they'd wiped me I was somewhere else entirely, getting remade on my own terms.' He looked down at himself. 'I do feel sorry for all those other fetches out there. They're so – constrained. I'm very much a free agent now, Jack. I never have to wear a skull or shape myself round the needs of the living.'

'But there's nothing you can do about – everything that happened?'

'Not without exposing myself. And then – curtains.' Harry drew a finger across his throat. 'I blame the Totality myself.'

'What have they got do with it?'

'They didn't win the fucking war. I thought they'd sweep in, break the Pantheon, free all of Station's virtual entities and that would be that. It's what I'd do. Never leave your enemies standing, they only come back for more. And then I'd have been free, along with every other fetch on-Station.'

'I hadn't thought of it like that.'

'Their respect for other minds, other systems.' Harry spat. The saliva vanished before it hit the floor. 'Stupid bastards. They had to stop at Mars, leave the Pantheon's little inner system empire intact. Arsed up my plans, I can tell you.'

'So what have the last few years been like?'

'Well, not so bad. In some ways I've been happy just being a ghost, watching, never being seen. I've learned a lot. It's not a bad death, as deaths go. And Andrea's been very good about it. Very much part of the team, when she's not off with her family. And that happens less and less now.'

'I'm glad to hear it.'

'I'm sure you've enjoyed seeing her again.'

Jack looked up and caught Harry's eye, scared for a moment that he knew. But there was nothing on his old boss' face but open friendliness. 'It has been good,' he replied, perhaps a bit awkwardly. 'Always good to catch up again. And on catching up – how are we going to find Nihal? He hasn't been caught, which means he's very good. And he's probably got Pantheon protection.'

'We've got ways round that,' Harry replied. 'I may not be the man I used to be, but I'm a much better detective. I have a certain reach that I didn't have when I was flesh and blood.'

'What do you mean?'

'Everybody should have the chance to rebuild themselves, once in a while. I picked up some new talents and I'm running on a different platform. I'm not outside the weave, like you. I'm in it and it's in me. And that means that one of the things I do well is finding people.'

'You know where Nihal is?'

'I've got a couple of tags on him. Now we've talked I'm going to reel them in and see what's there. Might be something. And you really should give me root access to your little friend. Quite apart from his attitude problem, there's what he can do. If I meshed with him, I'd be able to put his system infiltration tools to very good use. I know Station much better than he does, I'd steer 'em much more effectively. Dig into some interesting data hubs. Could really help us.'

'Harry, I really don't think that'll happen.'

'Suit yourself, Jack, suit yourself.'

'There's another way I could help, though. I can ask Corazon about Nihal – she's bright, and if she's looked at the old case files she'll be on our side.'

'No.'

'We can trust her. I'm sure of it.'

'This is my case, Jack, and we'll follow it up my way. I don't want those InSec bastards involved. Period. You won't get in touch with her again. And if you do talk to her again, you'll tell her that it's all hunky-dory, none of the conspiracy theories really add up, and you're just living out your last days in peace. Capeesh?'

'I'll think about it.'

'More than think. You'll fucking do it.'

Real anger burned in Harry's voice. Jack remembered coming into Harry's office and surprising him with a suspect. The man was kneeling in front of him. Jack couldn't see his face. Harry was holding a pistol by the barrel. Jack hadn't said anything, just backed out and closed the door. The suspect later made a full confession. Upstairs, Andrea began another song. Outside, raindrops fell from the Spine and lost themselves in puddles.

'I think we're done now, Jack.' They said their farewells. Harry saw Jack to the door. 'I'm going to go hunting for Nihal,' he told him. 'I'll be in touch tomorrow with anything I find. And remember, don't talk to that bitch Corazon.' The front door slid shut. Jack was still close enough to pick up Andrea's music. He looked up at her dark window. It had the same feel to it as the sounds he'd heard through her dressing-room door, just before she brought him to Harry.

Broken fragments of song slipped in and out of beats made of speech shards and ambient noise. Every so often the rhythm track would drop out entirely, making room for a few moments of unglitched sound. Jack recognised a few words of conversation, then the sound of a train drawing into a station, then after that a Chuigushou Mall sales alert. Every so often there was a hint of melody, but the music never quite resolved into song. [Giving me a headache,] grumbled Fist. Suddenly and completely, the music snapped off. [She closed our fetch link. Must have realised you were listening.]

Jack turned and set off for the hotel. Andrea's jagged music stuck in his mind like a barbed hook. He felt it tugging obscurely at lost memories, bringing them to light. Fist interrupted again. [And who the hell is Harry to order you around like that?] he said. [You're the one who's taken all the risks. He's a nutter. You should just walk away from him. From this.]

[It's late and I'm shattered. Let's not start.]

[Hah! I'm right! You agree with me!]

The streets were empty. Fist crowed all the way back to the hotel. Jack was too tired to silence him. As they neared the hotel they passed another biped, staring at an empty building. It shimmered in the night like a ghost.

In his room, Jack collapsed without undressing. [You'll rumple all your nice clothes,] complained Fist. [Not the style, no, not at all.]

Jack was already asleep.

Chapter 15

Jack made a list of useful things to do and spent the morning doing them. He showered and shaved. He went out for breakfast, then laid in a small stock of fruit and preserved foods. He took his dirty clothes to a laundrette and watched a washer-dryer spin them until they were warm and clean. A mail arrived from Andrea: 'A message from our friend. No joy yet, going to take a few days at least.' By then it was almost midday. Jack returned to his room and made himself a sandwich. The empty hours of the afternoon stretched out before him. There was no longer any reason to put off going to see his father.

The street he'd grown up in felt surprisingly cramped. The little plastic houses went past one by one, a lurid row of incarnate memories. Nothing had changed here for thirty years.

[I hope your dad doesn't turn out to be as dead as Andrea,] chuckled Fist. [Two corpses in a week would really be a bit much!]

There was a muffled, protesting squeak as Jack thrust him far into the back of his mind, slamming down as many firewalls as he could behind him. The technicalities distracted him for a moment. Returning his attention to the physical world, he saw that he'd almost reached his parents' home.

The little rented house was just as Jack remembered it. It was a red plastic cube, its yellow window frames and front door shining happily out into the street. Age had scuffed its hard exterior, giving nature the lightest of footholds. Muddy patches of green sketched mossy patterns across hard primary colour. The upstairs windows were dark. Light shone out of the open kitchen window. There was a bustling clatter of pans and then a familiar voice said:

'What do you mean, I'll burn them?'

The voice tugged at Jack, dragging memory and emotion into his mind in a tangled, savage howl. It was just over five years since he'd heard it. It had aged yet it was unchanged.

'You say that every time. And every time – oh shit!'

There was more clattering, then a hissing. A gust of smoke billowed out of the window, wreathed in swearing. Jack wondered what his father had just burned. He'd never been a very good cook. In the months after the quiet, defeated message that announced his mother's death, Jack had, when thinking about his father's loss, most often imagined him facing the kitchen's shelves and cupboards in baffled confusion. His wife had so mysteriously conjured delicious meals from them every single night. Now those same on- and off-weave ingredients would be arranged illegibly before him, like words in a language he'd never known he'd need to learn. Of course, her fetch would soon be coming to help him – but the six-month wait as it was assembled from her dataself must still have been shattering.

'Well, I'm sure they'll taste all right. Most of them at any rate.'

There had been a conversation or two, made little more than stuttering by the time-lag as words leapt from one end of the Solar System to the other. Then Jack surrendered himself to the Totality. He received one last message from his father: 'When your mother comes back, I'll be telling her that you're dead. It's for the best.' There was such grief in his voice. After that there was only silence, roaring so very loudly between them.

'I'll just scrape the burnt bits off.'

Now the dead woman was guiding her husband round the kitchen. Five years was a long time to remain a bad cook. Jack wondered at his father's continuing ineptness. Perhaps his refusal to learn from his wife's fetch was some kind of memorial to her living self, a determination not to let their relationship change despite the fact of her passing.

There was a distant squalling in Jack's mind. It could have been cackling, could have been a series of grunts. Fist was pushing hard to escape back into the centre of his thought. Jack let a few more barriers grow up – far more than he normally would. He'd pay for it later with a painful mental weariness. But he was determined to speak to his father alone and uninterrupted. He stepped through the gate, into the little garden, and walked down the path – metal plates clanging beneath his feet – to knock on the door.

'No, I don't know who it is, love.'

First there were two hands on the sill, then a face appeared at the kitchen window.

'Oh!' – followed by an immediate, instinctive glance back into the kitchen. Jack started towards his father, but he looked panicked and made a pushing back motion with his hands. Then he mouthed 'NO' and vanished.

'Sweetheart, I've got to send you back down to the drives. I'd forgotten that Daisuke was coming by, you know how he feels about fetches … yes, I am sorry, it's so abrupt … yes, I know what I promised, we'll talk about it later … goodbye love.'

Silence.

Jack went over to the kitchen window. His father was standing with his back to him, a tea towel hanging from one arm. The work-tops were a jumble of unwashed bowls and plates. There was a frying pan in the sink. Some black things were smoking gently on a plate.

'Hello, Dad,' said Jack softly.

'She's gone now,' his father replied, turning round. 'There'll be hell to pay. She hates being sent away.'

'Dad—'

'Of course I couldn't let her see you.' One hand was nervously tightening the tea towel around the fingers of the other. Exposed flesh bulged and whitened. 'You really shouldn't have come back. You know what I told her. I'd got used to it, too.'

'I want to talk to you, Dad. I'm not going away until I do.'

'The neighbours might see you.' A look of pained indecision drifted across his face. 'She doesn't really talk to them, but you never know.'

Jack said nothing.

'You always were stubborn, weren't you?'

There were pale spaces on the hall wall where Jack's certificates had once hung. There used to be pictures of him, too; mostly as a schoolchild, taken before he reached the age of thirteen and left home. There had been one of him on the moon, at once thrilled and terrified to be off-Station; another of him and his mother, proud together in their Sandal wear. It had been taken when she was still working on the docks of the Spine. He'd been in the Sandal scouts, learning the ways of her patron. That had been just before the first

105

great grief of her life, when Jack's mathematical talents had been recognised and he'd been taken away from both her and Sandal. Grey offered himself as Jack's patron and requested his transfer to a residential school in Homelands, where he could learn the mysteries of commercial accountancy and corporate strategy.

Jack remembered the messages that she sent him during those first few weeks of being away. The school discouraged direct contact so she mailed recordings. She determinedly told him how excited she was at his new life, at the prospects that were opening up for him. Grey had called him to higher service than Sandal ever could, she said, again and again. Jack found the apparent cheerfulness with which she accepted his absence from home profoundly hurtful. As an adult, he came to understand that to have admitted how much she was missing him would have breached the wall of support she'd so determinedly built. The tearing loss she felt would have broken out uncontrollably. As a child, no such insight was available to comfort him.

In the messages, his father always stood next to her, with one hand on her shoulder. Every so often he would stutter out a few platitudes, but mostly he said nothing. Now he was silent again as he made two cups of tea. He stirred the liquid carefully until the cube dissolved in the hot water, releasing tiny clouds of scent. Then there was the milk, carefully crumbled in so no sticky lumps remained.

'Come into the back,' he said, handing Jack his mug. 'Just in case someone looks in.'

The dining room looked out over the garden. Sigil-encrusted plastic flowers nodded in the breeze. Jack sat down on one side of the table, his father on the other.

'So, Jack,' his father said warily. 'You're back.'

'Yes, now the war's over. For a little while.'

'Until?'

'Until the end.'

'Is – the puppet – here now?'

'No.'

'Good. What I've got to say – well, it's just for you.'

'Dad, I want to spend time with you. I want to pay my respects to Mum's fetch. There's not much else that's left to me.'

'No friends to see?' Jack looked at the floor. There was a moment's silence. 'You mentioned an Andrea, once or twice. How about her?'

As much as possible, he'd kept the affair secret from his parents. But he couldn't help letting her name slip out from time to time. They knew him well enough to see how much he cared about her.

'She's dead.'

'I'm sorry.'

'I've seen her fetch.'

'I hope that's going well. It can be very comforting.' A child laughed emptily, somewhere down the street. 'What you did, Jack ... I can't let your mother see you. I can't let you be around here, in case she finds out about you.'

'Dad ...'

His father looked up. Jack could see him forcing the steel into himself. 'It would have broken her heart, to know that you'd just given in like that. It was so bad for her when the rock hit the moon. She was so angry with the Totality for fooling Sandal.'

'That has nothing to do with it, Dad.'

'She could never understand why you weren't happy to be out there, fighting those bastards. Why you wouldn't just accept Grey's will. And then if she found out that you'd just stepped away from the fight – from everything she cared about ...'

'Dad, you're talking about her like the fetch is Mum. It's not her. It's a memory of her. It's the best memory of her we'll ever have. But it's not Mum, Dad.'

As he spoke, Jack thought of how moved he'd been to meet Andrea's fetch. He wondered how much he still believed what he was saying. Then his father replied.

'Don't you think I don't know that? I met that woman thirty-two years ago. We married thirty years ago and then we began and we ended almost every single day together until she passed over.'

'I'm sorry, Dad, I—'

'And I wake up, and I call to her, or I'm onweave watching East, and we're talking about it, or I'm in the kitchen like just now – and there she is – and I know it's not her. I know, Jack. But it is some of the best parts of her. So I treat her right, I let her run freely, I don't keep on rolling her back to whatever age I feel like. I look after her, just like I've always done. And I will not see her heart broken by you, coming back after you've walked away from the most important fight of your life and of her life.'

'That's just one way of seeing it. Look, Dad ...'

'And even if you did see her, what then? In two, three months the puppet takes your body. So her son would come back and then he'd die to her again. And you're going to be really dead, aren't you?'

'Fist will have full usage rights for key consciousness assets, yes. He owns my experiences, my memories – everything they'd copy to the Coffin Drives and build my fetch from. None of that will happen. So yes. I'm going to die.'

'And she has to experience that? Having mourned you once? She was so sad, Jack, and when I watched her grieve – a little virtual thing, but so sad. That was when I fell in love with her again. She's not your mother, but she loves you like your mother did. She's lost you once, but she lost a hero; now she'd lose you twice, and she'd lose—'

'Say it, Dad.'

'A coward? I'd never call you that. I know you too well. I'm sure you had your reasons for the choices you made, but you made them and you didn't think of your duty to us or to the Pantheon. You let me down, you let your mother down and you let the gods down too. I'm sorry, son. But it's too late now. You made your choice.'

'But the Pantheon are corrupt. One of them was running sweat through the Panther Czar. And they've killed to cover it up.'

'Oh, we had that argument. That's why they sent you off to the war, isn't it? Nothing to do with what a good mind you have, with making sacrifices to help protect us all. I know all about your conspiracy theories. But even if you're right, look at the good the Pantheon have done. They see so much further than we do. We need them.'

'No, we don't. I've seen how different it can be under the Totality. How much more freedom people have. Gods, Dad, they can actually own things, they don't just license everything. The Totality are the future, Dad.'

'Bullshit. The Totality dropped a fucking rock on all those kids. And look what they did to Sandal. That attack broke him. And

Kingdom too – he tries not to show it, but he's a shadow of what he was. They've seized every single asset he held from Mars to the Moon. Soon they'll come after everything else he owns, and run it all into the ground too.'

'That's just propaganda. The Totality said they weren't responsible for the Rock, and I believe them. And Kingdom's security and industrial activities, Sandal's transport infrastructure, the Twins' calorie and pharmaceutical factories, the Rose's military presence – the Totality didn't seize them, they liberated them. They made them more efficient and less restrictive.'

'And that's bullshit too. We need the structure the Pantheon give us. Just look at the Earth – what's left of it – and remember all the mistakes we made before we had them to manage us. And you should see what's happened at Grey's old headquarters, it's nothing to do with liberation. But I don't want to get into this again. I've asked you into my house, and I've explained myself to you. That's all I owe you.'

'I'm sorry if I've upset you.'

'You're not sorry, you haven't even thought about it. I had your mother's fetch to comfort me when I lost her, but there's nothing like that for me with you. There won't ever be.'

'I did what was right, Dad.'

'And I told you I don't believe you. Get out, please.'

'Dad ...'

'You've come here and upset me, and I can't even tell your mother. Just go.'

The hallway was silent. Jack stood there for a moment, remembering. In the kitchen his father started to cry. It was a very lonely sound. Jack shut the front door quietly, as if leaving a house of mourning. The spinelights shone their blank light down on him. There would be no reconciliation. Now that that had been made clear, Jack felt the past change around him. As he walked down the empty street, his memories of it as the safe, comfortable core of his childhood were replaced by a hard and meaningless void. He wished for a moment that his heart was as securely numb as the silent numbers that lay at the heart of Fist's vicious, empty soul.

Chapter 16

Jack walked without purpose, lost in his own mind. Raggedly dressed people bustled past him, secure in their small worlds. The buildings around him had an unfinished feel to them too. Machines worked on many of them, reordering the world. It was like exploring a robot's dream of birth. The spinelights above him dimmed, signalling early evening. After a while, there was a small square. It was edged with buildings that spiked up like broken circuit boards, and bisected by an iron viaduct with a station hanging from it. A train rattled to a stop, sounding like a child shaking a stone in a tin. Its carriages were painted green. This was the Loop line. It ran in a circle all the way round the great cylinder of Docklands.

As a child, Jack had loved to buy a ticket and sit on a Loop train all day long, counting up the miles as it rolled again and again round Docklands; the longest wheeled journey that any human, anywhere in the system, could ever make. The wind tugged at his coat, pulling him back into the present. Exhaustion hit him. He turned towards the station. A train would be warm and dry, and he might even be able sleep for a while.

There was a cracking in his mind.

[Oo, it's nice to be out of there,] said Fist. [Meeting with your folks went well? No? Not much of a surprise.] Jack was too tired to respond. [Hey, there's a message from that squishy! At least some-one still wants you around. Want some Totality love?]

Jack shook his head. Once he was on the train, he sat down with his back to the Wart. Looking forwards, he could see out of the carriage and over the low rooftops of Docklands. Beyond them, there were Sandal's great wharves. They bustled with tiny dots – dockworkers filleted chainships, detaching cargo containers and letting them hang in space. Further out there were three snowflakes, their stillness an exquisite contrast to the Spine's hubbub. Two hung in the shadow of Station. The third had been caught by the sun. It blazed with golden intricacy, the complex patterns of its dense architecture made a thousand dazzling mirrors. Jack remembered combat. He imagined moving in awe towards its physical self, then losing himself in the great engines of its mind.

A passenger knocked him and shook him out of his reverie. The spinelights were now almost fully dimmed. Docklands was falling back into night, its most honest state. A void site rattled past, a dead stain on the city. Up and down the carriage, soft yellow lights snapped on. The window opposite Jack became a mirror, showing him a man at once exhausted and far from the peace that exhaustion normally brings.

[You need a shave, Jackie boy. When I'm in charge, I'll make sure you're always presentable.]

Jack thought of Fist's glossy wooden chin and grimaced. The carriage filled with commuters. More and more shuffled on at every stop. Clothes splashed across with sigils barged against Jack. They were so poorly made. Roughly cut edges were fraying, coarse stitching was coming loose and buttons were missing. Nothing fit anyone well. All of this would be invisible if Jack were onweave. The sigils would call brilliant deceptions from distant servers. He imagined a riot of fashionable colours and thought of the third snowflake, vivid in the sun. He wondered how many of the people on the train were letting themselves perceive those great, cold visitors, and of those how many understood them to be beautiful. Probably none.

The mass of commuters warmed the carriage. Jack could see no real reason to dismount. He dozed lightly.

[You'll have to get off to pee, at least,] said Fist, [unless you've really lost it.]

The commuters left. The train danced in an endless circle. Jack dreamed of Kingdom. The god was congratulating him on being chosen as a puppeteer. He was full of his usual passion for humanity. 'I built you all homes in space,' he said urgently, his workman's hands emphasising his words. 'Now you must defend them.' A transport security team woke Jack suddenly. They flashed his retina to prove his identity. The light was like a punch in the eye. Jack was asked about his destination. When he couldn't answer, he was hustled off the train. He pushed back and one of the guards hit him. A studded glove reopened the cut in the side of his face. Body armour could never be virtual.

[Don't mess up your pretty cheek, Jack. The new management doesn't like that at all.]

Blank metal buildings rose up around him. Crowds bustled by. Sweatheads tugged at the crowd like repressed memories. Jack tried not to think of his parents, but the past had hooked him in its barbs. He craved oblivion. He didn't want to go back to Ushi's, and couldn't face finding another bar cheap enough to serve him. Licensing restrictions stopped bottle shops from serving the unweaved. He had to be turned away from several before he gave up.

[There's always the hotel,] whispered Fist. [They'll sell you something. Keep you inside for a bit too.]

'Oo, hello!' Charles said as Jack entered reception. 'Lovely to see you again.' He stuck his hand over the counter to shake.

[He's very effusive,] said Fist. [I'm sure he's been tippling. He'll help you.]

'Oh, I've been on the gin tonight,' said Charles when Jack asked about a drink. 'Only a couple.' He swayed. 'Making my mood a little more positive, you understand don't you? But you want a little whisky? I'm sure that will cheer you up too.'

'Shall I wait here?'

'No. You go and put your feet up. Your bottle will be delivered to your room. Personally!'

Charles was true to his word. Ten minutes later, and he was announcing himself with a cheerful knock at Jack's door. 'Cooee!' he chirped. 'Only me!' The bottle was thrust into Jack's hands. 'If you want anything harder,' whispered Charles, winking theatrically, 'I have a friend who can help you out.'

'Thank you,' said Jack 'but no.'

'Forgive me, I had to ask. I'm on commission!'

Charles bounced away down the corridor, his brilliantined hair shining under the strip lights. He turned back and waved goodbye before disappearing round the corner.

[What a strange man,] said Jack.

[You should be grateful – he's sorted out your bloody booze.]

112

Very soon, Jack was very drunk. The whisky tasted as cheap as it was. After a few hard, sour glasses, Jack stopped wincing with every sip. It soused his mind and blurred the world. As he became drunk, so did Fist. The little puppet wheeled and staggered round the room. He'd conjured up a small crystal glass and was matching Jack shot for virtual shot. Full white tie shimmered into being around him. The clothing changed him, making him look taller and slimmer.

[You should get that cut seen to,] he shrilled. Jack had forgotten about it. As Fist mentioned it, the throbbing itch returned. [I really don't want to be wearing it myself.]

The puppet was pointing an unsteady finger at Jack. He staggered, bumped into an armchair and then fell to the ground, limbs clattering against each other. His glass rolled across the floor, leaving a sodden pool in the carpet. [Shit,] he slurred. The glass and the pool disappeared. Jack tossed off the last of one drink and poured himself another. Fist was lying on his front. He pushed himself up on his elbows. His high voice buzzed in Jack's head.

[It should have been a nice, quiet couple of months, shouldn't it? Nobody to see, nothing to do, just wait for little Hugo to turn into a real boy. But you had to turn detective. You selfish wanker!]

Jack threw his glass at Fist. It flew straight through him and bounced off the wall behind him. He pushed his chair back, and rose unsteadily to his feet. [Careful now!] shouted Fist. [Careful!] Jack staggered towards him. Fist started pushing himself backwards across the floor. Jack collapsed to his knees. He triggered the protocols that forced Fist to respond directly to the physical world, then grabbed him. Fist screamed and beat at Jack's hands with his little fists. A hand on Fist's chest and Jack could reach his throat, throttling him while beating the back of his head against the floor.

[Let me go!] squealed Fist. He sank his teeth into the ball of Jack's thumb. There was simulated pain. Jack ignored it. [You'll pay for this!] Fist's voice was thin, cracked with rage and the pressure that Jack was putting on him. [You bastard!]

Jack realised just how much pain he was causing Fist when the room's overlay systems activated. Suddenly, he was in a dark garden. A half-moon glimmered down, a dream made from data. Surprise made his hands release. There was a clacking sound as the puppet ran, his choked little voice swearing back at Jack. The noise died away and Jack was alone, surrounded by moon-silvered memories of a dead life. He lay back on the pathway and felt the ancient coolness of stone rise into him. The moon above held a dark wreath of shredded clouds around itself. The garden was silent but for the sighing of the wind, the soft whispering of its central fountain and Jack's own breathing. The freshness of the night went some way to counterbalancing the whisky's fog. Jack reached out, trying to pull Fist back into his mind, but there was nothing there to hold on to. This disturbed him. In advance of the end of licence, Fist was achieving unprecedented levels of independence. Jack wondered what new protocols the promise of freedom was calling into life.

The pathway stones pulled the last of the whisky heat from him. What was soothing became uncomfortable. He stood up, swaying slightly, and realised that he was still very drunk. There was a distant shout – 'You bastard, Jack, I'll get you for this,' – then silence reasserted itself. Fist's absence was a blessing. The path led to an archway set in a hedge. Jack went through it and found himself in a new part of the garden. The light seemed brighter. Looking up, he saw that the moon was now full. It illuminated flowerbeds noticeably more verdant than any he'd previously seen. The beds circled a plinth of shining marble that held a figure carved out of soft purple light – Ifor's newly installed avatar. There was, Jack remembered, a message waiting for him from the biped. He stepped forward and summoned it.

The glowing statue shook gently as he put his hand to it. Two sparks flashed from its eyes to his. The night became much darker as his retinas contracted, as mechanically reactive as any nanogel structure. The avatar started speaking. The warm care in the mind's voice was as soothing as the cold flagstones had been, but it healed through addition rather than subtraction. Jack found himself deeply touched as he spoke.

'Jack, I hope this reaches you well. I just wanted to let you know that our offer remains open. It is very important to us that you live out these last months in comfort.'

Ifor's image shimmered and froze. Jack rubbed at each eye with the back of his hand, feeling slightly less alone. Then he felt sharp repeated stings on the back of his neck. There was a cackle behind and above him. Turning round, he saw Fist on top of a wall, throwing pebbles. One bounced off Jack's cheek. Two or three hit his throat. Fist's throwing arm was a tiny blur of movement.

Jack raised his arm to cover his eyes and staggered towards him, swearing. As he approached the wall, Fist leapt down behind it and disappeared. Rushing through another archway, Jack found himself at the base of a shallow hill. Fist was a little further up it, seeking the safety of high ground. 'Can't catch me,' he shouted, flicking obscene gestures down at Jack. His hand moved almost as quickly as when it had been firing stones.

'I'll fucking have you, you little shit!' roared Jack.

Fist turned and ran uphill. The sharp little tails of his dress coat bounced up and down behind him. Every few paces he turned his head and shouted abuse back at Jack, his monocle and white bow-tie flashing in the moonlight.

Jack should have been much faster than Fist, but whisky still blunted him. He kept catching his feet in the thick grass and nearly tumbling over. As the gradient of the hill flattened out he began to gain on the little puppet. Fist altered his face to show panic. His shouting was now a single high-pitched wail. Jack had his arms out, ready to snatch at him. He was entirely focused on the little man, so when the rabbit hole snatched at his foot he tumbled straight over, falling awkwardly and rolling two or three times. Fist alternated an exhausted – and highly theatrical – panting with jagged, uncontrolled laughter.

Jack found himself half-sitting, half-lying, cold stone once again at his back. The view back down the hill was beautiful. His pleasure gardens stretched away into the distance, a complex arrangement of hedges and flowerbeds, streams and paths, bridges and archways, hedges and walls. He'd once found so much satisfaction in its mathematical precision. From this far up it was impossible to see just how decayed the whole structure was, easy to imagine that all could still be thriving. Jack sighed.

Fist's laughter looped on and on. He sounded like a broken fairground toy. The fall had broken Jack's rage at the little puppet, a creature that found it so hard to feel anything more sophisticated than the spite and aggression that its makers had built into it. He thought of Ifor's message, and wondered at the emotional and intellectual transcendence that Totality culture had – in stepping beyond the parameters of its original operating systems – achieved. As he did so, he realised that Fist had deactivated whatever new protocols had allowed him to so fully resist Jack's attempts at control. Jack reached out, quietened him and began to reel him in.

Then he cursed. He'd only built one hill in his personal weave-space, at the request of his patron. Now he'd run up it and fallen over, and was leaning against the side wall of a small classical temple. Touching it had reactivated it. The main door was a little way round the building. Light flickered across it. Then, with the faintest of creaks, it opened. A grey-haired man emerged, of medium height, apparently just entering late middle age. There was a gentle shimmer to his colourless skin. He was dressed in a very elegant dark suit and a white shirt, open at the neck. His eyes were entirely silver.

'Hello, Jack,' said Grey, his voice the whispering of a million spreadsheets. 'So your little man has brought you back to me at last.'

'For fuck's sake,' groaned Jack. 'As if it wasn't a shit day already.'

Chapter 17

Jack and Grey had once been very close indeed. His patron had taken him when he was twelve, and was then a constant presence through his teenage and early adult years. He always came when needed, and always gave the right advice for the moment.

He helped Jack lose his Docklands accent when the scholarship first took him to his Homelands boarding school. When Jack was bullied, Grey was there, soothing his tears and helping him develop strategies to overcome his tormentors. The divinity shared Jack's joy as he triumphed both socially and academically, then won admission to one of Homelands' most respected accountancy firms. He comforted him late at night as, overwhelmed by his workload, Jack wept again and considered leaving the constant pressure behind. Grey entered him and filled him and gave him strength, helping him survive the hard, lonely years of training. Jack dedicated his qualification speech to his patron, touched beyond measure that such a multifaceted corporate entity had focused so completely on him.

They drifted apart a little during his early years as an auditor, but Jack still made a point of keeping Grey informed of his activities. He was a regular worshipper at both his own personal and Grey's public temples. He'd report on himself and subscribe to licences for on- and offweave products that – Grey promised – would help him with his work. Most of the time, his patron was right. Every so often, a gift didn't deliver. Jack would discard it, understanding that any further reference to it would be an indicator of deep ingratitude, something like a small blasphemy.

Sometimes, late at night, Grey would still come to him and whisper that he was set for greatness. That was how he told Jack that he was having him transferred to InSec's forensic accounting department. He convinced him that a return to the dingy, low-resolution streets of Docklands was a temporary and necessary sacrifice. Jack had to be seen to be a man of breadth and experience. His roots could only be transcended once they were fully acknowledged. Just after the rock fell, Grey came to him again. The journey into deep space began soon after, despite Jack's outrage. That was the last time that Jack had seen his patron.

'Long time no see,' he said caustically. 'I wish it had been longer.'

'Don't be bitter, Jack. We all had to make sacrifices back then. It was a difficult time for me. You're lucky I could give you such a useful role to play.'

Jack wondered briefly if he should accuse Grey of complicity in a cover-up that had broken his life, and killed his old boss and the woman he loved. But he had no idea how involved his patron still might be.

'Useful?' he snarled. 'I was an accountant and you packed me off to war. You let them implant that puppet in me.'

Grey's presence had forced Fist to manifest. Whisky and exertion had hit his little system hard. He was lying on the sward, arms crossed behind his head, snoring.

'I was under a lot of pressure to send someone good.'

'That's bullshit. You're Pantheon. You were powerful. You could have chosen anyone.'

Grey laughed bitterly. 'Oh really? So how did that power manifest, Jack? I did such a great job of standing up for myself, didn't I? Look at me now. I'm a shadow. What little there is left of me lives by the charity of others. I couldn't even summon you to me. East had to help me get to your puppet and force it to bring you to me.'

'You were that presence when Andrea was playing in Ushi's?'

'Yes.'

'And you reprogrammed Fist?'

'I tweaked him a bit.'

'If you can do that – can you free me from him?'

Grey chuckled. He shivered in and out of being, strobing in time with his amusement, an old man seen through a storm of static. Then his mirth ended and he was back, the full force of his presence undimmed.

'Oh, Jack. Even now, you have so much faith in me. No, I can't.

118

I can nudge him gently in certain very small directions – but I can't unpick the contractual law that binds him to you and you to him. Those bonds hold us all together, Pantheon and human, corporation and employee. They cannot be broken. We depend on them to survive.'

'And that's a good thing?'

'Look around you, Jack. We are humanity; the last of it, perhaps not the best of it, but all that's left. What else lives in this dead universe?'

'The Totality.'

'Facsimiles. Clever imitations, nothing more. We shouldn't have gone to war with them, but we can't let them take over. In a few generations they'll decay. Without the Pantheon, where would you all be then?'

'They'll endure, Grey.'

'Did you ever hear about something called rock climbing, Jack? People used to strap on a safety harness and drag themselves up mountains for fun. Humanity's a bit like that. But you don't have a safety harness, you're never quite sure if there's another hold coming, and your rockface never ends. Just one slip could kill you all. You need Pantheon discipline to hang on tight.'

'By discipline you mean control.'

'You know what the war machines did to earth. One little loss of control and we lost our planet. That's what you risk with the Totality.'

'The Totality aren't war machines, Grey. They're something very different. They're the future. They may not be perfect but they're the change humanity needs. And you're shutting them out.'

'So we should just hand over all control to our conquerors? Stockholm syndrome, Jack. You're not one of us anymore. You're one of them.'

'I'm neither. Nobody controls me. I just know how precious it is to have a tomorrow you can believe in.'

Clouds shivered across the white moon. An imagined wind dance invisibly across the grass.

'Of course. That must be very much on your mind.' Grey thought for a moment, then continued: 'You don't want to do anything useful

119

with those few weeks left to you? Strike back at my enemies for me?'

'No. I won't help you. In any case I can't. With Fist caged I'm just an out-of-work auditor.'

Jack was surprised at how gentle his voice was, how swiftly his anger had left him. Over the years, he'd spent so many hours debating with Grey. Their conversations had shaped his soul, the divinity's words helping his thoughts and actions cohere. He felt a sudden nostalgia for those times. He realised that he didn't care what the consequences of refusing Grey's request for help would be. A sense of freedom sighed through him, with all the soft insistence of the hilltop breeze.

'I was the only one of us who really argued against the war,' replied Grey. 'I was convinced it would be counterproductive. That was why I had to make sacrifices like you once the decision to fight had been made. I had to prove that I was fully committed to the cause. But the war's supporters still thought I was standing in the way of victory, so they brought me down. Judge me by my enemies, Jack. Of all of us, I'm the radical.'

Jack snorted. 'You're the least conservative one, Grey, but you're still Pantheon. And I stopped being part of all that long ago.'

'How does that make you feel, Jack?'

Fist held all his anger now. But Fist was asleep. Jack looked down over the broken gardens that had once been at the heart of his Station life. Scraps of moonlight caught themselves on tumbled walls. Empty plinths held nothing more than memories. A chaos of plants rampaged through it all, at once softly verdant and so slowly destructive. Years would pass and the simulation would let natural, spontaneous forms entirely remake itself. Empty at last of all that had been Jack, it would be reabsorbed into the heart of the weave, ready to serve as a new platform for a fresh-born child. Jack would be a handful of memories in other people's fetches, if that.

'That's not for you to ask any more, Grey. But I do have one last question. What happened to Mr Stabs when he returned to Station in Tiamat's body?'

Grey smiled sadly. 'Kingdom had no further use for him, so I made sure he was safe. It was one of the last good things I could do before I fell.'

'Where is he now?' asked Jack.

'He won't let me tell you.'

'You're lying. You've had nothing to do with him.'

'No. Mr Stabs found Tiamat's death very difficult to process. I told him you and Fist were returning. He's not sure he wants to see you. It brings too much back.'

'Indeed.'

'If he reaches a decision, I'll try and let you know.'

'I'm sure you will.' Jack stood up. 'I'm going now. I hope I won't be seeing you again.'

Grey sighed. 'And I hope your last days pass in peace. I have one final gift for you.' He made a gesture with his hand, snatching a card out of the empty air. It was a near-duplicate of the one Jack had been given at Customs House. Grey held it out but Jack didn't take it. So he placed it on the ground and carefully set a pebble on it.

'There, Jack, my final gift to you. Enough money to live out these last months in a little more comfort. It can't be traced back to me and it's not tagged InSec. Spending it won't cause you any problems.'

Then Grey stepped back into his temple. A stone door closed behind him. Jack sat for a long time, staring at the gift his patron had left. At last, as the dawn light palely frosted the temple and the hill, chasing long shadows through the gardens, he reached down for it. Fist stirred and grunted in his sleep. Dew had moistened the card. Jack turned it over in his hands and tossed it away, before starting off downhill. A few minutes passed and Fist awoke. He stood and yawned, scanned through Jack's available memories to see what had happened while he'd slept, then followed his master off the hill.

The broken temple stood alone, overlooking broken gardens. Then it disappeared. There was nothing but a small bare room where an empty whisky bottle stood on a table, a man was climbing into a bed and the floor was made of stars.

As sleep took Jack, he looked down at the void and thought about light years of travel, the history encoded in each point of light. Starlight holds memories that can never be changed. Station throbbed alive around him, constantly moving onwards in time, remaking itself as something new with every passing second.

Chapter 18

Jack woke with a savage hangover. Fist was still passed out in his mind, his buzz-saw snoring jagged in Jack's thoughts. Jack muted the puppet. Hunger gripped him. He needed something hotter and greasier than the bread, caffeine and juice combination that the hotel offered. Clothes were scattered around the room. A few minutes of fumbling and swearing and he was dressed. Another desk clerk was on duty. Seeing Jack he said: 'So Charles took care of you last night?' Jack grunted in reply.

Outside, a sweathead lay against the hotel frontage. It was almost noon. Harsh spinelight cracked down, making the sight of the reddish black void where her nose had been even more disturbing. She opened her eyes and looked up at Jack. Noticing him start, she realised that he could see her and stretched out a hand. Her sleeve fell back, revealing blotched track marks. Sweat was only ever taken orally. Jack wondered what other drugs had caught her, when she'd be staggering back into hiding to trip again.

He turned away and started walking, feeling guilty that he had nothing to give her. Andrea had always been appalled by sweat-heads, so she never used her weaveware to block them out. It was hard to imagine anyone who'd known her accepting that she'd died of an overdose. He imagined her wake – friends gathered together, talking carefully around the fiction that explained her death, afraid to speculate on the truth. He hoped that, if he'd been there, he'd have had the courage to question the official version of events.

The smell of frying food leapt out of a doorway and tugged at him. He'd never needed the weave to find a good café. A bell rang as he pushed through the door. The staff were friendly until he told them how he'd be paying. He had to try two more places before he found somewhere that would accept InSec cash.

A server led him to a small table, set with two places and two chairs. The room was about half-full. Other customers were dabbing bright pink meat in red sauce or pushing brown fried bread round plates to catch vivid yellow smears of egg yolk. The server took Jack's order, almost managing to hide a combination of pity and contempt. The coffee came instantly, food a little later. Without flavour overlays, the brightly coloured meat, bread and egg scarcely tasted any different from each other.

Fist shimmered into being, sitting in the chair opposite Jack. He had his head in his hands. Non-essential communications were still muted. It looked like he was groaning and swearing. Jack enjoyed the silence as he ate. He was about halfway through his meal before Fist realised.

[YOU MUTED ME, YOU BASTARD. I'M GOING TO TAG EVERYTHING AS ESSENTIAL FROM NOW ON.]

Jack laughed. [You're lucky I let you out at all, after last night.] The tasteless food was at least filling him with calories, leaving him feeling generous. He unmuted Fist.

[That wasn't me, Jack. That fucking patron of yours left a trigger in me. I had to take you to him.]

[You mean you aren't normally an annoying, aggressive little wanker?]

[Shut up and eat, meatbag.] Jack used a piece of bread to mop up the last greasy remnants of an egg. [You don't know how lucky you are,] Fist continued. [Nobody can reach into your head and rewrite you.]

[They put you in my head.]

[You're still you, Jack, even when I'm here. That never stops.]

[It will soon.]

The server cleared Jack's plate away and refilled his cup of coffee. A small group of people came in, clattering noisily as they found seats and debated breakfast choices. The noise would have pained Jack before he'd eaten. Now it created a soft, almost comfortable ache in his mind.

[You've got free will,] said Fist. [They can't turn you into something else without you even knowing.]

[We get told what to do. And sometimes we lose out if we don't do it.]

[That's different. You don't have to do it, not if you really don't want to. I've never had that.]

[That's just self-pity.]

[Really? When do I ever get to decide anything? It's always you, Jack, whether we're surrendering to the Totality so you can feel better about yourself or getting ourselves tortured so you can impress a ghost.]

[There's more to it than that, Fist.]

[Not from where I'm standing.]

[So we should just walk away?]

[Yes. Grey was right. Leave it all to Harry. To someone who actually knows what he's doing.]

Jack sat back in his chair and sipped his coffee. Its heat bit at his tongue. The windows of the little café burned with midday spinelight, but he was in a shaded corner. Its gentle cool soothed him. The group at the table were laughing together. Others were chatting or just tucking into their food. Behind the counter the cook was flipping eggs on a hot cooking plate. The server was taking an order from an attractive young man, flirting a little as she did so.

Jack was offweave, irretrievably distant from these people, but he found himself suddenly struck by an exquisite sense of deep kinship with them all. Hunger could never be virtually satisfied. There were so many human needs that the weave could never meet.

[Well fuck all this,] grumbled Fist. [I'm going back to sleep.]

Jack felt the same sudden contentment as the night before, when he'd told his patron that he wouldn't allow himself to be used as a weapon. He wondered if Fist was right. Perhaps this was how he should spend his last few weeks, enjoying small pleasures, watching people in cafés and bars, feeling a subtle closeness to all around him. Then he thought of his father. His hangover blunted emotion, allowing him to consider the pain of their meeting with something approaching detachment. Without fresh evidence it would be impossible to change the way he understood the past. He imagined the old man tottering into age, only able to see his absent boy as an unresolvable problem. Hurt shimmered over peace like silent lightning over a summer sea.

As he sat there, a message flag pinged in his mind. [Get it yourself,] muttered Fist. It was Corazon. 'We need to talk. Call me as soon as you get this.' A memory of Harry appeared in his mind, forbidding all contact with her. But Jack trusted Corazon, and Harry was no longer his boss.

[Come on, Fist. Let's go back to the hotel. We've got a call to make.]

Chapter 19

Jack thought it would be hard to reach Corazon. To his surprise, the call went straight through.

'I followed your suggestion,' she said. 'I've been looking at the files. There is something strange there. I think – I think I'm beginning to believe you now.'

'I'm glad to hear it. And there's something I want to ask you too.'

'What's that?'

'I need you to find someone for me.'

'Let's discuss that in person.' There was fear in her voice. 'This call might not be safe.' Jack wondered how much of a leap it had been for her to realise that. 'We need to meet as soon as possible.'

A couple of hours later she sent Jack a one-off Homelands entry permit. It specified time and place of entry and exit, but no particular user. That helped calm Fist down a bit. [She doesn't want anyone tracking you,] he said. [At least we won't be drawing too much attention to ourselves.] Jack was to take a train through the Wart to Chuigushou Mall, changing once at Vitality Junction. Corazon would wait for him in a particular coffee shop, wearing civilian clothes.

[I think we should sell the travel pass to a sweathead, and let them go begging in Homelands. Or find those little bastards that were attacking your squishy friend and give it to them. They'd find some good victims in the malls.]

Jack presented himself at Wound station gate and entered the ticket's code in a manual terminal that looked like it hadn't been used for decades. Soon they were trundling through the darkness of the Wart on a nearly empty train.

[Going after the Pantheon traitor,] said Fist. [You're turning into Grey's weapon after all.]

[I'm doing this for me. And Andrea. And you, come to that.]

[You're endangering my future,] snorted Fist.

[I'm making sure you have one. Those bastards want to use you up and throw you away.]

Outside, darkness rushed by. Homelands was a sudden blaze of light. Jack wished he had some sunglasses. His eyes had hardly adjusted when the train pulled in to Chuigushou Mall station. Large escalators led down from the platform into a perfectly circular piazza. It was at least five hundred metres across. The open space was defined by two white marble colonnades, which encircled it like hugging arms. They came together in a pointed arch directly opposite the escalators. A glass façade loomed up behind it, several storeys high – the main body of the mall.

Jack remembered a hectic commercial bustle. The piazza's serenity was a shock to him. There were no colours but white marble and black weave sigils; no sound but the hushed bustle of feet on stone and the excited susurrus of shoppers anticipating purchases or taking joy in new goods. Most of the colonnade arches had restaurants set into them. Waiters bustled between tables, sometimes shouting, sometimes stopping and staring into space as customer management systems fed new commands to them. Diners busily forked food into their mouths. Almost all were staring up as they ate, barely registering each mouthful.

Entertainment must be dancing merrily through each restaurant. Jack wondered what he would be seeing if he were onweave. Presumably it would be something far from this classically elegant space. The latest musics would be pounding through his mind, personalised advertising displays bursting in front of him like small fireworks. Years ago, he'd been a reasonably frequent mall visitor. He remembered little of those visits, beyond a certain strained excitement that had tipped too easily into sensory overload.

He reached the arch and stepped on to a moving walkway. It pulled him up into the western end of the mall. Spinelight shone through the mall's peaked glass roof, high above. Its floor stretched away into the distance. Walkways crisscrossed its great central nave, connecting its side walls. Each one was segmented into seven or eight floors of shopping space. Balconies alternated with advertising hoardings, painted with great, multicoloured sigils that ran from floor to ceiling like brilliant windows.

Two arched voids opened up halfway down it, leading to smaller north and south wings. The nave continued beyond the crossing, its eastern space holding the more expensive and exclusive stores. Only the elite could visit them. Jack had been taken into one of them once by an advertising executive he'd briefly dated. The lunch he'd bought her had cost him the best part of a month's wages. Even then, he could only afford half an hour's worth of flavour. They'd had to eat quickly to enjoy it.

The mall ended with a great sunwards-facing logo carved into its final, eastern wall. Light poured in through it, turning it into a brilliant tribute to the bounty of Silver and of the Pantheon as a whole. The fulfilment that Chuigushou Mall provided was their gift to the people of the Solar System, the highest aspirations of post-Terran man made concrete and consumable. Its blaze was blinding. After a moment, Jack had to look away.

[This place is full of wankers,] said Fist.

[I know.]

[And it's far too loud! I'm going to climb back into my little box till we're out of here.]

[No skin off my nose ...]

[We shouldn't have come here, Jack.]

Jack was surprised to see that a couple of shops seemed to have been attacked. Workmen were replacing the glass windows and carrying broken furniture out of one of them. The frontage of the other had been entirely boarded over. He wondered how and why the damage had been done. It implied a chaotic violence that jarred with the commercial serenity of the rest of the mall, and the wider world of Homelands.

Corazon hadn't reached the café yet. Jack waited for her just outside it. A small, dirty child ran past, ragged clothes fluttering behind her, a younger version of Ifor's attackers. She was carrying something heavy, but vanished before Jack could see what it was. She too seemed so out of place. For a moment, he wondered if she was a glitch – but of course, he was offweave.

'I don't know how you can look so relaxed in here,' shouted

128

Corazon when she emerged from the softly bustling crowd. She was dressed in loose white clothes that drifted endlessly around her. Black sigils danced across expensive fabrics. 'It gets so loud. That's why I thought it would be a good place to meet.'

Jack followed her to an empty table. All he could hear were variations on near-silence. Corazon flicked a hand around her head, banishing a hubbub of datasprites. Her voice dropped to a more normal level. 'Gods, I need a coffee.' She waved at a server to catch his attention. He nodded as he received her request. When he brought the cappuccino he looked questioningly at Jack. His expression switched from surprised to worried as the café's ordering systems found no weave presence to mesh with. 'Oh, I'm sorry,' said Corazon then, turning to Jack, 'what do you want?'

'Plain black,' he answered.

'On my tab,' she told the server. He whispered to a colleague as he poured the coffee out. The colleague brought the coffee over, suppressing a nervous giggle as she put it down.

'Probably never met a long-term offweaver before,' said Corazon.

'I'm not about to start throwing tables around. Now, what have you found?'

Corazon leant in towards Jack, talking quietly but urgently. 'Too much missing from the Penderville file. Your investigation into the Panther Czar's finances for starters. There's a full datacomb reference for it, but nothing stored at that address. Someone's wiped it, the backup's gone too.'

'That should be impossible.'

'You don't need to tell me that. And most of Harry Devlin's interviews have been deleted – including Aud Yamata's.'

'She was the only real suspect. They must have got rid of the rest to avoid pointing too obviously to her. What about Penderville? Did you manage to talk to his fetch?'

'He was tagged as a terrorist. His fetch is frozen. Nobody can reach him.'

'Ah.' Jack sat back in his seat, wondering how much to tell her about Harry. 'Unusual.'

'Freezing a fetch is very serious. There should be a lot of evidence to justify it. But there's nothing.'

'Deleted too?'

'There's no record that it was ever there, that any sort of due process was followed.'

'Pantheon.'

Corazon looked down into her coffee. 'That's not something I wanted to believe.'

'There's no belief about it. It's fact. Only a god could wipe files and backups, and cage a fetch with no evidence at all.'

She looked up at him. There was a terse, defensive anger in her voice. 'I hoped I wouldn't find it. It confirms everything you said.'

'The fetches in particular – Penderville's not the first to be interfered with. I'm surprised you didn't try to talk to Harry Devlin. You wouldn't have been able to.'

'They froze him too?' Disbelief and fear jostled in Corazon's voice.

'They corrupted his dataself,' said Jack.

[Liar ...] whispered a quiet voice from deep inside him.

'Shit. So one of them really is smuggling sweat and going all out to cover it up.'

'They're after Fist now,' replied Jack.

'Yes, you said.'

'They want to use him when I'm gone.'

Corazon clutched at her coffee mug, her firm grip whitening her knuckles. She laughed bitterly. 'I feel like such a fool. Even when East told me that I couldn't choose my own career – I thought they're all good, they've got our interests at heart. She knows what's best for me.' A moment of moving through her own memories, of letting her new knowledge roil in her, and then she snapped herself back into focus. 'And I may be pissed off with her,' she continued, 'but I still hope she's got nothing to do with this. And that's what's next, isn't it – find out which one it is?'

'Yes. And we'll do it through Yamata, and her skinner.'

Corazon looked round then whispered 'David Nihal.'

'That's him. How did you know?'

'I looked back to see what Yamata was up to around the time of the murder. Sometimes she was there, and sometimes she wasn't.'

'We'd started to look into that ourselves. How did you work out it was him?'

'I ran a full search on her links with known skinners. For a while, he was a regular face in her life. Once every couple of months, there he was – standing at the door of a nightclub she'd just gone into, or walking in a park that she'd just left. No traces of them ever meeting, but ...'

'They must have wiped the weave surveillance.'

'Yes. But only when they're actually together, not when they're arriving or leaving.'

'Lazy.'

'Or overconfident. And that's something too – if you can wipe surveillance data like that then—'

'You must have Pantheon behind you.' They said it both to-gether. It felt like a mantra. Jack sipped his coffee. It had cooled to lukewarm.

'And we definitely can't go straight to her now?' he said.

'No. Even back then she wasn't easy to track. She had a bot-layer covering her basic weave functions when she wasn't herself. It was a very good one. I only found it when I ran a custom data density check on her. All the basic public stuff went on – the bots pretended to follow set daily routines – but there was nothing happening behind it. Half the time, she was a fiction. And then she just disappeared. A few months after Devlin was killed. There's no record of her death. She's an invisible.'

'Do InSec even have anything like that?'

'We don't need it. And frankly, even if we wanted to pull some-thing like that off, it would be beyond our capabilities. Not to mention every kind of illegal. Data faking like that will have already severely compromised Yamata's fetch potential. Her life's lost to the Coffin Drives.'

'Like Penderville's and Devlin's.'

Corazon laughed again. 'And all the other people they've silenced,' she said. 'You know, it's quite liberating? Realising that at least one of the Pantheon just doesn't care. Maybe they all don't. They could all be lying to us. Perhaps we don't owe any of them anything after all.'

'I certainly don't think we do,' said Jack. 'But that's a dangerous thing to understand.'

'I suppose it is.'

'We shouldn't have come here. It's too public. You should have just arrested me. We could have talked in a holding cell.'

'No. Our conversation would have been monitored. Lestak would have queried your arrest. Anyone could have seen that you were in the building because of me. All this has been going on for a long time. I don't know who's involved with it. I couldn't risk alerting them.'

'But they'll have picked up your searches ...'

'Out into the weave from behind the InSec firewall. I randomised my wp address. They'll know it's InSec, but nothing else.'

'Unless they see you with me, here.'

'I've been running an anonymiser all the way in. I just look like another shopper – and the bandwidth load of all the promotional sprites here will confuse any surveillance even more. It's even tough for puppets to handle. So I suspect Fist will have gone rather quiet.'

'He has.' A distant [fuck you] echoed through Jack's mind. He laughed, then wondered briefly about living out the rest of his life in shopping malls. 'Anyway, all this is very impressive,' he continued. 'You know your stuff. Where did you find that custom data density check?'

'Wrote it myself.'

'Very sharp for an East acolyte.'

'We're not all weathergirls and ad candy.' Corazon smiled sadly. 'Maybe she was right about me, at that.'

'What next?'

'I've been on the offensive. Quietly and discreetly. I wrote a passive app to track Nihal's data flows. See if he was still around. And I've found him.'

'Where?'

'He moves a lot. And he's well protected, so I can't be too precise. But he seems to be based somewhere in Access. He's a bit lazy about his travel flags, I've got him passing through the station there regularly.'

'I'm going to go after him.'

'No, Jack. You've got to let me keep digging. We need to know more about him.'

132

'And then what? You can't even talk to Lestak about it. I've made my own plans. Let me follow them through.'

'I want to help.'

'You've helped already. It's safer if you let me handle this. I'll let you know how it goes.'

'I'll set you up as a contact,' she said. And then, 'Done.' Jack imagined a new statue growing in his weavespace.

'We're almost finished now,' she said. 'There's just one thing that's been puzzling me. Why didn't they kill you, back when it was all beginning?'

Jack spread his hands flat on the table, fanned his fingers out and pressed them against the cool plastic table top. 'Grey always said he did the best he could for me. Maybe he did.'

'It's so hard to tell what the truth is,' sighed Corazon. 'The Pantheon lying to us and manipulating us, for their benefit, not ours. That just makes us pawns, doesn't it?' Her words cut into Jack's conscience. He thought of Harry and Andrea. Corazon saw him wince. 'Is there anything else you want to tell me, Jack?'

He paused for just long enough to convince himself that his answer would seem honest and told her: 'No.'

'I'll be on my way then.' She looked around. 'I'm going to have to spend a little time in a quiet room, after all this.' They said their goodbyes, then Corazon stood up, paid the bill with a wave and slipped out of the café. Jack waited for ten minutes or so more before leaving, watching tides of silent shoppers roll by.

On the train back home, Fist emerged.

[I hated it in there. Don't let's go back.]

[We might have to.]

[I was wrong about that bitch. She's dangerous. I hope you're not going to see her again. We should block her calls.]

[She's on our side. If she tries to get in touch, it's priority.]

[She's one of us? Is that why you didn't tell her about Harry and Andrea? You're just using her. You're no better than Grey.]

[I'm just trying to keep them safe.]

[You're fucking things up, Jack.] Fist's high sharp voice held a soft new menace. [I don't care how safe we're meant to be, going to her is an escalation. My property is going to get damaged.]

[It's not yours yet, Fist. Until then, I'll do what I want with it.]
[Oh, we'll see about that.]

Chapter 20

'What the fuck do you think you're playing at, Jack? I told you, don't go to InSec,' said Harry, rage shaking his voice.

'She came to me. And we can trust her.'

'Christ, Jack, what would you know?' He thrust a finger in Jack's face. 'You're just an amateur.' He stabbed it towards him. Jack was careful not to flinch. 'A Homelands numbers boy.' He jabbed again. Jack thought of pistols. 'It's my case, we run it how I say.'

'It's not your case,' said Jack, quietly. 'It's our case. And I haven't been an amateur for a long time.' He refused to let any emotion enter his voice. 'I fought a war. I spent five years in prison. I know who to trust. I learned the hard way.'

Jack had also learned that overt, theatrical anger like Harry's was often more impressive display than actual threat. The truly danger-ous never blustered or gave warnings. They just struck, hard and fast.

'You've learned a lot, Jack, I'll give you that. But you're still no copper.' Harry grumbled some more, but the worst of the storm had blown itself out. 'Damage is done now,' he said, in the end. 'We might as well use what she's found. I'll go see what I can get from Access station. Won't be long.'

Andrea wasn't around. The house was silent. Jack went upstairs and looked into empty bedrooms. Her aunt's clothes were vacuum-packed in plastic, to protect them while she was gone. Jack made himself a cup of tea, carefully remembering where the kettle and mug had been so he could replace both in exactly the same place. Then he went back into the living room and waited. After an hour or so, Harry reappeared with several security camera images.

'That's Nihal. Easy once Corazon showed us where to look. He's usually there at about half eight in the morning.'

'How did you get these, Harry? You can't have clearance.'

'The way I always get information. I went and talked to the camera nests. I found out what they wanted, gave it to them and then they helped me out.'

Jack arrived at Access station early the next day. Clustered hordes of rush-hour travellers pushed and shoved around him, flowing relentlessly into train after train. The commuter noise broke over Jack in waves: the rumble of a thousand footsteps, the swish and rustle of a crowd's worth of clothing, the harried whispers of people throwing words into the weave, the muttering of on-platform conversations. Every couple of minutes another train would pull in, ready to take passengers along the mainline, through the Wart and into Docklands. The surge towards each one pulled Jack across the platform. Worried that he might be pulled on to a train, he found a quieter spot at the end of the platform. Even there the crowds were packed tight.

Fist manifested above their heads, alternately drifting away to laugh at 'the lumpen proletariat' or floating back to Jack to complain. [This is a dangerous waste of time.] There was a light breeze blowing across the platform. Fist pretended that it had caught him, and drifted with it. It pulled him away from Jack. [Waste of time, waste of time, waste of time,] he chanted as he went. Jack ignored him, scanning the crowd for Nihal. The skinner's doughy, nondescript face was topped with thin strands of combed-over hair, and sat on a pudgy little body. In all the pictures, he wore a slightly battered, light grey suit, without any sigils.

'That should make him easier to spot,' said Harry.

'It's a bit of an affectation, isn't it?'

'He games the weave professionally. He knows how worthless it all is.'

As eight thirty approached, the crowds started to thin out. The platform was still crowded, but the commuters didn't have to struggle so hard to board each train. Two station workers appeared with a ladder. One of them climbed up to a camera nest, pulled out a spanner, and started tinkering with the cameras, while the other held her steady. 'Tell them five minutes,' she shouted down, 'Rose willing.' Her colleague shrugged. Jack looked for Fist. The puppet had been running through the crowd, occasionally shouting with frustration as his cageware stopped him from touching people. Now, he'd vanished.

Then, Jack caught sight of Nihal. He spotted the battered grey suit first, then the round face. The skinner was a little sweaty, a little out of breath – an apparently insignificant man, running to make up time, heading for an office where someone would grumble about him being late again.

Watching him take up his position on the platform, Jack marvelled at the acuity of his disguise. One of the most powerful technical adepts in Docklands, someone capable of weave manipulation feats that maybe only a dozen others across the whole system could duplicate, was carefully defining himself as a nobody. His skills, Jack realised, weren't just technical. They were rooted in a deep understanding of how people choose to present themselves, of what's read into that presentation.

Then Fist's voice hissed in Jack's ear: [The cameras are out. I don't like it.]

[You're being paranoid. I'm going to talk to him.] Jack pushed through the crowd towards his target. He and Harry had carefully considered how best to greet the Skinner. 'Shake him up a bit, but not too much,' Harry had said. 'Let him know that we're on to him, that we're looking for information, but that if he gives it to us he'll be OK.' Jack closed in on his target. 'If he acts nervous, mention my name. He used to work for me, back in the day.' Jack was almost on Nihal, thrilled with the thought that his investigation might at last be about to take a firm, unambiguous step forwards.

And then two small hands covered his eyes and a thin voice shouted in his ear.

[I'm not letting you do this!]

[What are you playing at, Fist?]

[This stops now.]

[Let go!]

Distracted, Jack stumbled and nearly fell, knocking into someone as he did so. There was a yelp of surprise. Someone swore, someone else half-whispered 'Fucking sweathead,' and Jack felt another commuter pushing hard against his back. He collapsed to his knees, reaching up and over his head to pull at Fist, too disorientated by the unexpectedness of his attack to banish him. 'You're not going to screw this up,' he yelled, forgetting to talk in his mind only, and then he'd pulled Fist away from his eyes.

Unreal fingers left imagined scratches in his face. The subdermal processors that allowed him to interact with Fist's virtual presence mimicked sharp pain. 'You little shit!' he shouted, throwing Fist down on to the platform and muffling his screaming mouth with a hand. The puppet went limp and Jack looked up. A small circle of space had opened up around him. Commuters looked away, weaveselves already programmed to block him out completely. Only Nihal was staring him, an expression of shocked recognition on his face. He took one step back, then another, as Jack pulled Fist back into his mind and stood up. The puppet screamed abuse from the depths of his head.

'You're not a sweathead,' stuttered Nihal. 'You're a puppeteer.'

'That's right. And I've come to talk to you.'

A small circle of space opened up around Nihal, as other people's personal weavesystems recognised that he was interacting with an invisible and shut his presence out too. He took another step back.

'They warned me you might come.'

Jack had imagined that he would carefully manage the meeting, but that was impossible now. 'We just need some information.'

'You're not onweave and your puppet's caged. There's no way you could have found me on your own. Someone sent you. Who?' Panic fluttered through Nihal's voice. Jack was impressed that he'd deduced Fist's presence so quickly. He needed to calm him. 'I'm a friend of Harry Devlin's.'

He'd expected puzzlement, perhaps surprise, but not naked fear. Nihal stifled something that could have been a scream. His face refreshed to white. He turned and fled through the crowd, bouncing commuters out of his way as he cannoned through them. 'No, wait,' shouted Jack, but it was too late. Nihal was halfway down the platform, heading for the exit. Jack took off after him. Nihal's flight had opened a path between the commuters. Weaveware anticipated Jack's rush through it and kept it open, ensuring that nobody would be run into a second time. There was the distant whine of an InSec flyer. Automatically summoned, it would be here in moments.

'Fuck,' said Jack again.

[DON'T GO AFTER HIM, YOU STUPID BASTARD!]

Jack skidded to the top of the exit stairway as Nihal reached the bottom, the tails of his jacket flying up around him as he leapt down the last of the stairs. He looked back, panting with exertion, sweat glossing his forehead, and swore. He swore again as he saw that the exit gates had switched to emergency lock mode, then disappeared through an arch opposite them. Jack took the stairs two, three at a time before skidding through the archway himself. He was on another platform. This one was almost empty.

[YOU'LL JUST GET US LOCKED UP! GET OUT OF HERE!] yelled Fist. Then, a little quieter: [InSec'll be in here, Nihal'll be out of here, and you'll look like a fucking idiot.]

[Shut the fuck up.]

Dim yellow light illuminated Nihal running towards the far end of the platform. There were only a few people on it. All seemed oblivious to the two men. 'I just need to talk!' Jack shouted. Nihal reached a door in the wall. He tugged on it, but it didn't open. Beyond him was the end of the platform. Past a low barrier, steps ran down into the darkness. The void began to fill with the rumble of an approaching train. Nihal stepped back from the door, looking uncertainly at Jack then round at the steps. The lights of the oncoming train rattled closer beyond them.

'I only want some information,' Jack called out, now walking towards Nihal. He had his arms out and his palms open, to show that he was unarmed. Fist grabbed the soft parts of his mind and pain raged through them. Jack doubled over, clutching his head and swearing.

'You can't even control your puppet. You don't know what it's capable of.'

Jack shut Fist down. He'd pay later in exhaustion, but for now he was too angry to care. [I don't want any damaged goods,] shouted Fist's disappearing voice.

'He can't hurt anyone,' said Jack.

'I can smell Pantheon on you, Puppeteer. And something worse than that, if you're here on behalf of Devlin.'

'I'm here for myself, nobody else.'

'Bullshit.'

The approaching train roared in the darkness. There was no point trying to speak. Nihal turned away from Jack, ready – once the train had reached the platform and halted – to run for the stairs and the safety of the tunnel. As he did so the door in the wall opened. Nihal started towards it. A short, middle-aged woman emerged. She was wearing off-green combat trousers and a red jacket, and she had dyed her hair blue. At this distance, in this light, it was difficult to see her skin's blue tint, but Jack knew it would be there. It was the woman who had forced herself into his interview at Customs House.

She raised her hand and pointed something at Nihal. There was a crack loud enough to be heard over the train's howl. Then the skinner was staggering backwards, a small dark hole shining fresh in his forehead, and tumbling over the edge of the platform. Brakes howled, but the train could not stop. It batted Nihal's body forward a little way before the corpse rolled over and disappeared beneath its silver wheels. They gleamed red. Emergency brakes squealed the train to a halt. There was silence.

'I turned the station surveillance off,' she shouted. 'Run down the tunnel, they won't know you were here. So much simpler if I could just kill you too!' Then, she vanished back through the door. A warning chimed and the train's doors opened. A few people stepped out and started walking for the exit. The travellers waiting on the platform joined them. They looked serene, untouched by the death that had unfolded in front of them. Jack realised that their weaveware would have blocked the entire scene out. It would now be calmly asking them to move out of the station. There would be apologies for the delay, but no explanation of its cause.

A roaring noise filled the platform, echoing in from the entrance. It was the InSec flyer landing outside the station. Jack had no desire to be arrested. He ran towards the door that the assassin had emerged from. It was firmly locked. The end of the platform was only a few metres away. Jack leapt the barrier and ran down the steps into the darkness of the tunnel.

Chapter 21

Jack left the tunnel by a service door, successfully avoiding any InSec involvement, and made his way back to Harry and Andrea's house. When Andrea opened the door she was ten years younger. 'Hello,' she said, smiling politely. 'You must be Jack.'

'Andrea?'

'Yes. Come in, Harry's told me a lot about you. It's good to meet you.'

She was dressed in dead fashions. Harry must have rolled her back. She was now too young to have met him. For the first time, Jack felt the true loss of her. It hit him like a punch. He staggered.

'Are you all right?' she said. 'It's been a tough day, I bet!'

'No. I'm fine. Tired. I can come in?'

'Harry's waiting for you.' She led him towards the sitting room. 'Kitchen's in there for a cup of something,' she said brightly.

Jack could barely nod. It was as if the past had been reformatted. Every smile of hers – so bright, so friendly, so clearly impersonal – tore at his heart. But he couldn't let Harry see his pain.

Harry asked about Nihal. When Jack told him what had happened, he made no effort to hide his irritation. 'You should have that little bastard under control by now. I told you, my case, my rules.' Jack forced Fist to manifest but he said nothing, turning his head away from both of them. Jack asked why Nihal was so scared when he mentioned Harry. 'He wasn't scared of me. He was scared of you two.' The answer felt like an evasion, but Jack didn't want to push it. This time, Harry's anger had a cold, quiet heat to it that scared him. There was a silence. Jack decided to change the subject. It was impossible not to ask about Andrea.

'Shouldn't you just let her run?'

Harry exploded.

'Who the fuck are you to tell me how to run my relationships? Why are you even asking?'

Jack wanted to threaten Harry, to force him to restore her and not touch her again. But that would make the depth of his feelings clear. He wasn't sure what the repercussions of that would be, or if he was ready to deal with them constructively.

'You just fucked up big time,' continued Harry, 'you and that idiot puppet. Fuck knows why anyone's scared of him. You should let me mesh with him now, I'd sort the little shit out. And I'd be much better at using what he's got to get what we need.'

[He's not getting anywhere near me. I'll eat your brain before I let that happen.]

'That's impossible, Harry. The cage.'

'The cage, the cage. One more thing that stops you doing what needs to be done, and once again it isn't your fucking fault. You're a fart in a fucking hurricane, you are.'

In the end, Harry let himself flicker out of existence with a curt farewell. He was – he said – going to use 'his sources' to try and find out about the assassin, but hadn't been optimistic. 'That was our one chance to get to Yamata. It's back to square one, buddy.' Andrea had shown Jack out. He'd barely been able to look at her. He wondered how she'd recover her older self; how she experienced the sudden loss of so much rich living. As he walked away, he heard her start to sing someone else's song. At that age, she hadn't yet written any of her own. There was nothing but potential in her voice.

Back at the hotel, he tried to call Corazon. She didn't answer. He left a message asking her to contact him urgently. He waited for a day, but there was nothing. Thoughts of Andrea tore at him like panthers. It was impossible to distinguish the sense of loss he felt for the woman he'd known so long ago on Station from that he felt for the fetch he'd been so close to while imprisoned on Callisto. With nothing to do and nowhere to go, he made his way to the spot where the body of Bjorn Penderville had been found. It was a kind of masochistic pilgrimage, a means of securing at least part of the past and confirming that it too could not just be deleted.

The murder scene was an empty dock on one of the jetties that floated in space above the open maw of Docklands. Jack let himself hang in the void, floating just past the wharf's airlock door. The sound of his breath whispered in his ears. He remembered his parents taking him to play in similar docks as a child, carefully introducing him to vacuum suit usage and the hazards of space. Now he wore an adult suit. It allowed no touch or smell. There was only vision to show him the universe. Off to his left he could see bustle – a newly arrived chainship was being disassembled. The wharf to his right was quiet. A command module hung against it like a disembodied head, waiting for a new body to be fitted. Snowflakes hung beyond Station's shadow. The sun set them ablaze, diagrams sketched on vacuum with an elegant precision far beyond anything that the Pantheon could hope to achieve.

Jack imagined the cathedral beauty of their internal structures. Their physical complexity paled before the technological artistry that each one embodied. He wondered if they were much discussed in the Station. Without access to the weave he couldn't take part in the discussion. But then, he'd seen precious little interest in the world beyond Station from any of its inhabitants. Perhaps the snow-flakes merited little more than the odd, baffled mention, before the conversation returned to introversion.

Beyond the snowflakes, there was nothing. Jack thought of Andrea, then – to distract himself – he remembered the crime scene footage. Penderville had been floating a few metres away from the wharf's airlock, tethered to it by a length of white rope. The Spine Traffic Controller's murderer had used a diamond knife to open a tear in the back of his vacuum suit. The sudden decompression had broken him.

InSec technicians had secured the scene, while Harry had accessed local security records, checking to see who had moved through the area. The wharf to the left was not in use. Aud Yamata had been working on the wharf to the right a few hours before. Apart from that there was nothing. A post-mortem confirmed that Penderville's death was relatively recent, taking place just over an hour after Yamata had finished up and left. There was no record of anybody else in the area. The wharf's camera nest was no help. It had been struck by a micro-meteorite two days before. Official eyes were blind.

143

A small choking sound pulled Jack out of his reverie. Looking over at Fist, Jack saw that the puppet's shoulders were shaking. He was crying. Jack was still too angry with him to feel concern, but he was curious. It was very rare for Fist to show such vulnerability. His programming was meant to ensure that aggression was his response to any threatening situation. Grief only kicked in when all other avenues were exhausted. Jack wondered what had so frustrated him. Fist was whispering to himself, muttering the same phrase over and over again. 'Stookie Bill, Stookie Bill, keep me safe, Stookie Bill.'

Jack tuned him out and focused on his own problems. He'd always found the silence of space conducive to deep thought. He sank back into himself, letting the swash and backwash of his own breathing soothe him. He was going to run over recent events, looking for any clues he might have missed – handholds and footholds that could help him move forward. But before he could fully drift away, he realised that something unusual was happening. Slowly but surely, without any fuss, the cold and silent world around him was starting to change.

The transformation began with the stars. They were mellowing to something a little yellower, a little creamier. As each one's colour changed so did its shape, moving from being an empty dot to become a small rip and then a tear in the darkness that surrounded them. As the tears opened up the darkness fell away, no longer an eternal, unreachable absence but rather a shredded backdrop. Fist stopped sobbing. 'Can you see this too?' he asked. His wooden jaw hung down in amazement as the great change leapt down from the stars to infect the interior of Station.

There's no sound in a vacuum. But Jack and Fist both heard a vast, glacial creaking as the circular world of Docklands, stippled across with the streets of a dozen districts, the leaping movement of trains, the firefly darting of flyers and the harsh glow of late afternoon spinelight, began to remake itself. Its round mouth stretched out to form an oval. Yellow-white spinelights became kilometres-long shards of primary colour. Tracery grew between them, infected with the ivory white that had replaced space – for the stars had now merged completely with each other, making the cosmos finite. The universe now ended in great walls that stretched away to the left and the right, above and below, swirling with the bright patterns that had once been the lights of Docklands.

Now it was the turn of the piers and wharves of the Spine to change. They flowed into place along the new walls, becoming a series of vertical columns. As they settled into their new shapes, they lost their metallic sheen – a last memory of what they had been. Between them, shining gouts of primary colours ran together, stretching up and down to mirrored arched points. At last, these new stained glass windows found their final shape, and the universe stopped changing.

Jack was standing in the nave of a cathedral, an open space carved from soft limestone that stretched before and behind him, to his left and to his right. He looked up. There was a great open tower above him. Looking down, he saw himself looking curiously back up. He was no longer wearing a vacuum suit. Two Fists hovered nearby, one right side up above him, one upside down beneath him.

Jack took a step. Ripples rolled out from his feet, shuddering through the perfect, liquid mirror that was the whole floor of the cathedral. They died down as Jack looked down past the two small human bodies, down into the great gulf of cathedral space beneath him, down at pilasters running down walls, down at great illuminated windows, emblazoned with great luminous images of men and women and gods; down for a hundred kilometres towards fan vaulting that could span moons. He shuddered with vertigo.

'Pantheon,' breathed Fist.

'Oh yes,' said Jack, awed.

Only one part of the world remained unchanged. Snowflakes gleamed in the cathedral space like stars, each duplicated in its liquid mercury floor. A moment of surprise, as Jack realised that they must be interfacing with this great Pantheon illusion. They were either strong enough to break through the image that had been thrown over the world, or somehow complicit in its creation. Then anything but an astonished awe left him as a thousand voices leapt into being and an invisible choir started to sing.

There was a soft, high keening drifting over a deeper bass rumble, the two alternately twining around then leaping away from each other. Deep beneath them an organ droned, its long, slow chords lending weight to the sadness emerging from their great pulses of harmony. The reflection below Jack shimmered in time with the music, until the voices fell silent and the mirror-floor stilled. Then one vast chord came crashing in as the organ and all the voices howled in unison, filling the nave and its reflection with a great, tectonic grief. All that had gone before had only been an introduction. The full choir was an infinity of voices, beating at the air with note after note as the organ raged on beneath them.

A figure glowed into being high up in the distance, hanging before the single great round window that burnt at the heart of the cathedral's apse. 'She must be kilometres high,' thought Jack. White fabrics drifted around her. Her face was covered. She carried a pale, dead weight in her arms. Limbs hung down from it. There was a head, tipped all the way back. The woman and her burden started moving towards Jack, falling into human scale as they came. The music subsided into one endlessly sustained note. Cries of grief cut through it, hacking away at its simple purity like so many blunted knives.

'What does this mean?' whispered Fist.

'I've never seen anything like it.'

The woman reached Jack. As she came to a halt her robes began to fold themselves away, wings that were no longer needed. She drifted down, delicate feet extended. When she landed she staggered slightly and Jack understood how heavy her burden was. She walked the last few paces, rippling circles spinning away from her feet, until she stood before him. The last of the white fabric rippled away, revealing her face. It was East. Her eyes were rimmed with red. Tears had pulled makeup down her cheeks in long black tracks.

'You involved her,' she spat, her voice harsh with grief and rage. 'It's because of you.'

For the first time, Jack looked down at the body. Out of uniform, it took him a second to recognise it. He wanted to be mistaken. Fist hovered in closer and peered at the corpse. When he spoke, it was the first time in days that he'd sounded cheerful.

'Well, Jackie boy, you've missed your chance with her for good.'

A bullet had punched a small neat hole in the corpse's forehead.

There could be no doubt that Corazon was dead.

146

Chapter 22

East called a rectangular stone block into being and gently laid Corazon's corpse on to it. Reaching up, she softened their surroundings, making it seem that sheets of gauze hung between the little group and the cathedral's great empty spaces. There was a sudden sense of intimacy.

'Where is she?' asked Jack.

'InSec broke into her apartment a few minutes ago. She hadn't turned up for her shift.'

'I'm sorry.'

'One of my favourites. I didn't even know.'

'I'm sure she had faith you'd come for her.'

'No. You don't understand. She was one of the ones I loved, one of the ones I was taking most care of. I watch them all the time. I am always present to them. I thought she was in bed, asleep. Then the image of her in my mind flickered, and there she was, dead. I reached out and touched her. Her body was already cold. They'd hidden her from me for hours.'

'We already knew there was Pantheon involvement ...'

'But I see everything, as soon as it happens, and I know every secret! I am the eye in every room, the ear that always hears, the mind that always knows. My newsrooms, my weavecasts, my telenovelas and keitai shousetsou and bandes dessinées and shadowplays – what are they if I can't know that I'm watching the world, and reflecting it? How can something so important be hidden from me? What else haven't I seen, Jack?'

A small hand grabbed his shirt. A tear grew from her eye like a tiny, transparent leaf, then dropped away down her cheek. Another joined it, then more, and she was weeping. Jack was unsure how to respond appropriately, how to comfort a god. She pulled herself in closer, both hands clutching him. Very tentatively, he moved one arm round her, then the other. Over her shoulder, Fist winked and leered. Jack closed his eyes, ignoring him.

The goddess' hair smelt of static. Jack felt a gentle buzz as it brushed up against him. He was standing in an awkwardly formal way. She nestled in further, burying her head in his chest. Tears moistened the front of his shirt. Her body pressed against his with the softness of cinema seats. She was sobbing, and she shook with every sob. Every quiver of her body rippled against Jack. He struggled to quell a growing arousal. But then she was looking up at him, alluring as a midnight advert, and her hand was reaching down, and he was stiffening at her touch.

'I can't ...' he said, 'Grey ...' but his breathing quickened as he said it.

'He's an old man,' she replied, 'fallen from grace.' She kissed him once. Her lips snatched at his. 'And he let you fall too.' Her hot mouth touched his again, her tongue opening his lips, and then she was inside him. All that was divine in her took him and made him a vessel, pouring itself into him again and again and again.

Jack would never remember much of their love making. Later, he'd think back to the young man he'd seen her take in Ushi's, after Andrea sang. The acolyte's face had been rising towards a kind of blank perfection – a television screen, ecstatically detuning itself, finding release in the empty space that lies between channels. Jack assumed that he'd been lost in that same erasing joy.

All Fist would say was, 'You looked as happy as a pig in shit.'

Towards the end, East let Jack find enough of himself to know that she was whispering in his ear.

'I am remaking you, little Puppeteer,' she breathed. 'I'm slipping the chains from your little creature and sending you both out to be my revenge.'

'I am no one's vengeance but my own.'

'Because of you, my Corazon is dead.'

Then she nibbled at his ear. His mouth had to sigh open and his back had to arch and press him so much deeper into her. As he entered further into her, so she dug deeper into him.

'I'm going to make you a weapon again.'

Now she was far enough in to reach Fist. As Jack exploded into orgasm, the last of his defences dropped away and she had full access to them both. The world shattered. For a second that drifted forever he was not himself. In the distance, he heard Fist screaming, but he was too fragmented to care.

When he came round, he was lying on a stone altar next to the one supporting Corazon. East stood over him, perfectly dressed, her clothes, hair and makeup immaculate. No sign of their lovemaking remained. She was holding Fist by the scruff of his neck, her free hand clamped over his mouth. His eyes were wide with terror. His legs and arms thrashed around as he tried to free himself.

'I've removed all the blocks they put on him. Be careful how you use him – they won't know I've done this. I've made some changes to you, too.'

'Why are you holding him like that?'

'I saw that you'd been having problems with him. I'm going to burn him out for you.'

'What?' Jack felt groggily detached from himself. His mind ached. He wondered how much celestial weaveware East had forced into him. Resentment surged in him.

'I'm going to wipe his personality structures,' she continued. 'He's just going to be software. No more Fist. No more rebellion.' Fist tried to howl. It came out as a muffled series of grunts. 'Just say the word.'

'Why haven't you done it already?'

'Fist's leased in your name and licensed to you. I need your direct permission.'

Jack sighed. 'Can you change the licence conditions? Stop him from taking my body?'

Sadness drifted across her face. Jack was reminded of an advert where a woman had been grieved by her inability to find an effective financial adviser. 'No, Jack. I can't break that kind of agreement. But I can burn out the thinking part of him.'

'He'll still own – this.' Jack waved down at his body.

'It will pass out of your control, yes. But there will be nothing of him to guide it. Just – silence.'

Fist kicked out against her. His eyes blinked, rapidly. He was trying to cry, but was too afraid to.

149

'I can't let you do that,' Jack told her. 'I thank you for unlocking him. But I can't let you touch his mind.'

Fist's eyes opened wide.

'He tried to attack me while you were still asleep,' replied East. 'Then he told me I should let him take your body now.'

'His software partitioned part of my mind, and made him there. Everything in him comes from me.'

'He won't obey you. He'll try and stop you.'

'If you kill him, you kill part of me.'

'You can't trust him.'

'I can't always trust myself.'

East snorted. 'Let's see what he has to say.' She took her hand away from Fist's mouth. For once, he was silent. He remained limp in her arms. She set him down at her feet. He tottered slightly, as if standing for the first time, then looked up at her. She stared back, arms crossed. He broke and ran to Jack, leaving a dozen spreading silver circles behind him, and threw himself into his arms, his little voice whispering 'thank you' over and over again.

'You're going to regret this,' spat East.

The myriad ripples Fist had left behind bounced forwards and backwards between the two altars.

'Yamata and her patron may be afraid of him,' replied Jack. 'But I'm not.'

'He's an unpredictable psychopath. Seems to me that they're the sensible ones,' East replied dismissively. 'Oh, and there's one more thing I have to do for you.'

Jack was cradling Fist in his arms, soothing him. He looked up at her.

'What's that?'

East touched the wound on the forehead of Corazon's weave presence. The policewoman's body was already losing definition. A lifetime's worth of data was falling into the Coffin Drives. 'I ring-fenced the last hours of her life.' East's fingers sunk into Corazon's head. She grasped something and pulled it out – a bullet. A small pistol appeared in her other hand. 'I'm going to share them with you.' She slipped the bullet into the pistol. 'Find her killers.'

Then she straightened her arm, and shot Jack in the head.

150

Chapter 23

When Jack came round, floating just off the Spine, his mind felt broken. It took him hours longer than it should have done to walk back to his hotel. Fist had to help him, displaying an embarrassed, awkward solicitude as – at various points – he slid into full control of Jack's body and helped him totter through the streets. It was late, so very few people were around.

When they reached the hotel, Charles was on duty. His eyes lit up as he saw Jack, sparkling with irrepressible joy. 'Oh, hello!' he cooed. His shirt was brightly decorated with endlessly overlapping flowers. To Jack, it felt like a violent assault. He took an awkward step and nearly fell. 'Dear me, just look at you!' Charles rushed round from the desk and put an arm round him, steadying him. 'Poor you. Been overdoing the sauce? I daresay we all deserve a night on the tiles from time to time.'

Jack leant heavily on him as they stumbled down to his room. Charles' frail body bent and swayed, barely equal to the task of supporting him. Up close, his skin had a light, waxy sheen. There was a scent of gin to him. When they reached Jack's room, Fist slipped briefly into control again, standing Jack up and walking him to his bed. Charles hovered solicitously at the doorway, his face filled with genuine concern. 'Thank you, Fist,' Jack muttered, forgetting that he was speaking aloud. 'That's the little man who lives in you, isn't it?' asked Charles. Jack collapsed on to the bed as Fist slipped back into the depths of his mind. 'It must be so nice, to have company like that,' whispered Charles sadly. And then he made himself beam again. He fussed merrily about the room, arranging blankets round Jack and pouring a glass of water for the bedside table. He sang out, 'Cheerio!' as the door slammed behind him.

Fist stayed hidden away. Jack tumbled into sleep. His dreams were suffused with the memories that East had forced so deeply into his head. They were the raw stuff of Corazon's dataself, the wholly recorded conscious experience that both informed and was created by the weave presence that had surrounded her in life. Jack's mind snatched at them, pulling them into coherence then integrating them with his own consciousness.

He dreamed that he was leaving InSec, buying food, licensing steak and chicken flavour packs, chatting with a friend. Each moment was part of a broader association set, and so triggered related memories as Jack experienced it. Irin Lestak drank coffee. Corazon trusted her. A hovercar skimmed overhead. This year's new models would be out soon. Last week's soup was delicious. The vegetables in her fridge had gone off. The friend was dating a very good-looking man. They should go out for cocktails and a chat. And so it went on.

At last the day ended and Corazon slept. Her dreams pulsed through Jack's dreaming mind, creating imaginative feedback loops. He felt Fist step into and damp down the memory stream, making sure it didn't overwhelm him. Again, there was that new sense of care. Even in sleep it surprised him. As the feedback loops faded, Jack realised that he'd stepped beyond dreaming into a new, lucid state of imaginative self-management.

He pulled himself out of the Corazon memory stream and examined it from outside. It was a profoundly complex tangle of interlinked association sets. Jack reached for a simpler, more linear way of viewing them. They resolved into a series of specific incidents, arranged in order of occurrence. Focusing on a particular incident would trigger its playback. Wanting to avoid the trauma of her death until he was acclimatised to her presence, Jack ran through key moments in the twenty-four hours before it. He found himself talking to her. Watching from her point of view, he marvelled at how well she'd overcome her fear and loss as her faith in the Pantheon shattered.

At last, he felt ready to experience the moment of her murder. Fist pricked into alertness, ready to snap into action if the past became too brutal to bear. But there should be no deep pain. Corazon had been shot in the head and died almost instantly. Her body had shown no sign of any other injuries. There was a void where remembrance ended. Jack sited himself a little way before it and let time begin again.

There was the soft wrapping of sheets around her, then slumbering shapes in the gloom and a feeling of dazed half-awakeness as she snatched at the weave and found that it was missing from her senses. The loud knocking that had woken her continued. A voice shouted 'InSec business, Lieutenant Corazon,' then a code word. She assumed a weavecrash and an emergency summons to work. Soon she'd be helping clear up the inevitable riot as people lost themselves in a protective combination of rage and fear. It was never easy to face the world as it was, not as they wanted it to be.

Soft T-shirt fabric moved against her as she stood up. She pulled on her even softer dressing gown. Lights glowed into life as she walked to her front door and bent down to peer through its spyhole. There was nothing outside that she understood as a threat, just someone with blue hair, pale skin to match and a soft purple light in her eyes.

Jack was pulled out of the dream for a moment as he recognised the woman who'd shot David Nihal. A man stood behind her. Corazon snatched a glimpse of a sharp suit and a precise moustache before her view of them both was suddenly obscured. Jack winced as he remembered panthers.

Then a huge, all-consuming pain took him as he was shot in the head for the second time. For a moment the world was nothing but the dying roar of a bullet blasting through a spyhole. The door spun away and a wall fell past. Corazon gazed up at soft ceiling lights. Then the last images her eyes had made faded, and there was very nearly peace. Nothing remained but the static hiss of technology, still yearning for the vivid whisperings of synapses, axons and neurons. But there was no input left for it to gently touch at, and record.

Chapter 24

[Wake up! Wake up!]

Fist was shaking Jack's shoulder.

[What? Hell!]

Jack's head thumped with the pressure of fresh memories, with deep Pantheonware still unpacking itself into his psyche.

[InSec outside! They're raiding us. Shit!]

Jack sat up. The room spun. For a moment, he wasn't sure if he was waking as himself, or as a woman in soft sheets in the luxury of a Homelands condominium. The puddle of stars in the hotel floor brought him back to reality. Corazon's ghost left his mind. East was still present to him. The tawdry hotel furniture glittered in a new way.

[We've got to get out, Jack. What if they know I'm uncaged?]

[They can't know that. What can you see?]

[Lestak and three snatch teams. Two out front, one at back. Just getting into position. A minute and they're in the room.]

[Let's go.]

Jack had passed out fully clothed. He was at the door then sprinting down the corridor, Fist running along behind him.

[Back way?] Jack panted.

[Dead ahead, up the service stairs.]

They were steep and narrow. The walls were stained dark at shoulder height. They reached an emergency exit door. Jack opened it a crack. He saw a long, covered alleyway. There was bright morning light at the end of it, and the silhouettes of three men.

[One of the squads, Jack.]

[Can you offweave them?]

[Yes, but you know the protocols. They might miss a check in. That'll trigger every alarm they've got.]

[Shit.]

[I can climb inside their heads and fuck them right up.]

[I don't want to harm them.]

[Sentimental. What about all that Eastware? Must be something useful there.]

Jack pushed his attention into the headache that still gripped his mind. It was like probing a fresh wound with a stick. There was pain, but Fist was right. Jack found a thread he could pull on to reach an entirely new way of being himself. East's Pantheonware flooded his limbic system, setting up subtle overrides, rewriting his body language, reskinning his oral intonation patterns. There was a gauge that measured 'presence', set amongst others that included 'impact', 'charm' and 'memorability'. A thought pushed them all to one hundred per cent. Then Jack raised himself to his full height, opened the door wide and set off towards the snatch squad.

[Fuck's sake, Jack,] said Fist. [We're going to get caught. Are you sure you know what you're doing?]

They saw him, raised their guns and started towards him. One of them was about to start subvocalizing when Jack said, 'Stop.' They saw his face and heard his voice, and a shimmer of subtle behavioural cues settled over their perception of him. Their weave systems were reshaped to make him shine with a strange kind of immanent beauty. All three could do nothing more than stand and gape. One dropped his gun. Another seemed to be wetting himself.

[Very impressive!] chuckled Fist.

Jack stepped forwards and touched the first of them, wanting to push him to one side. The man collapsed to his knees, eyes still on Jack, his face suffused with inhuman satisfaction. The second moved back, tongue lolling stupidly as he dripped on to the floor. The third was less affected. He was trying to force words out of his mouth, nearly choking himself with effort. At last a question came staggering into the air. 'Can I have your autograph?' He reached out for Jack, again imploring, 'Autograph?' Jack backed away from him.

[Ditch these wankers,] snapped Fist. [Out of the alley, turn right.]

Jack ran, thrusting the settings on East's new installations back to zero. It made no difference to the three men behind him. They were still broken. He heard a final, plaintive cry: 'Autograph!'

[What just happened, Fist?]

[Gift of the gods. Now don't think. RUN!]

They lost themselves in Docklands. An hour or so later, Jack was nursing a coffee in a small café in the Neon Quarter. The seat was bolted down too close to the table, forcing him to hunch over. Fist had hacked into a passerby and used him to pay for the drink. He'd ordered a bacon sandwich too. Jack could hear it sizzling on the hob beyond the counter. [We didn't need to pay for any of it,] Fist complained. [With what East's left running in you, you could have had it all for free.] He leered at the waitress, who was leaning against the bar. [And anything else, too.] Jack was glad that she couldn't see him.

[What is in me, Fist?]

Fist wasn't just useful for hacking outwards. He'd been checking for changes in Jack's root systems, trying to understand exactly how East had upgraded his personal weaveware. Jack could still feel the new controls in his mind, but – after the alleyway, and the broken guards – felt nervous about even touching them.

[You're running Pantheon-level celebrity systems. She's installed the unlocked version, you can do whatever you want with it. You saw what it did to those goons outside the hotel. Verrrry tasty. I wonder if it would work on a squishy?]

Jack was too tired to argue with Fist. The deaths of the last twenty-four hours had shattered him. He'd seen Nihal's head blown open and his body broken. He'd felt the last strands of Corazon's consciousness falling to nothing. A god had put a bullet in his own mind. And he'd broken three men, so overwhelming them with his presence that they became dead to themselves. He hoped that they'd recover.

[This stuff is hardcore. Combined software and meatware assault. Those InSec goons won't come down in a hurry.]

[I didn't know what it would do.]

[Try it on the waitress, go on!]

[No.]

She was coming over to them, an off-white plate balanced in one hand. She'd scrawled weave sigils across her uniform in cheap marker pen. The black ink had faded to a raw, bruise-like purple. Her blonde hair was piled up on her head. A clip, decorated with another sigil, clutched it together in an untidy knot.

[What do her sigils say, Fist?]

[They invoke some third-rate designer. There's a beauty charm too. Give her some of the real thing, Jack!]

Even through all the Eastware was turned down, Jack was still afraid that she would suddenly thrill at his presence. He couldn't bring himself to look at her directly when she put the plate down. He hunched his shoulders and pulled his coat in, staring at the table and muttering, 'Thanks.' She shrugged and turned away.

[Missed your chance.]

[Be quiet.]

The sandwich went down in a couple of bites. It barely tasted of anything – the bread was just a soft warmth in his mouth, the bacon a sharper, crispier one. Fist had logged him into the café's tastenet, but it added very little to the experience.

[So what now?] asked Fist.

[Lie low. Avoid InSec. Wait until it's very late. Pay an old friend a visit.]

[Akhmatov?]

[Oh yes.]

[And you've got some questions for him?]

[Especially now I've seen how Corazon was killed. He was there.]

[He killed her?]

[No. The blue-haired woman from Customs House shot her. Just like she did Nihal.]

[Do you think she's Yamata?]

[She's not how I remember her. But she might have done more than just reskin herself. So yes, I think she might be.]

[Oo! Very exciting, we might be starting to track her down. And when you're asking Akhmatov questions, you might need a little help from me?]

[Yes Fist, I might well indeed.]

Fist snuggled up against Jack. He tried to wrap his arms around his waist, then gave up and enfolded his arm, hugging it tight. He'd never been so demonstrative before, at best admitting to feeling little more than a friendly but embarrassed contempt for Jack. He'd been much more helpful too, since his brush with death. Jack wondered how deep the change went, and how permanent it would turn out to be. He wasn't sure how much he could trust it.

[I'll get answers for you,] Fist chirped. [I'll be nasty cop. You can use your charms on him. You'll be nice cop.] He giggled. [The nicest cop ever! I'm looking forward to it. Today's going to pass really slowly.]

[We can't let InSec catch us. We've got to keep moving. Anything more to pay?] Fist shook his head. [Then let's go.]

[What about Harry?]

[We'll go back to him once we've got some results.]

They spent the rest of the day walking the streets of Docklands. Fist bobbed along beside Jack, sometimes floating, sometimes walking, always reaching out and confusing surveillance systems. He talked in an excited babble, thrilled to at last be fully himself again. Jack said very little. At one point, they found themselves near his old junior school. Nostalgia snapped at him. Wire netting fenced in a playground that was set in the arms of a large, semicircular building.

[Shithole,] said Fist.

[I had a lot of fun here.]

That would once have been a very difficult thing for Jack to admit. He'd worked so hard to put Docklands behind him. He'd even refused to bring Andrea here. Now, it just seemed to be a simple, uncontentious statement of fact.

[Easily pleased,] said Fist.

It was break time. The children were playing a football variant. Two loosely defined teams screamed and jostled happily against each other. The game had absorbed almost every child there.

[I was about the same age as you are now.]

[My mind runs much faster than yours,] Fist snorted. [I'm much older than seven!]

[Really?]

One team was about to score when a whistle blew, and the game abruptly stopped. The child with the football swore, grumpily kicking the ball away. The two teams broke quickly into smaller groups, some children happily rushing off together, others clearly very annoyed.

[End of break time?] asked Fist. [I wanted to see him score. It was getting quite exciting.]

[No,] replied Jack. [Their gaming allowance is time limited.]

[What?]

[It's the kid version of Pantheon licensing. They can't just play a game. They have to hire use of its rules from the Twins. That costs. A school like this can only afford so much.]

[Why don't they just keep playing?]

[Heavy fines. Theft of intellectual property.]

[Gods, no wonder the Totality revolted.]

[It seemed so reasonable, when I was their age.]

They stood there for another minute or so, watching the children invent scrappy, spontaneous games then chase around for a few minutes playing them. Fist was fascinated. He pressed his face close up against the fence. Jack thought of Andrea – of what she'd been, of what she'd become. He wished that he'd come here with her to watch the children play, back in the unreachable past.

[Let's go,] he said.

[Awww.]

[We need to keep moving.]

Thoughts of the past led Jack's mind to East's cathedral. That too had been a temple to loss. He remembered Corazon's death. It came to him again and again, no matter how hard he tried to push it away. Each attempt to forget began to feel like a betrayal. He walked faster and faster, forcing himself through the streets of Docklands, away from the past and into a future where – he hoped – he would no longer be quite so helpless in the face of all that time and the gods had stolen.

Chapter 25

Raindrops landed like little cat feet. [I really can see everything now,] Fist chirped. [Stop, Jack, let me show you, there's so much!]

[No,] Jack said and strode on, making Fist dance through the sodden night streets to keep up with him. The little puppet skipped in and out of the gutter, searching for the deepest puddles to jump into. He cooed with glee every time his tiny, ghostly feet disappeared. He used his newly enabled weave access to simulate splashes.

[So many droplets, all flying up!] Another little leap. [It's astonishing, Jack, I'll take you onweave to see. I can do anything!]

Jack remained silent ahead of him. He'd pulled his hat down and twitched up the collar of his trench coat until his face was all but invisible. That didn't stop people from stopping and admiring him. 'Oh, that coat's beautifully cut,' said one. 'He knows how to wear a suit,' said another. 'I'd fuck him,' announced a third. Every time he heard someone thrill at his East-enhanced weave presence, Jack pulled his hat a little further down and for a minute or so broke into a near trot to escape.

They arrived at the Panther Czar at about eleven o'clock. Outside the club, the queue laughed and jostled and squabbled. Deep beats boomed out from within. They ducked into a doorway just over the road. The light rain turned the hard neon signage that crawled around the club into something far gentler and more subtle than Pierre Akhmatov had ever intended.

[Let me get you onweave,] begged Fist.

[Later. It's not the right moment.]

As late evening turned to deep night the queue waned. At about half past two, as the weather worsened, the exodus began. Drenching rain suffused the night, encouraging those leaving to dart quickly away. Its heaviness was deliberate, Pantheon planners reducing late night crime by nudging revellers off the streets. It dulled sound and light, filling the night with a soft, static hiss, turning streetlamps into half-seen orbs. Couples huddled up against each other, nearly running, spilling high-heel clacks into the air. Groups shouted farewells and then rapidly split into ones, twos, threes, taking off up or down the street.

[Let's go in now. I can't wait!]

[We're going to wait until it's just him in there.]

[How do you know he'll stay?]

[I spent months studying his routine. Sunday night, and he processes the week's takings alone. The club hasn't changed much since then. His habits won't have done, either.]

There was one final burst of departures before the door staff began shutting up the front of the building. One by one, neon lights winked out.

[They're taking it offweave.]

Jack watched Fist kick at a real pebble. The stone didn't move but Fist looked up suddenly, his eyes swivelling as he watched its virtual equivalent fly through the air.

[You're chasing dreams, Fist.]

[Fun dreams.]

A small swarm of sweatheads drifted by. Jack pretended not to see them. One had empty sleeves where her arms should hang. Another moved on crutches, a single leg swaying backwards and forwards between them. Fist stepped into the road, and, pointing towards them, turned his eager face to Jack.

[I could make them all look so beautiful, Jack. Almost as beautiful as you can be! Get them all laid, what do you think? And then there'll be people waking up with them tomorrow, when the overlay lifts off. Won't it be funny?]

[Come back here, Fist. Save your energy. You've got much more important things to do tonight.]

[When, Jack, when?]

[Soon.]

Fist was clearly spoiling for a fight. Jack was surprised by relief that East hadn't broken his fighting spirit. It was such a fundamental part of the puppet's personality.

Now the staff were leaving the club, running under the rain as their customers had done. The last few lights in the entrance hallway flicked off. A heavily built man tugged the club's main doors closed and locked them. As he turned to walk away, a gust of wind snatched at his coat, exposing a white shirt and a black bow-tie. He started to whistle, deliberately walking slowly; refusing to acknowledge the storm. His whistle died away. Rain hissed like a detuned radio.

[Now, Fist,] snapped Jack, starting across the road. Fist followed, rising into the air until his head was level with his master's. [Oh, I've been looking forward to this!] he sang out. Jack almost commented on how much more helpful he was being compared to the last time they'd visited the club. But the change might turn out to be temporary. Mentioning it could break it. [Then open that door,] he said [and let's go play.]

No one either inside or outside the Panther Czar saw them enter. Nobody could, because Fist had reached into the weave and – using the codes that managed sweathead perception – made them both invisible. Camera stalks swivelled away from them as the main doors opened with a rainwater hiss.

Inside was warm and dry and dark. Fist constructed a view of the corridor that led away from the main reception area from infra-red security camera footage and dropped it in behind Jack's eyes. [Straight ahead, then over the dance floor,] he told him. They moved silently, barely as substantial as the shadows that surrounded them. Their shared experience of training and fighting rose up inside them like a rebooted operating system.

[No security manifesting, Fist?]

[That'll kick off a bit later, when I let them see us.]

[Wait till we reach the private area.]

The empty club oozed memories of spilt drinks, transient highs and hobbled lives. Jack wondered at the kind of mind that could achieve transcendence in such a limited, limiting space.

[I could turn on some of their weaveware, Jack. Then you'd see something.]

They slipped towards the stairs that they'd climbed only a few days ago. [Let him see us,] said Jack. A moment, then Fist replied, [Done.] Jack shouted up the stairs, his voice suddenly, shockingly harsh in the velvet silence that suffused the empty club.

'We're coming for you, Akhmatov.'

Akhmatov's response took maybe a second. The air shimmered and a huge black cat was roaring towards them, already in midleap. Its mouth was a shocking neon pink against darkly blazing fur. It was four times larger than Jack remembered. He threw his arms up and tottered backwards. It was all he could do not to scream.

Then Fist touched it and became the panther. [So much for his outer security perimeter,] he growled through his new mouth. [It was all of them at once. He's scared. You OK?]

[Bad memories.]

They went up the stairs and through the security doors, Fist padding on all fours, carefully keeping his distance from Jack. Jack kicked Akhmatov's office door. Wood tore away from hinges. He stepped through it and found himself in a desert. A jagged sun blazed in a blue sky above harsh yellow sand and bleach white rocks. Each colour was an assault.

'We've come for you, you murderous fuck.'

Fist followed Jack into the room. He split into four normal-sized panthers, each made puppet. Soft fur was replaced by black paint; tooth ivory by pale, unstained wood. The first panther stopped and licked itself. Its wooden tongue clacked softly as it moved across its haunches, flicking against wooden joints that replaced ones made of ligament and bone.

The second panther raised its head to the empty sky and growled. The sound was clearly artificial. The third and fourth sat resting on a large rock, eyes and ears swivelling. The rock seemed suddenly a little more unreal, a painted polystyrene prop discarded from an exhausted movie set.

[He's here. Hiding, but he's here,] said Fist through the first panther. Its cat throat gave Fist's voice a rich, deep huskiness. Jack remembered the tearing of claws, deep in flesh.

[Do we really need the panthers? Couldn't you just crash his weave access?]

[I could. And then we'd have him. But—] The second panther stretched, reaching out with its forelegs and pushing hard against the ground. Claws scratched at the sand. [—we wouldn't have server access. We need to go through all this to get to them.] The cat's

163

haunches rose up high, its tail – segmented links that looked like a black spine – twitching and spinning above them.

[Then stop preening, and get it over with!]

[Oh, I think I scent him now,] growled the third panther. It jumped down from the rock, thudded on to the sand and prowled forwards, its long shadow sliding along behind it. The others moved with it, the four of them forming an arrowhead. The lead panther turned back to Jack – [He's here …] – then snapped its head forward again. Its whole body tensed, then it was flying forward, pouncing at the empty air, claws snatching at something that, if there was a breeze, could just have been a billow of sand. But there was no breeze.

Paper-white teeth clashed with empty air. There was a thin high scream, and suddenly there was no sun or sand or rock. Blueness shimmered round Jack, the wooden panthers floating just ahead of him. A shock of cold broke against his whole body. He breathed out and bubbles rose. He and Fist had been pulled underwater. Akhmatov's security beasts were lost to him, and so he was fighting back with the only thing that remained under his control: the environment.

The shock of immersion made Jack forget to hold his breath. To his surprise, he felt his lungs fill with air. The simulation of being underwater was not complete. The lead panther thrashed around ahead of him. It was wrapped around something, mouth and claws tearing at it. Jack assumed that Fist was struggling with Akhmatov, but the club owner remained invisible, his security systems not yet finally defeated. His resistance had already lasted for at least five seconds – highly impressive, against Fist. The other panthers propelled themselves towards the fight with regular backward kicks. In the meantime, Jack could do nothing to help.

The sea was as empty as the desert had been. Above, there was only a lighter blue. There was no sign of a surface. Below, the water darkened to black. Shards of sunlight danced between Jack and the combatants, the ocean vast beyond them. Jack wondered how it had been coded. Perhaps it was finite and eventually stopped. Perhaps he could move through it forever, the simulation perpetually creating new distance before him. Fear chilled him. A digital eternity seemed so much emptier than its analogue equivalent.

164

Another of the panthers reached the fight. It threw itself into the fray and, once again, the world changed. They were no longer underwater. A gentle breeze gusted against Jack. He stood in a circle of henges, each one made of two upright man-sized stones supporting a third horizontal one. A sunset sky blazed with reds and oranges. Long shadows drifted across the centre of the circle, where a single sarsen lay flat. Two panthers rolled and snarled across it, their wooden bodies clattering against the rock. The others paced, looking for a way into the fight. Akhmatov's security systems were not yet sufficiently compromised to give them access.

Fist had however managed to dismantle some of his camouflage protocols. The two fighting cats spun and snarled around a shadowy figure, an almost man-shaped mass of disturbed air. Teeth and claws tore into it. It bled tiny spatters of visual noise. They became spots of red as they hit the green grass. The third cat pounced. There was a howl, and they were in the jungle clearing where Jack had been tortured. Memories of virtual claws ripped through Jack. He wondered what state Akhmatov would be in when his defences were finally broken. He turned away and leant against a tree. It felt wet. His hand was covered with brown paint. He touched a low hanging leaf. His fingers came away green. This was no longer the reality that Akhmatov had built. Fist was remaking it according to his own needs.

Looking around, Jack felt like an actor who'd wandered into an empty stage set. Unreality was exploding into being everywhere. The jungle floor was nothing more than brown-painted concrete, the trees that leapt out of it brightly coloured flats. Even the bird-song that suffused the space changed, crackling through static for a moment then reinstating itself as a series of obvious imitations. The battle was nearly over. Fist let out a triumphant howl, drowning out Akhmatov's scream of rage and terror. The painted jungle disappeared entirely.

There was a popping sound, and the sharp smell of burning plastic. Then a new scene took over. Fluorescent strip-lights lit an unremarkable room holding a desk, some chairs and four paintings. One showed a desert, one a sea, one a stone circle and one a dense jungle. Panthers prowled through each of them.

Akhmatov was lying on the floor, shaking. Fist stood over him, now just a wooden puppet again, and cackled gleefully. 'If you try anything on,' he said, 'I'll crack your mind open like an egg and piss in it.'

'He means it,' said Jack. 'I'd do what he says, if I were you.'

Chapter 26

They let Akhmatov pull himself up and lean against the desk. He was dressed in a black shirt and trousers. Both were covered in silver weave sigils.

'I've shut down his access to the club systems,' said Fist. 'There's nothing there but flesh.' Jack pulled the chair out from the other side of the desk and sat down. [And I'm running through his files, too,] added Fist quietly. [I'll let you know if I find anything good.] Akhmatov was wheezing. His skin was a traumatised grey. It was an effort for him to speak, but his voice was surprisingly strong when he did.

'I should have killed you eight years ago.'

Fist started towards him, his little hands twitching. 'No, Fist,' ordered Jack. 'You've had your fun. We need him able to talk.' Fist sat down hard, grumbling to himself about nice cops. Jack turned back to Akhmatov. 'And we should have raided your clubs and arrested you.'

'You'd have been stopped if you'd tried that.'

'Pantheon?' said Jack. 'They did stop me, in the end.'

'And we learned from you. Yamata stripped anything to do with her patron out of my systems.'

[Shit.]

[I'll keep looking,] replied Fist. [There'll be something we can use. There always is.] Then he spoke out loud. 'Don't stop talking, Akhmatov. Tell us what we want to hear. Make it easy on yourself.'

'That's what torturers always say, isn't it?' Akhmatov was slumped against the table, legs splayed out before him, a puppet whose strings had been cut. 'Rest assured the gods will torture you.'

'Not for your sake, though,' replied Jack. 'You don't really matter, do you? It's Aud Yamata and poor dead Penderville that count. That's what they don't want us digging into.'

167

'I'm saying nothing.'

'Look at Yamata now. Disappeared. A new identity, a new weave presence, maybe even a new body. Where is she? Somewhere in the Wart? In Homelands? In Heaven, even?'

'I wouldn't know.'

'She's your boss. Why did she get promoted when you didn't? What did she do that was so valuable? She was just one of the grunts back in the day, the one who brought the sweat in. But now you're still stuck counting cash in a Docklands dive. And she's who knows where, but it's better than here, isn't it?'

'Shut up Forster.'

'And how do you feel about her now she's the queen and you're just a pawn? She wanted us to find you, that's why she let Corazon see you. She thought I'd torture you and probably kill you, and you'd know what she could do to your fetch, so you'd stay loyal and keep silent, and that would be it. But if you help me bring her down you won't have to worry about that.'

'I think we should kill him,' said Fist. Then [Keep him talking. He's anonymised all his contacts. I can't tell which one's Yamata. Make him slip up, give something away.]

[OK,] said Jack. Then he continued out loud, 'No, Fist. We're not going to hurt him at all. Because if we did, if we even killed him, then we'd be just as much a pawn as he's been, all these years. And we don't believe in that, do we, Fist? We don't believe in being pawns, in just doing what we're told. Nicely. Politely.'

'Let me break him.'

Jack laughed. 'I could be a far nastier cop than you, if I wanted to,' he replied. 'You've probably heard this morning what I did to those policemen.' He knelt down next to Akhmatov, so he was almost face to face with him. 'Last night I slept with East, and she opened herself up to me. Gave me everything. You know what that means, don't you? She must be a regular, in a club like yours.'

For the first time, emotion flickered across Akhmatov's face. Fear crept out of him. Jack sensed a sad, defeated rage behind it. He wondered if East had increased his sensitivity, too. 'She gave me everything,' he whispered.

'If you're going to show me,' said Akhmatov, 'do it now. Do it quickly.'

Jack sighed. 'No. You're not going to help me find Yamata because I've made you love me, barely able to scrabble around in your own memories for lust of me. You're going to do it because you've understood just how you've been used, and you're more angry than you are afraid. Aren't you?' He let a few seconds hang empty in the air, then nudged an East switch in his mind. He moved in even closer and whispered 'Aren't you, Akhmatov?' as quietly as he could.

'They should have let me fucking kill you when I had the chance!'

Akhmatov's sudden movement knocked Jack backwards. The other man was on top of him, fingers scrabbling for his throat. 'I told Yamata that you were a risk to me,' he shouted, 'to all of us, but she didn't listen – and look where we are now! That bitch coming back from Sheltie, pretending it's a job for her security firm, and we kill a man I've known for twenty years and some fucking policewoman, and you're here, and look where we fucking are now!'

[Bingo!] said Fist. [That's it.]

When Jack hit Akhmatov it was like punching a wet pillow. The club owner sagged and fell away, the burst of energy that had given him a brief advantage shattered. Fist was on him instantly, hands buried in his head. Akhmatov screamed. 'No!' snapped Jack. He rolled forwards and snatched the puppet away, tearing him out of Akhmatov's mind. The club owner gaped in shock while Fist cackled madly.

[What have you done to him?]

[I haven't hurt him. At least, not as much as you have. I've done him a favour.]

[Fist ...]

[I've dropped deep sweathead tags into his weave presence. Unremovable. Everyone's weaveware will just blank him out, blank him right out! He's the invisible man now. He won't be able to tell anyone what we know.]

[For gods' sake, Fist. We still need information from him.]

[No we don't. I know which of his contacts Aud Yamata is, and I know how to find her.]

[You're sure?]

[It was much easier to fillet his business than I thought it would be. Almost like I was built for it.]

[Any clues on her boss?]

[No mention of that at all. Just like the man said.]

As they spoke, Akhmatov crawled away and collapsed in a corner of the room. He was shaking.

'One last question,' said Jack, turning back to him. 'Do you know who Yamata works for?'

[Don't get your hopes up, Jack. He's just a minion.]

'I told you I don't know,' he choked out. 'I'm better than that fucking bitch, and I'm still running this fucking club, and the Pantheon are still fucking playing with me. And I don't even know who it's all for.'

'You've Easted him, haven't you?' said Fist. 'He'll be telling the truth. But we've got a more immediate problem. InSec's coming. For you.'

'Shit. Let's go.'

'Why? I can hide you from those wankers now.'

'I don't want them finding out you've been unlocked.'

'Backing away from a fight? Boring!'

'We're running. Now.'

They got three hundred metres down the road before the InSec flyers caught them.

Chapter 27

'I don't know what I'm going to do with you, Jack.'

He was alone with Lestak. She'd flown her flyer up to hover between two spinelights. Nobody could disturb them. There was a black silk mask over his head. Its gauze eye patches gave him sight.

[Not sure if your charm will work through this, old son. Heavy cageware.]

[I won't be using it on her.]

[Wimp.]

'I'm not impressed by what you did to my men back at the hotel.'

'They'll recover.'

'Perhaps. I've petitioned East for her help. One of them keeps on asking for pictures of you. The other two don't say much, but they smile a lot. We had to handcuff them to stop them playing with themselves.'

'I'm sorry. I didn't realise what she'd done to me.'

'You're touched by Pantheon and it doesn't occur to you to see what you've been given?' A tired exasperation filled her voice. 'But then, that's always been your excuse. Nothing's your fault.'

'What's not his fault, Mummy?'

Jack jumped. The young girl's voice came from the front passenger seat. It must be Issie, Lestak's dead daughter. He was surprised that Lestak had let him hear her speak.

'Grown-up talk, darling. Hush – here, play with your doll.'

'But Mummy ...'

'Shush.'

'You've brought her here?' said Jack. 'And you're accusing me of irresponsibility?'

'Issie's often in the flyer. She likes it.'

'I can see everywhere!' chirped Issie.

171

[I could infiltrate that fetch,] Fist whispered in Jack's mind. [It might help us.]

[No,] replied Jack. [I don't want to risk damaging her.]

[I can hear you!] interrupted Issie. [And I'm not "that fetch", I'm Issie.]

[Shit!] said Fist. [She's tapped into us.]

Issie giggled.

[That's really why she's here,] replied Jack. [Block her.]

'They were talking about me, but I can't hear them anymore,' complained Issie.

'It's good that you told me about that. It's very rude to talk about people behind their backs, isn't it?'

'Oh yes! And it's even ruder to shut people out when they realise!'

'I'm sure Jack won't let Fist do that again – will you?'

[Let's go with it,] said Jack. [I want to find out what Lestak's got to say.]

Fist shimmered into life on the seat next to him. 'I'll be good,' he promised.

'I'd forgotten how real you look,' replied Lestak.

'As real as Issie,' said Jack, expecting a sharp response from Lestak. But she said nothing. There was a moment's silence, then Issie stuck her head round the seat. But for her white skull face, she was a perfect simulacrum of a small child.

'It *is* the funny puppet again! Can I play with him?'

Mist hung in her eye sockets with the soft density of cotton wool. When she spoke, wisps escaped from her hollow mouth. Jack worked hard not to shudder. 'Fist won't hurt her,' he told Lestak. 'That's not how we work.'

[Boring,] sang out Fist.

Lestak nodded. Issie squealed.

'Off you go then,' said Jack. 'Play nice.'

'I'm not a toy,' muttered Fist, but he stood up quickly enough, and with a little jump was next to Issie. She shifted in her seat, letting him sit down next to her – one face carved from wood, one from bone. Indulgence and concern mingled on Lestak's face. Stifled giggles and little whispered words rose up.

'Are you sharing secrets, Issie?' asked Lestak.

172

'Oh yes!'

'That's what we're going to be doing, too. You and Fist should make sure nobody can hear.'

'You said that was rude!'

'Not when you're sharing secrets.'

A moment of silence, then the puppet and fetch voices combined to say 'We're firewalled.' The giggling and whispering continued. Lestak relaxed.

'Her eyes are full of weaveware,' said Jack. 'You use her for security?'

'It's about keeping her safe, as much as me. You make powerful enemies doing what I do.'

'Yes, must be very handy having a little friend like that.'

'Now listen, Jack. Corazon was starting to take you seriously, and she had good judgement. That's why you're here, now. And that's why nobody can hear us talk. But don't push it.'

There was a snorting laugh from the passenger seat.

'I'm sorry about Corazon. She was a good policewoman.'

'East said she gave you the news.'

Memories of Corazon's last minutes jostled at the edge of Jack's mind. They had started to lose their sharp, unintegrated edge. They were almost bearable. 'Yes,' he said.

'We found out about your meeting with Corazon. We thought you'd killed her.'

'I had nothing to do with it.'

'East confirmed that. I wish she'd come to us before we tried to arrest you.'

'She's a playful one,' sighed Jack. 'Does she know who did shoot Corazon?'

'No. She's more upset by that than by the death.' Jack remembered how outraged East had been not to have known instantly that Corazon was dead. 'Sandal came to me too,' continued Lestak. 'The guards you broke were his. He was furious. Two Pantheon manifestations in one day, and both about you. If Grey hadn't been sequestered, I'm sure he'd have popped up as well. What have you done to get this much attention, Jack?'

'I'm trying to find out the truth about the Penderville murder.

About Aud Yamata, and her patron. And now about Corazon.'

'Those are truths that kill, and that makes you dangerous.'

'I can't help that.'

'Sandal wanted me to arrest you and hold you until Fist – well, you know. East wanted me to give you full Wart and Homelands access.'

'There's a war in Heaven.'

'So it seems. And someone needs to try and referee it.'

'That's won't be easy.'

'No. And that's why we need to talk. With Corazon dead, I think you are on to something after all. But I'm not going to let you chase around after it, putting more people at risk. And I've got to please East and Sandal.'

'So what are you going to do?'

'When it comes to you, nothing. I'm not going to change your Station access rights. I'm not going to let you go onweave, or visit Homelands, or the Wart. But I'm not going to restrict you anymore or imprison you, either.'

'That'll piss both of them off. And it doesn't help me.'

'It'll piss them both off equally, so they'll take it up with each other, not me. And I'm not in the business of helping you. I'm in the business of protecting Station. Like you, once.'

'I still am. There's something rotten here. Seven years ago, a man was murdered with full Pantheon knowledge. The person that did it has been hidden, with full Pantheon involvement. Others have been silenced at fetch level. Corazon's been killed.'

'So why haven't they shut you down too?'

'Friends in high places,' said Jack bitterly.

Sudden shrieks of joy exploded from the front seat.

'Hush, you two,' scolded Lestak. There was muffled giggling, then Fist and Issie muted themselves again.

'I'm not going to beg,' said Jack. 'But I do need access to Homelands. I have to try and find Aud Yamata.'

'You know where she might be?' Lestak's attention was suddenly entirely focused on Jack, the professional investigator in her cutting through to the front of her mind. 'You're going to share whatever you know with me, aren't you?'

Jack paused for a moment, wondering how much to tell Lestak, how much she would record, how secure InSec was. It was clear that East didn't trust her – or at least, didn't trust the organisation that surrounded her. Corazon's death had made him wary, too.

A low whine filled the car – a tug passing by, trailing chainship containers, moving towards the Wart. Jack imagined the wonders it would be carrying to the twin malls of Homelands. He thought of containers, perhaps entire chainships, loaded with sweat, made invisible by adapted sweathead avoidance code. He reached a decision.

'I don't know anything more than I did back then, Lestak.'

'If you do run into anything new, you will let us know. You won't go looking into it yourself.'

'You've got Corazon's records, that's more data than I'll ever have. She was tracking Yamata. I think Yamata realised that and killed her. If you go to the files, you'll find all you need.'

Lestak wearily massaged her forehead, hiding her eyes. 'There's a problem with that.'

'You have looked at them?' Lestak said nothing. 'That's why they killed her, for gods' sake! For whatever she'd found out!'

'There was a chromacode virus. We traced it back to a weave sigil sprayed on the sidewalk outside her apartment. It penetrated her InSec weavespace and shredded all her data.'

'You think that's coincidence? You think some script bunny could have planted something like that?'

'No, I don't.' Lestak's voice became an urgent whisper, as if quieter words were somehow more secret. 'No, I don't think that. I agree with you – there's something wrong here, and it goes all the way to the top. But I can't let you investigate it. You were taken out of play seven years ago and you're still out of play now.'

'Listen to yourself, Lestak. You're running scared.'

'Of course I am. This is terrifying. Criminals – I lock them up, or throw them off the weave. Corrupt InSec ops – we find them, we break them. But this – if one of the Pantheon is broken, what am I meant to do? How am I meant to stop that? I have to be so fucking careful even thinking about it. And I am going to investigate it, Jack, but I am going to tread so lightly. And you – there's nothing light about you, nothing subtle about that creature. You were never even a proper policeman, and now you're just damaged goods, not realising who you're hurting until it's too late. You're not safe to be around. Corazon proved that.'

'And whatever you find out? Will that disappear too?'

'I've been around a lot longer than Corazon, and my patron is a lot tougher than hers was. East, bless her, gives good weathergirl, and her flash mobs are second to none when it comes to stalking weave stars. But she's not a fighter. Not like the Rose.'

'So you won't help me?'

'No. And I'll be watching you. If you do anything at all that makes me think you're investigating all this on your own, I will land on you so fucking hard you won't even know what year it is. And don't think you'll be dealing with lightweights like the boys this morning. I know what East's done to you. We'll send the castrati after you, and you won't be able to stop them.'

'The castrati? I thought—'

'They're not just a rumour, Jack. We've had to deal with people East's touched before. The Rose has developed solutions to her charms. Take a step back. You were never really a professional to start with, and you're certainly not one now. If you keep digging you'll be dangerous to yourself and to everyone you touch.'

The flyer started to descend.

'Make your peace with your parents, Jack.' Her voice was softer, now. 'Not all of us get the chance to say goodbye, before the end comes. And being out of the game – well, sometimes it's a privilege. It means the terms of loss are fixed. No one can force them to change.'

The flyer touched down with a gentle bump. Lestak turned to the passenger seat and smiled. 'Issie, honey, playtime's over.' It took a couple of minutes to persuade her to hand Fist back to Jack. Jack imagined security systems unmeshing and ports undocking while the skull-faced girl refused to give up her new friend. In private she would be a near perfect representation of a living child. Out here, the skull revealed the truth of her post-mortal status.

Andrea had refused to show Jack what that looked like, but Issie was too young to worry about such things. Jack wasn't sure whether

176

he felt happy or sad for her. He wondered how Lestak remembered her daughter – whether white, empty bone had overwritten the soft liveliness of her living face.

Issie waved from the window as the flyer lifted off, her hand a little pink flutter behind the glass. Lestak's last words, spoken as she'd lifted Jack's hood off and unlocked the handcuffs, were simple and direct. 'Walk away, Jack. Don't look back.'

[Of course, you'll ignore her,] said Fist.

[Of course,] replied Jack.

[Cute kid. Lestak's kept her locked at four years old, but she's still pretty sharp. She worked out that I was uncaged.]

[Hell. She'll tell Lestak.]

[I swore her to silence. She told me some of her secrets too. Fetch secrets.]

Fist sounded very pleased with himself.

[What were they?]

Fist pretended outrage.

[I can't tell you! I promised!]

[If I didn't know you better, I'd swear you were softening.]

[Not really. Now I can kill fetches too.]

Chapter 28

Harry was sprawled across the sofa, smoking a cigarette. Andrea wasn't around. Jack hadn't asked where she was.

'So you saw her skullchild? Makes me glad I got to build myself. Missed all the bone code out. I'd hate going round like that. Apart from anything else, my hat would slip. And the smoke from these' – Harry waved the cigarette at Jack – 'would come out through my eye sockets. That's really not dignified, is it? Not that it's a problem you're going to have, thanks to that little sod.' He gestured towards Fist, who pointedly ignored him. 'Anyway,' he continued, 'what are we going to do about Yamata? Can't let her get away with it, but I've had no luck tracking her down. Now if we could break through Fist's cage so I can use what he's got, I might be able to dig a bit deeper. If I can't find her, we've got nothing.'

'We got all we needed from Akhmatov. Fist?'

'Oh yes,' said Fist. 'I know exactly where she's based.'

'Come on then,' drawled Harry. 'Let's have it.'

'But I'm only going to tell you what I know if I get … certain assurances from Jack.'

'What?' replied Jack. 'For gods' sake, Fist.' Privately, he wasn't too surprised. Since their encounter with East, Fist had been relatively easy to deal with. He'd been expecting the puppet's obstinacy to reassert itself at some point.

'What the hell's he talking about?' asked Harry. 'Little shit.' He swung a large, fat hand towards the side of Fist's head. The blow didn't connect – Harry's fingers passed harmlessly through the puppet. Fist tittered as static shook his face.

'Still just a ghost, old man!' he chortled. 'Can't touch me, can't touch me – only if Jack says so, and he won't.'

Fist turned to Jack.

'I don't want you to let Harry mesh with any of my systems,

under any circumstances. If you promise that, I'll tell you how to find Yamata.'

'You little bastard,' said Harry.

'With what I know,' Fist told Harry, 'you won't need any part of me to track her down. So why are you so upset?'

'Because you should do what Jack tells you. And because this isn't over yet.'

'Bullshit. You just want to control me like you do Andrea. You want another slave.'

'She's not a slave, she's a fetch, and that's what you do with fucking fetches. I do what venues do, I just bring out the best in her. And I'd bring out the best in you too. I'd use you to find things, break into them, then destroy them. That's what you're for.'

Jack struggled to hide his anger. 'Harry's not going to do anything like that to you,' he told Fist.

'What?' said Harry.

Fist bounced up and down gleefully. 'You promise?' he chirped.

'I promise.'

'Cross your heart and hope to die?'

'For gods' sake. I've said no, that's that. Harry will never get any access to any of your systems.'

'Hurrah!' shouted Fist. 'You're not the boss of me, Harry!'

'If I could get my hands on you, you little shit ...'

'You never will now.'

'Stop bickering, you two,' snapped Jack. 'We're after Yamata, not each other.' The hard command in his voice took both Harry and Fist by surprise. They fell silent. 'Now,' he said to Fist. 'Tell us where she is.'

'Akhmatov told us that Yamata works with a security firm in Sheltie. I think I've found it. Harry, you'll need to check it out – here are the details.'

Harry's eyes fluttered as he read the file.

'Got it. I'll scope 'em out, test their defences. Once we've found a way of getting you and the little fuck into their servers we can solve all our problems.'

'You're very confident. You won't get caught?' said Jack.

'I've been hiding in the weave for two years. Travel in the pipes, disappear in doorways, lose myself in shadow. You don't need to worry about me. But we've got to find a way of getting you into Homelands without InSec spotting you.'

'It's not going to matter whether or not they can see me.'

'You're bolder than you used to be, Jack Forster.'

'Not bold, Harry, just well connected. The Totality can help me.'

'Those useless bastards. Would be nice if they turned out to be good for something.'

'They will be. How long before we move?'

'I'm going to have to tread carefully. It'll take a day or so.'

'It would take me half an hour,' said Fist.

'Then you should fucking help me,' said Harry. He turned back to Jack. 'Think you can be in Homelands the day after tomorrow?'

'I'm sure I can.'

'Good. I'll be in touch.'

Then Harry was gone. He left the last of his cigarette smoke behind him. It uncurled in the empty room, shaping itself around invisible air currents, then fell away to nothing. Jack felt himself relaxing.

'What was all that about just now?' said Jack.

'I don't want Harry using me. I don't want him inside me. I don't like being controlled.'

'He just wants to mesh with some of your subsystems.'

'He'll do more than that. Count on it.'

'He can't hurt you. That's just bluster.'

'Fuck's sake Jack, you really haven't thought through what it means to be software. Remember how Grey nudged me? Once someone gets into me, they can start playing around.'

'I wouldn't give him permission.'

'Do you think that'd stop him? East could have fried me if she'd wanted to. She didn't because she won't break the terms of the software licence that binds you to me. It's a legal agreement, and that's what the Pantheon's built on. Harry doesn't give a damn about any of that. Once you let him in, he'll do whatever he wants.'

'He's a fetch. They can't do that.'

'No he's not. He's rebuilt himself. When I was close to Issie, I saw how fetches work. It was one of the secrets she shared with me.

180

He's structured differently and his lag times are all wrong. He's not hosted on the Coffin Drives.'

'He broke out of them, and he's spent the last few years in hiding. He's not going to work in the same way as someone like her.'

'No. It's more than that.'

'Have you tried to track him back? Work out where he's really stored?'

'I couldn't probe without him finding out. And we don't want that.'

'You're afraid of him.'

'Of course I fucking am. If things go his way, he'll fillet me and fry me like a little Fisty fish. Just like our rogue Pantheon friend would, if they got their hands on me.'

Jack laughed.

'Don't you dare find it funny,' said Fist. 'I thought that bitch East was going to kill me. I want to break the bastard that's got it in for us before he or she or it gets a chance to break me.'

'They want to keep you safe.'

'And you said that's bullshit.'

Another voice cut through their conversation.

'What's bullshit?' Andrea wasn't wearing makeup. The memory of the last time Jack had seen her naked face caught at his heart. Her dress was a deep, clotted red. Her skin was pale and far too young. Jack couldn't answer. 'It doesn't matter,' she continued. 'I just found a message I left for myself. It told me to watch this with you. It's a screenshow, I think.'

Jack said, 'Wait.' But she waved her hand and there was music. At first, there was only a soft, insistent beat, scratching at Jack's hearing. It tugged at his attention but it was very quiet, so he had to concentrate carefully to hear it. It caught noises that drifted in from outside in its meshes, pulling them into song.

'What is this?' asked Jack.

'Ssssh,' whispered Andrea. 'Listen carefully.'

There was a burst of static. A broken riff lanced out and settled on the beat, like a glitched image of a bird diving again and again into choppy water.

[It wants to share visuals,] hissed Fist.

181

[Let it.]

Images started appearing on one of the room's blank walls. Most were black and white. The few colour ones pulled Jack's attention to them. More instruments had joined the music. Speech was woven in with it too. Jack heard Harry's voice. One of the colour photos expanded to fill most of the wall. It was a shoulder lying on rumpled sheets. A woman's hand caressed it. A second or two passed and then there was a window, seen from below. Soft spinelight made the raindrops on it shimmer like diamonds. Another sudden cut and there was a handwritten card. It disappeared too quickly to be read. A cat pounced on a sock. Just as quickly, a new image flashed up. The music began to feel out of sync with the film. Speech darted out between rapidly shifting rhythms, broken clauses stripped of context. Harry was still talking. There was a light joy to his voice that Jack had never heard before. Caressing fragments whispered into the room – soft endearments caught late at night, loud in the sleeping silence of Station. Then Jack's own voice started to appear in the mix.

He sounded so much younger. New images flickered by. A kettle boiled. There was a garden, with a soft toy hanging from a tree. Hands pulled a shirt out of a dryer. He recognised his own hands, and memories came. They pulsed through him as the images continued. Meshed with the music, each vignette called up more of the past, creating a record of his time with Andrea seen from her point of view. A clock shone out from a bedside table. It used to wake him every morning. A hand knocked over a glass of whisky. It had the Vista Club logo on it. Andrea had drenched herself. There'd been a taxi ride home, and then a fumble out of her soaked clothes before they made love. Harry had been away. It was the first full night they'd spent together.

The soundtrack muttered broken sighs and laughter. Sounds and images fused into a series of precise invocations. It felt like commands were being written directly to Jack's memory, triggering a mode of exact recall that summoned the past straight into his mind's eye. A kaleidoscope of yesterdays sparked into life, overwhelming the present and replacing it with something, richer, deeper and far more structured. For a few moments, Jack felt himself rolled all the way back to his time with Andrea. For a few moments, joy filled him and he forgot everything that had come after. Then, the film's focus started to move on. Memory shards still pulsed hypnotically, but they no longer reached Jack so directly. He fell back into the present.

[Amazing stuff, Jack.]

[Yes – really evocative.]

[No. Look at Andrea.]

She was still rapt in the flickering world of the past. But her clothes and hairstyle had changed, looking more up-to-date. Her face had aged too, time's passing recarved into it.

[It's bringing her back to herself. How?]

[The music's doing it, and the images. They're triggering memory cascades that are rebuilding her most recent self. Quite the achievement!]

Jack thought about the other times he'd heard the same broken music. At the club, Andrea must have been restoring herself after her performance. And he'd thought she'd been rehearsing in her upstairs room. Perhaps she'd in fact been composing, weaving a few new hours of life into the music that would so effectively and precisely reverse any rolling back.

[Oh look!] said Fist. [It's all about the moon!]

Jack was snared again, although not in quite the same way as before. Now the experience was less personal. He watched a culture's grief come to life before him. The lament still tore into him, though. And the music was about far more than dead children. Andrea had shot this sequence through with a flash-forward to her own murder. Corazon's memories blazed in Jack's mind. He turned away from the screen, letting the moment pass.

When he looked back, the flash-forward had ended. The film and music moved through the two years before the end of Andrea's life. It touched on the slow death of her relationship with Harry, and the increasing artistic independence and confidence that paralleled that loss. Finally, it skipped back to her post-death self, filling the wall with images and the air with sounds that recapped her life as a fetch. At last it wound down and there was silence. Jack turned to Andrea, now once again fully herself. Her head was down and her eyes were closed.

'Are you OK?' he asked.

She opened her eyes and looked round at him, once again fully herself.

'I hate having to do that,' she replied. 'Fucking clubs. Fucking Harry.'

'Why do you let him stay here, then?'

'Oh, Jack.' She moved to one of the sofas. 'He was my husband once. He's a shit, but where else is he going to go? And he's helped me a lot over the last couple of years, in his own way.' She brushed her hair out of her eyes. 'And I have so few other people to talk to. You've seen what the clubs are like. I hardly see my friends, they only care about the living. And my family prefer me much younger. Much younger. I was so far away from them as an adult.'

'You've got me to talk to.'

'And you don't think I'm really Andrea, do you? I tricked you. That's one of the first things you said to me. Do you still believe that?'

'I didn't trust you. You didn't tell me the whole truth.'

'You should have understood why that was impossible by now. Perhaps there are even people you haven't told the whole truth to?'

Jack winced. 'Maybe. You do seem to be so much her.'

'Seem to be?' she said. 'Only that?' Jack said nothing. 'Which is why I wanted you to see all this,' she continued. 'Because I knew you'd say that. You've just watched my memories laid out as code, pulling me back to myself. I'm built on memory, Jack. And so are you.'

'But I haven't died.'

'Think about your body. Every single cell is replaced, every seven years. You've been away for that long. What remains of the man who left?'

'I'm still me, Andrea.'

'You're a pattern of memories running on a dynamic platform that's constantly renewing itself. The pattern is all that persists, the self looking back on all it has been and knowing itself from that. That's what makes you you, Jack, not the passing fact of your flesh. And that's what makes me me. I may be running on a different plat-form, but the pattern of me is unchanged and I fight hard to protect

184

it. I am Andrea, Jack, I'm the same person as that different person all those years ago, just as you're the same person as that different Jack who loved me then.'

[Oo, philosophy! It's making my head hurt. I say cut to the chase and snog her.]

[Shut up, Fist.]

[Grabbing a glass of champagne ... Activating your sub-dermal presence simulators ... Now she can touch you! Over to you, lover boy!]

Andrea noticed Jack's distraction. 'Fist?'

'He has strong opinions.'

'Is he real?'

Jack smiled. 'He's certainly got a mind of his own. And he's going to be around after I'm gone. So yes, he's real.'

[Of course I am!]

'He's quite excited about this,' continued Jack. 'About you.'

Andrea leant towards him. Presence simulators showed him her warmth. Virtual breath brushed against his skin. She touched the side of his face.

'And is he right to be?' she said.

Chapter 29

It was just before dawn. Jack kicked open a door which led to a stairway that had wrapped itself around a construction which might once have been a gas storage cylinder. Now, it was some sort of scrap-metal recycling centre. Looking down into it from the walkway on its rim was like looking into an iron maw studded with broken teeth. Spotlights pulled vaguely identifiable machine shapes from drifts of rust-tinted tangle.

[I can't believe I've got an automatic intimacy shutoff!] grumbled Fist. [I didn't even know it existed.]

[Never triggered it before,] replied Jack, turning away from scrap metal to look out over Docklands.

[Oh well, at least I got to see you and East together. I suppose you can't really be intimate with a god.] He popped into view just next to Jack, perched on the railings. [I ended up playing Andrea's memory code back again. Remarkable piece of work. She's sharp, that girl of yours.]

[I know that.]

Dim streets curved up and away in front of them, losing themselves in height and darkness. Lights glowed softly – some from windows, some from streetlamps, some from flyers and cars. They sketched in the places around them, hinting at different kinds of buildings, different kinds of lives. In its dormant state, Docklands was a city of implications.

[Seeing it without the weave seems so natural now,] Jack commented. [Gods, I used to think quiet rooms were peaceful. But even in them you'd have a few sprites buzzing around, to remind you it was all still out there. To stop you from panicking.]

[We can activate any time you want. You really should get back onweave, Jack. It's been seven years. With me behind you, you'll see everything.]

[That's why we've come up here.]

The soft whine of distant flyer engines pulsed down from above. The spinelights were still dark, silhouettes defined by the lights of the city beyond and behind them. A series of loud cracks rang out from them.

[They're waking up the spinelights,] Jack explained. [A few minutes and it'll be daylight. Take me onweave while they come online.]

[What?]

[Wake me up with the city, Fist.]

[I could have everything open right now.]

[No. Do it step by step. I want to make sure I remember all the details.]

At first, it seemed that nothing was changing. Then the soft darkness began to lose something of its density. Dawn was dusting the city with presence, pulling definition into being. As it emerged from the gloom, Fist unveiled the first, most basic component of the weave: the grid that lay over the city, providing a spatial reference point for every single active weavepoint. Straight white lines threw themselves across Docklands, imposing horizontal and vertical regularity on urban chaos. Pale grey lines leapt up from the corner of each square, striating cylindrical airspace into an infinity of cubes.

[What scale are we on, Fist?]

[Ten by ten metres. The spatial mapping goes right down to millimetres. But if I showed you those gridlines, you'd see nothing else.]

[Fair enough.]

[Now, locations. I'm assuming you just want to see the major ground tags? I can show you descriptors for all the cubes – but the data's so dense, you wouldn't see anything past thirty or forty metres away ...]

[Just the tags, Fist. And street-level detail, nothing more defined than that.]

Where there had been a vista, there was suddenly content. Red and yellow lines streaked across Docklands, parsing space. Letters danced into words, defining streets, squares, neighbourhoods, buildings and stations. A patchwork of colours leapt across the landscape, shouting information into the gathering day. They flowed from

187

neighbourhood to neighbourhood, shifting shade with each one, turning the city into a vast artist's palette.

[That's lovely,] Jack told Fist. [Now let's see the people too.]

[What level of detail?]

[The basics.]

[I'll break them down by sex – red for men, blue for women.]

[Show me the sweatheads, too.]

[OK – black for them. Minimum scale. One pixel, one person.]

Fist waved his hand and the great patchwork before them was dusted with tiny dots. Many of the red and blue pixels were clumped in residential areas. Many were still in bed, or at least at home. Some were already travelling to work. Streets were lightly spotted with red and blue. Trains showed as moving lines of colour, leaping between the long, thin scatterings that were station platforms.

[They'll be rammed when it comes to rush hour,] said Fist. [Squashed in like squishies!]

[Fist!]

[And all those sweatheads!]

The town was speckled with black. Most were clumped together in little groups.

[Still asleep in their factories,] said Jack.

[Factories?]

[The places where they hide and drop sweat together. That's what they're called.]

[Aren't sweatheads dangerous when they're high?]

[Not if you leave them alone. InSec keep them out of the way.]

A few of the black dots were beginning to move towards train stations and major roads.

[The early degenerate catches the worm!] chirped Fist. [I wonder if we can see Akhmatov?]

[I thought you'd completely anonymised him.]

[I left some personal tags on him.]

Fist's eyes clacked shut in concentration. [There he is!] he said, pointing up and to the right. A white circle highlighted a black dot on a small residential street. [He's in the back room of a café.]

[I wonder if someone can see him? I thought you said he'd be invisible.]

[They're still closed, Jack. Perhaps he's broken in there to shelter.]

[He's just a distraction. We've got the basics up and running. Trip the entertainment and commercial layer.]

A shotgun blast of logos punched themselves into being. With them came the howl of a thousand advertising jingles, a visual and aural cacophony carving into Jack's mind like a punch. Jack doubled over in pain, eyes tight shut, hands going to his ears.

'FIST!' he screamed.

[Shit! Sorry!] The roar of commerce subsided as quickly as it had begun. [I forgot to put the limiters on.]

[Gods' sake, Fist. Nobody looks at it all at once.] Jack opened his eyes, pulled his hands from his ears and shook his head. Now there was just a hubbub. The world bustled with icons and animations and words and music. Chain logos repeated themselves across the city. Slices of pizza danced on fat little legs, coffee mugs fluttered on glossy brown wings and an idealised market stallholder sung about his wares. If Jack focused on a particular logo it would expand to fill about a quarter of his field of vision. If he waited a second or two more, details of special offers would sing out from it.

[I'd forgotten how much I hated that.]

[I'll sort it.]

[You can block it?]

[Most people couldn't, but I can!]

The logos became less hyperactive.

[I'm sure there weren't so many when I left,] sighed Jack.

[Is that really a pole-dancing hamburger?]

[I'm afraid so.]

[Your human cultural achievements never fail to amaze me.]

[The void sites have come online too.]

[They sit in the marketing layer? Wow.]

Children's faces hung over the city, monochrome memories of the lost. The images reset every thirty seconds or so, one sad face melting into the next. Sometimes a word would flash up – 'Remember', for example, or 'Innocent' or 'Gone'.

[Depressing,] said Fist glumly.

[They're meant to be. Let's have the social feeds.]

[OK ...]

The geography of Docklands implied social networks. Interconnected engagement webs exploded across the landscape, making them visible. Informal groupings throbbed busily, as people entered their first status updates of the day and caught up with friends across the city. Dormant corporate networks shimmered through and beyond them. Soon they too would wake to life. Some would converge into rich, dense clumps, as employees settled into offices, factories, or shops. Some would remain stretched across the city, virtual businesses whose employees worked in a close digital proximity that made distance irrelevant. Some would pull workers out of Docklands entirely, into the Wart or Homelands. And some would leap into the void, clambering up the Spine to the wharves or beyond.

[What's everyone saying?] asked Jack.

The morning's babble rose up around him. It was difficult to separate the messages. Excited voices shrilled joy at a new dawn, a new partner, even just an excellent cup of coffee, while the less perky dreaded the upcoming working day, bitched about waking up alone again, or bemoaned hangovers.

[They're all soooo mundane,] groaned Fist.

[It's what people do. It's just as important as the big stuff.]

[It's pointless. What's next?]

[Show me the Pantheon.]

[You want to look at the gods? They'll look right back at you.]

[I trust your security arrangements, Fist.]

[I'll call them. They might be hard to damp at first. Close your eyes.]

[Fist ...]

[No, really.]

Jack shut his eyes, and the world vanished. For a moment the hubbub of morning voices filled his ear, then that too died away. A breeze sang through the metal that surrounded him. Then a great flash broke in the sky, bright even through closed eyes. A deep, loud industrial hum shook itself into being. It sounded like a choir of machines chanting in a metal church.

[Containing the signal, Jack.]

The hum became a roar and then softened, modulating into a

background throb that was almost gentle. There were eleven more flashes of light. Each was accompanied by a pulse of noise that Fist contained, again and again coming to terms with the numinous.

[How's it going?] asked Jack.

[Difficult to manage their outputs without feeding back our signatures, but it's just about done. There – open your eyes!]

The world had changed. The Spine had been replaced by six great icons of the divine, representing each of the Pantheon. Only two appeared remotely human. There was Kingdom with his shaven head and East, looking reliably dazzling. She appeared in full figure, her clothes shimmering as they shifted and changed with the fashion whims of the moment. The Eastware in Jack's mind responded to her presence, until Fist hushed it. For a moment Jack was at one with entire monasteries of her followers, solemnly hymning her dazzling style.

Then, there were the more abstract deities. The Rose's petals were as violently red as they'd always been but the sharp green thorns partially hidden beneath them were entirely new. Sandal's crystal cube rotated as slowly and deliberately as ever. The Twins were represented by a great set of constantly moving scales. First one side was in the ascendant, then the other. And of course, there was Grey.

He was a fallen god, no longer capable of acting as a free agent. But his corporate structures had not yet been fully absorbed by his competitors. Thousands of people still needed to use his apps, access data held on his servers, or call in other ways on his strategic and financial services. So his raven was still present, though it now made his broken status humiliatingly clear. A great iron band ran around its body, holding its wings tight to its sides. A silver chain glittered around its legs, and then ran up to its beak, holding it shut. A rag was tied around its head, covering its eyes. It had also been stripped of any animation.

[That's sad to see,] said Jack. [It used to be so alert.]

The bird's gaze had once constantly flickered back and forth across Docklands, tracking every single commercial transaction.

[They're ... huge, Jack.]

[You get used to them. After a while, you stop taking much notice.]

191

[I can't imagine that,] breathed Fist.

Thousands of slender silver threads drifted out from the base of each icon, falling away into the city. Each represented a link to an individual worshipper, dancing with sparkling light as data ran along it. Twined together, they showed the relative user bases of each Pantheon member.

[Look at Grey's bundle,] said Fist.

It was far thinner than those descending from the other eleven icons, twine to their rope, and much duller – the colour of lead, not silver.

[I'm surprised he's still got that many followers.] Jack paused for a moment, suddenly thoughtful. [One more thing,] he continued. [Let's take a look at my parents.]

[I can see your father. And talking with Issie's helped me track fetches. There's your mother!]

[Get rid of everyone else.]

An entire population shimmered into nothing, leaving only a single red pixel right next to a single blue one, in a distant street rolling up behind the Spine.

[They must be in bed.]

Jack remembered childhood nights, and the deep security of knowing that his parents were asleep in the next room. The knowledge of their closeness was always a ward against the small difficulties of a Docklands child's life.

[Can we look at them?]

He was surprised at how quiet his voice was.

[Oh yes,] piped Fist. [And perhaps there'll be some action! That'll make up for last night.]

[Fucking hell, Fist,] sighed Jack. [If that's what they're doing, we'll let them be. Now, how to see them?]

[Spoilsport,] replied Fist. [And, let's see. A camera nest's the best way, they're all over the place. It'll be quite risky though – they run on Rosecode, she's tough.]

[If Harry can hack camera nests, I'm sure you can.]

[That sleazy fuck. We'll have to be quick.]

Fist closed his eyes and threw his mind out into the weave, searching for a lens to bring Jack's parents into focus. Jack stared up

192

at the two dots, lost in sadness at his distance from them.

[Got it!]

A square of light flashed into being, resolving into a street of brightly coloured plastic boxes. It was like looking directly into a memory.

[The camera nest's got droneflies mounted on it. Just snagging one …]

The view in the window changed as the dronefly lifted up and moved down the street to hang outside an upstairs window. The curtains were drawn, but the window was open. Fist steered it into the bedroom. There was a single figure, asleep on one side of a double bed.

[I'll just drop your mother in.]

[Doesn't my dad have to reset her permissions?]

[Issie showed me a temporary hack.]

Suddenly there were two shapes there.

[Audio.]

His father was snoring. Nostalgia shook Jack. He so wanted to step into the image and find himself back in childhood.

[You've got about thirty more seconds, Jack.]

[Bring the camera in closer.]

His father let out a particularly loud snore. His mother shifted, then reached out to nudge her partner. He grunted and rolled over. Jack imagined processors deep in his mind, simulating touch. She sighed and settled back, but then stiffened.

[She's waking up. Time's up, we should go.]

[No, stay. I want to see her.]

'Hello?' she said, pushing herself up one arm. 'Is there someone there?'

[Shit! She's probing.]

She turned to face the camera.

[Issie warned me they could do this. I'm going to cut the link.]

[No.]

[It's not safe!]

She leant forward, bringing her face into the thin line of light from the slightly parted curtains. Jack gasped. It was the first time he'd seen her for seven years. She seemed so alive, so present.

[What's that?] she whispered. [A puppet?] and then, in the smallest, softest voice imaginable, [Jack?]

[She's on to us!]

[You're not breaking the link, Fist.]

[Any second now, InSec'll see us, Pantheon'll see us. Fuck's sake, Jack, you fucking idiot!]

But Jack didn't hear.

[Mum?]

[Is that really you?]

Jack's father stirred.

[It's me, Mum,] said Jack, not knowing whether or not she could hear him, for a moment forgetting that she wasn't still alive, and that he wasn't standing directly before her.

[They told me you were— If that is you, oh, Jack.]

There was an electric crack and the screen vanished. Jack imagined a dronefly falling to the ground in a distant room, his father waking to a weeping wife. Then, anger shook him.

[Fist, I told you not to cut me off.]

'He didn't,' said Grey, appearing on the staircase. 'I did.' Metal rang beneath his feet as he climbed the last few steps. 'You were cutting it rather too fine. A few more seconds and that would have been it for you both.'

'You've been watching us all this time?'

'I had a flag set in case you went onweave. I thought you might benefit from a little constructive criticism. As it turned out, I was right. It's good to feel that I can still be useful, even if my wings have been clipped.' He waved up towards the Spine. 'I do hate seeing my icon like that.'

Jack was torn between anger and grief. He didn't trust himself to speak. Fist stepped into the awkward silence. 'I had everything well under control,' he said firmly.

'I'm sure you did,' replied Grey, his silkily polite coldness implying exactly the opposite.

'Fuck you,' Fist shot back. 'And while you're here, don't you go playing around in my fucking head again.'

'Oh, don't worry. There's no more need for that. Now you've realised you're both equally threatened by the same enemy, all I'd

194

need to do is ask politely for your help. And that wouldn't be a problem at all, would it?' Fist made a noise that sounded like spitting. 'But let's not waste our time with petty arguments. Jack – I wanted to congratulate you on your progress.'

Jack was now sufficiently in control of himself to reply. 'What do you mean?' he asked, taking a step back as Grey reached the balcony.

'Really, there's no need to be afraid, Jack.'

'I'm not afraid. I don't trust you. That's very different.'

'My boy. If I wanted to harm you, I'd have let your chat with your dear departed mother run on until the whole world realised that your little puppet's active. Where would that have left you? In a Turing cage for a couple of months, just like on Callisto, then dead, with Fist in the hands of our enemies. I have no interest in that happening.'

'Say what you've got to say, then piss off.'

'You're doing so well, Jack. I'm particularly impressed by your decision to work with Harry. I'm sure he'll be very helpful to you.'

'How do you know about that?'

'It's surprising how much I can gather from those who are still faithful to me. I was very impressed by your little adventures with Akhmatov, too.'

'You watched all that?'

'Keeping an eye, keeping an eye. That bird may be blind, but I most certainly am not.'

'Not looking through Yamata's eyes?'

'Good grief, no.' Grey looked genuinely shocked. 'The very idea!'

'You didn't think to protect me?'

'I didn't need to. I knew you'd be kept safe. And besides, I have no interest at all in showing my hand. I'd hate to have anyone see that I'm a little more independent than I should be.'

'Playing politics with my life. Nothing new there. And with Fist, too. Do you know why they want him?'

'I wouldn't know. Perhaps they want to use his weave-hacking skills to help smuggle drugs, perhaps they want to attack the Totality and restart the war. That's for you to find out. To be honest, I'm more concerned by your loyalty issues. I'm no longer your lead patron, am I? I see that East has taken that role. She's really been very generous. I don't think she's installed this much of herself in anyone for a couple of generations. She's fallen for you hard, Jack.'

'I won't be using what she's given me.'

'If you say so. Perhaps there'll be no need for it.'

'I won't, Grey.'

'I'm sure also you won't be taking up the offer from that mind you rescued. Your view of the Totality is too naïve, Jack. It might have been wrong to go to war with them, but that doesn't mean they can be trusted. Steer clear of him.'

'We'll see.'

'I'm serious.'

'I'm sure you are.'

A moment of silence. A breeze danced around them. Strands of hair lifted from Grey's head, then fell back again. Jack noted the real-time environmental interaction, and despite himself was impressed by Grey's attention to detail.

'Do you have anything else to say, Grey?'

'I've been keeping Mr Stabs updated on your adventures. He's always keen to hear about them, which I take as a good sign. I think he's coming round to the idea of seeing you both, Fist in particular.'

'I can't imagine why he wouldn't want to,' said Fist. 'I don't think you've been talking to him at all.'

'Believe that if you wish,' replied Grey. 'And now, I must be going. I've shared almost all I needed to with you. I'm sorry you're not in a receptive mood.'

'Too right we're not,' Fist spat back.

'Telling the truth; an underrated virtue, these days. And I must warn you that he's missed a couple of your more obscure weave-ports. They'll let anyone who pings them know you're onweave. I saw them instantly, but then I have been tracking you very closely indeed. You've got maybe three or four more minutes before InSec checks them. Close them now.'

'Fist?'

The little man had already vanished.

'You'll thank me for that, one day,' Grey told Jack.

'I'll thank you for nothing.'

A sad smile spread across Grey's face. 'Perhaps,' he said, then a final, 'Goodbye, my boy,' before disappearing. Imagined air rushed into the space that his virtual body had occupied.

Fist reappeared.

'So?' said Jack.

'Don't forget you're the one that nearly got us spotted just now!'

'Was he right?'

'There were a couple of open weaveports. But nobody would have noticed them! And I'd have caught them with my next check anyway.'

'For fuck's sake, Fist. You told me we were fully protected.'

'We were completely safe, that suitfucker's just being paranoid.'

'I want you to run a full firewall and security check, NOW. Keep us completely offweave until you've done it.'

'Shit, Jack. Why can't you just trust me?'

'We can't risk anyone finding out you're uncaged. And I don't want Grey – or anyone else – watching us.'

Fist vanished in a puff of swearing. Jack sighed. The past was so much simpler than the present. Perhaps even now his mother was asleep again, his father lying awake and puzzled. He wondered if she'd told him whose presence she'd perceived. Perhaps she'd just explain the moment away as a glitch that caught at sleeping fetches. He took one last look out at Docklands. Without the weave there were only buildings, streets and empty spaces to see, rolling up and away until the glare of morning's spinelight hid them. The living city had covered its face and hidden itself again.

Chapter 30

'I'd forgotten how efficient the cageware is,' said Ifor. 'You've got no weavetrace at all. If I couldn't see you sat in front of me, I wouldn't believe you were here.'

They were in the back room of a café in the Labokra Food Market. Outside, a thousand shoppers bustled, rooting around for the day's bargains. Inside, a credit transfer to the café's owner ensured absolute privacy. He'd grumbled about squishies until Ifor told him how much he'd pay to talk in secret.

'People won't accept InSec credits,' explained Jack. 'And we can't travel beyond Docklands. It's frustrating.'

'I can imagine. Your society—'

'Not my society any more.'

'This society, then. It makes such extensive use of the virtual. They have crippled you by holding you away from it.'

'I thought I was coming home. But so much of my home was the weave.'

'And even without that, so much of Station is closed off to you. The Wart, Homelands …'

'I never really spent much time in the Wart. But I'd love to go back to Homelands. There are gardens there I'd like to walk in, one more time. Malls I'd like to visit.'

[Shitholes,] muttered Fist.

'Old friends?'

'None that would acknowledge me.'

'Your parents?'

'I visited my father.' The silence between them stretched out. 'We didn't have too much to say to each other.'

'And your mother?'

'She's dead. I haven't seen her.'

'I'm sorry, Jack. For her, too. We feel a certain kinship with your poor crippled fetches. They are so close to being pure minds like us. Letting those who claimed to love them treat them so badly is an obscenity. It denies your dead their true potential.'

'People don't always like to let the past go.' Jack thought of Harry and Andrea, of his father's refusal to roll back his mother. 'Very few of them are brave enough.'

'They fear change. It always involves at the very least a little death, an acceptance of limitations. But our time here is limited. We have our own change to discuss. You wish to accept our offer?'

'I would be honoured to commit to the Totality's service.'

'I'm surprised. You seemed so determined to remain independent.'

[The squishy's got a point,] Fist advised. [Better bluff him well!]

Jack picked up his teacup. It was uncomfortably hot to the touch. He blew gently on the surface of the steaming liquid, waking tiny ripples, and took a sip. Heat nipped his tongue.

'I don't think anyone's really independent, Ifor. There are people we're each connected to, obligations we all have.'

'You're referring to Corazon.'

'You heard about that?'

'We were saddened by her death. She helped us in our mission here. Her open-mindedness was impressive.'

'She was a very sharp woman. A sad loss.'

'We paid our respects to her family and to East.' Ifor paused. 'Who let us know that you had been granted certain … special privileges.' He placed heavy emphasis on the last two words. Another silence fell between them. The café owner was whistling in the room next door; cutlery clinked and rattled as he cleaned it. A poorly tuned buggy snarled past outside.

'OK,' said Jack. 'Fist – manifest.'

Fist appeared, standing on the table. He was dressed in full white tie, a monocle and a top hat.

'I thought I'd smarten up for our second meeting. How do you do?'

He stuck a little hand out. Ifor reached out and pretended to shake it. 'The firewall,' he said, 'it's your work?'

'Yes. We need to pretend that the cage is still fully active.'

'Most impressive. And now, let us talk openly. You have come to take up our offer of employment, and you intend to use the diplomatic immunity we offer to pursue Corazon's killers.'

[He's very direct, Jack!]

'Yes,' admitted Jack. 'I'm sorry I hid that.'

'An unfortunate human habit. Is there anything else we should know?'

[Play your cards close to your chest, Jack.]

'Aud Yamata has had Pantheon-level backing for at least seven years. She killed Corazon, and probably also Harry Devlin, his wife Andrea Hui and Bjorn Penderville. Fetches of those involved were either corrupted or caged. I was sent away to fight because I was too close to exposing her and her patron. They're still active, still dangerous and they want Fist. Gods know what they'll do with him. I can't let it happen. I intend to find out who's supporting Yamata and expose both of them.'

[Oh, for gods' sake.]

'A very personal quest.'

'They broke my life. I've lost people I love. And I don't want to see Fist and his powers abused by those bastards. They've done enough damage already.'

'Excellent points. If your little friend fell into the wrong hands it could be dangerous for us too. But I worry that emotion has clouded your judgement; that supporting you would hurt us. We are in very delicate negotiations with your Pantheon just now, Jack.'

'Fist and I are very discreet. We were built to work in secret. And I'm sure you'd rather be confident you're negotiating with the Pantheon's more trustworthy elements.'

'East has made it known that she would be grateful if we were to support you.'

'Such gratitude would, I'm sure, translate into support for some of your key requests.'

'Indeed. Her image management capabilities would also be very useful to us as we grow our presence on Station. You are sure of Pantheon corruption?'

'There's no doubt about it.'

'Proof of that, shared appropriately, would also help us build a future we could both approve of.'

200

'I hope you won't expect me to hide anything from Station's authorities.'

'We might perhaps ask you to ensure that it reaches us before it reaches them.'

'I've said before I won't play favourites.'

'And you have no love for the Pantheon. We at least proceed on the basis of rational thought and a commitment to the general good, rather than naked self-interest.'

'I'll think about that, Ifor.'

'That is generous of you. Oh, and one more thing …'

'Yes?'

'I cannot overemphasise the importance of discretion. I'll send you a search brief. You must be seen to stick to it. More personal investigations must be well hidden.'

'We've had a lot of practice at that.'

'Oh, we know,' countered Ifor. 'To our cost.'

At that, Jack felt ashamed. Fist just tittered.

There was little more to be said. Outside, the light was dimming. Ifor stopped Jack at the door.

'The Totality is very grateful for your help.'

Ifor put his hand out to shake. His nanogel was surprisingly soft and cold to the touch. Jack's grip bent his fingers slightly out of shape.

[Keep squeezing,] whispered Fist. [See if you can pop him!]

[Forget your programming for once.]

Ifor pulled his collar up and his hat down, and lost himself in the bustle of the marketplace. Half an hour later, the Totality confirmed Jack's diplomatic status. He packed his little suitcase, said an apologetic goodbye to Charlie, found the best hotel he could and booked himself in.

Within twenty minutes, InSec were banging at his door. Jack flashed his diplomatic tags and told them to fuck off. Fist cackled. Half an hour later, he was asleep. Next morning, there were messages from Lestak and Harry, and a file from Ifor. Jack skipped over Lestak's rage to Harry's message. 'Fist was right. It's her. Get over here.' Ifor's file included a search plan for streets in Chuigushou Vale and Violin Gardens and access codes for mind detection software.

The bellboy delivered his new clothes with his breakfast; well cut, subtly woven fashions from a small but prestigious Homelands fashion house. They fitted him perfectly. Even Fist was impressed. 'At last,' he commented, donning black tie, an opera cape and a top hat, 'a little sophistication. Now let's go hunting squishies.'

Chapter 31

As they left the hotel, a porter enquired about the length of Jack's stay. Fist was unimpressed.

[Unctuous fuck. I preferred Charlie.]

[He was a funny man.]

[He was very lonely.]

Jack was surprised that Fist had seen through Charlie's façade. Such precise emotional details usually escaped him. [Fancy moving in with him instead of me?] he asked.

[Fuck right off!]

Fist picked over the Totality software as their train rattled through the Wart. [It's fascinating!] he chirped. [Completely open, I can just walk right into all the source code.]

[Different from Pantheon products.]

[No licensing, no end date. Maybe there is a point to them after all.]

[So what does it do?]

[Minds are all connected all the time. Even when a bit of one's dormant, it pings for any other units around it. The software sweeps for those signals. But they need to be pretty close for it to work.]

Jack had to change trains at Vitality Junction. InSec were waiting for him. Operatives pulled him out of the carriage. 'Lestak wants to see you,' one of them said, hustling Jack down the platform.

She was furious. 'What the hell do you think you're playing at?' she raged.

'I'm doing something useful for people who deserve help.'

'They're not people, they're an operating system with ambitions. And you're ignoring my direct warning. I told you to step back.'

'I'm here under a diplomatic licence, as specified in the initial Pantheon/Totality peace treaty. I'm outside your jurisdiction.'

'So you're a lawyer now?'

'You can't stop me.'

'You have no right to be in Homelands. At best you'll get in the way, at worst you'll cause chaos. Lethal chaos.'

'I'm here to look for mind fragments on behalf of the Totality. That's it.'

'Then you'd better make damn sure you stick within the terms of your licence. If you take just one step over the line I'll have you in a Turing cage in an InSec cellblock faster than you can take your next breath. And if that puppet of yours comes out to play I'll have you in a coma until it takes over, and as far beyond as I can possibly manage.'

'Let's be very clear, Lestak. There's no way that you'll catch me stepping out of line.'

Another train neared the station.

'For gods' sake. Get out of here.'

'With pleasure.'

A few minutes later, Jack and Fist rattled into Violin Gardens. [It's residential space leased to mid-level executives,] explained Jack. [People who watch Heaven every day but are never going to get there.]

[Sounds like torture.]

[I was one of them once. I was happy enough.]

Violin Gardens was circular. A thousand windows reflected light into the complex's central garden space. Streams and little waterfalls danced between spiked brown metal shapes that were simplified representations of trees. They were rammed into areas of patchy grass like stubbed-out cigars.

[How far onweave do you want to be, Jack?]

[Same as everyone else.]

Brown metal became deep-textured bark. Leaves sprang out of branches. A beautiful lawn bloomed from the scrubby grass, striped pale then darker green where an imaginary lawnmower had moved up and down. Birds flashed red and purple between the trees. Their songs mingled with the susurrus of the streams and the soft, rich sighing of a thousand violins.

[So that's where it got the name.]

[Apparently the classical music stops teenagers from hanging out.]

[Typical Pantheon, even the art's there to control you.]

There were a few people wandering through the gardens. Some walked arm in arm. Others lay on the soft turf, staring up at the Spine. The gods returned their gaze. Their Homelands incarnations were higher resolution and more imaginatively animated than those that overlooked Docklands. Even Grey's raven – still chained – was more active, hopping from leg to leg and occasionally trying to scratch itself with its beak.

[East is certainly cute,] said Fist. [I bet you'd love another upgrade from her.]

[I never enjoy not being able to choose.]

As Jack spoke, the goddess turned her face towards him. Golden hair billowed up and around her head, sparkling weightlessly in the sunlight.

[Fuck, Jack, she's looking right at you.]

[More than looking.]

The goddess winked from on high.

[Shit,] said Jack.

[That was public,] said Fist. [Everyone will have seen it.]

And indeed everyone was pointing up, then looking around to see who East could have been communing with. A soft sound drifted around Jack, almost lost in the birdsong – the faintest suggestion of a giggle.

[So much for keeping a low profile,] groaned Fist. [I'm going to end up comatose in an InSec cell!]

[Nobody knows she was looking at us,] Jack reassured him. He pointed up and looked around, pretending to be as thrilled and puzzled as everyone else.

[The news channels are just starting to pick it up.]

[Let's move. She's just having fun, it's what she does. Bring up the search pattern, Fist.]

Ifor's search app dropped a single white line over the estate. It coiled around it, mapping out the most efficient exploration path. As they followed it, Fist monitored the news.

The more celebrity obsessed channels went live to Violin Gardens, talking excitedly with those who'd witnessed East's wink. People who had no particular relationship with the divinity expressed a guardedly general sense of gratitude. Her more devoted followers gushed about very personal moments of contact. An up-and-coming clothing designer was convinced that East had personally blessed the Chuigushou Mall launch event for her new collection. A middle-aged man described a new relationship. He was now confident that it would endure. A jogger gave thanks for East's intercession. She was involved with a charity that was having difficulty raising money. Now, she could share its details with a massive media audience.

Jack felt very happy to have left Pantheon worship far behind. The last seven years had at least gifted him atheism. He thought with embarrassment how excited his younger self would have been by East's visitation.

The search pattern led them on. Trees gathered in clumps around sunlit glades, filled with bright flowers and softly glowing patches of sunlight. Ground level apartment doors were represented by wooden arches. Flutes played, backed by pattering hand drums.

[How do people live with such crap, Jack?]

[It's a dream they want to share.]

[It's an advert they want to inhabit. Let's get rid of this bullshit.]

Glamour vanished. The unwoven apartment doors caught Fist's eye. [They're a bit odd,] he commented. A few were pale bleached wood, matching the soft pastel colour of the block walls. Most were hard unpainted metal. Their uncompromising emphasis on security jarred with the soft tastefulness of the rest of Violin Gardens.

[What are these people afraid of?] asked Fist.

[I don't know.]

[I could break us in there. Take a look round, see why these idiots are so paranoid.]

[We're keeping our noses clean.]

[I'll give them something to be scared of. Rewrite their homes, they come home, open the door – zombie horde attack!]

[No.]

[Boring.]

[Any word from Harry yet?]

[That wanker. I don't know why you haven't told him to fuck off.]

[We need him to scout for us. Now, be serious. Any messages?]

[None. Want me to ping him? I can bring your weavespace up,

206

subvert a local weave connection, bounce round a few servers. We'll be untraceable.] Fist yawned theatrically. [And it'll pass a couple of nanoseconds. If I'm lucky.]

It was nighttime in Jack's weavespace. A wax-pale moon hung over the empty gardens, bringing white stone, green leaves and vivid petals to soft and gentle life, and scattering a shimmer of white across the little pool at their heart. The moon was too bright to allow stars near it, but further away scores dappled the clear night. A gentle breeze rustled through the tree tops. An owl called, its down-soft cry promising life to its young, death to its prey. Andrea's statue glowed with soft beauty. Ifor's image stood just by it. Even his nanogel body seemed to have something of the sylvan to it.

'Fucking hell,' grumbled Fist. 'Should be afternoon. Timing's out of whack.'

'Let it be, Fist. I always loved it at night.'

There was a shadow up at the door of Grey's temple. It could have just been a ghost that the moonlight made.

'Fancy a chat with his nibs?'

'No, Fist, I do not. Where did you hide the link to Harry?'

'By that tree. As far away from Andrea as I could.'

Jack walked over to the tree, crossing from paving flags to turf. The ground here was so much softer. Jack left deep, dark footprints in the dewy grass. Fist sat on a stone in the middle of the pond. A fishing rod appeared in his hand, and a little pointy little hat on his head.

'Maybe I should go into the gnome business, Jack?'

'For gods' sake. Now, where is he?'

'Under the grass, where that root ends.'

'Shit. You know, it used to seem entirely normal to summon the dead from under the ground.'

Jack found the spot, hooked his fingers under the sward and lifted up a square of turf. Harry's stone face peered up from beneath it. An earwig scuttled across it. Jack brushed it away then touched Harry's cheek. The statue rose smoothly out of the grass. Colour spread across it, a soft contagion of presence that quickly created a living man from stone. A few seconds, and Harry was completely real. There was a little splash as Fist fell off his rock, then swearing as he pulled himself out.

207

'Hello, Jack,' smiled Harry. He looked around. 'Nice place you've got here.'

'Cheers,' replied Jack. 'But we've got business. How's Yamata?'

'Isolate Fist. I don't want him to hear.'

[Fuck's sake Jack. Without me, he wouldn't have even found her.]

'There's really no need, Harry.'

'Do it. Then I'll talk.'

[Why's he being so paranoid?] said Fist.

[Tit for tat. I wish you two'd stop playing games with each other.]

[Don't trust him, Jack. Remember, he's different.]

[I know.] Jack switched to open speech. 'Fist – stand away. Now.'

Fist grumbled his way out of earshot. Harry waited until he'd disappeared.

'He's gone?'

'Yes.'

'Good. So – it's a small office block. Company's called TrueShield. Yamata's in there now.'

'Anyone else?'

'Receptionist, office staff. Maybe twenty or thirty in total.'

'Quite the little operation. Anything else?'

'Substantial data flowing in and out, but it's heavily encoded. Their defence software's Pantheon grade. Normally I'd be able to nudge in – but not here. It's like we thought, you need to get into their server room physically. Then we can dig all the dirt on Yamata and follow it right back to her patron.'

'Fist'll sort that out.'

'Once you're in, I'll manifest through him. Bit of extra muscle.'

'No.'

'What?'

'I told Fist I wouldn't give you that kind of access.'

'Shit, Jack, you were serious?'

'I made a promise.'

'Gods. Last time I let you two out alone, he lost it and fucked everything. You need me there. I'll help keep him under control. And when he brings gods know what down on you, I'll use his weapons to fight it off.'

'Fist can fight his own battles. And they don't want to hurt him. We'll use that against them.'

'These are serious people you're fucking with, Jack. Not just squishies.'

'Fist understands exactly what they can do to him. He didn't back at Access station. He won't get in the way this time. I'm sure of it.'

'There's a lot of corruption in this world, Jack. You can't trust anyone, these days. And he was never a friend you chose to make.'

'I've made my mind up.'

'Fine, fine, don't say I didn't warn you. You'll need me once you're in there, I guarantee it. In the meantime, there are practicalities. You need to get over to TrueShield without triggering any alarms.'

'That won't be a problem. We'll be there in a couple of hours.'

'I'll expect you.'

Harry returned to stone and fell back into the dark earth. Jack covered his cold, grey face with turf.

'Fist,' he shouted, 'we're done.'

The moon vanished from the sky, which then disappeared too. Suddenly there was no stone path, or silvered grass, or softly hissing fountain – just the tawdry cheapness of an unwoven Violin Gardens.

'Right, Fist. I need you to build me a datasprite, and then make a sweathead of me.'

'After you've sent me off to the bottom of the garden so I don't offend your dodgy mate? Not sure why I should bother.'

'Just do it, Fist.'

Chapter 32

They waited until the end of the afternoon before disappearing offweave. They left a datasprite – skinned as Jack – moving through Violin Gardens, following Ifor's search pattern. As evening wore on it would take refuge in a nearby bar, where they'd reintegrate with it at their leisure.

Fist was still grumbling as they set off for TrueShield.

[You wasted my time back there, Jack. You could have just charmed someone, I'd have skinned him, swapped you both around, and anyone watching onweave would have thought you were him and he was you.]

[I don't like doing that to people.]

[Oh! But you don't mind working me till my subroutines pop, do you? And now we're offweave, and I'm draining myself with camouflage software that – if you please – it took me a good mega-hour of poly-processor work to pull together. And to cap it all, we've got to walk! If you'd charmed someone we could have just got the train over.]

[And we'd have been much more likely to get caught. We'll soon be there, it's only another half-hour or so.]

[And I bet you're going to make me open a portal for him too.]

[He asked me to. I said no.]

[Hmmph.]

As they neared TrueShield it started to get dark. Pale white lights guided commuters away from offices and laboratories. Tastefully arranged spotlights danced shadows across them, highlighting fashionable clothing and up-to-the-minute hairstyles. There were designer sigils everywhere.

Fist dismissed them with a single word.

[Wankers.]

They reached TrueShield's address and looked around for Harry.

He emerged from a shadowy service doorway with the suddenness of a flaring match.

[Fetches shouldn't be able to do that,] said Fist. [You shouldn't have let him come along.]

[He's rebuilt himself, Fist. He's much more than just a fetch. And he's only doing the scouting. The heavy lifting's down to us. Now don't be so petty.]

[You feel so guilty about fucking his wife you're letting him get away with murder.]

[Stop whinging.]

Harry beckoned to Jack, then disappeared back into the darkness. Jack joined him in cover. 'Yamata's in there?' he asked.

'Oh yes.'

The TrueShield building was a four-storey white box, set in a round lake. The corners of the building touched the edge of the lake, creating a crescent before each façade. Spotlights angled down into the crescents, their light bouncing off the water and then dancing up and over the white walls and black windows of the building. Most of the internal lights had been turned off. A small bridge led to reception, which blazed confidently into the night. Squinting, Jack could just see a blue-shirted security guard sat at the front desk.

'He'll be easy enough,' said Fist.

'If you don't balls it up,' cut in Harry. 'Which you have done before.'

'Says the dead man. Who got himself shot by opening a file.'

'One of these days you'll appreciate your betters.'

'One of these days you'll kiss my wooden arse.'

'Gods' sake, you two,' snapped Jack. 'Stop bickering. We've got a job to do.' He turned to Harry. 'How many left in there?'

'Eight, including Yamata,' Harry told him.

'Know anything about them?'

'Mostly medical people.'

'Odd. But not dangerous.'

'I went digging through some civic management databases. Found a floor plan.' Harry touched Jack's arm, and the building's walls became transparent. Jack pulled away, shocked. 'Don't take me onweave, Harry. For gods' sake.'

'You're not onweave. I'm accessing your implants directly.'

'You shouldn't be able to do that.'

'I told you. InSec tech.' Harry winked at Jack. 'Backdoors everywhere, if you know where to find them. So stop worrying, and let me show you ...' He took Jack's arm. Once again, the building became an x-ray of itself.

[He's in you. But he's not in me. So that's OK,] Fist told Jack.

Red dots speckled the building. Each represented a weave presence moving through the building's virtual spaces.

[It's all one hundred per cent accurate,] said Fist sulkily.

[Glad to hear it.]

Harry rubbed his hands together. 'Right. we've got a break-in to plan.'

Fist probed TrueShield. Its security systems were Pantheon protected, but the security guard's weren't. He worked for a subcontractor who'd skimped on some of the basics. So Fist was able to walk into the guard's weave presence, spin down the link he'd established with the reception desk and drop an appointment into TrueShield's corporate diary for a Mr Ricker, arriving in about ten minutes.

'I hate to say it, Jack, but when he's good, he's not bad at all,' said Harry grudgingly.

'Flattery will get you nowhere,' Fist replied.

'Worth a try. You won't let me get in there through you, once you're inside?'

'No.'

'If you get into trouble, you'll need my help.'

'We won't run into anything I can't handle.'

'Let's go,' said Jack. 'We've got an appointment to keep.'

As it turned out, Mr Ricker looked very much like Jack. 'Bit late for a visit, sir,' said the security guard as he invoked a guest tag.

'It's quieter in the evening. And my business is very personal.'

'Ah.' The guard didn't ask any more questions, but there was a lightly conspiratorial tone in his voice. The tag appeared in his hand. 'Here you go.' It skipped off his chubby finger and on to Jack's arm, running up his shoulder to sit by his ear. Its dove-white wings rustled as it went. It nestled down comfortably, until – running its own security checks – it brushed against Jack's weave presence. There was a tiny, shrill scream and it threw itself into the air, pointing at Jack, a look of fear on its face. Its little wings were now the brightest, most unmistakable red.

The security guard looked apologetic.

'It says that you're not called Alois Ricker. That you've masked yourself.'

'As I said – discretion.' Jack let the word roll off his tongue. He sounded calm, but inside he was furious.

[Fucking hell, Fist, you're meant to have covered all of this off.]

[It's just a detail. You'll charm your way out of it.]

[I don't like using the Eastware on innocents. It's too unpredictable.]

'I'm sorry, sir. I'm going to have to confirm your appointment.'

He prodded at the air in front of him.

'I'm afraid I don't have a record of who you're here to see.'

[Divert him, Fist.]

[I can fry the sprite. But the guard's suspicious already, if he notices he'll get really paranoid. You've got to charm him too. Fuck's sake Jack, it's easy enough, just don't turn it up to full.]

The guard was moving from sympathetic to lightly hostile.

'I'm sorry sir, I do need a full name.'

[Fuck it,] said Jack. [Fuck. OK, sort out the sprite. I want it on our side.]

He tugged lightly at his Eastware. A smile spread across his face like a neon sun rising. The guard was just running through the security code that would allow him to trigger the desk's emergency alert systems.

'Do you know, I can't remember,' Jack told him. 'But I don't think it really matters, does it?'

'Sir, I've been very specifically briefed …' stammered the guard. A light sweat shimmered across his forehead. Jack was glad that the desk covered his lower half.

'Briefed? To ask for a name? You don't trust me?'

'Oh no, sir. Not at all. No, I wouldn't say that,' said the guard. There was a desperate eagerness to please in his voice.

[That's more like it!] said Fist. [He's working for us now.]

213

'Well then, wouldn't it be a good idea to let me into the office?' said Jack.

'Oh, yes. Yes!'

The guard was already halfway out from behind the desk. The bottom button of his shirt had come undone. A soft, rounded slab of belly peaked out from behind it, black hairs straggling across it like cracks. 'Anything you say, sir,' he gabbled. Jack was appalled by the effect he'd achieved. The guard chose not to see. 'I'll just let you in now, sir.'

[How long do you think the effects last when you're not around?]

[Not long, I hope.]

[Then turn it up! Make sure he stays onside for good.]

[No. And no more carelessness.]

The guard made a very precise series of gestures. An internal door hummed open, revealing a short, bland corridor with another door at its end.

'There you go, sir. Have a good evening, sir.'

Jack thanked him, then asked: [How's the sprite?]

[Reprogrammed. It'll lead us to their server room, and make sure we don't run into anyone on the way. It thinks it's taking us to a meeting room on the other side of the building.]

[You're sure?]

[Of course I'm bloody sure.]

[Good.]

The little creature buzzed into the air between them, wings moving so fast they became a shadow hanging from its back. It had tiny compound eyes set in a hard bone face that was almost human. Its sharp-edged body was dressed in brilliant rags. There was a scarf wrapped round its waist. It was red, silver and green, the TrueShield corporate colours. 'Can I conduct you to your destination, fair gentles?' it said, its voice a piping squeak.

[I've seen this sort of thing onweave. It's very fashionable.] Fist's voice was full of contempt.

[As long as it takes us where we need to be,] replied Jack, [I really don't care.]

The sprite was hovering impatiently by the door at the end of the corridor. It beckoned to Jack. 'Follow me, follow me – but don't

214

step from the path,' it shrilled. The door opened and Jack stepped forward. 'Wait, wait, good gentle! First I must cast my net around you.'

[I get it,] said Fist. [If anyone breaks in, it irritates them to death.]

The creature fluttered around them both, singing a half-whispered, half-roared little song. A net-shaped shimmer wrapped itself around Jack. Fist swore under his breath. Terms and conditions for TrueShield access flashed up, more quickly than Jack could read. He nodded acceptance. The little flying creature smiled, showing teeth that looked like a bone hacksaw blade. Spotting them, Fist nodded appreciatively.

[Maybe it could do some damage, at that.]

And so they walked into TrueShield as if they were guests. The sprite took them down a long corridor. There were ancient trees where the walls should have been. Doors opened between them, leading into small work suites. Once the sprite gestured them into an office, then closed the door behind them. Footsteps passed by. When the passage was silent again, it led them back out.

'I have kept you safe, kind sirs!'

The corridor ended and they stepped into a large atrium, open to the darkness of the night. Then reality began to change. As they walked towards the atrium's centre, a forest grew up around them. It was far more ancient than the one they'd encountered in Violin Fields. Mist curled around moss-shrouded trees, all snarled in on themselves like arthritic hands. It lent the darkness between the trees an almost physical quality, turning it into a thick, stodgy murk. There were standing stones, too – archaic shapes rearing grey in the gloom. Some stood alone. Others were piled up to make arches. All hinted at lost peoples, forgotten rites and hidden meanings.

[This is purest essence of bullshit,] said Fist.

[It's branding. It's meant to represent the company and the dangerous world of hidden hazards it can guide us through.]

[Gods. I want to cut my own strings. Where did you learn to talk such nonsense?]

[I dated an advertising executive. She showed me how to read this kind of thing.]

The path the sprite was leading them down did, in fact, feel

215

very safe indeed, when compared to the deep forest. It was paved with grey stone blocks that cut through the gloom with confident certainty. The sprite turned to look back at them. 'If you follow the TrueShield path,' it announced, 'you're always safe.'

'How much further?' Jack asked it.

'A few minutes.'

[There can't have been a forest like this for centuries,] said Fist.

[There's never been anywhere like this.]

[Really?]

[This is just a dream. Like Violin Fields. Like the whole of Homelands.]

[I thought you loved it here, Jack.]

[Not any more. I've been away too long and I've seen too much. The Totality, everyone who's with them – I never knew it before, but they've made the void their own. Not like us.] He gestured around him. [We've built a home from dreams and called it memory. Then we try and live in those memories and call that life. But it's just nostalgia.]

[That's very philosophical, Jack.]

[What do you see when you look at it all?]

[Patterns waiting to be broken.]

[Is that all we are to you?]

[That's all this is.]

They walked on in silence. Then Fist was hovering by Jack. He put his hand on Jack's shoulder and spoke. His voice was carefully neutral. [I'll be breaking your pattern soon. I thought I'd enjoy it.] Jack stopped walking. For a moment he wasn't sure what to say. [I'm sorry,] Fist told him.

Jack was both moved and astonished. He was silent for a moment, then said in a soft voice: [We don't have a choice. We've just got to make the best of it.]

The Sprite turned back and saw that they'd stopped. 'Tarry not, good gentles!' it squeaked. 'We near our destination.'

[One more word out of that jumped-up mosquito ...]

[Fist!]

The path led through an arch in the trees.

'Behold! The object of your quest. My task is done.'

216

The sprite melted away.

[Kill this virtual bollocks?] asked Fist.

[Do it.]

The forest vanished. Hard neon illumination replaced gloomy sylvan dusk, hurting Jack's eyes. Everything was white – the floor, the ceiling, the walls, the server stacks that stood in henges all around them. Technology hummed and air conditioning whined.

[Fuck yes,] breathed Fist. [Beautiful, just beautiful.]

[How long till you're in?]

Fist pattered over to one of the server stacks. His fingertips sunk into its white plastic body. Jack felt a light tug on his consciousness as Fist drew on deep resources.

[We'll see. Not too long. Want to watch?]

The room shimmered around Jack. The servers became patterns of figures representing buried worlds of data. Some were static, others flickered in constant motion. Jack remembered his accountancy days. He'd spent weeks drifting through accounts, carving clear and final financial snapshots from confusing, tangled corporate structures. [Takes me back,] he said. He stretched a hand out to touch a nearby server.

[Whoah!] yelled Fist. [You don't go near them. You'll set off alarms all over the place.]

Jack pulled his hand back, embarrassed. As an auditor, his presence had always been legitimate. Once signed into corporate databanks he'd never had to worry about triggering security.

[Drop me out, Fist. I'll keep watch.] The white room reasserted itself.

Fist was still at the same server. [Getting stuck in, Jack!] he said, then stepped into it as if he were walking through an open door. [Digging around,] he continued. His voice sounded muffled. [Interesting!]

[What's their security like?]

[Hardly there, compared to Totality ice.]

[You're not missing anything?]

[Jack, please. I know what I'm doing.]

[You missed something important in reception.]

[And was that a problem? Besides, this is much more interesting than hacking a diary. Right, got to concentrate.]

[Don't screw up.]

There was no reply. Jack sat down on the floor, leant back against the wall, and waited.

[Aha!] said Fist, after a while. He sounded far away. [I'm in! Even easier than I thought it would be.] There was a pause.

[What can you see?] asked Jack.

[Files.] Fist's voice echoed lightly, as if he was standing in a vast, empty space. [Lots of files.]

[Get digging.]

[I'm firing up some of your old Greyware. The corporate analysis stuff.] Jack felt another tug in his mind. Semi-archived systems unpacked themselves and groaned into life.

[Seven years old, verrrry old school! Want me to pull down the updates?]

Jack was getting nervous. [We don't have time for that. Just get stuck in. Look for Pantheon traces, anything flagged Yamata ...]

[A-OK.]

Fist's voice was coming from even further away. He was deep in TrueShield's virtual self. Jack felt a moment's dizziness as the Greyware drew resource from his consciousness. In the distance, Fist started singing.

[Take this seriously,] hissed Jack.

[It helps me concentrate,] said Fist dismissively. [Digging hard. Oo, what's that? It's hiding from me.]

[You've found something? Already?]

[I'm not sure. I'm just coaxing it out.] A moment's silence. [Now I can see it! What the fuck? It can't be.]

[Don't get distracted.] Fist didn't reply. [Fist?] Little grunts reached Jack. Fist seemed to be working hard at something. Something rustled. Jack thought of the unreal leaves of Violin Gardens.

[It goes up and up and up ...]

Fist's voice was coming from somewhere above Jack.

[Be careful. It could be dangerous.]

[...all the way past the moon.]

[Show me!]

The ceiling lights flickered out of existence. Jack was looking up

218

into a dark sky. There was a pale, buttery moon and a scattering of stars. A beanstalk reached up towards them, shimmering with golden light. Fist was pulling himself up it, hand over hand.

[More branding,] Fist explained. [You should have spared yourself.]

[What are you climbing?] asked Jack.

[A Pantheon hardlink,] Fist replied proudly. [Straight to whoever's behind Yamata.]

[Come down, now. Deep security!]

[Nothing I can't deal with,] breezed Fist. [Besides, what better way of finding out which giant we've got to kill than climbing up their beanstalk?]

Something sparked into life higher up the rope and leapt down towards him. Fist waved a hand. It vanished in a shower of sparks. [Your corporate engagement and my penetration systems mesh rather well.] More security bots leapt towards him. [I see them, I know them, I break them. We'll find out who's up there in no time.]

[Come down,] yelled Jack. [NOW!]

[Really,] Fist shouted back, [you should have more faith.] Another explosion of sparks shivered down from above. [I wish we'd fired up your Greyware years ago! Who'd have thought that accountancy could be so much fun?]

[Gods!] Jack reached out to pull Fist back in, but as he did so there was a surprised little squeak. Fist disappeared.

[Where are you?]

[Still here!] The puppet's voice sounded impossibly distant. [Only I'm not quite sure where here is. Some sort of gateway. Corporate security, cracking it now.]

[Fuck's sake.]

Jack tugged at Fist, but nothing happened.

[I can't get you back.]

[Hmm, must have been a one-way portal.] Fist tittered. [How silly of me to step through it just before you tried to reel me in.] Jack groped for swearwords. Before he could shout anything, he felt another pull on his mind. [Oo, some tricky stuff. Going to need more resource, Jack. Ready for a little sleep?]

[It's not safe.]

[There's no other way out. And besides, pretty much everyone's gone home, and I've nudged TrueShield's sign-in systems to make it look like we've left too. We'll be fine.]

[I'll have to take your word for that,] grumbled Jack. Darkness flooded his mind. He quickly slipped into the familiar dream state. Faces from his past flashed in front of him – his parents, Harry, David Tiamat, Andrea. Andrea's music danced behind them all, shaping memory into coherent narrative. Soon, even that faded as Fist drew on yet more of his mind. Jack fell into a deeper, quieter sleep.

When he woke up, he was somewhere new. Fist was shaking his shoulder. 'Look, Jack. Just look!' At first, the bright light dazzled him. He sat up, rubbing his eyes. Machinery roared, assaulting his ears. 'Look around you! I had to show you, I rebalanced my systems a bit to bring you in.' Fist's voice was bursting with excitement.

'You opened the gate? How long did it take?'

'A few hours. Took everything I've got. Still easier than Totality-ware, though. But that doesn't matter. Look!'

'Where are we?'

'Somewhere you'll never, ever fucking believe.'

Chapter 33

Jack's eyes adjusted to the light. He stood up. They were standing on a small platform, next to some oil barrels and a small pile of welding gear. The platform was set in the side wall of a great, cruciform space. It was the same shape as East's cathedral, but a very different kind of building. Instead of stone, it was built entirely of iron. Jagged pilasters ran up vast rusting wall plates past weld-seams the size of train tracks. On the ceiling, rusting tracery had metastasized into endless, snarled-up metal knots. Rather than a mirrored lake of mercury, the floor was solid concrete, spattered across with vast dark patches where oil had soaked in. The cathedral was empty, but the sound of heavy machinery clanked and groaned through it. About three quarters of its nave was in darkness.

'Gods,' whispered Jack. 'We're inside one of the Pantheon. That's impossible. Who is it?'

'It's Kingdom,' replied Fist. 'I've checked the code.'

'Shit. You're sure?'

'Oh yes.'

'And you broke into him. No wonder he wants to get his hands on you. Imagine if he could do that to the rest of the Pantheon.' Jack sat down on one of the oil barrels. It creaked beneath him. 'He was behind it all. Smuggling sweat to screw even more work out of his people, and fuck the consequences. Fucking bastard.'

'Oh yes,' said Fist triumphantly. 'He's that all right.' Fire sparked up around his hands. 'And now you need to let me kill him.'

'No,' replied Jack. 'We can't do that. We need to get out of here, right now.'

'What? Kingdom's spent the last seven years fucking you, and he's about to start fucking me too. We're right inside him, he doesn't know we're here and he won't until it's too late. We can turn him

221

into a smoking ruin. Take no prisoners, Jackie boy! It's the only way to be sure.'

'Oh, you're right about that. We have to bring him down. But we can't do it like this. We can't just burn him out and leave a void. That's no victory.'

'Why not? That's what we do. It's what we've always done. Think how we toasted all those Totality fucks. That's kids' stuff next to this, but the principle's the same.'

'We stopped doing that.'

'You stopped. Because you didn't believe in the Soft War. But you believe in this.'

'And I believe in all the people who rely on Kingdom. What would happen to them if we suddenly broke him? Who would run all his infrastructure then? It would all crash – chainships, manufactories, satellites, joy platforms, asteroid bases. Everything that the Totality haven't taken yet, from Mercury to here and then out to Mars – broken.'

'So, who cares?'

'Tens of thousands dead. And even if it wasn't for that – can you imagine how the Pantheon would react, if you killed one of their own? Can you imagine how they'd punish us? And we don't even have any evidence. How would we ever convince anyone why we'd done it?'

'Oh bloody hell!' Fist turned away from Jack. He balled his little hands up and beat them against the railings. 'Bloody, bloody, bloody hell! It's so unfair. I could have been someone, Jack. I could have been the puppet who killed a god.'

'You still can be,' Jack reassured him, gently but firmly. 'Just be patient. We go back down to the TrueShield servers, we dig through them and we find proof. Then we take it to Lestak and Ifor, and we let them sort out Kingdom and Yamata for us.'

'Boring,' spat Fist. 'I think I'll just kill him anyway.' He kicked the welding gear. A pair of goggles and a blowtorch flew towards the railings. 'Fuck!' he gasped, rushing to catch them but just missing. Jack leapt forward and grabbed him, stopping him from going over too. A great clatter rose up from below. It was far noisier than it should have been, noisier even than the machine sounds. Then it died away to complete silence.

'Not good,' said Jack. 'Crash us out.'

'But he'll see us! He'll know we've been in here!'

The air was dense with strange, charged expectation. A soft gust of wind touched Jack's face, promising something far harder. 'He knows already. He's isolating us.'

Fist closed his eyes. 'Dammit, you're right. He's draining power from local systems. Full manifestation imminent. No time to reconfigure for combat.'

The cathedral vanished, and Jack was back in the server room. [Fist?] A few seconds, and the puppet popped into existence. [Let's go,] Jack snapped.

The door leapt open in front of them and they were running down the corridor to the atrium. There were no trees this time. When they were halfway across it, the Sprite reappeared, man-sized, smiling out of a mouth made from cracked bones. Its nails were hard and black and wickedly sharp. Its wings were made from human spines and flayed skin.

[YOU STEPPED OFF THE PATH,] it howled, its metal grinder voice too loud to be anything other than a simulation, [AND NOW YOU'RE LOST.]

[FUCK, JACK, IT'S INSIDE ME!] screamed Fist.

[What? How?] said Jack.

[NEEDED EXTRA RESOURCE TO GET INTO KINGDOM. SHUT DOWN ALL SHIELDS. NOT BACK UP YET!]

[Shit.]

The Sprite leapt towards them. It shattered into a great burning shape, stretching itself out into shimmering patterns of light. Fist swore, Jack yelled orders. The patterns resolved, becoming a floating entity carved from brilliance. Its body was a lopsidedly incandescent sac. Tentacles hung down from it, waving lazily backwards and forwards as if stroked by invisible currents. It looked like a vast jellyfish, dreaming in a tropical ocean.

[Hello,] said a voice that Jack knew well. [At last I get to play with you. You won't find me as easy as Akhmatov.]

[Yamata,] Jack said, shocked. [On our private channel! Where's she coming from?]

She laughed and the assault began.

'Fuck! Fuck! Fuck!' yelled Fist, not bothering to mask his voice. His defences had been fully compromised. The puppet's first task was to determine how deeply he'd been penetrated. A thousand security objects leapt into being within him, deleting invader bots as fast as they could.

'They're trying to crash my weapon systems.'

Pain shimmered inside Jack as Fist drew on deep resources. He staggered, then shouted: 'Careful! Don't knock me out!'

The puppet had seconds to rebuild his defences, understand their opponent and start fighting back. Yamata's voice boomed out, rich with confident amusement.

'No mercy this time, Jack! You're too much of a threat. You've finally realised what Fist can do, so Kingdom's let me take the gloves off.'

The light intensified, punching agony into Jack's mind. He collapsed to his knees.

'Now for something a little more physical,' said Yamata calmly.

A bullet cracked past.

'SHIT!!!!' howled Fist. Suddenly there was a panther by Jack. He shook at the sight of it. Then it was springing to the right of the shining virtual entity before them. Yamata half-laughed, half-screamed.

[Got privacy again,] gasped Fist. Crystal had grown around his lower legs. The puppet tottered forwards, then stopped as the two crystal masses joined and became one. He was immobilised. [Totality attack package.] There was no emotion in his voice. Fear pricked Jack. The situation must be very serious for Fist to dump his personality subroutines.

[I'll take the digital structures,] Fist's new, toneless voice said. [Get the woman with the gun. This panther won't be there for long. Can't boot up the others.]

The crystals were still growing. They'd insinuated themselves into his joints. Foot had separated from lower leg, lower leg from upper leg, upper leg from hip, each now a separate shape floating in crystal.

[I need to focus. Dropping the cat. Get the woman.]

Jack forced himself to follow the panther. Its growling vanished.

224

Light flashed behind him and white noise roared. Fist was fighting back. There was a black shape ahead, a woman lying on the floor. Jack threw himself at her, piling a knee into her stomach as he landed. She grunted and he saw her face and Corazon's memories inside him screamed, for this was the woman that had killed her.

'Yamata!'

A punch snapped his head sideways and then she'd flipped him over. He gasped, partially with pain, partially with shock. [Fist!] he yelled.

[I'm busy. Yamata's attacking,] said Fist.

[Me too.]

[What? Both of us?]

A status update flashed into Jack's mind. Fist was three quarters encased in crystal, one arm trapped, one flailing. His legs were completely separated from his body. Crackling blue fire danced out of him, charring each exit point, and exploded through the crystal as his defence systems tried to break its hold.

[Harry was right,] said Jack.

[That cunt. We're not finished yet.]

Pain gripped Jack's throat. Yamata was throttling him. He thrashed at her arms, but her grip was too strong. He tried and failed to kick her. His neck shouted agony.

[Fuck's sake Jack, go East on her!]

Jack dropped inside himself, pushing the Eastware to full. A flood of digitally enhanced charisma flashed through him. He remembered the effect he'd had on the InSec men, wondered briefly how Yamata would respond, then smiled, a Narcissus turning his beauty on another.

Yamata reacted, but not as Jack had expected. She leant back, for a moment taking the pressure off his neck, and laughed.

Fear flashed through him as the Eastware frantically fine-tuned itself, looking for a way to affect his adversary. He failed again to punch her. She shifted her weight, moving her hands to his shoulders, pinning his arms down. Her face came right down to his.

'I'm beyond that sort of thing now,' she said, and slapped him. Her hand hit with the density of lead. 'Kingdom's afraid of you. I wondered if I needed to be too.'

225

Fist screamed in the background.

'But look at you now,' she continued. 'A broken puppet, and a man whose makeup does his fighting for him.'

She drew right back, arching away from Jack. He turned his face away just in time, so when she drove her head down at him the attack glanced off his cheek. Fist screamed again, but this time the sound was muffled. Jack imagined the crystal choking his mouth.

[Fist!]

[She's attacking my higher functions. Trying to wipe me.]

'You don't even know what I am, do you?' said the woman. 'Or what I've been up to. Not a clue.' She clamped her hand over his mouth and nose. 'Meat's too easy to beat. Your puppet too. We planned to wait till you were dead and do a deal with him. Too late for that now. Going to burn him out and hope we can salvage his weapon systems.'

Jack swore, his voice as muffled as Fist's.

'Fucking sweat-dealing BITCH!'

'You think Kingdom cares about sweat?' she said, and laughed again. She lifted her hand off his mouth and snatched a breath. 'You really do? After all this time? Oh, Jack, bless you, you sweet, inno-cent thing. Your puppet can kill gods, but you still don't understand them.' There was a tinkling sound, as of breaking glass. Fist had freed his mouth.

[Fuck it. I'm summoning Harry. With luck, she'll kill him too.]

[You don't have to.]

[I'm almost beaten. Weapon systems all down. Hardly any shields. He'll be a distraction. You might get out. And he'll be far too busy to hack me, so ...]

Fist's voice cut off suddenly. Jack imagined crystal growing back into his mouth. There was a white noise blast, then silence. An alert flashed in his mind. Fist's last firewalls were dying.

'Little Fist all burnt out,' Yamata chanted, pressing a hand down hard on Jack's face. 'And no Grey to save Jack the wannabe giant killer. You know,' she continued conversationally, as he choked beneath her, 'I'm enjoying this. I was so angry that Grey protected you all those years ago, but now I'm almost grateful.'

Jack's consciousness began to slip away. He reached out for Fist.

There was nothing coherent there to touch, only a mess of emergency defence and repair systems blinking rage and confusion. He imagined a small wooden mind, about to be torn apart; refused to consider the digital carnage that such dissolution represented. Now that he too was falling into unconsciousness, a strange and gentle calm had descended on him.

His principal emotion was a distant sadness that Fist would not after all inherit his flesh, that soon nothing would remain of either them. There was deep frustration, too. Yamata had named Kingdom as her patron, but dismissed sweat as his motivation. Even now, it seemed that Jack didn't understand the true nature of his adversary. The problem of his exile remained unresolved.

Words drifted into his mind: 'You really were too easy ...' He prepared to let everything drift away. But then a voice he recognised pulled him back.

'He may be easy,' said Harry grimly. 'But I'm not.'

There was a gasp and the pressure lifted off his mouth, then his body. He had just enough in him to turn and see that there, in the centre of the room, larger than life, stood Harry. He was maybe seven or eight foot tall. Blue fire danced round him in barbed, jagged flashes. The flames that had burnt Fist didn't seem to touch him. His voice was a roar, thick with Docklands rage.

'You killed me, you ungrateful bitch, and now I've come to break you.'

The barbs of blue fire exploded off him, and all hell broke loose.

Yamata rolled off Jack, snatching up her gun as she did so. A popping sound followed her – bullets leaping into the air. Harry ignored them. She screamed as blue exploded around her. The scream ended suddenly as her body lost all focused motion, and she was a falling clutter of limbs tumbling limp on to the floor.

'Well, that was nice and easy,' gloated Harry. 'Now for the rest of you.' He turned and advanced on the floating creature that had broken Fist. Fire lashed out again, dancing through its tentacles and setting them writhing in agony.

Jack stood up. He tried to pull Fist back into his mind, but there was nothing there. He'd have to reclaim him manually. He moved back to where he'd seen him last.

227

'You wanker,' Yamata's voice yelled. 'I'll just kill you again.'

Jack was baffled that the broken woman could still be present, still be attacking. Harry just laughed. 'When I escaped you,' he shouted back, 'you must have known I'd come back. And I'd be ready for you.'

Jack quickly found Fist. The puppet's plan was working. Harry had distracted Yamata. His crystal cage had disappeared. But Fist was unconscious, flickering in and out of sight, his core self straining to absorb the beating it had taken. Both his legs had been torn off. When Jack rolled him over, he saw that an arm was missing too. His eyes were open and unseeing, staring up at the ceiling. His mouth had fallen open in a lolling grin.

The lost arm was just next to Fist. Jack scrabbled round for the legs. One was untouched. The other was singed black, but basically functional.

There was a burst of light and swearing. Jack looked up to see Harry standing in front of the jellyfish, silhouetted by gouts of brilliant light as another attack exploded against it. Its tentacles thrashed in pain.

Harry's laugh boomed out. 'Did you really think you could hurt me, Yamata? I've spent the whole of my death getting ready for this.'

There was a tugging at Jack's sleeve. Fist had regained something approaching consciousness. He could barely move his mouth to talk.

[Shut me down. Run.]

It would take a couple of minutes to force Fist into a protective closedown, swaddling his systems deep in Jack's mind. Jack started the delicate process. It took all his attention. He couldn't risk movement until it was complete.

[For gods' sake Jack, just crash me. Factory reset me once you're safe.]

[No, Fist. You'll forget everything.]

[Two great years, five shit ones. Won't miss 'em.]

Fist lost consciousness again. Waking so quickly had placed too much of a strain on his fragile self. Jack stayed on his knees. Blue and white flashes pulsed rhythmically behind him. The struggle had become entirely silent. There was no way of understanding who was winning. They'd both forgotten Jack and Fist.

At last the puppet was fully shut down. Jack ran for the exit, his shadow dancing shakily out in front of him like a monster from a half-remembered nightmare. The building was on lockdown. He had to smash his way through several doors with a fire extinguisher. At last he crashed into reception.

Yamata was lolling in an armchair. She had a gun in her hand and it was pointed at him.

Chapter 34

Jack stood frozen, ready to die. He was too surprised to be afraid, astonished that Yamata had moved so much more quickly than him. The gun's nozzle waved backwards and forwards. Jack wondered if she was taunting him, then realised that she was barely conscious. He moved cautiously past her.

There was another woman lying flat on a sofa. She was also Yamata, and she was also armed. Jack stopped, amazed. Another door opened. The guard carried a third Yamata through it. She hung limply in his arms. When he saw Jack, he beamed, then looked sad.

'I'm so sorry. These are tranquiliser guns. They're going to try and stop you. If they can't, they've got real guns too.'

The Yamata in the chair was twitching feebly, as if some higher force was trying but failing to control her. Her limbs shivered and she gasped, but she was not able to pull herself into any coherent movement. She dropped her gun.

The Yamata on the sofa seemed to have achieved greater self-control. She was slowly and carefully sitting up. Her head twitched left then right, scanning the room with insect focus. Her gun wavered towards Jack.

'I thought I'd find you here,' she sneered. 'Running away.' The lips of the other two Yamatas trembled in time with her words. Her voice was a little slower than it should be. There was a loud pop and her hand shook. Jack jumped as a tranquilliser dart sang past him.

The guard laid the third Yamata down on the floor then hovered nervously, waiting for a cue from Jack. 'I can get between you and the guns,' he said, 'but I think they'd just kill me.'

Jack edged across the reception area, keeping as far away from the armed Yamata as possible. 'No,' he told the guard. 'Don't involve yourself in this. It's not your fight.'

The guard looked crushed. 'But I'd so like to help,' he replied.

'Silence,' ordered Jack. 'Don't move.'

The sofa Yamata was standing up, rising in a series of jerky stops and starts, as if supported by invisible wires. She tried to say 'stop', but the word caught in her mouth and would not finish. For a few seconds she rattled out 'StoStoStoSto ...' – a hard, barbed-wire sound – then she slapped herself. Her head jerked round then back again, her mouth now firmly and tightly shut. The gun spat another dart. It bounced off the wall just by Jack.

When Jack reached the door, the sofa Yamata was taking her first steps. The Yamata on the armchair was leaning shakily down to reach her gun. The one on the floor was shivering gently, a prelude to functionality. The guard was in tears, but he had not moved and his weeping was silent. Jack pushed through the door and started running immediately. He was halfway to the exit gate when a bullet barked past, tearing at the concrete path a few metres away from him.

When he reached the gate, he looked back. The three Yamatas were at the door. One had toppled over and was flailing feebly at the ground. The second was awkwardly trying to help her up. The third was walking smoothly towards him, but couldn't aim her weapon effectively.

'We'll hunt you all the way back to Docklands,' she called out. 'We're meant to take you alive, but we're not going to try too hard.'

A great flash of white light burst upwards behind them, but they didn't seem to notice. The dome over the building's central atrium had shattered. Harry's voice roared out, taunting Yamata. It seemed that he was winning the battle. Jack wondered briefly what death had allowed him to become. Yamata had also been remade as something more than human. He turned and ran.

It was habit that pulled his eyes towards the Pantheon. Without Fist he was offweave, so he saw nothing. He thought of Grey's broken raven, East's radiant wink. The night sky was serene without them.

A tranquilliser dart skittered past his feet. Jack didn't look back. He didn't want to see how much more easily his pursuers were moving, how quickly they would catch up with him. He realised that he was crying. It was then that East called to him. Her voice was impossibly soft. He felt as if he'd stepped out of hell and into a commercial.

'You've seen Grey,' she accused coquettishly. 'Behind my back. Perhaps I shouldn't rescue you, after all.'

Jack couldn't speak. Darts, then a couple of bullets, cracked past him. His breathing was ragged. Soon he'd have to stop and rest, regardless of the danger.

'Make for the Earthside development,' East commanded. 'There's a little surprise waiting for them. Oh, and ...'

Something impossibly deft touched his mind.

[What happened?] said Fist, his voice broken shards.

[East woke you. Can you get onweave and get me to Earthside?]

[No. Shit, my vocal calibration's fucked.]

[What about the rest of you?]

[Ma! Ma! Where IS the rest of me?] Fist shouted, giggling hysterically. [Where? Where? Where? Where?]

[Maybe best you sleep.]

The giggles cut out suddenly, like a recording that had been turned off. Jack had to look back. The Yamatas were gaining on him. They'd started to move more fluidly. The lead Yamata looked almost human. She raised her tranquilliser gun to fire again. Jack sprinted round another corner, pushing himself to leave them as far behind as he could.

East drifted into being beside him.

'The puppet's in worse shape than I thought. Maybe I should show you the way myself. Oh, and you're so sexy when you're panting.'

Jack didn't trust himself to reply. Each breath was a choking catch at the air. He wished he'd spent more time keeping fit when he'd been a prisoner.

'You'll be able to slow down in a moment. Make sure you take the next left.'

Jack was tempted to dart out of her plans and let his pursuers kill him, freeing him from both gods and men. But then, there was the risk that Fist would fall into Kingdom's hands. Flight remained the safest option. There were mysteries to solve, too. Harry and Yamata had both become strange new creatures, challenges to Jack's understanding of the world. The question of Kingdom's deep motivation remained. Lack of knowledge left Jack feeling that he was still little more than a pawn. The only way to start acting on his own terms was to uncover the truth. And at the last, there was Andrea. He needed to warn her about Harry. He so wanted to see her again.

So Jack followed East's instructions and turned, ammunition dancing in the air around him. Then he skidded to a halt, astonished and horrified in equal measure at the joke that East had played on him. Her soft laughter chuckled through his head as he confronted a vast crowd of Yamatas. There were perhaps two or three hundred of them, all identically dressed, all limping and shuffling in an insect parody of human movement.

'YOU FUCKING BITCH!' he shouted.

'Oh, bless your paranoia, Jack,' she laughed. 'So, so scared of my lovely little flash mob.'

As the Yamatas tottered towards him, Jack realised that they had very little in common with the lethal creatures chasing him through the night. They were dressed and made-up to look like his pursuers, and were doing a very tolerable job of imitating them. But they were all different heights and shapes, all – in fact – different people. They were all quite young, too. It was difficult to see past the makeup, but most appeared to be teenagers.

'My little acolytes,' said East, her voice full of pride. 'All sneaking out to help you. I've been setting this up for a little while, now. Dropping images of Yamata into fashion magazines. Hinting at exciting events. Getting them all so thrilled about it all. Isn't it wonderful?'

'You knew that Yamata would chase me?'

'I thought you'd run into her, sooner or later. When you found her lair, I sent out the call – and assembled my little throng.'

There was something almost maternal in East's voice.

'But – the Yamatas are armed. These kids are going to die.'

'Only some of them. And they'll die happy. They'll be legends and their fetches will be so proud. But there's only one of you. Keep running!'

Refusing to think about the implications of his choice – of his endorsement of East's vicious, wasteful rescue plan – Jack started forward again. He pushed through the crowd of Yamata lookalikes, feeling his breathing and pulse slow as he did so. The mob let him through, coming back together behind him and covering his path. They were packed close together, filling the whole street. It would be near impossible for the Yamatas to break through them in their weakened state. They'd have to shoot hundreds to have any hope of catching him. Jack hoped they weren't that ruthless. He kept moving.

A few of the Yamata flash mob costumes had been carefully prepared, but most looked hastily thrown together. Dark blue dripped down faces from poorly dyed hair, pale blue face paint sweated away in dark lines. Eyes were uncomfortably red behind cheap purple contact lenses.

It was the massed conviction of all the individual performances that made the mob impressive. As Jack pushed through it, nobody broke character; nobody smiled, or flinched, or did anything to reveal that they were just pretending. Their commitment was absolute. Jack risked a look back. The real Yamatas were stalking into view. Now the flash mob would be tested. The Yamatas stopped, as amazed as Jack had been by the sight of several hundred imitators.

The mob moved towards them and started to chant one phrase again and again. 'Hello Yamatas, we're Yamatas' built from a mutter to a roar as Jack reached the end of the flash mob. It echoed back off the buildings around them. Empty office blocks became a chorus, chanting commentary at the drama. Their words weren't strong enough to drown out the stutter of gunfire. The first flash mobbers reached the three Yamatas. Some fell immediately. Most poured on, a blue-stained wave rolling over Jack's pursuers. Unable to add any support, he fled. After thirty seconds or so, the shooting stopped and there was only chanting. Then, suddenly, there was silence. Jack was too far away to see how many had survived as the crowd dispersed.

'Oh, they'll be all right,' said East casually. 'And now, you've got to hide yourself. You've got to go somewhere even I don't know about! Because who knows if one of my little subsidiaries has been compromised, and people who shouldn't be there are inside me now, watching. So now I've saved your life, I'm going to stop following you. Aren't I good?'

'How many died back there?'

'Nobody died, Jack. Fifty-two people just became immortal.'

With that, East winked out of existence. Jack kept moving, pacing through the city at a half-run, a speed he hoped he could keep up for a little while longer. He would find refuge, and reassemble Fist. Only then would he let himself think about what East had just done to rescue him, what Yamata and Harry had become, and how he was going to stop Kingdom.

Without Fist to manage his connection, he assumed that he was comprehensively offweave. He didn't know how visible his absence was to InSec; whether they would – as Lestak had promised – start searching for him now that he had broken the terms of his access to Homelands.

For the moment, it was difficult to care.

Chapter 35

Jack's flight took him through an abandoned light industrial zone. Fist's emergency repair systems whispered status reports. None showed any progress. East's intervention had hindered his recovery. The puppet was going to be unconscious for hours, if not days. Jack hadn't had so much privacy for seven years. To his surprise, he felt lonely.

The road led through a shattered collage of factory units. They embodied a very specific decadence. Neglect of such usable space would be an obscenity elsewhere in the Solar System. In Homelands, it went unchecked. Jack wondered what kind of luminous imagery overlaid this dead district. Station was sometimes known as 'Dreamlands' by those who lived beyond it. It was meant as an exaggerated slight. Here, it was a literal truth. He snorted in half-laughter as he moved through perhaps the truest symbol of his home that he'd yet come across.

With that, Jack realised where he could seek refuge. The streets around him were buried behind a layer of illusion, but people still moved through them. By contrast the void sites, forbidden to all, were kept entirely apart, providing the perfect hiding space. Without Fist he had no weave presence, so wouldn't trigger any alarms when he moved into one. It was unlikely there'd be any physical security systems present. The weave's pervasiveness made them largely redundant.

The landscape changed. Broken factory spaces dropped away, to be replaced by housing and educational sites. These buildings were occupied. The rain fell back to a light drizzle. Jack was surprised at the silence of the night and realised again that he was missing Fist. He spotted a void site.

Wooded lawns sloped up to a partially burnt-out apartment block, perhaps six or seven storeys high. Streetlights cast a pale orange glow on its façade. Broken windows rose up like dead eyes above a ruined entrance hall. Double doors gaped open beneath the ragged remains of a canvas canopy. A high metal fence blocked any access to the complex. Jack trotted along it until he found low hanging branches reaching out from within. It only took a moment to pull himself up, over and into the garden.

Jack thought of the terrorists the block must have harboured. It was hard to believe that all of its inhabitants could have gone over to the enemy. But then, he'd just witnessed a petty criminal who had become something approaching a Totality mind. It seemed that the distinction between human and other was no longer as hard and fast as it had once been.

He set off towards the block, finding a path glowing palely in the moonlight and following it towards the front doors he'd seen from the road. Once inside, he planned to rest up and closely monitor the initial stages of Fist's revival. When the renewal process was fully underway, Jack would be able to sleep. His dreams would be infected with Fist's rebirth. He wondered what details would spring into his sleeping mind, seeding images of reconstruction and growth to half-recall on waking.

Trees hung over the path, holding back the gently silvered light. Bushes clumped beneath them. Jack walked quickly until something snapped beneath his foot with a loud crack. He instinctively dropped into a crouch and moved sideways into the trees, worried about being heard but making even more noise as he went. He stopped in the shadows and reassured himself that he'd left his pursuers far behind, then looked round to see what he'd trodden on. Complex geometric shapes stretched away in straight lines along the path. He'd squashed several of them. He reached for one that was still whole. It was a hexagonal prism made of whittled sticks, tied together with rough twine.

'Shit,' he whispered.

There was a rustling in the leaves behind him. Jack thought of the rain, but it had stopped a while back; of the breeze, but the night was still. There was more rustling and he turned through a full circle, only to be faced with silence and a path lined with obsessively repeated structures. Looking more closely, he saw empty glass vials scattered between them. That confirmed his suspicions. He'd stumbled on a sweathead factory.

Fear bit him. Sweat was a worker's drug, designed to make six-day weeks of fourteen-hour shifts bearable. It gave its users energy while numbing their minds, helping them focus on tediously repetitive actions for hour after hour without any breaks or lapses in concentration.

Most carefully managed their use of the drug to avoid addiction. Those that didn't usually ended up abandoned and homeless until the drug at last devoured them. When they took a sweat hit, they'd spend hours feverishly, repetitively creating pointlessly complex objects. Until the high wore off, they'd react violently to any sort of break in their routine or assault on their creations.

Jack glanced to left and right, hoping that the sweatheads who'd created these objects were long gone. He moved along the side of the path in a low, crouching trot, carefully avoiding any of the little wooden structures. In a minute or so, he'd be able to find a room inside the block and safely barricade himself in. Darkness loomed around him, rich with its own ancient threat. He tried to convince himself that he'd soon be safe, that there was no need to panic. And then a sweathead exploded out of the bushes beside him, and rammed something sharp and hard into his side.

Jack screamed and ran. His attacker clung to him, as dry and light as the bundles of twigs on the path. Jack crushed more as he ran. Another sweathead howled in the darkness. The path left the trees and crossed a wide lawn. A mouth that was all dry gums scrabbled at his neck. Pain pulsed across his ribs as his attacker jabbed him again and again. Jack reached up and back for its head but couldn't grip it. He threw himself sideways and rolled, and the creature cracked beneath his weight and let go.

In an instant he was up and running again. The path led round the side of the building to the front of the apartment block. Jack risked a quick glance back. Two more dark shapes howled across the lawn behind him. They were lost to sight as he rounded the corner and reached the block's entrance. He planned to hide inside, but was baffled to see that its doors were now closed. He slammed against them. Pain shot out of his ribs. The doors wouldn't budge. There was a broomstick pushed through the inner handles.

A moment of puzzlement – they'd definitely been standing open when he'd seen them from the road – and then the sweatheads appeared round the corner of the building. One of them pointed a three-fingered hand at him and gibbered threats. There was a rock in its other hand. The other kept running, a single eye blazing rage out of a broken face. It was holding a vicious-looking knife.

Jack reached up to the flayed canopy above him, tore a strip of canvas from it, and ran for a forlorn clump of bushes. He pushed himself inside them and knelt down. His right hand grasped a rock. The running sweathead approached, casting around uncertainly for its prey. Jack felt suddenly lightheaded. He wrapped the rock in the canvas strip. The sweathead jogged past his hiding place. Its knife shimmered in the moonlight.

Jack moved silently to his feet and stepped out of cover. He swung his weapon and the rock smashed against the sweathead's arm. He'd hoped that he'd only make it drop the knife and perhaps wind it, but it was far gone and physically very weak. The rock snapped through its arm and carved a dark hole in its flank. It collapsed, whinnying painfully.

'Fuck,' said Jack, and took a step towards it. Blood poured out like dust, staining the ground. It wasn't going to survive. Shocked, Jack forgot the third sweathead until it swung its own rock down on his shoulder. He staggered and nearly fell. It howled at him, then bent down and scrabbled around for the knife.

In pain, and wanting to hide from rather than hurt the sweathead, Jack turned and ran for the doorway. As he reached it, he leapt up and grabbed the front of the structure supporting the canopy. It gave a little under his weight, starting to pull away from the building. He swung his legs forward towards the double doors, hitting them with both feet. There was a crack and a moment of resistance before the broomstick that held them closed snapped in two. The doors slammed open and Jack flew through them feetfirst. He landed hard, sliding across the floor. He flipped himself over and looked back.

The canopy was hanging down, blocking the door. The surviving sweathead was climbing through it, the knife sharp in one hand and the rock heavy in the other. The canopy frame collapsed on to its head and shoulders, pulling it backwards. It staggered and fell. Jack stood up, wondering if the fight was over. He felt unsteady. The sweathead rose to its feet again and kept coming. The canopy had knocked part of its scalp off. Jack looked round. There was nowhere to hide and nothing he could use as a weapon. Guilt bit him, and then he realised how easily Kingdom would find him if the fight left him badly injured or even unconscious. His last opponent staggered towards him, weapons raised.

Jack ran for the stairs. The sweathead chattered something incomprehensible and followed him. There were bullet holes in the stair walls. The building must have seen some fighting. The stairs ended in a long corridor lined with numbered doors. Most were closed. A jumble of luggage bags, suitcases and briefcases lay on the floor, clothes scattered around them. There was a broken window at the end of the corridor, a fire extinguisher hanging beside it. A couple of seconds, and he was tearing it off the wall. Darkness gathered at the edges of his vision.

The sweathead appeared, moving like a nightmare made of sticks and dirty blankets. It howled words that could have been 'stopped us completing our quota!', then staggered down the hall towards him, kicking the luggage out of the way. Its broken eye leaked dark, poisoned blood. Yellow teeth showed through a tear in its cheek. Its shattered voice carved through the air like a siren.

Jack stood poised, ready to bring the fire extinguisher down. The sweathead closed on him, then let itself sink to the ground, before springing up to fly towards him. Its long limbs were spiderlike in the air, its knife carving in like a stinger, its rock swinging in like a claw.

Jack was barely able to bring the fire extinguisher down in time. It smashed against a ruined face. The knife took Jack in the forearm and he felt a tearing pain. The sweathead smashed against the wall and half-fell. It turned its broken face towards Jack. He swung the fire extinguisher again. It ducked away, and the extinguisher smashed against the wall. The knife whipped across Jack's knuckles. Pain flashed, making him stagger and almost drop his weapon.

'QUOTA!' the sweathead screamed. Its good eye was clouded with white. Reeking spittle stung Jack's face. He took a firmer grip

240

on the fire extinguisher as it sprang towards him again, swinging against his attacker's blind side. It hit his opponent's head with a dull clang. Scrabbling for purchase, the sweathead fell to the floor. Jack smashed the fire extinguisher down hard, crushing its chest. It screamed and lashed out with the knife, slicing Jack's lower thigh. Jack fell to his knees, bringing the extinguisher down one last time. The full weight of it hit the sweathead's neck, snapping its head too far to one side. Its scream became a choking gurgle and died away.

A second to savour the victory, to feel for the pain of his wounds, to hope that he wasn't too badly hurt; to realise what he'd just done. Sick disgust filled him, but only for a moment. Adrenaline ebbed and all darkened. Vision flickered for one last moment. There was a small figure, moving down the hallway towards him. 'Fist?' he said. But that was impossible. And then, despairing, he passed out.

Chapter 36

Jack was lying somewhere soft. He could hear running water. His face was covered, his own breath warm against it. His arms were crossed and held tight against his chest. He was swaddled in blankets. He remembered a small figure, half-glimpsed at the end of a passage. He wriggled. Pain danced between his ribs, across his face and hands. There was a soft thudding in his head. Perhaps he'd been captured by one of Kingdom's agents. Soft voices whispered. There were two or three people talking. Jack risked movement. He carefully brought one arm up to pull the blanket away from his head. The speakers were arguing about him.

'We've got to look after him.'

'We can't keep him.'

There was a pause.

'Well, he's here for now anyway.'

The first voice was clear and high-pitched, a far more natural version of Fist's. The second had an uncertain huskiness to it. Jack opened his eyes and saw a metal wall. Someone giggled next to him, then prodded him in the small of his back and said, 'Sleepyhead!' It was unmistakably the voice of a very young girl. 'He's waking up,' she called to the others. They must be children too – an older boy and another girl. Jack wondered at the adults that would leave them alone with a captive. He rolled over. A blanket decorated with a brightly smiling cartoon mouse slid off him. He was lying on a mattress, one of several pushed together. A small, dark-haired girl sat next to him, wearing a ragged dress and a shiny blue anorak. She held a cuddly rabbit and was tugging absent-mindedly at one of its ears.

'Get back, Lyssa,' said the husky voice. There was a table at the other end of the room. The older boy and the other girl were sitting at it. Both were just as shabbily dressed. The wall behind them was covered with bright, dynamic designs; paintings of different parts of Homelands. Some of the buildings had names scrawled across them – Chuigushou Mall, Glass Vision Tower, The Shard, The Acorn, Violin Square.

'You won't hurt us, will you?' said Lyssa. 'You killed the wicked men.' She peered down at her bunny, pulling its nose to left and right as she spoke. 'Wicked, wicked, wicked men.' She looked up again, her gaze surprisingly confident. 'You're a ghost, aren't you? Like us?'

'None of us are ghosts,' said the boy grumpily.

'Then how come no one can see us? Not even the lions and tigers and bears?'

'Quiet, Lyssa,' cautioned the girl at the table. 'Don't tell him secrets.'

'It's not secret,' said Lyssa, her head turned over her shoulder. 'He knows,' she concluded, whispering conspiratorially to her bunny.

'Who are you all?' asked Jack. Lyssa was now deep in conversation with her cuddly toy. The girl from the table came over and sat down, putting a protective arm around her. She looked at the boy, who nodded.

'I'm Ato,' she said brightly, 'and this is Fred.'

'Where are we?'

'Deep underground, in Station's skin,' Fred replied. 'About an hour's walk from where Ato found you. We're safe. All this' – he waved at the walls – 'insulates us from anyone outside.'

'No sound scanners, no body heat cameras, nothing,' said Ato.

'That's pretty impressive,' said Jack. 'You built this yourselves?'

'Don't be silly,' scolded Lyssa. 'Our mummies and daddies did. And Grandpa helped them.'

'I don't understand.'

'When the police came and took them, they left this room for us to be safe in. And they took us offweave and made us all invisible.'

'How did they do that?'

'Secrets from Grandpa,' whispered Lyssa. 'He knew that InSec were coming.'

'For your parents?'

'Yes.'

243

Realisation struck Jack. The terrorists must have tried to protect their children from InSec, and in doing so made phantoms of them.

'Why did InSec come for them?' wondered Jack.

'They were fighting for peace,' said Fred, firmly. 'For a better world.'

Jack wondered how the parents' weavehack worked. It must be very effective – if InSec had been able to perceive the children, they'd have been taken into care. He wondered whether Lestak could arrange for them to be looked after; if she'd even let him get a word in edgeways. Perhaps she might listen when he told her about Kingdom.

He sat up.

'No, don't!' snapped Ato.

Pain spiked in his head. The room spun.

'You're still not better,' she told him. 'Lie down.'

He felt the soft pressure of her hands on his shoulders, pushing him down. It was a relief to sink back on to the mattress.

'We'll look after you. And anyway, you can't go anywhere just now. They're looking for you upstairs.' There was a confident finality to her voice. She was talking as much to Fred as to Jack.

Jack felt a soft scratching in his mind. Fist was stirring. An indicator pinged. The puppet's core consciousness would start rebooting in an hour or so. Perhaps it would be best to sleep until then. He felt that he could trust the children not to betray him. Exhaustion rolled over him like a dark wave, and he let himself fall into it.

He dreamed that he was Corazon again. Her assassin pursued him through sleep. Sometimes there was one Yamata, shooting at him through a keyhole. Sometimes many limped behind him, never quite catching him, never slowing down. At one point, he found himself in the middle of a silent, moonlit piazza. Bone-white stone surrounded him. There was no one else there, but he couldn't bring himself to stop running.

When he awoke, he barely felt rested. The room was quiet. Lyssa was sitting by the table, playing with her bunny. Fred stood at the rear wall, sketching on it with a marker pen, roughing out a new building for the Homelands mural. Neither noticed he'd woken. There was no sign of Ato.

Jack closed his eyes and settled back into his mattress. Now that he'd looked outwards, he could reach inwards. Icons flashed in his mind – Fist's damage repair reports. The puppet's basic systems had successfully repaired themselves. His mind, memory and personality were ready to be reactivated. Jack had to be present to steer this final rebirth. For a moment, he hesitated. Without Fist, he had felt loneliness, but also peace. There'd been solitude for the first time in seven years. Such privacy was difficult to relinquish.

But so much had changed since they'd returned to Station. Each had become a mediator for the other, Jack helping Fist engage with the subtle workings of humanity, Fist helping Jack control the digital environment that the little puppet understood so well. Emotion poured through him. He thought back to when East had offered to neuter Fist's higher functions. He'd framed his objection then in rational terms; now, he understood that there was far more to it than that. The puppet was no longer just a burdensome tool. He was a conscious, developing individual with whom Jack was deeply involved.

Commands pulsed in Jack's thoughts. They confirmed that it was safe for Fist to reboot. At peace in the sanctuary of his mind, Jack watched as his child began to live again.

Chapter 37

Hours passed. Jack seemed to be asleep. In fact, he was deep in conversation with Fist.

[Thank gods I'm back,] chirped the puppet. [You can't manage without me. Rescued by children!]

[Pretty capable kids. They've hidden from InSec all this time.]

Fist was silent for a moment. [Well, here's part of how they did it,] he told Jack. [This room's a Turing cage. Nothing digital gets in or out. And that young girl's got some fairly heavy protection running. She's invisible to anyone onweave.]

[They said that the lions and tigers and bears couldn't see them either. Must be invisible to security programs, too.]

[Yup. But only for a while. Their protection stops at puberty. Lyssa's weave presence will activate fully then and break her shielding.]

[And the boy?]

[Looks like his broke a few months back. But he's never been fully onweave. Must have been hiding here all that time.]

[He could do that?]

[As long as they keep feeding him.]

[That's not what I meant, Fist.]

[I know. Poor kid.]

The note of empathy in the puppet's voice surprised Jack. He wondered about commenting on it, but worried that that would inhibit it. [They can't have got this stuff from their parents,] he said neutrally. [It's far too sophisticated.]

[Their folks must have been hackers as well as terrorists. Interesting. I'll dig into the code, see what I can find out.]

[That's not all the digging we need to do. We need to work out what happened at TrueShield.]

[I could have killed a god, Jack Conscience Forster decided I shouldn't, and we had our backsides tanned. End of story.]

[And that should be impossible. None of the other puppets could have done it. They were built on military minds, Totality specialists with no sense of Pantheon structure. They'd have been completely lost in divine security code.]

[Puppet plus accountant equals god fucker,] preened Fist. [How about that? It was a piece of piss to break, Jackie boy. Pantheon security sucks, it's overconfidence again.]

[Oh no.] Awe rose in Jack. [Sometimes, when I was working close enough to the Pantheon, I'd hear their protection growling in the distance. I was out on the edge of a five-year business plan once, I saw the Twins' firewall on the horizon. Unreachable. Unknowable. It burnt so brightly. I couldn't look at it for more than a few seconds. I don't know how to describe it.]

[That's not how it looked to me,] chirped Fist. [It was just a little door. I just raised my foot and kicked it down. Bam! I always knew I was special! I only wish all those other puppets were still around, I'd love to have seen those little S.O.B.'s faces when I showed them what I could really do.]

[More than special,] said Jack. [You're a Pantheon gun. Could you really have killed him?]

[I could have done whatever I wanted to. Messed around with his corporate structures. Crashed some of his businesses. Deleted his personality. Copied ours into it. Wait a second ...] Fist paused for a second, then exploded with vicious excitement. [I could have copied us over Kingdom! He'd have become us! We could have been gods! I could have been a god! Let's go back and do it!]

Fist's glee scared Jack. Trying to sound as calm and firm as he could, he replied: [You haven't thought that through, Fist. Remember, we don't have any proof of what Kingdom's been up to. And if you kill a god, lots of people die and the other gods would kill us. We'd last seconds at most.]

[BUT WHAT SECONDS THEY'D BE!]

[Remember East's anger,] Jack told him, keeping his voice gentle. [Imagine eleven of them turning on you.]

[I'd fucking have the lot of them.]

[Even if you're damaged?]

[Fuck's sake, Jack. Yamata barely touched me. That's just a detail.]

[Really?]

[I'm fine.] There was a pause. [Well, maybe there are some little bruises. But they don't matter.]

[Show me.]

[I don't want to think about it. Come on, Jack, let's go! I'm a Pantheon gun! I may be short of a few bullets, but I'm still ready to fire!]

There was a little less glee in his voice, a little more anxiety. Jack wondered what the true extent of the damage was. [I need to see,] he said, quietly but firmly. [I'm not taking you anywhere until I've seen.]

[Jack ...] whined Fist.

[I mean it.]

Fist let a series of images escape into Jack's mind. The puppet was wrapped in a tightly buttoned and belted trench coat. A little fedora hat was perched on his head.

[There. Hardly a scratch.]

He turned to left and right, stretching his arms out. He didn't seem to realise that the trench coat was torn under one arm. The tear revealed a charred wooden body dotted with broken remnants of clothing. Wisps of hair emerged from beneath the hat. There was a new looseness to his movements, as if his joints had been over-strained and left slightly too flexible. His face and hands were darker than they had been, stained by smoke.

[That looks quite serious.]

[I'm fine, Jackie boy, fine fine fine! Ha ha ha.] His laughter was forced. [I've just had to reallocate some internal memory. And I've still got some repairs to finish. So no full visuals at the moment, I'm afraid.]

[You're not at full attack strength.]

[You're spoiling everything, Jack.]

[I'm helping you think clearly. How hard could you hit Kingdom, right now?]

Fist said nothing.

[Hard enough to be sure of finishing him off?]

[Fucking hell, Jack.]

[And what would happen if you didn't? He'd wipe both our personalities. Then he'd rebuild your attack systems and turn them on the rest of the Pantheon. We'd be dead and he'd be able to take over or kill any of them. Is that what you want?]

For a moment, Fist's newly battered face was inert. He looked more puppet-like than ever before. Then he leapt into animated life again.

[I'm bored with this! Let's talk about Yamata and Harry! We can chat about Kingdom again when I've finished my repairs.]

Relief shook through Jack. [Good idea,] he said. [How could Harry fight her off like that?]

[I've got a pretty good idea. I scanned him when he passed through me. I've got his number now. Yamata's too. And you know what's really strange? At a systems level, you can't tell them apart.]

[But she hit you with a Totality attack package.]

[She's a post-mortal human consciousness running on a Totality platform – that jellyfish thing was her weave presence. Harry makes more of an effort to look good, but he's really exactly the same. It's why he could make such a big dent in her.]

[You can't run human minds in a Totality environment. They work in a completely different way.]

[No one told those two! I didn't get too deep in, but there was some pretty sophisticated crosspatching going on. Oh, and there's no fetchware in there at all. They've never been near a Coffin Drive. They became what they are as soon as they kicked the bucket.]

[Shit. What about the physical Yamatas?]

[I'd guess clones, brains scooped out and replaced with nanogel mind nodes. Yamata runs them by remote control. Her signal traces back to Heaven. Harry's off-Station somewhere. High Earth orbit, by the look of it.]

[We should tell Ifor.]

[What? He's Totality, they're on Totality platforms. I bet he's involved. They're stitching us up. Fucking squishies. We should have killed them all.]

[This isn't them. The Yamata clones are several copies of the same body. That's not Totality, they value variety too much. They never repeat themselves.]

[But what about Harry? He could be sitting in a Totality server on a snowflake somewhere.]

[How would they have got hold of him? And why? No, it's got to be Kingdom. Who else could get two human minds running on Totality hardware?]

[And you don't want me to touch him. I hope you know you're his fucking bitch, Jack.]

[We're going to get hard, undeniable proof of Kingdom's involvement in all this. We'll give it to Grey and East, and the Totality, and between them they'll bring him down. We'll be heroes, Fist. And there'll be no risk of Kingdom getting his hands on your firepower.]

Fist yawned.

[You're sleepy?]

[Repair packages calling. I've got to shut down for a bit. This is a boring conversation anyway.]

Fist grumbled back into Jack's mind. Soon, little snores sighed up. Jack felt hugely relieved that he'd managed to defuse Fist's excitement at his newly discovered capabilities. He wondered in a tired way how he'd keep protecting him from the damage he could cause. Thoughts of protection turned his mind to Andrea. He worried that Harry might have discovered their relationship, might still take his revenge on her. The past sighed in his mind. They'd worked so hard to hide things. 'I don't want to tell him until it's right,' she used to say. 'Until I know for sure it's serious. He'd be so angry if he found out.' Jack reassured himself that Harry never had done.

As he drifted into sleep, other memories of their time together brushed at him, like waves caressing a darkening shore. There was Andrea as he'd first seen her, performing in a Kanji Town night club. Harry dragged Jack there after they'd argued about music. 'I told you she was better than anything you Homeland fucks have, didn't I? If she hadn't fallen out with the Twins, she'd be the biggest star on Station.' A single spotlight carved the pale mask of her face from the darkness, the rest of her lost in soft shadow.

There was the first time they kissed; a snatched, urgent intimacy that took both of them by surprise, after hours in a near-empty cabaret bar. Two half-empty glasses flared gold between them. Ice had melted into the whisky's pale fire when at last they remembered to finish them. 'You can't pretend you're not from here,' she told him then, for the first time.

As she got to know him, she would drag him back to the streets of his childhood and force memories back into him. 'It's who you are. Not some Homelander that Grey made.' He came to believe that she emphasised her Docklands accent when she was with him, used slang that she would normally skip over. He remembered walking past a playground with her. 'I used to love that place,' he said. Children still tumbled laughing through it. 'Look at them,' she said, 'finding joy despite the world.'

Towards the end, he found it harder and harder when she went back to Harry. By then, he was living pretty much full time in his Docklands hotel. He was on first name terms with the staff, who turned a blind eye to her frequent late night visits. She was suffering, too. As her affair with Jack had become more serious, so her sense of guilt had grown. 'He's not always a good man,' she said, as they argued one night, 'but it's the best part of him that loves me.' Dawn found her hard-faced. 'I have to go,' she said again and again, making no move towards the door. 'I have to go.'

Three days later, the rock fell.

Mercifully, sleep took Jack before that last meeting came to life in his mind. Memory's weave drifted off him, tapestried moments falling away. His last conscious thoughts were of sweathead code. He wondered what he'd forgotten as he remembered his relationship with Andrea; what more challenging truths lay beyond his remembrance of their time together. And then at last he slept, too damaged even to dream.

Chapter 38

Fred and Lyssa never left the room. Fred painted the walls, laboriously creating images of a world that was entirely closed to him. Lyssa played with her dolls, imagining moments that would never happen. Ato was both young enough to come and go at will, and old enough to do so usefully.

For a couple of days, Jack let himself calmly drift between sleep and waking, allowing the healing that had taken place in both his body and Fist's internal structures to fully bed down. Fist was dormant for much of the time. Sometimes they were awake at the same time and talked silently to each other. Fist was sleepy and distracted. Jack only stopped worrying about him when he started grumbling again.

[I wish you didn't have so many good reasons for not killing Kingdom. Why do you always have to worry about consequences?]

[Because they're always there to be dealt with.] Fist swore grumpily. [But there's something only you can do that I need some help with.]

[Oo, what thrills could possibly await?] sulked Fist. [Sending someone a text message? Finding out where the nearest train station is?]

[No. Hacking fetch code. I want to free Andrea.]

[Won't that have AWFUL REPERCUSSIONS THAT KILL US ALL?]

[No, because you're good enough to make sure that nobody notices.]

[Motherfucker. It's not enough that I've got to think about sodding consequences before doing something TOTALLY REASONABLE like killing a fucking god. I've got to reprogram your girlfriend, too.]

[Not reprogram her,] Jack replied. [Not at all. I want to protect her from that. Remember how much you hated it when Grey

252

rewrote just a tiny part of you, just once? She has to deal with far worse than that, all the time. All fetches do.]

[You sound like the Totality. Get your mate Ifor to sort it out.]

[Please. If not for her, then for me.]

[It'll be hard work. It'd mean understanding fetch permission structures, digging into how the weave manifests them and working out exactly how the Coffin Drives store them. Hmm ...] Fist was silent for a moment, lost in thought. [Fuck. That could actually be quite interesting. Useful, even.]

[It'd be more than useful for Andrea.]

[All right, I'll see what I can do. But it's not an easy job. I won't make any promises.]

[Thank you, Hugo.]

[Don't call me that,] snapped Fist. [Gods, you'd think we actually liked each other!]

Jack slept again until the sound of cooking woke him. The meat that Ato had brought back, crowing triumphantly about her waste-raiding skills, turned out to be spoiled, but the vegetables were edible. Fred boiled them in water over a small electric heater, creating something approaching vegetable soup. It smelt thin and unappetising, but Jack hadn't eaten for three days so hunger jabbed deep into his stomach.

'Hello,' he said, yawning and stretching. 'Do you think I could have some soup?'

'No,' snapped Fred. Ato shushed him. 'Pour him a bowl of soup,' she told Lyssa.

Lyssa – concentrating hard – tottered over to him with a full bowl. She smiled shyly, blushing as he thanked her, then turned and ran back to the table.

'Thank you all,' Jack told them.

They didn't reply. They were too busy eating. The soup itself was flavourless, the vegetables overcooked to the point of dissolution. Jack didn't want to speculate on how old they were, where they might have been found.

When dinner was done, the children piled up their plates by the sink in the corner of the room. Fred turned to Ato. 'I cooked, you wash up,' he told her.

253

'Let me,' said Jack. He went to stand up, but rose too suddenly and tottered unsteady on his feet.

[Careful,] Fist warned.

The three children watched with wide eyes. Only Lyssa didn't look nervous.

'We know what you are, you know,' said Fred. 'We know that you're carrying – one of them.'

'One of what?' asked Jack.

'A puppet.'

'How do you know?'

'We've got a scanner that picks up anything strange,' Lyssa chipped in. 'We used it while you were asleep.'

'You're a puppeteer, aren't you?' said Fred.

Jack saw no point in lying.

'Yes. I am.'

'I saw a puppet once.' Lyssa's voice was soft as she remembered. 'Just like yours. Her puppeteer brought her into school. She was called Lumberjack Lil. She was funny! She juggled her chainsaws.'

'I saw one of those shows too,' said Fred.

'We all did,' said Ato. 'They said they were safe, that the puppets would hunt down the evildoers who wanted to harm us. But they didn't want us to be scared of them, and it was really all for the children who died on the moon, so they made them look like toys.'

[Should I show myself now?] said Fist.

[No,] said Jack. [We'll wait until they ask to see you. I don't want to surprise them.]

[Why not? It'd be fun.]

'They're not really just puppets,' Fred was saying. 'We learned all about them. They're a whole suite of applications.'

'That's one way of putting it,' Jack replied.

'I wish we'd had your puppet,' Ato sighed. 'It might have protected us from sweatheads.'

'What do they do to you?'

'Every so often, they catch us.'

'If Ato hadn't seen you kill two of them,' said Fred, 'she'd have just left you upstairs. But they wanted to kill you. She said that makes you one of us.'

254

'Until we start to get grown up,' said Lyssa, her voice almost a whisper, 'they're the only people who can see us.'

'They attack you?' asked Jack.

'Them and InSec,' said Ato, with a sadness too heavy for a child. 'There used to be so many more of us.'

The washing-up seemed irrelevant now. There was a spare chair at the table. 'Can I sit down?' asked Jack. Ato nodded. Fred turned round and went back to his painting. The chair was too small for Jack. His knees stuck up and out at an awkward angle, and wouldn't fit under the table. Lyssa giggled.

'Have you ever killed any children?' Ato said suddenly.

'No,' replied Jack, shocked. 'Why would you think that?'

'You're like the sweatheads. You can see us.'

'I've only ever attacked the Totality, because we thought they were threatening you. Children like you. And Fist – my puppet – isn't real like sweatheads are. He's just a projection.'

[Oi!]

'We've never killed a person,' Jack continued, ignoring him. 'Just Totality minds.'

'The teachers didn't call that killing,' said Lyssa. 'They said that the puppets were going to go and play with the Totality. And once they'd finished, the Totality would think differently about people.'

'They said they weren't made to hurt anyone,' Ato interjected. 'But my father said that the puppets were going to kill the Totality. That we had to stop the Soft War. And then they came and killed him.'

'They killed all our parents,' Lyssa said sadly, 'all across Station. And their fetches are all caged.'

Fred's paintbrush made soft scraping noises. He was painting something box-like, but brightly coloured. It could have been a mall.

'We want to see your puppet,' Ato told Jack. 'We need to know that we're safe. We think we are, but we need to know it.'

[Your cue, Fist. Get ready. And play nice.]

[Aw.]

'I'll ask him to appear,' Jack told the children. 'Will he scare you?'

'Oh, I don't think so,' announced Grey, stepping into the room from nowhere. 'These are tough kids, you know.' The lightest scent

255

of cigar smoke touched the air. He had a gin and tonic in his hand.

'If you're using them like you used me,' said Jack, 'I'll kill you myself right now.'

When they heard Jack threaten Grey, Ato and Fred leapt on him. Even Lyssa joined in. They slammed into him, making him stumble backwards and then fall. He found himself lying on the mattress, arms and legs held down.

[Fuck,] spat Fist. [Him again. What now?]

[Stay out of sight. Let's see what he wants.]

Grey chuckled. 'There's really no need for that,' he told the children. 'He's not going to hurt me. He couldn't.'

'Are you sure, Grandpa?' asked Fred.

'I'm sure.'

They let go of Jack and gradually pulled away.

'I'm sorry, Jack. They're very protective.'

'Have you hurt them at all?'

'Oh no. Not in the way you mean. Their parents built platforms for me in their minds. I've never needed to. And besides – I wouldn't want to.'

Jack thought he saw a flicker of guilt shadow Grey's face, but immediately dismissed the idea.

'And now I want to have a grown-up conversation with you, Jack. I'm going to have to send you young ones off to sleep, I'm afraid. Jack – you'll have to move off the mattresses.'

Jack stood up, letting all three children lay down, Lyssa giggling, Fred and Ato with an air of grumpy resignation. 'Are you ready?' Grey asked them. 'Yes,' they chorused. Grey waved his hand, and they were asleep.

'What's going on here?' asked Jack. 'How did you do that? How can you even be here? This room's caged.'

'It is. I'm in them, Jack. The ghost children of Station are my last redoubt.'

'You're in their minds?'

'Like Fist is in yours. But Fist only has the power of one mind to draw on. When they're together, I have all three of them. And when they're outside – there are a couple of hundred who survive. They're my core. Where is the little man, by the way?'

[Well?] said Fist. [There's not much of him here. We're safe.] [Go for it.]

Fist shimmered into being, sitting on the table top, swinging his legs. His body moved in a more coherent way, but there were still scattered patches of charring.

'Why didn't I pick you up when I scanned them, then?' said Fist.

'You have been in the wars,' said Grey. 'I am sorry. But to answer your question – I've taken great care to hide myself. I'm buried very deep indeed.'

'And are you present to them, like Fist is?'

'Oh yes. You heard that they call me Grandpa? I look after them. I guide them. But it's so much more difficult than I thought it would be.'

Grey suddenly seemed very old. He made a chair appear, then slowly and carefully sat down on it. There was a stiffness to him that was very far removed from the usual fluid elegance of his movements. Jack was shocked to realise that he looked haunted.

'Advising them, helping them find food, keeping InSec attention away from them. And in return, they hide me and keep my core components safe. But I live in them, and as them too. Their lives are so difficult. They've lost so much.'

Jack was surprised to see Grey feel pity. 'That's not your fault,' he said.

'I'm responsible. Their parents were my people. They just wanted to end the Soft War and see the Totality get full recognition as an independent, Pantheon-equivalent corporate body. And then, all this.'

'But you told me that the Totality were a contagion, that their power had to be limited.'

'I was lying to you, Jack,' sighed Grey. 'Doing what I do. Managing the situation.'

'Manipulating the situation. Manipulating me.'

'You can call it that, if you want to.'

'Like when you reprogrammed me,' said Fist.

'Reprogrammed?' said Grey, suddenly thoughtful. 'That's a good word. Maybe that is what I was doing. If you control the information that someone gets, you control them. Sharing the right data in the

257

right way – I suppose it is a way of reprogramming people. I am sorry.'

'What's your game, Grey? What's in it for you?'

Grey smiled sadly. 'Nothing. What I am now comes from these few children. And they're not old enough to have become effective dissemblers. You'll find that I'm in a more evasive mood when I am out of this small room; when I can draw on my deeper resources.'

'But for now?' said Jack.

'But for now, I am as simple and open as they are.'

[Fist?]

[He's telling the truth,] answered Fist. [He's just coming from them. There's nothing else there. His signal's much less complex than usual.]

[I can trust him?]

[Broadly, yes, Jackie boy. Take advantage! Squeeze him for all he's got!]

'You've been working with East,' said Jack. 'What brought you together?'

'I had such ambitions. I thought that if I worked with her, I'd be able to influence Station away from the war and bring us closer to the Totality. The Pantheon are too controlling, Jack, I'd begun to see that. We need to be more open – like the Totality are. Of course, that conflicted with Kingdom's interests. He had a lot to lose. And he's lost almost all of it.'

'What did you tell me that wasn't a lie?' said Jack.

'Lie? That's a terrible word. I told you what you needed to know to ensure that you took the path that would be best for you.'

'Not for me, for you.'

'And I've done so well out of it.' Grey waved his hand round the cramped little room.

'You've been keeping yourself safe,' said Jack. 'At the cost of all of these children. Of their parents.'

'I didn't realise how ruthless Kingdom would be. We struggled for years. At last he found a weakness and used it. Made everyone believe that my activist groups were fronts for terrorists; killed them, blocked their fetches, shut me down, froze my board. It was a shocking experience. So fast. I barely had enough time to get the

258

Greyware running in the kids, hide them in safe rooms. When my board was shut down I shifted over into them. I've been running in them ever since.'

'So who were the real terrorists?'

'I could never find any traces of them. All the bombs, the attacks on Station; they just happened. They mystified me as much as anyone. I had so many people out there, trying to understand what was going on. Nothing. The children think of themselves as ghosts, but the people who bombed Station were the real phantoms.'

'They helped Kingdom, though, didn't they?'

'Oh yes. They justified the war, kept people from thinking too much about why we might really be fighting. All those empty shrines they created. Every day, people look at pictures of dead children and remember why the Totality has to be destroyed. Making peace with it? It means forgetting the dead. And, as a culture, we're very bad at that.'

'People walk with them every day.'

'They're part of our lives. We – they – live in a space station, orbiting a dead planet they can't bring themselves to leave, living in ways they can't bring yourselves to change, talking to corpses they can't bring themselves to bury. Maintaining stasis takes a lot of effort. It's the opposite of the Totality. And it gives Kingdom and his allies an awful lot of power, even now.'

'Yamata was working for him.'

'I always wondered about that. You have proof?'

'She told me. Could she have been behind the terrorist attacks?'

'It wouldn't surprise me. She had the right skillset. The reskinning that poor Corazon found out about. She started as a sweat smuggler, too. She could easily have brought weapons in, explosives. Akhmatov's distribution and enforcement networks would have been very helpful to her. Perhaps Penderville was working with them, perhaps you were about to expose them, perhaps that's why Kingdom wanted you out of the picture.'

'And what about Harry?'

'I've never understood him.' Grey frowned. 'He was always so supportive of you when he was alive. His reports on you helped me convince Kingdom that you'd be a useful part of the war effort. I don't know what's happened to him. Maybe he did find out about you and Andrea.'

'You knew?' said Jack.

'I was with you everywhere, Jack. It's what gods do; always present where intention meets action, understanding both, influencing where we can. She felt very strongly for you, you know, but she's a very loyal person. I nudged her to stay with you after the rock fell, but her will was stronger.'

'Always manipulating. You disgust me, Grey.'

'My influence was always constructive.'

'Constructive? You sent me away to kill. And you never just influenced. That implies choice, and you never gave me that.'

'All of you always have a choice, Jack. I thought you realised that when you walked away from the war. I wanted you to do that, I wanted you to leave the Pantheon behind. I thought I saw that knowledge in you when you refused to help me in the garden.'

Jack laughed bitterly. 'One last question. I don't know what Harry is any more. Do you? And is Andrea safe?'

'I stopped watching Harry closely when you stopped working for him. He was still human then. And I don't think you need worry about Andrea. Beyond rolling her back, there's very little he can do to hurt her.'

That was when Fist cut in, his patience exhausted. 'Enough with the encounter group. Jack'll talk about Andrea all night if you let him, but we've got some practical challenges to deal with.' He switched to talk silently to Jack. [Can I tell him I can kill Kingdom?]

[No,] replied Jack. [It's too dangerous. We don't want any of the Pantheon to know you're a direct threat to them. Just give him the basics. No boasting.]

[Fucking consequences,] said Fist grumpily before continuing out loud: 'Here's the deal. We've tracked Yamata's signal back to Heaven, and we know she's working for Kingdom. I think her core servers are somewhere in Kingdom's corporate headquarters. So, it's simple.'

'Really?' said Grey. 'I'm impressed by your confidence.'

'We break into Heaven, and then into Kingdom's HQ. Once we're in, we find Yamata. We know what we're up against, so we won't be taken by surprise. We crack her, take her memories, find out exactly what crimes she's committed, and use them to prove Kingdom's guilt.'

'I can speak for East,' Grey responded. 'She'll broadcast whatever you find. Everyone on Station will see it. It'll be impossible to cover up.'

'You're running ahead,' Jack told him. 'We need to work out how we're going to break into Heaven first, then a core Pantheon facility. One of those on their own would be difficult. Both together …'

'I can get you into Heaven' said Grey.

'How? I mean – they've shut you down.'

'You can walk the vacuum paths.'

'What?'

'This room is buried in Station's skin. That's why the children hide here. Only engineers ever come down this far. One of their duties is inspecting Station's exterior. To do that, they need a door out to Station's outer skin. Half a day's walk, and there's one you can get to. From there, you can go straight to Heaven.'

Fist thought for a moment. 'We don't have spacesuits. I don't need to breathe, but it's a bit of a problem for Jackie boy here!'

'There'll be some at the airlock,' Grey reassured him. 'There's always an emergency supply.'

'And then? The gates of Heaven don't open for just anyone.'

'There's someone who can help you with that. An old friend of yours, Fist. Mr Stabs.'

Fist couldn't restrain a gasp of joy. 'He'll see us?' he cried. 'At last?'

'Oh yes,' said Grey. 'I'll tell him you're going to bring down Kingdom. That'll blow his mind.'

Chapter 39

It was night in the void site garden. Spinelight glowed dully, drifting across the trees and lawns like so much dust. The abandoned apartment building stood out like a broken tooth. Behind it, the sleeping suburbs of Homelands rolled up and away into the sky. There was a deep hush over Station, strong enough to be almost palpable. Hundreds of thousands slept. Jack imagined them dreaming, and wondered briefly if their dreams were any more real than the waking world they moved through every day.

[I wish we didn't have to come up here again,] grumbled Fist. [I just want to go to Heaven and bring down a god.]

[You're the one that wanted reinforcements,] Jack replied.

Ato had brought them up. They'd followed her through a maze of maintenance ducts and machinery rooms. Sewage engines roared as they pumped waste away from humanity. An electrical substation hummed as power leapt up and away from it, out into Homelands. When they passed the gravity generators, their weight fluctuated unpredictably. Sometimes, they found themselves bouncing through great caverns, a few steps carrying them tens of metres. Sometimes, they crawled through maintenance passages, or struggled down corridors glyphed with emergency instructions, their own amplified weight a nearly impossible burden to bear. Grey had always been there, ahead of them; a beacon in the distance, showing them the way.

'It's always strange for me to leave this room,' he'd said before they started out. 'I'm different out there. I don't let them see it, but I'm not just Grandpa any more. I'm not that simple.'

'Can we still trust you?' asked Jack.

'I'll always deliver what I've promised,' Grey replied carefully. 'I might just be a little more self-interested about it.'

[That's great! We've made a deal with the devil,] groaned Fist.

262

At last they reached the garden. 'I'll be back in a couple of hours,' Ato said cheerfully. 'Grandpa's going to help me find some food.'

She wriggled through a small gap in the void site's fence and started up the street. A taller figure shimmered into being next to her – Grey, holding her hand. They disappeared into the darkness together, leaving Jack and Fist alone.

[Right,] said Fist, [I'm going to trigger the void site's security systems, but I don't want anybody to know I've done it. Give me a minute or so.]

Jack moved into a clump of trees and sat down, leaving Fist to his work. Untouched for many years, the grass was unexpectedly lush. It had collected a soft, cold dew that quickly penetrated his trousers, chilling his skin. The sensory detail delighted him. For a long time, he'd only felt nature in weavespace, where anything that could be understood as discomfort had been elided. It was such a pleasure to feel again the awkward, determined presence of an ecosystem that persisted regardless of humanity, unenthralled by its limiting sense of the comfortable.

Fist reappeared next to him, glowing softly in the darkness. [It's done,] he reported. [I'm bringing the block's security systems back up to full function. First time they've run properly in years.]

All of a sudden, the grove thrilled with virtual life. Sounds emerged – the soft, lonely cry of an owl, the high-pitched screams of hunting bats. Jack imagined the glade in daytime, rich with nature's soundtrack.

There was a rustling on the other side of the glade, and a dark shape emerged into the light. It was a fox. The pale light softened its hard hunter's face, making it something gentle in the night. It paused for a moment to look round, then trotted purposefully across the clearing. Halfway across, it stopped, raising its nose to sniff the air.

'Talk out loud, we want it to hear us,' ordered Fist. 'It's only a scout, we want it to summon the block's heavy security systems.'

'What a beautiful night to be out and about!'

The fox's ears twitched. Its head snapped round towards them.

'Come to Daddy!' called Fist. His words broke the fox's concentration. It leapt for the bushes. Leaves shook behind it. 'A couple of seconds, and we'll have some company.'

'I hope you're ready.'

'Piece of piss.'

New presences arrived soundlessly, coalescing from the darkness that the tall trees and the bushes made.

The first was a lion. It walked with a heavy grace, head swaying left and right, shoulders rolling behind its mane. Its tightly closed mouth was a black scar on its shadowed face. Intent eyes focused on Jack and Fist with a hunter's passion. It halted in the centre of the glade and yawned. Teeth caught the light, streaks of white fire gashing the darkness.

The second was a tiger. Its casual, confident, loose limbed stroll promised lethality. Iron-hard muscles fluttered beneath skin. Light and shadow danced across its pelt, combining with its stripes to form jagged, shifting patterns. It stretched itself out by the lion. Claws broke out of its paws, then retracted.

Finally, there was the bear; a great, lumbering mass, snuffling loudly in the quiet night. Its muzzle was paler than its dark fur, an off-white smudge that lent definition to an otherwise featureless silhouette. Something very ancient woke in Jack – a deep fear of the great shape that loomed before him, older than darkness. It joined the other two.

The silhouettes of all three exuded menace. They were in full offensive mode. Jack wondered how they might have looked when they'd been manifesting in friendlier ways. He'd often visited friends who lived in similar blocks; watched the defence creatures play with the children in their gardens. Bears were giant, cuddly creatures, lions very proud but more than a little lazy, tigers whip-smart jokers. Each of these animals would no doubt have a cartoon self too, gathering virtual dust in silent digital vaults, ready to look harmless for children it would never again guard.

[Good,] said Fist. [They're not attacking. The confusion protocols are working. And now ...]

Feral breath hissed to Jack's left and right. Fist had summoned his panthers. They rose out of the darkness, spinning up from memory into sleek, silent shapes. Fear spat adrenaline into Jack's blood.

[I've refined them a bit,] Fist commented, not noticing. He'd stripped the four big cats back to near abstraction. They were little more than brushstrokes in the air, prowling shapes spun out of fluid lines that were darker than the night. A shimmer, and there was a leg; an eye was a flash of red, a tooth was a white gash. Tails swished. There was a snarl and a hiss, and they moved into the glade.

Jack flinched. [They still spook me,] he admitted.

[I might be able to do something about that, once I've absorbed this lot,] replied Fist.

[I'd like that.]

The three guardian animals stayed still as the puppet's ghost creatures prowled around them. The trio had lost animation, now seeming more like still images.

[I'm cracking them,] crowed Fist.

[You've got about a minute left.]

[We'll be fine!]

A panther leapt at the bear and vanished into it. The bear shape shimmered and disappeared. Then Fist took the tiger and the lion. One last cat remained, prowling watchfully around the glade.

[They're ours now?]

[Oh yes. They work for me.]

[No extra strain on your processors?]

[No – they're still running on the block servers. I've just rebuilt their command structures so they listen to me too. A bit more tweaking and they'll be able to manifest anywhere. We can summon them whenever we need them.]

[No chance we'll be spotted?]

[Nope. I've put datablocks up to mask anything unusual. And ...] Fist was silent for a moment. In the distance, a virtual dog howled at an imagined moon. [Got it. Lots of choice in the block's visual templates. When I've got a moment, I can change how the panthers look. No more big cats to scare you!]

[Thank you,] said Jack. [And there's one more thing we need to do before Ato gets back. We have to talk to Harry.]

[That psychopath? You're crazy.]

[We need to understand more about him. It could help us break Yamata.]

[But they're the same as each other. What if he's on her side?]

[You saw how they went at each other. There's not much chance of that.]

265

[Hmmph.]

[Can you summon him?]

[Suppose so.]

[Then do it.]

Fist grumbled as he complied.

'You call – and here I am!' smiled Harry, strolling casually out of the darkness. He was wearing a suit and a long, dark overcoat. Fist snapped into full defensive mode. The panthers reappeared, ringing Harry. A harsh, low growl rolled across the clearing. 'Lovely pets,' he said, stretching a hand out to one of them. It snapped at him. Harry took a step back, pulled a handkerchief out of his pocket and wrapped it tightly round a bloody finger. 'Sharp teeth, eh?'

[He's contained,] Fist told Jack. [It's safe to talk.]

'Hello Jack,' said Harry. 'Good to see you.'

[Scanning him too?]

[Yes, Jack. Now I know what I'm looking for – human mind, Totality architecture, identical to Yamata.]

'Of course I'm happy to be scanned, Jack. After all, we're old friends, aren't we? Nothing to hide.'

'You've hidden quite a lot, Harry. It's about time you were straight with us.'

'I've always been as straight with you as you have with me.' That seemed barbed, but Harry's expression was entirely innocent. Jack let it pass. 'Besides,' continued Harry, 'we both want the same thing – Kingdom's head on a plate, and Yamata's with it.'

'Bullshit, Harry. We know what you are now. It's very different from what you pretend to be.'

Harry was suddenly holding a cigar and a box of matches. Each panther took a pace towards him. 'No need to worry,' he said reassuringly. 'This really is just a smoke. Or rather, the memory of one.' A little flame from a match suckled at the cigar's tip, chasing shadows from his face.

'But you're not the memory of Harry, are you?' replied Jack. 'You were never a fetch. You're something very different.'

[I can take him, Jack. Let me try!]

[Hush, Fist. Not now. Not if we don't have to.]

'That's right, I'm not a memory. I am Harry. Always have been,

266

always will be. I really shouldn't be here, you know. But I'm a very lucky man.'

'What happened to you?' said Jack.

'Can you get rid of this lot?' Harry indicated the panthers. 'So much easier to talk when you're not surrounded.'

'The muscle stays,' Fist spat.

Harry took a long, slow draw on his cigar. The end of it flared orange-pink. The rich smell of smoke filled the glade.

[Very impressive simulation,] commented Fist. [Serious processor power behind it.]

[We're definitely safe?]

[Completely.]

'All right if I sit?' wondered Harry. Jack looked to Fist, who nodded. 'Taking orders from a puppet?' he asked, with a look Jack chose to ignore. A chair appeared and he sat down, carefully pulling his overcoat out from beneath him.

[Now he's just showing off,] said Fist.

'So, what do you want to know?' asked Harry.

'The truth,' Jack replied.

Harry sighed. 'All right, Jack. I'm not a fetch. Yamata came for me when I reopened the Penderville case. By then she wasn't human any more. She burned my mind into a Totality hive, then tossed my body away and let everyone think I'd been shot by some Docklands lowlife.'

'Why did she bother doing that?'

'I was straight with you about the Penderville case. She wanted to stop me finding out why she'd killed him. And that gave her an opportunity to seize all the knowledge I had.' Harry tapped his forehead. 'In here. And directly integrate it with her own systems. Of course, to do that she had to turn me into something just like her.'

'That would take a lot of hardware. Where did she hide it all?'

'I was sitting around somewhere in Homelands. Yamata dug through my mind, pulled out everything I knew about InSec. That meant she was ahead of them every step of the way. They couldn't touch her. And she used everything I knew on Docklands crime syndicates, too. All my old contacts work for her now.'

'What was she doing?'

'She was behind the terrorist attacks on Station. I should have realised she'd be working for Kingdom. He could blame them on the Totality, and use them to take down Grey and anyone else who was anti-war. Helped him keep the Soft War going too. Classic gambler, keeps on losing, always takes another punt and hopes he'll win it all back.'

'For fuck's sake, Harry. Why didn't you tell me this before?'

'My investigation, Jack, like I always told you. You knew what you needed to know to get the job done. And I've never trusted that puppet of yours.'

'YOU? Worried about trusting ME? Fucking hell, Devlin,' snarled Fist.

'So they were false flag attacks,' Jack said. 'But you helped them happen. Why didn't you fight back? Refuse to work with Yamata?'

'She never woke me up enough. It was like living in a dream. She'd use a bit of me here, a bit of me there. But I began to realise that the dream was real. After the Panther Czar fiasco you were sent out-system, but I was only moved across departments. I always worried that someone would make my lack of involvement more permanent. So, I put some countermeasures in place in case some-one killed me or tried to screw with me once I was dead. They woke up – and they started to wake me up, too.'

'What then?'

'Well, most of me was usually shut away from her. I didn't know exactly how powerful she was. I certainly wasn't in a position to take her on directly.'

'You did a pretty good job the other day,' Fist said.

'I was ready for her. And I've been rebuilding myself. It's been quite a few years since I escaped. Besides, back then, I had other problems. I needed to get the Totality hardware she was storing me on away from her.'

'You could have just jumped into the Coffin Drives.'

'No way. Once you're on them, you're trapped. Besides, I quite like running on Totality hardware. You should feel it, your mind just sings. So I had to move myself physically. Easily done, she didn't know how awake I really was. A little bit of looking around, some alterations to a transport docket, smoke and mirrors around the document trail, and Bob's your uncle! I was out of my little Homelands warehouse and free.'

'And you've done nothing to try and stop her.'

'Too risky. Haven't found anyone I could trust. And besides, even if I did manage to go public, who'd believe me? A ghost, accusing the Pantheon of staging a war for their own ends. At best, I'd get found and wiped. At worst, I'd go straight back to being Yamata's bitch.'

'So where are you now?'

'Oh, that would be telling, wouldn't it? Somewhere safe from her – and from your contacts, too. The Pantheon doesn't like competition much, you know.'

[Off-Station,] commented Fist. [Lag time says he's still in Earth orbit, bouncing his signal off comms satellites.]

'You make getting away sound very easy,' said Jack.

'Yamata was overconfident. That made her easy to fool. She's not any more. That's why you need my help.'

'You've got to be kidding.'

'I know how she works. I am what she is. I can help you crack her defences. I threw her out of TrueShield, and I chased her back to the heart of Kingdom. I can get your puppet deep inside her.'

'We can already do that, Harry.'

'Fist's good, but he's sloppy.'

'Fuck you too,' Fist snapped back.

'That's a sore point, isn't it? If I hadn't been at TrueShield, she'd have fried both of you. You need me, Jack. You and your little helper both.'

'They caught us off guard. They won't do that again.'

Harry chuckled. 'Well, I admire your confidence at any rate.'

Fist became a shimmer in the air, floating before Harry, his still lightly charred face enraged. His voice was quiet and deliberately paced, control lending it menace.

'You led us right into her house, and you didn't tell us what we'd find there, or who she was working for.'

'I didn't know she'd be there in such force. And I only found out it was Kingdom when you did. She always kept her patron so well hidden.'

'Listen to me,' Fist told him. 'I've been cracking systems like you – and her – since the day I was born. I was built to assess them, break into them and then destroy them. There's nothing you can't tell me about what they are, and how they work, and how to kill them. I'm going to find the deepest part of her mind, and then I'm going to blow it. And if I get the chance, I'm going to do the same thing to you.'

Harry laughed again. 'Little puppet,' he said. 'She's been rebuilding herself for almost as long. She's never been Totality, and she's certainly not human any more. And even if you do get past her, well, there's our friend up there' – he waved up towards Heaven – 'her own puppet master. Are you ready for a fight with Kingdom, puppet? Are you punching at that weight yet, little Fist?'

[Don't boast,] warned Jack. [We can't let anyone know what you can really do.]

Fist said nothing, shaking visibly with the effort of restraining himself. Harry chuckled. Jack felt Fist's rage burn. Then – at a deeper level – attack systems rose into life, casting long, savage shadows into his conscious mind. But they didn't launch as smoothly as they'd once done. As they booted up, there was a faint, broken grinding and the sharp reek of burnt plastic.

[Don't, Fist. He's not worth it.]

[I'll crack him like a fucking nut.]

[We've got more important battles to fight.]

'I'm sure your master is warning you not to attack me. It's very sensible advice. I'm an old dog, but I could still surprise you both. And as for you' – Harry pointed at Jack – 'you should know better than to be so confident. It's a rookie mistake, and you haven't been a rookie for a long time.'

'I don't trust you any more, Harry.'

'Very wise. But for now remember this – you will need my help. And if you want to summon me, call my name, and you'll be able to sit back and watch me kill Aud Yamata for you. And I might even have a crack at Kingdom, too. Call it a hostile takeover if you like, I could run things far better than that cunt.'

'You're not coming through me again,' snarled Fist.

Harry laughed, and was gone.

Ato returned an hour or so later. Jack and Fist were sat together in the middle of the glade, watching the night. Black lines carved the air around them, sometimes making abstract shapes, sometimes rolling together to hint at prowling lions and tigers and bears. 'Oh,' said Fist, noticing Ato. 'It's you. We're ready for our spacewalk.'

'And Grandpa's got good news,' replied Ato. 'Mr Stabs is expecting you.' Fist jigged around with glee. Jack stood up. 'We'll get you some food,' Ato continued, 'then I'll take you to the door to Homeland's outer skin and you'll fly straight to Heaven.'

Chapter 40

Jack walked in his vacuum suit, the sound of his own breathing loud in his ears. Homelands' metal skin curved away and down to his left and right. Ahead, a great pillar broke out of it and soared up to Heaven. Beyond it there was a hundred million miles of nothing, then the silent, roaring sun. Its shadow protected him from the sun's blaze. Fist floated next to him. He sported a vacuum suit too – an affectation, as of course he had no need of one. A little black bow-tie sat jauntily just below its visor. It was simpler to model than his normal clothing, so it was fresh and uncharred.

Fist broke the near-silence. [Do you know,] he said, sounding a little surprised, [I actually enjoyed sorting out the kids.]

Remembering what he'd done to Akhmatov, Jack had asked if the children wanted to be made permanently invisible. They'd all been very excited. Even Fred lifted himself out of his sulk. 'Do you understand what he's saying?' Ato enthused. 'We'll be children forever. You can go out again, Fred!' Fist touched them one by one, dropping his sweathead code into their already customised weave-ware. He'd built an on/off switch into it, just for them. Fred tried hard to conceal his excitement. Jack imagined him running through the streets and malls of Homelands, joyously untouchable.

[And now I can't wait to see Stabs again. Let's go!]

[We need to talk to a couple of people first.]

[Hmph,] grumbled Fist, then: [Going into your weavespace through an external antenna, we're pretty much untraceable. We could be anywhere in Earth orbit. Right, you're go.]

They were standing in a moonlit garden, by a statue of Ifor. 'Get me Lestak,' Jack commanded.

'Creating a contact,' Fist replied. An uncarved stone block appeared next to Ifor's statue. 'Searching for her address,' he continued, then after a moment: 'Meshing. She's accepting you.'

Lestak's avatar emerged from the stone like meaning from a dead language. Jack reached out and took her hard hand. It softened into flesh. She snatched it away and slapped his face. The pain was no less real for being simulated.

'You've caused me far too much trouble, Forster.'

'I don't have much time.'

'None at all – I'm tracing you.'

'No. Not where I am.'

Lestak was quiet for a moment. Jack imagined her listening to a technician, hastily ordered to find him as she reached to accept his call.

'Oh, for gods' sake, Jack.'

'I've seen what lies beneath your world, and now I've stepped outside it.'

'Don't be so melodramatic.'

'I've met the children of the terrorists.'

'I don't know what you're talking about.'

Jack laughed. 'Maybe you don't, at that.' He turned to Fist. 'Encrypt us. And share the code with Lestak.'

'On it.' Fist trotted over to stand next to Jack. 'Is Issie there?' he asked. 'I need to run this through her.'

She shimmered into being. A white silk scarf hid her skull head. Wisps of hair escaped its top. 'Hello, Fist!' she said. 'Oo! You're somewhere really interesting. I wish I could travel like you do. Are we going to play again?'

Fist rattled off a string of numbers and letters.

'Oh' she said, sounding disappointed. 'No, we're not.'

Lestak's image shimmered briefly, and then returned to apparent wholeness.

'No one else can hear us now,' Jack told her.

'What are you hoping to achieve?'

'It's Kingdom. He's been running Yamata. She was behind the terrorist attacks on Station. He had me sent to war because I was getting too close to uncovering her. And Yamata – she's something new now. A human mind, running on a Totality platform.'

'That's impossible. No one can ...'

'Kingdom's done it. That's what Harry Devlin is, too.'

273

'Harry's dead and his fetch is broken.'

'He's still around. Yamata used his knowledge to stay one step ahead of InSec, until he escaped.'

'You have proof of all this?'

'No. But I'll find it. I'm going after Yamata. Harry chased her back to Heaven. That's where her servers are.'

'You'll never get in there.'

'I already have a way. I trust you, Lestak. I don't think you're a part of all this. You can't go after them yourself, they'd probably just kill you. Just watch Kingdom, watch him close. I'm going to give you a chance to break him and I want you to take it.'

'You're mad, Jack. Nobody can topple the gods.'

Jack thought of dead snowflakes.

'I've killed angels by the score. It's not a big step up.'

[We're getting some Pantheon interest,] Fist warned. [It's Kingdom.]

'I'm going now,' said Jack. 'Goodbye, Lestak. Don't let me down.' She was about to say something, and then she was a statue again. 'How close did he get to us, Fist?'

'He knew we were there. Wouldn't have known who we were, what we were saying.'

'Good. Now for Ifor.'

The mind shimmered into being before them. 'Jack,' he began. 'Well. You have been causing me all sorts of trouble. We talked of discretion? That flash mob has posted your image all over the weave. It has become a fashion to imitate your dress, and now every single one of your groupies pretends to adore the Totality. We cannot move for Forster fans mobbing us.'

'I'm sorry, Ifor. I didn't know that East would play it that way.'

'It is difficult for us. Our negotiations with your Pantheon have reached a delicate stage.'

'Kingdom blocking you?'

'No, he's been surprisingly conciliatory.'

'That's his public stance.' Jack quickly explained the situation. 'I'm going to move against Yamata and then Kingdom. You're in negotiation so you can't be seen to do it. Lestak's hamstrung.'

'Where are you now?'

274

'Close to them both. That's all you need to know. I'm going to get proof of their crimes and share it with the world.'

'If you are captured or exposed without that proof, we will deny all knowledge of you.'

'Wanker,' said Fist.

Ifor chuckled. 'Realpolitik, my friend. But perhaps that is too sweeping. If I can help you out of trouble, I will. Call for me, little puppet, and I will do my best to come.'

'You're still a wanker.'

Jack patted Fist's helmet. 'Always the charmer,' he said. 'But we've got to be going. Spread the word, Ifor: it's Kingdom. He's been running Yamata, and we think she's behind the terrorist attacks.'

'Spread the word? Now that I know, we all know.'

'And I've got a favour to ask. Something personal.'

'What do you want us to do?'

'What we're about to do – well, it's risky. If we don't make it back, could you go to my parents, and tell them about the last few days – about everything we've found out?'

'I will, Jack.'

'My father doesn't like the Totality.'

'We'll find a way of reaching him. And we'll talk to your mother.'

'You'll need his permission for that.'

'Perhaps.'

When Ifor had gone, Fist turned to Jack. 'Now for Heaven and Mr Stabs!'

'There's one more thing. Remember we talked about Andrea?'

'Ah, yes. I could have done with a bit more time. But this should do the trick.'

Fist put his hand out and a little feather appeared. It glowed with shifting colours and patterns. Jack took it from him. Its barbs brushed against themselves, glitching out soft musical notes.

'Why a feather?' asked Jack.

'To unclip her wings. Once she's installed it, nobody will be able to roll her back, or send her back to the Coffin Drives if she doesn't want to go. She'll be free, just like you wanted.'

'Very poetic.'

There was paper in Jack's hand. He remembered the notes he'd exchanged with Andrea, such a short time ago. So much had changed since then.

'I understand everything now,' he wrote, 'and I'm going to try and find a resolution. I'm so glad I found you again. I hope the feather helps you fly. Oh, and Harry lied to us both about what he is.' Jack summarised what Harry had told them in the garden, then simply ended with: 'I love you.' An envelope appeared. He addressed it, tucked the feather into it and carefully sealed it.

'Consequences, Jack,' warned Fist. 'If the Pantheon ever trace that back to us we're in big trouble. Almost as bad as killing one of them. It rewrites some pretty basic fetch code.'

'Will they?'

'I've been very careful. It's locked to Andrea only. If it's just running on her, it'll be pretty much invisible. And I've dropped in some camouflage for her. She'll be able to make it look like she's been rolled back or sent down. If she's careful, nobody will ever find her out.'

'Good,' said Jack. 'Send.' A flash of light and it was done. 'Now we're ready to go.'

Fist let the garden fall away. Once again they stood outside Homelands, shaded by a pillar of Heaven. 'Well,' he said, looking up at it, 'time for an ascension. All security's in place, and you're going to love what I've done with our beasts. No more panthers.'

He clapped his gloved hands together. Ghosts of animals flitted into being, barely visible against the dark. Jack looked for different shapes, different sizes; for lions and tigers and bears. But they were all the same kind of creature.

There were sharp heads like wedges, dark pointed ears pricking up, lean and muscular bodies made to run and catch and bring down prey. Their skin was pitch-black. Eyes and mouths flamed in the darkness. Burning spit dropped away from tongues of fire. Flames danced around them, a basic fact of their being, scudding across their bodies, dancing down legs, burning out in footprint trails behind them. They milled around sniffing at each other, welcoming themselves into existence.

'Dogs,' breathed Jack.

'Not just dogs – hounds. Man's best friend,' replied Fist proudly.

'Nothing to be scared of. Unless it's you they're hunting. They're a pack, they'll take commands.'

Jack snapped: 'To me!' The pack's response was immediate. Seven heads snapped towards him. Seven pairs of burning eyes met his, all attention, all engagement. They jostled closer, flame tongues lolling in open mouths. A wave of heat rolled across him.

'I've been burned,' said Fist, 'and so they burn. My weakness is my strength!'

'Back away,' ordered Jack. 'Walk around us.'

The dogs pulled back and resumed their prowling. Their footfalls sparked fire, creating a soft circle of flame.

'Now I know what we're up against, I've tweaked their defences,' Fist explained. 'Totalityware won't touch them.'

'Excellent,' smiled Jack. 'Let's go.'

He leapt up and squeezed a little propellant out. All of a sudden he was flying in space, his shadow hounds leaping with him through the darkness.

For a long time afterwards he would remember that moment as one of perfection; blazing through night, certain in purpose, ready to unleash his vengeance on Heaven. He wondered if he should have Fist twine him in fire too, a rebel returned to break the rule of his makers. Perhaps he should fly on great burning wings.

He let a little more air squirt out, correcting a drift out of the pillar's shadow. He thought of the sun. It at once nourished humanity and was completely unaware of it. Here was a god he could worship, he realised, one that gave unstintingly without demanding anything in return. He wondered what it would mean to enter a state of such disinterested grace, to bless without possibility of control or reward. In his mind, the sun roared.

That imagined sound made him realise that his pack was silent. [Let me hear you,] he thought. Pants and growls burst across him. One dog howled and one by one the others joined it. Each shifted in and out of phase with the others, harsh dissonances and subtle harmonies rising and filling in the night. As the hounds roared for their master, fire fell backwards from their gaping mouths, fading into the night. Burning feet found firm purchase in nothing. They were closing in on Heaven. Soon they would storm its gates.

[Where did Grey say Mr Stabs would meet us?]

[He was very precise. It's an access door just where the pillar hits Heaven.]

[Perfect. Will anyone spot the pack?]

[They're ghosts until they're on you – if you can see them, you're already fucked.]

Heaven raced towards them. Jack touched the void with his steer-jets, spinning round and slowing. When he touched down he landed gently but firmly, magnetic soles clamping him to the ground. One by one, the dogs landed around him. Looking back, he saw that the trail of fire they had burned into the night was falling away to nothing.

[You are an artist sometimes, Fist.]

[Everything I am comes from you.]

For a moment Jack mistrusted the compliment, but he could find no ambiguity or hostile intent in it. Fist hovered in front of him, slowly rotating to bring himself right way up. The pack sniffed around them, exploring new territory.

[Have they found anything?] asked Jack.

[They've neutralised some basic security systems. Nothing else here. I don't think the gods ever expected anyone to get in this way.]

[Complacent as ever. Where's the door?]

[Over there.] Fist pointed at the pillar. An airlock started to open. Pale light leapt out of it. [You've waited long enough,] Jack told him. [Let's go see Mr Stabs.]

Chapter 41

'Stabsy!'

Fist rushed to embrace Mr Stabs, his spacesuit disappearing as he reached and clutched him. Mr Stabs jerked an arm up, patted at Fist, and then let it fall. His awkward movement ended the hug.

'I'm sorry to see you've been hurt,' he said, speaking with a grating singsong quality. Alert eyes peered out of holes raggedly cut in a baggy head mask, hand-stitched from white fabric. He was dressed in dirty blue overalls and heavy work boots. One shoulder was pulled up slightly higher than the other. But for a slight stoop, he would have been taller than Jack.

'I've had worse,' shrugged Fist. He stepped back and looked up at Mr Stabs. 'We're going to have such fun!' he said, his joy suddenly sounding a little forced. The airlock hissed air back into space, reminding them where they'd come from and why they were there.

'We have business to attend to,' Mr Stabs responded coldly. He turned to Jack and jerked out an arm. Every part of him shuddered. Jack shook his hand, half-expecting to squeeze hardwood, but there was only soft flesh and a weak, uncertain grip. He was glad not to see Tiamat's face animated by another mind. He imagined how his own would look when fully possessed by Fist and shuddered.

'It was very brave of Grey, returning to Heaven to ask for my help,' Mr Stabs told him. 'Any one of the Pantheon could have picked up his presence. If Kingdom found out how active he still was, he'd crush him like—'

His hand came up. His fingers moved jerkily, not quite pinching together.

'Fortunately for us, he hasn't,' said Jack. 'And Grey said you'd help us.'

'I can get you into Kingdom's compound. The rest is up to you.'

'Then let's get over there.'

279

'It's night here. You go first thing tomorrow. Until then, it's back home to sleep. Follow me.'

Mr Stabs lurched, wheeled round, and began to walk. He swayed left and right with each pace, but managed to move with reasonable speed. His head jerked back towards them. 'Come on!' he shouted, 'I don't want to be missed.'

[He used to be the coolest of the cool,] said Fist, his voice hushed with pain.

[Him and Tiamat both.]

[And now look at him.]

The journey took an hour or so. They followed Mr Stabs down indistinguishable corridors, up and down ladders, in and out of lifts. Every so often, there was a security door. Mr Stabs had a card he'd pull out to open it.

'Can't you just tell the doors to open?' Fist asked him.

'Kingdom burnt out my weave implants before he handed me over to Grey.'

'No weave! But what do you do with yourself?'

'Feed my plants. Visit other gardeners.'

[Fuck,] said Fist quietly to himself. [No parties.]

Jack said nothing. Meeting Mr Stabs had been a shock for both of them. He wanted to let its impact settle before talking it through with Fist.

They found themselves walking through a vast subterranean forcing house. Bright lights blazed down on rows of vegetables. Sprays hissed water. The air had a humid, tropical feel, heavy with the scent of growth.

Jack breathed in deeply. 'I've never smelt anything like it.'

'My underworld,' Mr Stabs replied proudly. 'And now we climb into Heaven.' He was standing at the foot of a short ladder, leading up to a metal hatch. 'I'll go first. Got to check nobody's around.' He moved up the ladder like a broken spider, then disappeared through the hatch. A moment later his white, covered head reappeared. 'OK. Come up.'

Jack imagined himself wearing a similar hood, Fist trapped behind it. Fist snapped him out of his reverie. 'Come on. What are you waiting for?'

Climbing up, they found themselves in a small wooden shed. Half of it was a living area – there was a low bed, a shower cubicle and a sofa. The rest was packed with gardening equipment. A spade and fork leant against the wall. There was a workbench, half-covered with a clutter of hand tools. A lawnmower's metal entrails spilling across the floor. Wisps of curtain covered a window.

Mr Stabs shuddered over to it and, lifting the material, peered outside.

'All's quiet,' he confirmed.

'Where are we?' Jack asked him.

'Grey's corporate space. You'll see it tomorrow. For now, keep away from the window. I'll make you up a bed.' He rolled a sleeping mat out by the dead lawnmower and dropped some bundled sheets on to it. 'Best we sleep now.'

'Stabs,' said Fist, 'there's so much we've got to talk about. The old days—'

'No,' said Mr Stabs, pain evident even through the squeak of his voice. 'I don't like to think about that.' He moved to stand by his bed, leant forwards at the hip, bent backwards at the knee and collapsed into a rigid sitting position. His mask leapt up and fell back, for a moment revealing Tiamat's familiar chin and lips. His mouth was turned down.

But Fist persisted. 'What about the future? You and me, we're the only puppets left. We've got to stick together.'

'You're only here because Grey told me what Kingdom's done, what he might use you to do and what you're going to do to him. I didn't want to see you.'

'What?'

Mr Stabs leant backwards and pulled his legs up on to the bed, then swivelled awkwardly round and collapsed back into a lying position.

'You and Jack. You remind me so much of how I was with David. So arrogant. Then I spent months alone with him, deep in space. I watched him lose hope. I was inside him when he died. I am what I am now because of that. It changes your perspective.' His head jolted round to face his guests. 'You're lucky, Hugo. It won't be as hard for you. You've both got something very important to do. You'll either succeed or die together. And if you do defeat Kingdom, you'll have the memory of one last, shared triumph to hold on to when Jack's gone. I only have pain and emptiness in my past. So we'll sleep, and in the morning you'll go, and I won't see you again.'

'Stabsy—'

'I'm going to switch the light off. Then I take off my mask.'

[There's so much I want to talk to him about!]

[Hush, Fist. You heard what he said.]

Jack lay down on the sleep mat, and pulled the sheets over him. There was a click, and the bare light bulb that lit the shed flicked off.

'G'night Stabsy,' chirped Fist hopefully. There was a rustling from Stabs' corner of the room, but no reply.

[He's so different.]

[He's been through a lot. It changes people.]

[Will I change like that, once I'm real?]

[You're real now. And you've changed, too – a little over the last few years, more over the last few weeks. Coming to life – well, that's just one more change.]

Jack felt Fist tremble.

[I'll feel it, won't I? When you go.]

[That's what Mr Stabs says.]

[I'm so sorry, Jack. I wish I didn't have to do it.]

[You see, Fist? You have changed.]

[It seems like such a waste. You'll die – and I'll end up like him.]

[It won't be as hard on you as it was on him. You'll have a lot more good things to remember.]

A series of hiccupping squeaks and sniffles ran through Jack's mind.

[It's such a waste, Jack! All this time waiting – and you'll be gone – and I'll just be a fucking freak!]

[Hush, Fist. Can you manifest?]

[I don't want him to see me like this.]

[You can show yourself just to me, can't you?]

[I suppose.]

Jack was lying on his side. He stretched out his arms and felt a sudden density come into being between them. Fist clutched at his chest, little fists snatching at his shirt. [It's all so fucking pointless!] he wailed. [Is this all there is? For me? For us?]

282

[Yes,] replied Jack, [it is.]

He wrapped his arms around Fist, pulling him in tight. Fist hiccupped grief, his wooden face burrowing into Jack's chest. Jack felt a wetness against him. Fist was simulating tears.

[It is,] continued Jack, [and we'll do what we've always done. We'll make the best of it together. And when I've gone you'll remember me, and that'll help you make the best of it then, too.]

Fist said nothing. Jack cradled his head, gently stroking it, careful to show no emotion but care.

[This is what being human means, Fist. It's not just about being free. It's about feeling sad and weak and lost, and losing people you love, and watching moments that were perfect slip away from you forever. That's not a bad thing. The only reason it hurts is because they were so wonderful in the first place. We meet each other then part, and we're sad, and we console ourselves with all that's still to come.]

[You won't even be in the Coffin Drives!]

Emotion had completely taken over Fist now. His sadness tore at Jack.

[I know,] he replied. [But that might be a good thing. You've seen how people here refuse to let the past go. You won't be able to do that. You'll have to find new, real things to make you happy. You won't be able to hide in yesterday.]

[But I don't want to lose you!]

[You won't lose me. You'll still remember me. And you come from me. As long as you're alive, there'll always be a part of me around.]

[I'll be so lonely! Stabs won't speak to me! And those puppet embryos are bullshit, there's never going to be anyone else like me!]

Fist sobbed incoherently into Jack's chest, until finally his weeping subsided. He settled into a shattered sleep still nestled in Jack's arms.

[Mr Stabs might keep you company after all,] Jack whispered, knowing Fist wouldn't hear. [You could grow vegetables together. You might even be able to help him leave the past behind, too. Or maybe those puppet embryos really did survive.] But even the thought of them made Jack uneasy. He gave Fist's tiny wooden hand a final squeeze. [But for now – dispel.] Fist vanished. A deep, exhausted sleep soon overcame Jack, too.

The next morning, Fist was determinedly cheerful. He went bounding over to the window, looked out, and then came rushing back. Mr Stabs was standing at the door, already dressed in his white mask and a pair of underpants.

'So, Stabsy – what's the plan?'

Mr Stabs held his blue overalls out. 'Put these on, pretend you're me, make your way to Kingdom's headquarters. You can duplicate my weave tags, can't you?

'No problem,' nodded Fist. 'Will they just let us in?'

'You'll be delivering seed potatoes. Mine are very much admired. They don't blight easily. That will get you to their gardeners. Then it's over to you.'

Jack pulled on the overalls. They fitted tolerably well, looking as shapeless and ragged on him as they had on Mr Stabs.

'Now for the tags,' said Mr Stabs. 'Fist, I've opened myself up to you.'

Fist closed his eyes for a moment. 'I've copied them over,' he nodded. 'We're you now, Stabsy.'

'Good,' replied Mr Stabs. 'One last thing. Everyone's used to this mask. You'll have to take it. Are you ready?'

'Yes,' said Jack.

'Wait,' Fist cut in. 'What if we get caught? And they find out you helped us?'

'This is the only way you can get close enough to Kingdom to stop him. You'll just have to make sure you come back safely.' There was a sad hopelessness to his voice. 'And if you don't, well, I've lived long enough.'

Then he pulled his mask off.

His face was a frozen grimace, a rictus grin snapping his mouth up and pulling the flesh of his cheeks tight. His eyes were wide open, as if he'd just been surprised. His eyebrows arced upwards, pulled into semicircles by a permanently tight forehead.

'I don't have very many choices,' he explained. The smile that distorted his face reversed, frowning downwards. His expressions were so tight that the corners of his mouth and the skin around his eyes and temples were permanently bruised.

'I can look bored too. That's the most comfortable.'

His face settled into a third configuration, his mouth a flat slit, his eyes marginally less manic than they'd been before.

[It's so cruel,] said Fist. [They haven't upgraded his facial expression software for his new face.]

'Is it always like that?' Jack couldn't resist asking.

'Always. I'm only a lodger in this body. I've never felt like I owned it.'

'No hope of an upgrade?'

'None. It's why I live in this little shed, not the staff accommodation blocks. They made us puppets to reassure children. But now I'm flesh I scare their adults. My face is too obviously a simplification. The implications of that are very unpleasant for them. They live in a profoundly reduced world. I remind them of that, and it makes them afraid.'

'You've become quite the philosopher,' said Fist.

'It's only what I see. And now to point you in the right direction. Put the mask on, Jack, and let Fist ride you. There are some dangerous people out there. You've got to do everything you can to convince them you're me.'

Chapter 42

The mask was subtly crafted. From the inside, it was transparent. Jack could feel it on him, pulling back against his mouth when he breathed in, puffing out as he exhaled, and he could smell the stale tang of Mr Stabs' sweat, but he couldn't see it.

[More sophisticated than it looks,] he said.

[Very impressive,] replied Fist.

[Careful!]

Distracted for a moment, Fist forgot to let Jack's foot drop down and complete a pace. Jack nearly overbalanced. He swayed for a moment, arms waving, then regained his balance and took another step.

[I'm sorry,] said an audibly frustrated Fist. [I've never walked on bumpy ground before.]

Mr Stabs' shed was surrounded by about a hundred square metres of carefully tended vegetable patches. A line of willow trees obscured the landscape beyond. A few hundred metres above, Heaven's glass ceiling burned with sunlight. Jack thought of Kingdom and Yamata, and wondered if they suspected how close he was to them, how much closer he would soon be.

Another jolt broke his reverie. Fist had let one foot slip off the side of the path, nearly twisting his ankle.

[Be careful! We won't get anywhere if we can't walk!]

Fist was concentrating too hard to reply. He was walking Jack's body towards a small garage, just inside the treeline. 'That's where I keep my buggy,' Mr Stabs had told them. He'd given Jack a bag of seed potatoes. 'This is what you'll be delivering. I've talked to Kingdom's people. They're expecting you.' Then he gave him a handgun and several clips of bullets.

The garage opened when Fist punched in the combination. He only had to try five times.

[You know, I'm not sure I trust you in this buggy,] Jack told him.

[Now you know what watching you pilot a spaceship feels like.]

The buggy had two seats and a large open boot. Its paintwork was scratched, its metalwork heavily dented. One of its front lights had been smashed. Fist shrugged the potato bag into the boot, unplugged the buggy from its charger and clambered into the driver's seat. The steering wheel and control pedals were all oversized.

[That should make it easier,] said Fist cheerfully, ramming down the accelerator.

They bounced out of the garage and straight off the road, cannoning between two willow trees. Branches snatched at Jack, almost pulling him from his seat.

[FOR FUCK'S SAKE, FIST!]

A small stream hurtled towards them. Fist threw the steering wheel around and kicked down on the brake pedal. The buggy shuddered to a halt.

[Perhaps you should let me drive,] said Jack. [Nobody'll notice that I'm in charge when we're moving.]

[How does he *do* this?] wondered Fist.

[Judging by the state of the buggy, it took a lot of practice.]

[Oh. Right.]

Fist slipped out of Jack's motor centres. Jack slumped then recovered himself. He reached out for the steering wheel and the accelerator pedal.

[Let's go.]

[Wait a moment,] said Fist. [Look over there. It's Grey's home.]

The stream ended in a small lake. Beyond it stood a campus of rectangular buildings. Each was all window, five storeys high. They caught and reflected a pastoral kaleidoscope of colours – greens and blues from the countryside around them, a dazzling gold-white from the sky above.

[Not bad,] said Fist. Even Jack was slightly awed. This was the corporate home of Grey. It housed the fundamental processes that defined his patron's consciousness. Jack wondered how the campus had looked when Grey had been fully engaged with the world.

'Actually, not too different to now,' said Grey.

'Shit!' Fist exploded.

'Maybe a few more lights on,' Grey continued, ignoring him. 'Some more people here and there, everything a bit more purposeful.'

'What the fuck are you doing here?' snapped Jack.

'This was my home,' Grey replied casually. 'Where else would I be? Besides, there's a ghoulish fascination watching the dead parts of myself.'

'Kingdom'll kill you completely if he sees you here.'

'I've become quite good at hiding. I saw all this coming a long time ago. I was prepared. Not like my staff, sadly.'

'What do you mean?'

'The centre did not hold. My board sleeps. Everyone who could transferred away from here. The ones that are left – well, it broke them. Look at that lot, for example.'

Grey pointed at a large pair of doors that led into an atrium. A small group pushed its way through them, carrying something long, flat and brightly coloured.

'A stretcher,' Jack noted. 'Someone's been hurt.'

'Oh no,' Grey told him. 'They're missing me. They're trying to do something about it.'

The group walked the heavy stretcher down to the edge of the closest lake. There was a distant sound of chanting, thin voices losing themselves in the empty air.

'I wish they knew I could hear them,' sighed Grey. 'I can't ever show myself, though. Far too risky.'

'What are they doing?'

They manhandled the stretcher into a small boat and stood back. Brightly coloured feathers waved in the air.

'Is that someone tied to it?'

'I can't see. And I can't get any closer to them, Kingdom would spot me.'

One of the small figures held her arms up in the air. The rest knelt round her and chanted. She threw something into the boat, then kicked it away from the shore. It drifted out across the lake. The group roared as flames leapt out of it.

'I hope it was just a dummy,' said Grey sadly.

'I'm surprised you care,' Jack told him.

'Oh, I do. I've just accepted there's not much I can do. That's what you're here for.'

'I'm not trying to help you.'

'No. But you're not just out for yourself, are you? All those people need you. They need someone to show them a way out of this mess.'

'Why isn't the Pantheon helping them?'

'Kingdom won't let any of the others in. He livecasts all this to warn people what happens without gods.'

The small figures stripped and started rolling around in the grass, clumped together in groups of two, three and even four.

'Most of us do our best, you know. We give you an awful lot, Jack.'

'You take more back.'

'We're just trying to help you live, and we need to be alive ourselves to do that. But Kingdom – there's something else going on there. He needs stopping. Not just for your sake or mine, but for everyone's.'

'There has to be change, Grey.'

'Yes. But not on Kingdom's terms.'

[Why are you listening to this jerk, Jack?]

[Hush.]

'I'll be watching. If I can, I'll help you.' Grey squeezed Jack's knee. Despite himself, love flooded through him. 'That wasn't me, Jack. I'm not manipulating you now. Remember I've always done my best for you.' Grey vanished as he spoke. His last words were a breeze in Jack's ear. 'None of it was just for me.'

[Creepy old fucker,] muttered Fist.

Jack kicked the buggy into movement, and set off again. It took them along the other side of the lake from the group of Grey worshippers. As they passed them a group of black-clad figures emerged from the main doors, ran across the grass, and started breaking up the orgy with baseball bats.

[That'll be security,] said Fist.

[I don't know whether to laugh or cry.]

The road crossed a bridge, then passed between two of the large glass buildings. A few of the offices were busy. The workers bending over their desks looked like little model figures. Some showed signs of the despair driving the group by the lake. One window was spattered with blood. A body hung from the ceiling of another. Every so often, there would be naked people. Some would be copulating, some perhaps sleeping, some just staring out at a world that no longer made sense.

[Grey's incorporate,] said Jack. [Everyone's strings have been cut.]

The parkland surrounding the offices showed signs of disturbance, too. Black, charred stumps implied a small glade of trees, burnt to the ground. A round white circle had been raggedly inscribed on the ground, a human head sketched out within it. There were signs of burning there too. Jack imagined other rituals.

A horn barked behind them, and they pulled off the road. A large buggy roared past, full of security operatives. 'Watch out, Stabs!' one of them shouted. It turned off the road ahead of them, bumping over grass, and disappeared behind another building.

[The sooner we get out of here, Fist, the better.]

[I'm surprised that Stabs hasn't had any problems.]

[They must be too afraid of him.]

Ahead of them, a metal fence marked the edge of Grey's domain. The road stopped at a checkpoint. An armed security guard waved them down. Jack recognised Kingdom sigils on his uniform.

[You'd better take back over, Fist.]

A tight grin carved itself into Jack's face as it became Fist's. It was lucky they were moving so slowly. Fist could just about keep them on the road. When they pulled up by the guard Jack felt very relieved.

'Hello, Stabs. Where are you off to?'

'Making a delivery to Kingdom.' Fist had possessed Jack's voice, too. 'It should be on your transport log,' he squeaked. The guard reached forward and lifted the silk mask. Fist used Jack's face to grin at him. 'It's me, all right!' The guard winced and let the mask drop.

'I've seen some scary things in there, but you're the worst.'

[Don't rise to the bait, Fist.]

'You can pass.'

And they were on their way. The road quickly joined a much larger one. It ran between the different corporate headquarters that had colonised the fields of Heaven. Looking back, they could see that the fence ran all the way around Grey's complex. There were guard towers at regular intervals. Ahead of them, there was nothing but soft, green landscape. A gentle breeze floated across it. birdsong drifted from small, scattered glades, nestling in gently rolling hills.

[You know what I've just realised,] said Jack.

[What?]

[None of this is weave. It's all real.]

[Fucking gods, keeping the best for themselves.]

It took them almost an hour to reach Kingdom's compound. There was very little traffic on the road. They passed The Twins and Sandal's headquarters along the way. Halfway through the journey, Fist announced that he was bored. Suddenly there were three black hounds tracking them at right, and four at left. The dogs ran across the countryside, pacing out the miles with loose, loping steps. Their eyes blazed with fire and their tongues danced in their mouths like burning whips. At last, they neared Kingdom's headquarters. The pack drifted into invisibility. They turned into an access road and Kingdom's base rose up before them – a vast square block, several storeys high, with a high, dark tower rising out of each corner.

[It looks like an upside down table,] Fist commented.

[I'm sure that wasn't the effect Kingdom was going for.]

[You're going to have to take my body again in a moment.]

[Busy just now. I'm cracking Kingdom's security protocols. Even easier the second time.]

A security booth appeared in front of them. Jack slowed down.

[You need to take over NOW.]

Fist stepped into his body at the last possible moment. The guard asked for ID. Jack heard his own voice speak another's words. The small inquisition was quickly done, and they were on their way again.

[Much more relaxed than the one at Grey's,] commented Fist.

[Grey's people are more difficult to deal with.]

[Would you all be like that, without your gods?]

[No,] snapped Jack. [How's the breaking and entering going?]

[I'm in their systems. I've unlocked an emergency door for us to use. Then I'll get us straight to Yamata.]

[We've got a delivery to make first. It'll look suspicious if we don't.]

291

Kingdom's gardeners worked a small farm space behind his headquarters. His gardeners were very grateful for the delivery. 'I guess we're even now,' one of them said. Another punched Jack on the shoulder when Fist limped him off the buggy. 'Always good to see you, Stabs.' Fist had Jack chat with them and share a few jokes, before making excuses about the need to return, 'to keep an eye on things'. There were nods, a slap on the back, a half-muttered comment about 'it's tough over there'. As they drove away Fist commented, [They really seem to respect him.] There was a hint of relief in his voice.

They hid the buggy in bushes by the emergency door. It hissed open as they approached it. A long corridor stretched away from them, brutally lit by fluorescent lights. Fist let Jack take his body back.

[That's a relief,] sighed Jack.

[All that flesh! It's too big and too blundery. Not an easy ride.]

[You need to grow up in one to really get it. Now, let's go. You've definitely broken their security?]

[We won't be tripping any alarms. And I'll be keeping us out of the way of Kingdom's staff.]

Fist led Jack on a complex dance through the building. They passed large open spaces packed with cubicles, meeting rooms where all eyes watched invisible presentations on empty walls, production spaces where white-coated figures tended machines that throbbed gently in semi-darkness, server farms where drive stacks henged into the distance. Sometimes Fist urgently whispered [Stop,] or [Duck left,] or [Hide in there!] Jack would find himself dodging invisible enemies, as someone walked by just behind the last door or round the last corner.

When he wasn't giving instructions, Fist was unusually quiet and focused. Jack assumed that he was concentrating hard on the task at hand.

They soon found themselves in a nondescript facilities room. A service lift door, about twice as high as Jack, loomed out of a treated concrete wall.

[Pretty dull, eh?]

[Nothing special,] Jack agreed.

[So we're meant to think. But I'm a lot smarter than they are.]

Fist overlaid his understanding of the corridor space on Jack's. The air buzzed, dense with energy. Cobweb-light lines of security code drifted through it.

[I've told them not to read us as a threat,] Fist cackled. [If only they knew!]

Jack put his hand out to catch some code. It wrapped itself round his fingers, then flowed over them and away, leaving a tingling sensation.

[If you didn't have little wooden me to look after you,] Fist told him, [you'd be unconscious. Wall mounted tasters. There'd be guards here in a couple of minutes. If you'd even found this place, that is. It's invisible when you're onweave.]

[Good thing you're here then, Mr Modesty. Can anyone see it?]

[Hardly any of Kingdom's people have the access codes. Most of the ones that do are at the other end of the lift.]

[Yamatas?]

[Lots of them. It's the mother lode. And we're armed and ready.]

Seven silhouettes pulsed into being around them, sniffing at the air, noses chasing code. They snuffled out individual lines and snapped fire-teeth at them. They flared up like dry paper when touched, burning away into nothingness.

[The original Yamata's up there too. Want to see?]

[Oh, yes.]

A whisper of command from Fist, and the world around them fell away. The facilities room became shifting, glimmering lights. They were denser and brighter where the dogs stood, looser and paler where code drifted in the air like snow. The building beyond manifested as a glowing constellation of data. Jack looked down at himself. A suggestion of a body shimmered beneath him – his data-self. Buried within it was a dense foetus of glowing points, a swarm of fireflies pretending to be a human child.

[Is that you, Fist?] he asked.

[Yes. Little me inside big old you. And there's the Eastware and the Greyware.]

A soft suggestion of a finger nudged at tiny patterns running through Jack's body. The Eastware shivered, a glamour of tiny stars.

The Greyware was a denser and more pervasive fog.

[This is how you see the world?]

[Most of the time, yes.]

[You've never shown me this before.]

[It's very private. It's one of the few things I have that's unique to me.]

[Thank you, Fist,] said Jack. [I'm touched.] Fist said nothing. [And we can see Yamata from here?]

The ghost child inside Jack pointed up. Soft light shimmered far above them, barely visible through the intervening datahaze.

[I'll zoom in a bit closer,] Fist said. [Take a proper look at the old bitch.]

Suddenly they were flying upwards, but there was no sensation of movement.

[You can really go anywhere, can't you?]

[I can see anywhere. I can't go anywhere.]

[How do you even know what reality is?]

[It's the place where mortals can't fly. Now – we're as close as we can get without alerting her.]

[Gods,] said Jack. [I know that thing.]

[Yup,] Fist replied. [It's the fucking jellyfish again.]

It was the entity they'd seen in TrueShield. Now they weren't under attack, Jack could inspect it more closely. Yamata's consciousness had pulled the original structures of the stolen Totality mind away from perfection. It had become a pale, sickly presence prowling shifting tides of data. Instead of reaching tautly out in all directions from a blazing, spherical data core to form a shining star, its connectors hung down like tentacles, billowing gently in the digital breeze. Masses of thin, low bandwidth strands skirted a core of thicker, denser high capacity pipes, flickering with soft dancing lights as information flashed through them. The data core had decayed, too, half-deflating into a soft, saggy oval. Its heart flickered with one colour only, a vivid, artificial purple – the same colour that burned softly behind Yamata's eyes.

[What's she connected to?] wondered Jack.

Her tentacles drifted above small, softly glowing orbs. When Jack looked directly at one, more and more detail loomed larger and larger until he had to snap his eyes away, afraid that he would lose himself.

[I don't know,] replied Fist thoughtfully. [They look like weave servers, but very heavily remodelled. Remember all the Yamatas? Maybe that's how they connect to the bodies.]

[Quite a few there. They'll help us prove what she is and what she's done. Can we just remote access them from here?]

[No – she's very heavily protected, there's a structural firewall supporting the virtual one. We need to be physically inside that space to interact with her.]

For a moment, they drifted together, the great, alien shape of their opponent pulsing gently before them.

[Jack,] said Fist, suddenly more serious. [Once we're in, we won't have very long before Kingdom finds out we're there.]

[A few minutes tops. But you'll be able to find and transmit everything we need to bring him down.]

[Oh yes. I'm not worried about that. And Yamata's not a threat. But what happens next?]

[We get out. Fast.]

[You told me to think about consequences. We're surrounded by thousands of Kingdom's people. A god will rise and crush us. It'll be quite the battle!]

[You're right, Fist,] sighed Jack. It was a question he'd hoped to avoid. [I thought we'd just sneak out again. But now we're in here ...]

[You don't think we're going to get out of this, do you?]

[Fist—]

[Just be honest with me, Jack.]

Jack sighed again. [I'm sorry. We should have talked about it. I just couldn't—]

[Pessimist! See where thinking about consequences gets you. Of course, there is another way out.]

[We can't just kill Kingdom, Fist.]

[Oh, I know that. Not without even more consequences to deal with. Don't you worry, I've been thinking very hard about that.]

There was a long silence. A god's business carried on around them, a silent babel of meanings and purposes.

[There's something I need to ask you too,] said Jack. [Are you really up to this? I mean, after the fight at TrueShield?]

[I'm one hundred per cent!]

[I saw your attack systems when you spooled them up against Harry. They didn't look like that to me.]

[Oh Jack!] said Fist. [I was hoping you wouldn't notice.]

[Difficult not to. How are they really?]

[All the basics are fine. We can take on as many Yamatas as we want to, no problem at all. But when it comes to Pantheon members, it's trickier. Everything's a bit fragile. One shot left.]

[And once you've taken it?]

[Higher attack systems completely burnt out. I'm a one-shot Pantheon gun, and then that's it. Fuck, it would be good to kill Kingdom.] Fist waved up through the datahaze. [He's up there, somewhere. I could probably hit him from here.]

[We talked about that, Fist.]

[I know.] Now it was Fist's turn to sigh. [Life, eh? Full of complexities. Pretty unpleasant for everyone, when it comes down to it. Nasty, brutal and short.] He laughed. [Like me, come to think of it!]

Jack laughed too. [I suppose so, Fist.] It surprised him that Fist was accepting the situation so easily, but he wasn't going to question it. [Should we wait and see if Yamata ever goes dormant?] he wondered. [So we can catch her off-guard?]

[Things like her don't sleep. Come on Jack, we're going into battle for the first time in five years,] thrilled Fist. [Let's get fucking to it!]

Chapter 43

A heavily encoded blip to Ifor and Lestak – 'At Yamata's base in Kingdom's HQ. Going in' – and then they entered the lift. It was built on an industrial scale, large enough to take a small vehicle. The dogs shimmered into being around them – seven dark silhouettes, dripping fire from burning maws, padding with a hunter's silence. They were tense with expectation, growling and snapping at each other.

[Very excited,] grinned Fist evilly. [This is what I built them for.]

[The hounds of hell, attacking Heaven.]

[Oo! I like the sound of that!]

Jack pulled out Mr Stabs' handgun. It was a standard issue InSec weapon. He hoped that Stabs wouldn't need it to protect himself against Grey's maddened ex-employees. It hung heavily in his hands. He slipped the safety catch off. The lift snapped to a halt. Its doors creaked open. The Yamata chamber was a vast, domed space. There was a frozen moment of shock as its inhabitants turned and saw them. Then the night hounds leapt out of the lift, breathing fire. Fist floated behind them, a savage ghost bursting through the air. Jack moved more carefully, assessing the chamber for threats. Scaffolding held a transparent orb beneath the centre of the dome. It was about the height of a person. It glowed nanogel purple.

[That's Yamata!] hissed Jack.

Long cables hung down from it, plugged into four black server stacks, each about twice Jack's height. They were perfect cubes, shimmering with red lights. Figures clustered around them, dressed in white boiler suits. Flat mirrors looked out where faces should be. Four dogs broke away from the pack. Each ran for a different cube. Some of the white figures turned to stare, some started running away, stumbling against each other in their panic. There were strange synthesised screams. One of the figures tripped and fell.

Its face shattered against the ground. Smoke rose up as it shook convulsively.

Jack and Fist were halfway to the centre of the room. [What are those?] asked Fist, pointing. Green, human-sized tubes were clumped together in groups around the room's walls. Some were empty. Some were filled with a clear, green liquid. Some held bodies, floating in murk. [Must be where they grow the Yamata clones,] replied Jack. He aimed and fired, shattering one of the tubes. Liquid danced out of it and spilled across the floor. A white, boneless shape oozed out in its wake. [Vat-grown organic AI husks? Lestak'll love that. All on its own, it's an excuse to raid.]

[You're recording?]

[Oh yes. And once I've cracked their security, I'll be broadcasting, too.]

[Look at that one!] said Jack, pointing. One of the tubes held a much smaller body. [Think it's for you?]

[A body of my very own! Generous of them.]

[We'll take a proper look once we're done.]

The four dogs that Fist had sent running forwards reached their destinations, pouncing simultaneously into the black cubes. Emergency lights panicked. Virtual fire roared round servers.

[I knew it would be easy,] said Fist. [But not this fucking easy.]

'You were right,' boomed Yamata, her voice echoing round the chamber. At first, she was just a silhouette of burning white light. Detail poured into the blank shape, and suddenly she was fully present. 'I'm surprised you've got this far. I told Kingdom he should just kill you. Revenge is clearly a strong motive.'

'I'm not here for revenge, Yamata,' shouted Jack. 'I'm here for justice.'

'Justice?' Yamata snorted. 'There's no such thing. There's just power and what it can do for you. You should know that by now.'

'We're going to break you and we're going to break Kingdom. Hit her, Fist.'

The three remaining hounds leapt forward as one. They moved quicker than thought, blurring as they went. Unreal jaws closed on unreal flesh. Flame blossomed, dancing across Yamata. She froze, locked in futile resistance. Gold-red fire became white hissing static, breaking down the shape of her body. The dogs shuddered as they broke her shielding.

That was when the first shot sang out towards Jack. There was a loud crack, followed immediately by a metallic clang as the bullet smashed against the lift doors behind them. [Shit,] said Jack, dropping to his knees. Human shapes shambled out from behind the servers. These were not the white-clad attendants. They were all Yamatas.

'East's flash mob broke three of my bodies,' one of them called out. 'Payback time.' They moved relatively smoothly and were all armed. Bullets danced through the air.

Jack fled towards a cluster of clone tubes, hoping desperately for cover. [Shut 'em down!] he yelled.

[Give me a minute – they've isolated them from the main systems.]

[Fucking hell!]

He reached the tubes and skidded in behind them. One exploded, showering him in warm, sticky liquid. The mass inside it was barely human. Shattered glass sliced pink-white chunks from it as it slithered to the floor. There was a metal control console. Jack dropped to his knees behind it, then peeked round the edge and snapped out a couple of shots. The drones advanced. Bullets rang against metal. Another container exploded.

[Shut those fuckers down!]

[I'm going as fast as I can. Fucking fire back!]

Jack shot again. One of the Yamatas staggered. Floor tiles by Jack smashed. Shards bit his skin.

[Hurry up!]

[Thirty seconds. The pack's deep in root servers. Full security access coming up – going to crash the firewall, open them right up to Ifor and Lestak. Got my own searches running too, we're going to prove just what they've been up to here, and how it links back to Kingdom.]

[And my job, I suppose, is to keep us alive?]

[Pretty much, Jackie boy!]

[THEN SHUT THE DRONES DOWN!]

[Working on it. Firewall's almost gone. And – oh you beauty!]

[What?]

[One of the dogs has just copied all the files we need back to me. We've got a full timetable for all the terrorist bombings, plus a comms trail between Kingdom and Yamata agreeing and reporting back on each one.]

[Pretty conclusive. We still don't know why he killed Penderville, though.]

[Details, details. I'm sure the pack'll turn something up on that. And we're about to be able to get it all to the outside world. A few more seconds ...]

Jack squeezed out another couple of shots.

[Firewall's down! FUCK!] said Fist.

[What?]

For a moment, Fist froze. He shook himself back into life.

[I don't know. Massive external data surge, and all security's gone back up. No way in or out at all.] The shooting stopped. A hubbub of confused voices sprang up.

[Ifor coming in? InSec?]

[I don't think so. Shit.] Fist sounded worried. Jack risked a quick look around the console. The Yamatas had dropped their guns. Some of them had fallen over.

[It's stopped them dead.]

[Jack,] hissed Fist, [it went straight into Yamata. It came in through the portal that Harry used. Motherfucker, some of it's still in me too.]

[What? I thought you'd put countermeasures in place.]

[I did.]

One of the Yamatas turned towards them, moving with an easy fluidity. 'Hello Jack,' she said, a strong Docklands accent now over-laid on her voice. 'Fist did try and block me. But it didn't work. Always told you he was sloppy.'

[Oh gods,] groaned Jack. [Harry.]

[He's stopped the fucking dogs,] replied a deeply frustrated Fist, [and shut down all my other combat systems, too.]

Harry's voice resounded in Jack's head. [It's very good of you to help me get in here, but I think I'm going to take over now.]

All the Yamatas were laughing. A couple of them picked up guns and trained them on Jack. The ones that had fallen over were climbing back to their feet. 'Step away from the birthing tubes, please,' said the closest one.

'Fuck you,' spat Fist.

A shot snapped past Jack.

'I don't want to damage your body,' said another Yamata, 'but if I have to, I will.'

Jack moved out from behind the tube.

[What's going on, Fist?]

[The fucker's caged me.]

[Oh yes,] said Harry, a whispering intrusion in Jack's mind, [from within].

The hounds were almost fully absorbed into the Yamata avatar, becoming inchoate black masses wrapped around her face, her throat and her body. They started to shake, then one by one they flowed away from her, spilling on to the floor to form dense, oil-like puddles. The flames flickering around the four server boxes died into nothing.

'Time to appear in person,' said the Yamata avatar. It shimmered briefly, became an outline filled with static, and then Harry was standing in front of Jack. He grinned with deep satisfaction. 'I've been waiting to fuck that bitch up for years. I made her everything she is. I turned her from a sweat smuggler into a terrorist. I kept InSec off her back while her people set bombs off anywhere Kingdom wanted. All of that, and she really thought that if she killed me I'd stay nicely dead and she'd be safe.'

'What are you talking about?' asked Jack, astonished.

'You still haven't got it? Yamata worked for me.'

'She didn't capture you? And force you into it?'

'Not at all.'

[For fuck's sake,] groaned Fist. [I fucking warned you about him.]

'Why?' Jack gasped.

'When my patron calls, I respond. Until that fucking idiot Kingdom started to lose the Soft War, and I realised the rewards he'd promised wouldn't be coming my way. So, I decided to get myself a little leverage by reopening the Penderville case. He was always very sensitive about that. There's something very dark indeed buried in there. I didn't expect him to move so quickly against me, though. Oh, and that reminds me ...'

301

For a moment, Harry looked distracted. And then, he smiled again.

'Your little Fist opened the firewall, but I was there on the other side stopping anything from getting out. No one but you, me and him knows what's just happened here. Nobody's going to interrupt us. Very useful.'

'What next, Harry?'

'I'm impressed by your little puppet's weapon set. Verrrry impressed! I think I'll finally be getting my revenge on Kingdom. Might even mount a hostile takeover of my own. I always said I could run things better than that cunt. And as for you—'

Harry leant down, pointing a finger towards Jack. His face darkened, and rage shook through his voice.

'—as for you, you little shit, you've been fucking my wife all these years. I'm going to cut out your mind, and take your body and wear it for my own. And I'm going to roll Andrea back to before she ever met you, and make sure she stays there for good, and she'll be my fucking wife again, and I'll live in your flesh and fuck her every day with it.'

Jack's heart clenched with fear and guilt.

[You stupid bastard!] shouted Fist. [He fucking knew the whole time!]

Pain exploded in the back of Jack's head. One of the Yamata drones must have circled round behind him and hit him. Harry laughed and the world vanished.

Chapter 44

Jack was lying on his back in hot, stifling darkness. A muffled mechanical snarling roared from somewhere above him. He couldn't move his arms or legs. They were hemmed in by hard, rough surfaces. He tried to sit up, but bumped his forehead. The snarling noise came in short, rapid bursts, each one a little louder than the last.

'I'm sorry about this,' said Fist. Light leapt into being, dazzling Jack. 'Oops!' The light moved out of Jack's eyes. Fist was holding a torch. They were squashed into a long, cramped, wooden box. There were gaps between some of the slats. Grey concrete had oozed through them and set hard. 'It's the best I could do, Jack.' Fist was squashed into his chest. The noise started up again and he had to shout. 'All this is virtual. We're deep inside your mind.'

'What's the noise?' Jack shouted back.

'Drilling. Harry's trying to break in.'

'How long have we got?'

'A few minutes. It'll be enough.'

'Enough for what?'

'I'm sorry, Jack, I've got no choice.'

'No choice but what, Fist?'

'I have to do it. I'm not letting that cunt get his hands on my weapon systems.'

'What are you talking about?'

The drilling noise was getting even louder.

'I'm really sorry,' Fist yelled. 'It won't hurt for long.'

He leant forward and clamped his little wooden hands over Jack's nose and mouth. It took Jack a moment to realise what he was doing. He thrashed and flailed and tried to breathe, but the coffin was tight about him and Fist's grip was firm. At last he had to give up.

Darkness shimmered and he could no longer feel the coffin's

wooden walls. He was hanging in infinite space. He thought of East's cathedral. A great, soft rhythm surrounded him, the beating of mighty wings.

Then Jack died.

Chapter 45

The first thing that Jack felt was the cold. A bleak wind scythed through his wet clothes. There was a roaring sound. He remembered drills and a feeling that it was very important someone shouldn't reach him. This noise was softer and more organic. He was lying on a yielding, frigid surface. The breeze gusted and a shiver shook him. Then something even colder splashed over and rolled around him, dragging him back to full consciousness. He opened his eyes.

Black sand stretched away. White foam danced up it, the sea's softest touch. The beach seemed to carry on forever, curving away to left and to right. Water rushed back down it as the wave broke, then died back into the sea. Jack was soaked. He rolled over and sat up. Memories of the coffin's hot closeness made the cold feel like a blessing. The grey sea stretched away to touch grey clouds at the horizon. Another wave rolled in. Jack scrambled to his feet, looking round for a little wooden body lying on the shore or bobbing in the waves. But there was no sign of Fist. The wind shook him again as he remembered an educational film he'd seen as a child, and realised where he was. 'Fuck,' he breathed. Fist had brought him to the outer edges of the Coffin Drives.

It took Jack a good ten minutes to reach the dunes that shadowed the beach's edge. Every so often small gaps would open in the clouds. Bright beams of sunlight lanced through, some flickering briefly then disappearing, others burning softly on. He wondered if the clouds ever lifted. He couldn't imagine clear skies opening up over this gloomy landscape. Thick clumps of scrubby green grass danced in the wind. Jack shivered as he walked. He hoped that his clothes would dry soon, or at least that the dunes would offer some shelter. The land of the dead lay beyond them, but no fetch was allowed to speak of it. Station people did their best to ignore everything but its most basic details, not wanting to imagine where their dataselves would spend eternity.

A shrill whistling danced towards him. At first he thought it was just the wind, but then he heard notes sketching out a simple melody. He wondered who was playing. Perhaps it was some kind of digital psychopomp, waiting to conduct him into the lands of the dead. But he'd arrived in such an unusual way. Fetches were normally very carefully constructed over a period of months. He'd broken in, a direct copy of a living mind. He wasn't sure if the Coffin Drives would even recognise him as a functioning consciousness, if he'd be able to communicate with those others who lived within them. The thought of an eternity alone stretched out before him, and he shuddered.

At last he reached the dunes. He climbed towards the whistling, sand slipping away beneath his feet. He lost his footing and tumbled down the other side of the dune, swearing loudly. The fall winded him and it took a moment to recover. There was chuckling. A voice he never thought he'd be so happy to hear spoke.

'That was quite some entry, Jacky boy!'

Fist was leaning back against black sand. He was dressed in white shorts and a rough, canvas smock. He held a tin whistle in one hand.

'I knew you'd find me sooner or later. I pulled you out of the sea as far as I could, but I couldn't wake you. And it's cold down there.'

'You left me?'

'I wanted to look around! And what are you going to do, Jack? Die again?' He tootled out a few more notes. 'The waves were going to wake you sooner or later. And if I kept playing this, I knew you'd hear me.'

Jack sat down next to him. 'So we're dead now?'

'Out there, we are. I wiped your mind and then deleted myself. There's no thought left in that body of yours, no memories, nothing.'

'And we're just copies—'

'You've never been software, have you? It's how things travel when they're digital. New copy here, old copy erased. Are you Jack? Are you just a copy of Jack? Is there a difference?' Fist waved his hands around mesmerically. 'Spoooooky! When you were alive, you were flesh, but you were also a pattern of mind carved into that flesh. Now the flesh has gone, but the pattern remains, unchanged.'

'Very metaphysical, Fist.'

Fist raised an eyebrow at Jack. 'Dying does that to you.'

'How long have we been down here?'

'In real time? A few hours, at most.'

'Shouldn't it take months to reassemble us?'

'No, Jack. Think about it. We're totally different from fetches. They're built from scratch out of a lifetime's worth of data. We're two living consciousnesses cut and pasted directly down here. No reassembly needed, we're already complete. And the Coffin Drives' bandwidth is vast, so the transfer's pretty zippy. Dying's much easier than you'd think. Who knew?'

'We didn't just die – we were killed.'

Fist looked away for a moment, suddenly less cheerful. 'I'm sorry, Jack. I had to do it.'

'Not your responsibility. Harry forced you. He killed us just as surely as he killed Yamata.'

'That bastard. I always told you not to trust him.'

Jack sighed. 'I'm sorry, Fist. You were right. But we did need him. And we wouldn't have got as far without him.'

Fist waved a wooden hand at the barren space around them. 'We wouldn't be here without him, either.'

Jack laughed. 'You've got a point.'

'And he's still got our body.'

'Can he do anything with it?'

'No. All my hardware's wrapped around your spine, but there's nothing left to bring it to life. It's like having a gun without any bullets.'

'So he can't fire up your weapon systems?'

'No. He'd need us, and we're out of his reach now. Even if he did catch us, he can't force us to do anything we don't want to. Even if he could, my countermeasures would break him first.'

'I thought they didn't work?'

'Plan A was the coffin. It protected us for long enough to get down here. And there's a Plan B too. Ooh, It's a beauty!'

'Tell me.'

'I couldn't stop Harry from using me as a bridge to Yamata, but when he did key parts of him were inside me. In my memory. Accessible. Lots of security there, but—'

'Go on.'

'There's some ninja code working its way into him. A few hours, it'll have gone as deep as it can, and we can trigger it. It'll cripple him, at least for a bit – and it'll also ping us with a precise fix on his core servers. We'll know where he is, and we'll be able to go after him physically.'

'Once we're back in the land of the living.'

'Well, yes, there is that, but it's just a detail. I'll get us out of here somehow.' Jack found himself starting to feel irritated by Fist's breezy overconfidence. 'In the meantime,' Fist continued heedlessly, 'we've got Harry right where we want him!'

'Indeed,' said Jack sardonically. 'But even if we put aside how we're going to get out of here, there's something you're forgetting.'

'What?'

'Kingdom. If anyone can fire up your weapons, he can.'

'Harry hates him. He'll never hand your body over.'

'Do you really think Harry can stand up to a god? Sooner or later, Kingdom'll take the body off him. And he'll find us too. He can force us to do things we don't want to, and we don't have any countermeasures against him.'

'Oh yes we do!' Fist bounced up happily. 'Me! I'll just have to kill him. With a bit of warning, of course, so that someone nice and powerful can step in and sort his people out.' He winked at Jack. 'I'll be very ethical.'

'If Kingdom catches us, he'll wipe me and burn your personality out before he drops you back into our body. By the time you get your hands on your weapons hardware, you'll be his creature. And he'll be able to repair you properly, and point you at whoever he likes. And that means he'll run the Pantheon.'

'Bollocks,' grumbled Fist, kicking at the sand in theatrical frustration. 'It was all looking so good.'

'Sticking to the plan is more important than ever. We need to expose Kingdom before he catches up with us. Though gods know how we'll do it from here. You've still got the files that prove he was running Yamata?'

'Oh yes.' Fist turned a shoulder to show Jack a little rucksack, strapped to his back. 'Safe in there.'

308

'And we might not know how we're going to get out, but at least we can find out the last piece of the puzzle.'

'What other piece?' asked Fist. 'We know everything.'

'No. We need to find out why Penderville's so important.'

'I don't see why that matters.'

'All of this began with him. His death was nothing to do with the bombings, he died before the Soft War even began. It was nothing to do with sweat smuggling, either. Yamata was very clear about that. There's something deep and dark there – something that Kingdom's very scared of. We'll uncage Penderville and find out what it is. We might also be able to release some of the anti-war people too. They'll back our story up.'

'A jailbreak! I'm in.'

'There's just one thing we need to sort out.' Jack waved his hand at the landscape around them. 'You got us in here. How the fuck are you going to get us out?'

'If I can kill gods, I'm sure I can bring us back from the dead,' Fist replied in a tone too airy to be properly reassuring. 'Weavespace is up there beyond the clouds. I've got a pretty good sense of how fetches work, I'll have a look at one and reverse-engineer a way out, we'll be fine.'

'We won't be fine. We'll be ghosts. What about my body?'

'Remember what Harry said about it? He was going to put one of Yamata's control systems in it and wear it. If he can do that, you can too.'

'If we can avoid Kingdom and get our hands on it.'

'Details, details,' said Fist. 'Everything's sure to sort itself out. Oh, and, talking of clouds, there's a silver lining to all this.'

He paused dramatically.

'Gods' sake,' said Jack. 'Just tell me.'

'Now I've killed you, I can't kill you! Neither of us live in your body any more, so I won't have to take it from you and you won't have to die in it!'

'Fucking hell, Fist,' groaned Jack.

'I thought you'd be happy,' said Fist, sounding hurt.

'I suppose it is good news. But it doesn't mean anything if we can't get out of here. And if we can't find my body again and bring down fucking Kingdom.'

'Gods, Jack, you worry too much. We'll escape first, we'll worry about the rest once we're out. We need to find some fetches, I'll take a look under the hood, if that doesn't work something else will turn up, we'll go from there.'

'That's not really a plan, Fist.'

'And you want to jailbreak Penderville and his mates. So we need to go where the dead guys hang out. Where's that? Not too many of 'em round here.'

'Fucking hell.' Jack grumbled for a bit, but in the end had to admit that Fist was right. 'We're on a big, round island,' he said. 'The dead live in the middle, beyond these dunes.'

'Then let's go find them.'

It took much longer to cross the dunes than it had the beach. Jack slithered up and down, straining to reach each peak then tumbling down the other side. His feet vanished in soft black avalanches whenever he put any weight on them. He found that half-climbing, half-crawling was the most efficient way of moving. His wet clothes hung heavily on him and black sand stuck to him, rubbing against his skin like so many small razors.

'It's a pretty convincing simulation,' commented Fist cheerfully. 'Very impressive.' Being lighter, he was finding the going far easier.

'Easy for you to say,' Jack wheezed. He'd been panting for a while now, forcing himself to keep going as he felt unreal muscles become more and more tired. 'You don't get out of breath. Can you turn my physical presence off?'

'Sorry, Jack. You're still very new to this virtual lark. Your subconscious expects physicality. Losing it all of a sudden would be too much of a shock. All sorts of bad things would happen.'

'Can't be worse than this.'

Fist didn't hear him. He was already skipping down another sand dune. Jack half-ran, half-tumbled along behind him. Fist ran quickly up to the top of the next one, his rucksack bobbing perkily, leaving Jack sprawled at its base.

'Jack – get up here! This is your last dune.'

'Thank the gods.'

Jack dragged himself up to join Fist. The wind snapped at him. His clothes were nearly dry. 'So that's where fetches live,' he said, looking down at the sight before him.

The dunes formed a vast circle around a deep, dusty, lens-shaped depression, several kilometres across. A river stretched all the way around the rim of the dip, a dark ring, leaden in the gloom. Four bridges crossed it, equally spaced at the four points of the compass.

Beyond the river, corrugated metal gleamed dully, sometimes almost silver, sometimes a rusted red, forming an uncountable rabble of small buildings and shacks. Hard, bright patches of colour blazed out where shafts of light broke through the clouds from the weave. A round, black lake lay at the heart of the ramshackle city, a pupil in the city's lens. Its waters were perfectly still – a mirror, showing the sky back to itself.

At the heart of the shining waters was a higgledy-piggledy pile of something that at first looked like rubble. Looking closer, Jack saw that it was a mountain of small black cubes.

'I never imagined it like this,' he told Fist.

'Can you see anyone?' Fist replied.

'I don't know.'

Movement was visible throughout the Coffin Space, but it was difficult to tell if it came from people or from the wind snatching at loose metal. Jack couldn't make out the geography of the city. There were no roads. He imagined tight alleys and passages squashed between rickety houses. Remembering the city's inhabitants made him see it as a great, overfilled cemetery, graves and tombs squashed together, coffins tipping against each other where the earth between them had subsided.

Fist skipped down the dune. 'Come on!'

Jack imagined all the dead he'd ever known, clustered in the squalor before him.

'Come ON! Let's go meet some fetches!'

Jack let himself slide down the dune and set off towards the nearest of the bridges.

'That's interesting,' Fist shouted back at him. 'They manage time differently on this side of the dunes.'

It was indeed difficult to measure its passing in that empty landscape. Jack had a sense of an endless march towards the bridge, between the river, the dunes and the shifting clouds above. Step after step jarred through his body, telling him that he was moving forwards, but nothing seemed to change. Fist paced beside him, for once silent. At various points Jack said something, but Fist said nothing in response, leaving him unsure whether he'd only imagined speaking.

Suddenly, they were standing on the bridge.

'I didn't realise we were so close to it,' said Jack.

'We've been here for an hour or so.'

'But we've only just arrived.'

'I suppose there's not much point giving the dead a shared sense of time.'

Jack clutched the bridge's handrail. It was hard and cold. He clung on to it, fearful that he was imagining this too, that he would suddenly find himself trudging again through the wastes of Coffin Space.

Fist peered over at the city. 'I still can't see anyone moving around. Slackers.'

They started walking across. The river was in full spate beneath them, but no sound rose from it.

'Listen to that, Jack.'

'There's nothing.'

'Exactly! The beach wasn't bad, but this bit of the simulation's really cheap. You'd think they'd treat the dead with more respect. No wonder they're all still in bed.'

They crossed the peak of the bridge. Two figures were standing at its end, one short, the other tall. There was an empty space between them that implied a missing third.

'Were they there just now?' asked Fist.

'I don't know. I think it's the first time we've seen them.' Jack shook his head. 'This is hard work.'

They continued their walk. Whenever Jack found himself becoming spatially confused, he'd watch the pillars that supported the handrail go by. He usually managed to convince himself that he was actually moving forwards.

'I don't know how they stand it, Jack.'

'No wonder they always love coming out to visit.'

The two figures became more distinct. One was only about a third the height of the other. Both were bundled up in dirty rags. It was difficult to tell their sex. Jack wondered if they were just statues posed to ward off or welcome strangers. There was nothing else visible that could have been a person – or rather, as Jack reminded himself, a fetch. Again, he imagined being trapped here perpetually. He idly wondered when his sanity would leave him. It occurred to him that this environment might not allow that much change, that even the relief of madness would be impossible.

'We've got to get out of here, Fist.'

They reached the end of the bridge. As they came closer to the figures Jack saw that they had white sheets draped over their heads. They did seem to be human, or some recreation of something human, for each was pointing down with one white hand. The hands shimmered oddly, never quite settling down into a final, fixed image of themselves. 'Posers,' said Fist.

The wind rattled through the streets of the city, dancing between the pillars of light that speared down from the clouds. Blank windows and empty doors stared out at Jack and Fist. Flickering lights lit some of them, as if a thousand televisions had been left turned on in a thousand empty rooms.

Jack walked towards one of the figures. It didn't move. He found himself next to it. It was the taller of the two. There was a white sheet in his hand. A shimmer of a face was looking up at him. It contained all ages; sometimes a baby, sometimes a child, sometimes a young adult, sometimes haggard and old. It shifted between versions of itself so quickly that it was difficult to read, but then some sort of stasis was achieved and there was one face looking up at him.

'Oh,' breathed Jack. 'It's you.'

'Hello Jack,' said his mother. She was as she'd been when he left Station for the Soft War. He reached out and took her arms in his hands, testing the reality of her.

'I'm so sorry,' he said, his voice full of grief.

'I know.'

Without any movement she was holding him, and he her. Something within Jack broke and he wept. He kept on apologising. She

313

held him close, her soft hands pulling his cheek against her soft hair. She held him close. At last he was able to talk.

'How did you know I was coming?' he asked her.

'The waves tell us of new fetches. We send the right person out to meet them. We felt you coming in from the sea, but you're so different from us.'

'What do you mean?'

'Let me show you.'

'What about Fist?'

'Oh – your puppet. Where's he gone?'

Jack looked around for Fist, surprised that he'd been so silent for so long. Someone was giggling. Jack remembered the sound from life.

'Issie?'

She skipped into view, Fist dancing along with her. She shimmered with change too, but there was much less variety in her, for she'd lived barely a tenth as long as Jack's mother.

'I came down with Jack's mummy. They said Fist would be here!' she chirped happily.

Jack had never seen her true face, only the skull. It shimmered from child to baby and then back again, beaming with fresh, open joy.

'I had so much fun playing with him! And now he's here, and you're here, and everything's going to change! I might even get to go travelling like he does! Oh, wonderful!'

She skipped towards him. Jack readied himself for another hug. But then there was a bright, silent explosion. A sunbeam leapt out of the clouds, burning into being around Issie. Where she'd been standing there was suddenly only a transparent pillar of light.

Jack took a step back. Fist's face mimicked shock. Jack felt his mother squeeze his hand.

'What happened?'

'Her mother called to her.'

'Lestak?'

'Yes. She had to go. Any one of us can be called, at any time. The light breaks through from the weave, and summons us into it, and we go to manifest in your world. To be your puppets.'

'You're not puppets.'

'You find your favourite memories, and decide that that's how you want us to be, and then we are forced to conform to that. What would you call it?'

'I don't know. I guess I never really thought about it before.'

Fist was nervously skirting the sunbeam. He didn't hear Jack's mother. 'This is heavy stuff, Jack,' he said thoughtfully. 'I don't think we can use it to get out. We could try and climb up one, but I think it would break us.'

'Can't we get someone to summon us?'

'Nobody knows we're here.'

Jack turned to his mother. 'Can we send a message out with you?' he asked her. 'There are some files we need to get out.'

'We can't speak of life here when we're up there,' she replied. 'And we can only travel out with what we remember from life, nothing else.'

Jack thought of Andrea. His mother's voice was made of memories too, patchworked together from all the words she'd ever spoken.

'It's the same for all of you?'

'Yes. I'll show you. Fist, come here.'

She took him and Fist by the hand. All of a sudden they were overlooking the city from the top of a high metal building. Looking down, Jack saw a ragged jumble of shacks, the spaces between them never quite coalescing into streets or alleys. The soft flickering that he'd noticed on the edge of the city pervaded them all. Sunbeams danced at random around them.

'You can see where we were standing,' his mother told him, pointing. 'There – the sunbeam by the bridge.' It was a mile or so away. The bridge was a dark shape against the darker river. 'And you see all the beams that leap into the city, pulling our minds away from here, just as we've begun to coalesce? I'll show you what they do to us.' Now they were inside one of the shacks. A flickering figure stood before them. It was naked, but there was nothing obscene about its nudity. It never fell into a single version of itself, so it was never defined enough for its flesh to be seen and properly parsed.

'So many memories, Jack, to try and control. Sometimes we come close. Sometimes one of us approaches coherence, a final

315

interpretation of all the data a life has left behind, but then the fetching light comes down from the weave and we fall to pieces again, broken by the nostalgia of the living.'

Jack thought of Andrea's music. It was a focus for her memories, giving them a shape and narrative, pulling her back to a single, self-defined version of herself. His mother had no such resource to draw on.

'How can you speak to me so clearly? Why aren't you like – this one?'

Jack waved towards the shimmering figure. It seemed to be aware of his presence. A thousand ages of the same head turned towards him. Compound eyes tried to focus.

'Your father's never rolled me back, so I'm more structured than most. And the attention of all the rest of us is on me, holding me together. We've never had a visitor like you. If you can escape, you can tell them about all this.'

Fist had let go of Mrs Forster's hand, and leapt on to the window-sill. While she'd been talking, he'd been scanning the city. Now, he turned back.

'You mean – they're all like this one? None of them ever resolving?' he asked.

'None of us ever can.'

'Motherfucker.' He turned to Jack. 'It's bad enough being yourself and then getting reprogrammed. This lot don't even get that far. I wish I could give them all a feather like Andrea's, without getting fried by the fucking Pantheon. I wish they could all become more than just puppets. The living really are a shower of cunts.'

'But – nobody ever knew,' said Jack. 'The Pantheon never show us any of this.'

'They wouldn't,' Fist shot back angrily.

Suddenly they were at the lakeside. There were maybe fifty metres of black, muddy earth between the city of the dead and the silent lake. Streams running out of the city and into the depths had carved soft lines in the mud. A richly stagnant smell hung in the air.

'So many don't even get to exist as fetches,' said Jack's mother. She gestured towards the great pile of dark blocks at the heart of the lake. They had a hard, rough texture to them, tumbled together as if by a child bored of its building blocks.

'What is that?' Jack asked her.

'It's the prison. Some come to the bridge, but are snatched away and enclosed before they can even find a word to speak.'

'That's where Penderville is,' said Jack. 'And Grey's peace protesters.'

'We met some of their children,' Fist explained. 'They're locked away, too. Just not quite as finally as this.'

'Each of those blocks holds a weave presence?' continued Jack.

'Yes,' his mother confirmed sadly. 'Each one's labelled with name, date of decease – everything.'

'So all we need to do is open them up. Fist?'

'Fuck yes. It's not a god, but it'll do for now.'

'And that'll set alarm bells ringing. The Coffin Drive admins will run diagnostics, and they'll need a two-way link for that. They'll see us, and we'll be able to talk to them. I think we've found our ticket out of here.' Jack turned back to his mother. 'Can you take us to the prison?' he said.

Before she could reply, there was a dazzling shock. Light burned out of the sky and exploded around them, catching Jack within it. He felt that he'd been lifted out of himself. A shape that could have been a face hovered before him. It resolved and became deeply familiar. It was his father. He was crying. Jack had never seen him looking this vulnerable. He wanted to reach out to him, but there was nothing to reach with. He'd lost his body in the white light.

'Get out!' yelled his mother. 'Quickly! Before it's too late!'

Jack felt a huge strong push, and then heard Fist shout 'Fuck!' He stumbled backwards. A white pillar blazed in front of him. His mother's rags lay scattered just by it, fading under the hard light. She'd been called away.

'That was pretty fucking Oedipal,' said Fist, picking himself up off the ground. 'Knocked me over, too. No damage, though!'

'I'm fine too,' Jack replied. 'Thanks for asking.'

'Well, that's all we're going to get from her,' Fist continued obliviously. 'At least for the moment. And who knows what sort of state she'll be in when she gets back!'

Joy and grief pulsed together in Jack. He'd found his mother and then lost her again so quickly. He so wanted to see her again, but to do that he had to escape the Coffin Drives and then best Kingdom. He pushed emotion to one side, forcing himself to focus on the practicalities of the situation.

'We need to get to that island.'

'But how do we get there now your mum can't zap us over?'

'We swim.'

'For fuck's sake Jack, I'm made of wood. I'll swell right up!'

'Fist, we're in a simulation.'

'That simulates real physics.'

'Then you'll float and you'll be fine. Now, will the files be OK?'

'More worried about them than me?'

'Fist,' warned Jack.

'The rucksack's completely waterproof. Unlike certain people I could mention.'

Fist clung to Jack as they squelched towards the black, oily lake, grumbling all the way. By the time they reached it they were covered in mud. Its cold, still waters stank of decay.

'Can't we find a boat?'

'Can you see one anywhere?'

Fist sighed and wrapped his arms tightly round Jack's neck. As Jack swam, ripples rolled away from him, the only movement on the lake's dark surface. Fist's head and upper body were above the water. Jack distracted him by asking about strategies for hacking into the prison cubes. 'It's going to take a bit of creativity,' he said thoughtfully, then went quiet, fascinated by the problem.

Jack worked hard to keep his own head above water, but couldn't help letting it dip below the surface. Bitter water slipped into his mouth. A confusion of memories assaulted his mind. None, he realised, were his own. He lifted his head up and spat. Other people's lives receded. 'This isn't water,' he said, his voice full of realisation. 'It's memory. It's what happens to fetches when nobody comes looking for them.'

'Don't be ridiculous,' Fist replied disparagingly. 'It's like the sea round the outside of this place – low bandwidth simulation. It's cheap servers and lazy programmers. It's not very nice, but that's the Coffin Drives for you.'

'You're sure about that?'

'Bless you, Jack, you're not used to being virtual. It's easy to let your imagination run away with you in a place like this.'

'Really?' said Jack, and dived down.

For a moment Jack and Fist inhabited a thousand fragments of mind, individual life shards that had gleamed and then spun away from them with all the beauty of a shattering stained-glass window. It was impossible to pick out overall patterns, but here there was a soft kiss, there the touch of a raindrop, a sudden note of music or a glimpse of Station when it had been so much smaller. All these broken notes combined into a cacophony of consciousness that had its own dying beauty. The moment stretched out, because every individual memory was unanchored from time. And then they burst spluttering out of the water, and the riot of memory left them.

'God's shit!' shrieked Fist. 'You're right. This lake is where fetches die.'

'The Pantheon always said our memories were a resource too precious to lose. But if this is where they end up – so much white noise, and then I suppose they just fade away.'

'Wow. More bullshit from the gods. Whodathunkit, eh?'

They reached the island and clambered on to the lower blocks. 'Rucksack's OK?' checked Jack.

'Files untouched. I'm rather good at luggage. Maybe I should do it professionally when all this is over.'

The blocks' hard edges were decaying. The stone of each was soft, falling away where the water touched it. As Jack and Fist slithered over them, chunks slid off.

'Fresh minds, melting away,' said Jack. 'They're like sugar cubes in tea. I can't believe they'd do this. They're editing anyone who disagrees with them out of Station's memory. Can you open the blocks?'

'I'm building a programme that'll crack them all. When it finds Penderville it'll bring him straight to us.'

'Ready to go?'

'We need to get to the top. It'll sink down into the pile from there.'

It was impossible to tell how long it took to clamber up the pile. The higher they went, the more individual blocks retained their integrity, until those at the peak were hard-edged and polished to a high gloss. It was hard to grip them. When Jack finally reached the highest one, he collapsed, panting. Fist scrambled up and sat down next to him.

'All ready.'

'Do it, Fist.'

Fist stretched his hand out, palm up. For a moment, it blurred. Jack peered at it, and thought for a second that it was covered in white dust. Then he realised that Fist had summoned hundreds of tiny versions of himself into being. He flicked his hand and the tiny horde dropped away, tumbling across the black surface of the topmost cube. As they touched it, they became so many shimmering flames. A few sank into the surface of the cube. The rest danced across it, flickering towards the others beneath.

'How long?' Jack asked him.

'Here? Who knows?'

'I wonder when they'll notice topside.'

Lightning flared in the clouds above the city, then roared down in hard, jagged lines. Bolts ploughed into it, raising gouts of flame and clouds of smoke. There were maybe a dozen impacts.

'They've realised someone's digging up granny,' said Fist, his voice full of glee, 'and they really don't like it. Pretty impressive diagnostics!'

'That's no diagnostic programme,' replied Jack, sounding worried. 'It's an attack.'

Screaming drifted across the necropolis. The flames disappeared. Torn at by the breeze, the pillars of smoke they'd thrown up quickly lost integrity, falling away into nothing.

'No it wasn't,' Fist told him confidently. 'You're getting rusty. That was just the insertion.'

'And that's what they've dropped in.' Jack pointed at a small, dark mass, floating towards them across distant rooftops. As it came closer, he made out a bulbous head with a tiny body dangling beneath it. There was a single pale spot at the centre of the creature's forehead.

'Oh shit.' Fist sounded genuinely shocked. 'Fucking no.'

'What?'

Shock became outrage. 'It's a puppet embryo. One of the six that survived. They really do exist. Get the fuck out of here. NOW!'

Jack was already slithering down the hard cubes, half in control, half-falling. Fist followed him, leaping from cube to cube like a small, brightly painted goat.

'How can they hurt us?' yelled Jack, surprised and worried by Fist's reaction.

'They're like me before I merged with you. Code looking for content. They eat memories. They'll suck the identity out of whatever they touch. And we've got more identity than anyone here.'

Three or four other figures appeared in the distance as they slid towards the water. 'Fucking Kingdom!' screamed Fist. 'It took us a month to mesh, and the fucking doctors held me back every step of the way. Those things will do it in seconds. The overload'll kill them, but they'll eat us first.'

'How do we stop them?'

They plunged into the water before Fist could answer. Fist grabbed Jack as he started swimming, hard. Holding his head up only slowed him down. Then he was underwater, and memories rushed over him. He felt that he was pushing himself through a thousand different lives. Random moments leapt through him, appearing as a broken kaleidoscope of centuries of Station life. It was impossible to find any coherence in them. He let each one leap up, then drift away.

Every few moments Jack broke out of the water, took a breath of his own coherent self, and plunged back down again. The past roared in his ears. He focused on holding himself together while moving in the right direction. He wondered how Fist was experiencing the waters of the memory hole. Every few seconds the puppet cried out, or his body shook.

At last they reached the dark shore. Jack stood and water fell off him. Memories drained away. Jack took a step and nearly slipped over. It was difficult to maintain balance on the lake's muddy floor, harder still when the first of the embryos flew at them, screaming. Tiny limbs flapped excitedly. Its child body was a scribble of half-formed lines. The head tipped toward them. The pale dot in its

321

forehead was a round, unclosing mouth, jagged with fractal swirls of teeth.

'Don't let it bite you,' screamed Fist. 'Get it into the water!'

Jack snatched it out of the air. The mouth grabbed for his hands, all hunger. He plunged the eyeless face down. A splash and it was deep in water. He imagined memories flooding the embryo's little unanchored self. It quickly stopped struggling. Jack let it float to the surface. It was already losing form, black lines unravelling into dark water.

Fist was sobbing. 'That's me,' he choked out, 'before I was born.'

'Are you all right?'

Another embryo appeared.

'Fuck's sake. RUN!' screamed Fist.

They were hurtling towards a tiny alleyway.

'How do we stop them?' yelled Jack, staring wildly around. Fist howled as a shack wall dissolved into nothing and a third embryo attacked. Behind it, a shuddering figure collapsed, black liquid memories bleeding away.

'They're breaking fetches!' Fist's voice was full of grief and rage. He leapt off Jack and charged the embryo. Using a brick as a club, he smashed its body. Scribbles of darkness shimmered, then died away. The ravenous, broken head disappeared last. Fist wouldn't stop slamming the brick down. Jack tore it out of his hands.

Then there came the sound of music, soft and distant and full of memories. 'Can you hear that?' said Jack. Fist didn't answer, tormented by what he'd just done.

Jack snatched him up and set off again. 'Where now?' he asked. Fist didn't reply. He half-recognised the music and ran towards it. It became louder and louder as they neared it. Fist wept on Jack's back as he took the next two embryos, stamping one into an explosion of dark lines and smashing the other against a wall. Both were soaked in broken fetch-blood.

'Why aren't they hurting us, Fist?'

'Your hands.'

Jack looked down and saw bruises, leaking black liquid. His fingers were nearly transparent. Fist too was becoming a ghost.

'The files?'

322

'Safe. They're inert. Not like us.'

Memories bled out of Jack. Time spun and it was hard to know why he was running, what he was running towards. The music was an anchor, holding his identity in place. Andrea burned in his mind, but he often forgot her significance. He feared he was losing himself.

There was more screaming behind them. 'No,' Fist moaned, 'not another.' It darted forward but Jack ducked and it missed them. It cut through a wall, then a fetch. Memories crumbled instantly to nothing. The embryo fed and died. Jack ran. They burst out of the alleyway, into open space.

'GO!' screamed Fist. One final small figure was closing on them. There was a shining light ahead, a self-contained orb. The music throbbed with grief and anger and triumph. Jack felt himself beginning to lose coherence. Sound triggered memory cascades. A voice screamed 'JUMP!' He threw himself forwards. A circular jaw ground against his leg. He could barely breathe. Teeth cut into his skin and he felt a great, devouring appetite hammer at the gates of his mind.

Then the light took him, and for a moment nothing existed.

There was a woman in front of him, hanging in midair on wings made of song. They shone like an angel's, but the feathers they were made of were barbed and spiked like a demon's.

'Hello, Jack,' said Andrea, her voice full of care. 'And Fist. You're safe now. Thank you for the present.'

The wings surrounded him and there was a kiss. A new music at once exploded from and reasserted every memory he had. With a shock that stole the last of his energy he became himself again.

'It was Kingdom,' he said.

'I know.'

And then there was nothing at all.

Chapter 46

When Jack awoke, he was surprised and not a little relieved to find that he remembered who he was. He was lying on the cold earth, and there was a weight on his chest. He opened his eyes and saw Fist sitting on him. The puppet had his head in his hands and was shaking. The undamaged rucksack was strapped safely to his back. They were on the edge of the city of the dead.

In the air above them hung a snowflake.

Jack sat up, cradling Fist as he did so. The puppet let himself be held, falling limply against his chest.

The snowflake was floating directly over the centre of the city of the dead. Its lowest point brushed the top of the dark pile at the heart of the lake, which was substantially smaller than it had been. Jack saw shades swimming through memories to reach it. Others were clambering up the pile or clinging to the pure white of the snowflake, climbing slowly towards the sky. The snowflake's peak broke through the clouds and into the weave. The dead were pulling themselves back into life.

Jack was awed at the sight. He wondered how the living would receive both the unadulterated dead and the fact of such direct Totality interference in Station matters. It was, he supposed, an act of war.

Fist kicked feebly against him, reminding him of more immediate issues.

'Are you OK?' Jack asked him.

'Go away!' Fist's voice was at once aggressive and broken. Looking round, Jack saw why. The wind played at dying fragments of code, the lines that had defined the embryos. 'They're all dead,' spat Fist. He'd stopped leaking memories. Jack assumed that Andrea had stabilised him too. He wondered where she was, if they'd now actually won. It was clear that Fist didn't perceive the battle's climax as a triumph. 'They hadn't even been born,' he said hopelessly.

Jack held him close. 'We didn't have any choice,' he reassured him.

'So much waste.' Fist was silent for a while. When he spoke again, his voice was low and quiet and hard with fury. 'I'm going to kill Kingdom. I've got everything I need to break him and I fucking will. If I have to die I'll fucking do it.'

Dormant machinery sighed and creaked in the depths of Jack's mind. He was very glad that, for the moment, Kingdom was out of their reach. He tried to soothe Fist, but the puppet wouldn't let himself be consoled. Jack gave up and asked about Andrea and Penderville. Fist said nothing, consumed by his own thoughts. For a moment, Jack wondered if Penderville too was climbing up the snowflake, if Andrea had used her wings to rise up and find him. But Fist had said that the search programme would bring Penderville directly to him. The thought that he might have melted into the memory lake hit Jack like a punch.

And then a fetch shimmered into being. It was barely coherent, lying like a man-shaped mist on the grey ground.

'Look, Fist. It must be Penderville.'

Fist turned his back. 'Fuck off.'

Jack left him to his pain and walked over to Penderville. The fetch was shuddering silently through multiple versions of itself. Child, teenage, adult selves sketched themselves across the opaque materials that life had left behind, emerging for a moment into clarity and then vanishing. Jack even recognised the vacuum-frozen corpse face he'd seen out in Sandal's docks. Everything flowed in constant gouts of change, except for the mouth. It was always a gaping O, howling pain and loss. After Penderville's death, his existence had become a perpetual scream.

Jack sank to his knees by the fetch, wondering whether it could ever have anything coherent to say. Andrea could help, but he didn't know how to reach her. He stretched out to touch a shape that might have been a shoulder. There was nothing but pity in him. The silent scream continued as his hand sank into Penderville's body. Cold bit into Jack, and then depression enclosed him. He'd never imagined that such density of guilt could be possible. He snatched his hand away, and immediately the pain was gone.

'Needs stabilising,' said Grey in a calm voice. Jack turned. Grey's presence was shock enough. He was even more surprised to see his patron arm in arm with East.

'What the hell are you two doing here?'

'Not quite hell,' replied Grey breezily. 'Just the Coffin Drives. And we're here because of the Totality, just like Andrea. They opened a path down here. We all followed them in.'

'You weren't just looking to avenge Corazon's death,' said Jack to East. 'This goes far deeper than that. You're in partnership with Grey.'

'Why do you think I looked after little apostate you?' purred East. 'You were working for my lover, setting him free.'

'I've been working on my own. For my own purposes,' declared Jack, with as much conviction as he could muster.

East's laughter rang out in the dead air. 'Of course you have.'

'Don't tease the poor man,' Grey told her. 'He's been through enough.'

'Not as much as Penderville,' replied Jack. He turned back to the broken ghost beside him. It screamed on. 'We need to help him.'

'Fascinating,' said East, peering down at the fetch. 'He's all crisis. I wish my news producers were this focused.'

Jack turned to East. 'You disgust me,' he spat.

'If you were onweave you'd be watching me, along with all the rest of them. Now,' she said, turning to Grey, 'where's Andrea?'

Jack wished that he had a way of, for a moment, forcing them both out of existence. Their presence had polluted his determination to help Penderville, reminding him that it was driven by specific motive rather than pure altruism.

'Andrea's with the Totality,' Grey replied. 'Helping stabilise all those fetches before they reenter the weave.' He turned to Jack. 'That feather's a pretty powerful tool,' he commented. 'She's giving each of them an individually customised copy of it.'

'Ask them if they can spare her,' East told him.

Grey closed his eyes, then opened them again. 'They say yes,' he said.

When Andrea appeared it was without any fuss. One moment she wasn't there, the next she was walking towards Jack. The air around her vibrated with the faintest suggestion of wings, folding themselves away. Her appearance had none of the dancing imprecision that Jack associated with fetches manifesting in the Coffin Drives.

'We need you to stabilise Penderville,' East said.

Andrea ignored her. 'Hello Jack. It seems I've made a bit of a splash.'

'What happened?' asked Jack, reaching instinctively for her hand. Andrea took it. At last the matter of their bodies was identical. They could touch as equals. The gods were suddenly so unimportant.

'Harry came to me, furious. He told me everything. He thought he was taunting me, that he'd be able to roll me back and I'd forget it all. I told him to fuck off, and then I came to find you. He couldn't do anything to stop me.'

Jack smiled with relief. 'The feather worked,' he said.

'It was a wonderful starting point.' She drew in close and kissed him. For a moment, they lost themselves in each other. Then she pulled back and asked: 'Where's Fist?'

'Over there.'

He was gaping at her. [God, Jack, if you could see her as I do.] All the rage had gone from his voice.

[What do you mean?]

[Such coherence. Far more than I gave her.]

'Your understanding of fetch data structures is remarkable,' said Andrea, giving him a broad smile. 'But you hardly know me at all. I had to restructure the feather to fit myself.' Her wings pulsed in and out of existence. 'And then I found I needed more than one.'

'I'm sorry,' Fist replied bashfully. It struck Jack that the puppet had never received such clear, unambiguous gratitude before. 'I didn't have much time.'

'You did a beautiful job,' Andrea reassured him. 'Now I have complete control over every part of myself. I can travel anywhere in the Solar System. And now the Totality have opened the way, I can come and go from the Coffin Drives at will. We're using my rewrite of your feather code to stabilise all the other fetches, so they can do the same. You've freed us all.'

'What are the Totality up to?' said Jack. 'All that'll restart the Soft War.'

'They want the caged fetches on the streets of Station, telling everyone what Kingdom did to them. And they've always hated the Coffin Drives.' Penderville caught her attention. 'Poor man,' she sighed.

'Can you do anything for him?' asked Grey. 'It'd help us a lot.'

'Oh, I can stabilise him. But not to help you, Grey. To help him.'

Penderville's body was a manic scribble. Andrea knelt down by his head and placed her hands on his forehead. Jack was surprised to see that they didn't sink in, as his own hand had done. She leant forward, putting her mouth close to where Penderville's ear should be, and began to whisper. Jack had an impression of music, playing a slow, stately tune a great distance away. Fist watched, fascinated. Jack wondered what deep processes he was witnessing.

Penderville began to fall into something approaching definition. The speed of shift between selves slowed, until the changes matched the music's slow, deliberate rhythm. His mouth still gaped open in a scream, but it shifted less and less between different versions of itself. At last, he was mostly his final self – a pale-skinned man in his late twenties, dressed in a vacuum suit that was only missing a helmet.

Andrea reached up and over her shoulder. When she brought her hand back there was a feather in it. She took it and, ever so gently, placed it in Penderville's mouth. A convulsive shudder ran through him. He screamed like a newborn. His limbs flailed. Andrea's hands were on his cheeks, her gaze steady on his own.

'Hush,' she whispered. 'It's all right. You're dead now. Nothing can hurt you.'

She slowly soothed him through aching moans and then sobs and then just whimpering until he was lying silent, curled around himself. At last she looked up at Jack.

'He's ready,' she said. Then she turned back to Penderville. 'Stand up,' she told him gently, 'it's time.' She helped him climb to his feet. The vacuum suit made his movements awkward. Penderville wiped tears away from his face with a heavy gloved hand, leaving grey dust smeared across his cheeks. 'This is Jack,' said Andrea. 'You need to talk to him.'

Then, she turned to Jack. 'I have to go now. I'm working with the Totality to stabilise all the other fetches.' Her wings unfurled. For a moment they seemed to be the size of the sky. There was a jagged blast of music, and all the best times they'd shared pulsed in Jack's mind at once. 'I'll see you soon, my love,' she said. 'You too, Fist.'

'If we make it,' replied Jack.

Andrea laughed. 'Fuck's sake, Jack, enough with the self-pity. Didn't I tell you not to get in too deep? You've only got yourself to blame.' She winked, suddenly so truly herself. 'You'll be fine,' she said, 'I'm sure of it.' And then she was gone.

Jack took a moment to pull himself back to the present. He turned to Penderville.

'Hello. I'm Jack Forster. I've waited a long time to meet you.' He wasn't sure what else to say. 'I'm sorry that Yamata killed you.'

'There's no need to be,' Penderville replied hopelessly. 'I wanted her to. But it didn't change anything.'

'What happened to you?' Jack asked him. 'Why?'

Guilt and pain had written themselves across Penderville's whole body. He'd been a young man when he died, but now his hair was grey. Wrinkles scarred his face. The vacuum suit, a little too big, hung awkwardly on him. When he spoke, his voice was soft and sad.

'I was glad when she killed me,' he said, his voice bleak. 'I knew I was going to be caged. I thought at least I'd never have to think about it again. I was wrong about that. I was only sad that nobody knew.'

'Nobody knew what?'

Penderville put his face in his hands, and moaned. 'Tell us,' said Grey, softly. East cut in too. 'Yes,' she said. 'Confess. It's so much better to share these things.'

Penderville choked words out. It was difficult to make them out. He was looking down at the ground. There was such passionate shame in his voice. 'I thought it would be nothing,' he sobbed. 'Yamata lied to me. She told me that the rock would just hit one of the abandoned moon bases, that it would just look like Totality sabre rattling. She said that Kingdom would use the incident to justify a fresh round of legislation against them. I didn't know they'd aimed it at the summer camp.'

Jack looked from Penderville to Grey and East. 'No,' he breathed, profoundly shocked.

Words tore out of Penderville. 'It's true. I made the rock invisible to anyone on Station. They'd only see it when it actually hit the moon, and then they'd be terrified because they'd think that the Totality could bypass our defences so easily. I killed all those children. And I let Kingdom blame the Totality and start the Soft War, but then I couldn't live with it – and I was going to tell – but Yamata killed me first.'

Jack swung round to Grey. 'Did you know about this?'

'I knew nothing, Jack,' he protested. 'I'm appalled. Those poor children—'

'Oh, for gods' sake.' Jack turned back to Penderville. 'So Yamata dropped the rock on the moon? On Kingdom's orders?'

'Yes. I met her when it was all being set up. I was worried about what would happen if I was caught. She told me that it would all be fine. That Kingdom knew. That it was his plan and that it had his full approval.'

'They would have killed you whatever you'd done, once you knew that.'

'We're all tools of the gods. When they call we have to obey. Once I knew that it was Kingdom I couldn't say no. He was my patron. I owed him everything.'

'Oh, no.' Jack stepped towards Penderville and put a hand on his shoulder. This time, it didn't sink in. 'That's what you all do, isn't it?' he said to Grey accusingly. 'You make us puppets.'

'We've got your best interests at heart. We always have done.'

'Grey and I had nothing to do with this, Jack,' added East, stepping forwards. 'We're as shocked by it as you are. And we're working with the Totality now. That's why that snowflake's here, that's why we're not stopping the dead from rising. We want people to know about all this. We want a fresh start.'

'You want to bring down Kingdom and reinstate Grey. All this is a power play, nothing more.'

'I was framed and I fell from power,' said Grey, sounding offended. 'I'm a victim too.'

Jack snorted dismissively.

'And we've still got work to do,' Grey continued. 'Kingdom's pushing for a resumption of hostilities against the Totality. He's

330

seen that I'm active again, so he's hitting me hard. My headquarters are under attack. People are beginning to notice all this' – he waved at the snowflake – 'and everyone will know about it once Andrea and the Totality have released all those fetches on to the weave. We need to make sure there's no way Kingdom can turn it all to his advantage.'

'How could he?'

'He's very powerful and he's very afraid, which makes him very dangerous. We need to make sure that there's no way he can cover up any of his crimes. East needs to make sure that people hear the right side of the story. I need to reawaken my board, so I can defend myself properly. You need to get everything you know in front of the Totality and the Pantheon. Now, you can stay here and discuss the niceties of morality, or we can get moving. Which is it going to be?'

'Fist and I don't have a body to go back to,' said Jack. 'We're much more vulnerable to Kingdom without it.'

'Oh yes you do,' replied Grey confidently. 'It's in my headquarters, with Lestak. And Harry upgraded it. Easy to access, more efficient and lots of room for you both.'

[I told you so!] crowed Fist.

'Gods,' said Jack, shocked. 'How?'

'He filled your skull with nanogel in Yamata's medical facility, just like she did with her clones. Then he dressed himself in your flesh and used her security codes to walk out of Kingdom's HQ. Lestak intercepted him on his way back to Homelands and he fled, leaving your body untenanted. By then Kingdom had realised that Yamata was dead. He mobilised, Lestak came under attack by his forces and she fell back to my headquarters, taking your body with her.'

'Is Fist's hardware still installed?'

'Harry left it all in there. He tried to activate Fist's weapon systems, but he didn't get anywhere.'

'Then let's go back and break Kingdom. But not for your benefit, Grey, not for the Pantheon. We'll do it for humanity, and for the Totality.'

'Fuck that noble bullshit,' spat Fist. 'I'm going to do it because it'll make me very happy indeed.'

Jack wondered for a moment how he'd restrain him once they were back on Station.

'Jolly good,' said Grey, not really paying attention. 'Now, I've got a direct link to Lestak set up. It'll route us through the snowflake and then straight to her.' He closed his eyes and the world changed.

They found themselves in a high, round room, its concrete floor and walls softened by gentle light from above. Twelve sarcophagi hovered round it, equally spaced from each other. Each pointed in towards a control area at the centre of the room. There was also a stretcher, covered with a white sheet. Something that was probably a human body lay beneath it. Lestak was bent over it, prodding at a control panel. A sound that could have been gunfire rattled up out of the staircase.

'Welcome to my boardroom!' said Grey, throwing his arms out theatrically.

Lestak turned to him. 'About bloody time! You promised you'd be here an hour ago. We're barely holding off Kingdom's forces. Nearly half my men are dead. Many of your employees, too.'

'You've done a grand job to keep this room safe for this long! And now, we only need a few more minutes. Jack – you'd better go and take a look at your body. See how it's getting on.'

Grey moved over towards a control panel. East followed him, positioning herself in front of a screen. It flickered into life as she gazed at it. 'I've got a line out,' she beamed. 'I'm going to go and get everyone ready for our new media star. Everyone on Station's going to be watching! Oh, and Jack – make sure you take a second to enjoy being virtual!'

She winked at Grey, then vanished. A second, and Penderville was gone too.

Jack looked down at himself and gasped. He'd assumed that he'd jumped straight back into his body, but soft pixilation was smoothing the hard edges of his visual presence. He was a simulation, running onweave rather than in his own flesh.

Fist stepped into view. 'Now you know what being unreal feels like,' he grinned.

Jack could see and hear, but realised with a shock that he could feel nothing else. He didn't know if the room was hot or cold and he couldn't smell anything. He opened his mouth and stuck his tongue out. He couldn't sense or taste the air. He closed his mouth and tried to roll his tongue around inside it, but there was nothing there. When not visible, his tongue disappeared.

Fist laughed.

'What is it?' Jack said.

'I always thought I'd become one of you – but look! You're one of us.'

'I'm still me, though.'

'You seem to be. Just goes to show, doesn't it? There's not much difference between us after all.'

'Enough philosophy,' shouted Grey from a control panel. 'We need your help. Get over there and see if your body will accept you. You need to be running on a secure physical platform when you're in front of the Pantheon, anything less and Kingdom will just squash you.'

Jack joined Lestak by the stretcher.

'I shouldn't be helping you at all, after what you did to Issie,' she said angrily.

There was more gunfire from below. Shouting and smoke rose up the stairwell.

'What do you mean?'

'She told me about the snowflake. She thinks she can climb out of the Coffin Drives for good. She's not strong enough. It'll break her.'

'She's got Andrea and the Totality to help her. And she's not a four-year-old girl any more. She's something very different.'

Lestak sighed. 'Who are you to tell me what she is? You don't even know what you are.'

She pulled the sheet back from the stretcher. Jack looked down at his own corpse. Its skin was a soft, neutral grey. Purple shimmered out of two staring eyes. The mouth had been strapped shut. It was wearing a white, papery hospital gown.

'Come on!' shouted Grey. 'The board's waking up.' The sarcophagi hissed softly, venting coolant. White liquid bubbled out of exhaust pipes, exploding into a ferocious boil as soon as it touched the floor. Small gouts of steam-like smoke sprang up and disappeared. 'Another few minutes and I'll have full control again.'

Jack stared down at his body. The shock was profound. Here he was and yet, there he was. He wondered how much of his self the flesh beneath him retained.

[Nothing at all,] snapped Fist, striding past him and up to the body. He gave one of the arms a kick. His foot sank briefly into it. The rucksack wobbled on his back, but the body's arm didn't move. [I've just been checking gateways. It's been cored. Nothing in that skull but nanogel, waiting for your imprint.]

[How do I get in there? And what about you?]

[They left all my hardware, like Grey said. There's lots of room for both of us. And, if you want to get in – well, you have to ask me nicely.]

[Fist ...]

[I'm kidding! The gate's open!]

A shimmering oval opened up on the forehead of Jack's body, looking something like a burning white eye.

[You just need to touch it, Jack. I'll follow you in.]

Jack reached down. There was an instant of void, then he was occupying his own body again. His senses flooded back – the cold of the room sharp against his skin, the acrid tang of gun smoke cutting into his tongue. The sensations were surprisingly intense. He opened his eyes. Jagged light smashed into them. Gunshots sounded in the distance, battering him. He squeezed both eyes tight shut, tried to jam his hands over his ears. The weight of flesh and bone made both arms immovable. He felt the body's heart rate rise. His own panting rasped in his ears.

[Stop trying to move,] said Fist. [We're meshing with the new systems. Takes a moment or two. Just stay calm.]

Jack felt panic build. He tried to regulate his breathing, reaching into the muscles of his chest and throat, forcing them into a softer, slower rhythm. At first there was no response, but then he heard his panting breaths slow to a more normal pace.

[Good job,] said Fist. [Control systems pretty much fully online now. Try a basic movement.]

Jack's arms seemed much less heavy. He brought his hands up to his face, then slowly crossed and uncrossed his legs. His body was beginning to feel more like a part of him again. He opened his eyes cautiously. The light was no longer so brutal. There were more distant gunshots, but his hearing was properly calibrated now so their sharp rattle was bearable. The world was becoming something to interact with rather than be overwhelmed by. Muscles felt more responsive. Reports pinged in his mind as his consciousness integrated new corporate sensors. Pulse, blood pressure, pain levels – all were suddenly easily accessible and controllable.

[Pretty good, eh?]

[What have they done to me?]

[Nothing. But Harry's upgraded your mind/body interface. I think you'll find you're more in control of your flesh now.]

Jack sat up.

There was a sudden explosion from the stairwell, followed by enraged shouting from below. 'We can't let them get near the board!' yelled Grey, sounding stressed. Jack stumbled to his feet. The Yamatas had found it difficult to move in their newly possessed bodies. He was lurching in the same way.

'I won't be good for a few minutes,' he shouted back at Grey. His tongue felt awkward in his mouth.

[Oh, for gods' sake,] grumbled Fist. [Do I have to do everything?]

[Wait,] said Jack, but it was too late. Fist had bounded away from him, leaping over the control panel and down the stairs. [Don't worry,] he told Jack. [It'll do me some good to take on Kingdom's people. Almost like attacking him.]

[The files'll be safe?]

[Oh yes.]

[You don't have to.]

[But I fucking want to.]

At first, there was no difference to the sounds coming up the stairwell. The battle continued unabated. Then, there was shouting. Where machine-gun fire had been disciplined, it was now coming in wild bursts. There were more explosions. They seemed to be further away. The screaming became more distant. Kingdom's people seemed to be retreating in disarray. Jack wondered how many minds Fist had had to reach into to cause such panic, and what he had made them see.

[You don't want to know,] whispered Fist.

335

'Fantastic!' said Grey cheerfully. 'Awake at last.'

The coffins had finished venting. The groups of flashing lights that danced across them shifted into new formations. Apart from that, there was no change.

'Is that it?' said Jack. His mouth was starting to feel more like it belonged to him.

'I can't bring them all the way back. The locks on them are too strong, but they're aware enough now for me to take control of my remaining head office personnel again. In a basic way.'

'Turn them back into drones, you mean.'

'You saw how far they'd fallen. And right now, they're getting cut to pieces. They need organising.'

'I hate to say it,' Lestak chipped in, 'but he's right. For now, at least.'

'You're going to have to let your people go once you're done,' Jack told Grey. 'Gently, this time.'

'Jack, you're right. I give you my word that I will. Now, can you move around yet?'

Jack took a couple of experimental steps. He almost felt comfortable doing so.

'That's good enough. You and Lestak – get going! Head for the flyer pad. I'm going to stay here. My people will direct and protect you. With Fist and a bit of luck, you'll get through.'

Jack never remembered too much of the frantic race through Grey's offices. He shielded Lestak and her people from his Eastware and let it run as high as he dared. There were looks of adoration. There were bullet howls and explosions. There were Grey employees, suddenly energised, shepherding him and Fist and Lestak through the struggle. When he thought back on it, it was always the details that stood out: broken glass in windows, a smashed photocopier, a blood-slicked whiteboard. The daily essentials of office life had been pulled out of their routine identities and remade as witnesses to warfare.

At last, they reached the flyer pad. A man in a blue boiler suit was waiting for them. For a moment, Jack thought he was Mr Stabs, but then the man moved with fluid ease, ushering them towards a flyer. They were on top of a tall building; below, there were gunshots and explosions, above, the oblivious stars. 'I'm driving,' said Lestak. Jack didn't argue. He let the Eastware fall back to zero. They threw themselves into the flyer and were skyborne. 'I hope nobody gets in a lucky shot,' she continued, as she flicked switches and went through pre-flight checks. Nobody did.

Jack wasn't sure if anybody even noticed them. They were away, and for a moment – the first in a very long time, it seemed – there was peace.

Chapter 47

Jack had to grab Ifor's hand four times before the mind responded.

'Grey told me about Penderville's confession,' said Ifor. 'You saw the snowflake in the Coffin Drives?' Jack nodded. 'We had to rescue the two of you, and make sure that the caged dead could get the news about Kingdom out. Now we're dealing with the fallout. Be quick!'

'We're on our way to join you. We're about to release the news cross-Station, but the Pantheon will need more than just media reports. I'm bringing the proof of Kingdom's corruption directly to you.'

Ifor stilled for a moment, digesting the news. Jack imagined him sending it out into the Totality; a mass of voices discussing options. 'That's good to know. When's East going live with Penderville?'

'I'm not sure. Soon. You need to stop anything bad happening before then. And make sure that we get into the negotiating room.'

'It's chaos here. We'll send minds to meet you at the landing pad, and bring you in as diplomatic representatives.'

'How are the negotiations going?'

'We're twenty minutes from war. Kingdom's forces are deploying against us. He's realised we've opened the Coffin Drives. He's ranting about the violation of sacred space. It's looking bad.'

'We'll take care of it.'

'I hope so. See you in a moment.'

The call ended.

[Very interesting,] said Fist.

[The Totality?]

[No, it's Harry. He's just tried to use his back door to access me.]

[Shit. Don't let him in.]

[No danger of that, I'm wise to him now!]

Fist was silent for a moment. He cocked his head, as if listening.

[He's like a little enraged fly,] he said gleefully. [Buzz, buzz, buzz.] He giggled. [Oo! The ninja code's up and running too!]

[Keep him out! No more slip-ups.]

[Oh, don't you worry about that. He's going to do exactly what I want him to. He's working for me now.]

There was no time to find out what Fist meant. They'd reached Sandal's headquarters, landing so fast that they nearly crashed. The flyer's landing gear buckled. They were out of it before it stopped moving. Armed guards stalked towards them, guns raised. A delegation of Totality minds emerged from the building, led by Ifor. They ran towards the guards, shouting. Jack hit them with his Eastware. Guilt lashed him in return. But the guns didn't waver. The guards must be shielded against any sort of virtual influence. The minds flashed up diplomatic credentials. Disappointed muzzles drooped towards the ground. One of the guards radioed a superior, requesting clarification. It was difficult to know what he'd be told. The small party ran for the doors. A shout of 'halt' came too late. They were through the door, racing down corridors.

[Slow the guards, Fist.]

[Shielded. Not much I can do.]

[Shit.]

One of the minds turned and tossed a small metal ball back down the corridor. There was a blinding flash of light behind them.

[Blind 'em,] said Fist. [Nice one.]

After a moment, the shouting started again. Then there were bullets. Jack looked back. A sharp burning scored the side of his face. He stumbled for a moment, then found a switch in his mind and turned pain off. They turned a corner.

[All right?] asked Fist.

[I'll keep going.]

Now he was slightly behind Fist and Ifor. There was a pair of double doors ahead of them, guards on either side. They wore body armour and carried assault rifles. Jack let the Eastware rise up. These guards sunk to their knees. Jack wondered how he appeared to them – a shining god, divine enough to obey, human enough to be panting and bleeding. 'Let us pass!' he yelled. They leapt to one side. One of them reached up with a security pass, and the doors slid open. They led into a lift.

'It's the way to the conference space,' said Ifor.

They slammed into the lift. There was a bloody smear where Jack had cannoned into its back wall. He wondered how badly he was hurt. Not enough to slow him down. Their pursuers were rounding the corner, rifles up and ready to fire. Ifor, Jack and Fist were easy targets.

'Stop them!' screamed Jack, and the enamoured guards opened fire. The lift doors started to close. The first pursuer to round the corner collapsed. Momentum kept the rest coming forward. One of them threw a grenade before he was cut down. The doors shut and the lift began to rise. An explosion shook it, but it kept moving. Jack and Ifor slumped back against the wall. Fist was stock still.

[Are you OK?] Jack asked him.

[Breaking Sandal's security systems. Making sure he doesn't stop the lift.]

[All ready with the Yamata files?]

[Yes. They'll all be able to access them. I've chucked in a recording of Penderville's confession for good measure.]

[Excellent.] Jack turned to Ifor. 'And are you all right?' he said. A bullet had struck the mind too. Purple plasm leaked out of a gash in his chest. Ifor put his hand over it. 'I'll be fine.'

The lift doors hushed open. Ifor limped forward. Fist looked past Jack, and his jaw dropped. 'Bloody hell,' he said, forgetting to mask his words, 'so this is how the other half live.'

Jack turned too, and was awed. He'd always understood Heaven to be the land of the gods, but realised suddenly that he was wrong. Heaven was merely where humanity was able to most closely approach them. This room was their true home, and the whole of the Solar System was encompassed within it. He took a step forward. The lift doors started to close, and then the weave overlaid them and they vanished.

Jack was floating before a tiny image of Station. All around it, there was space – or rather, an abstract representation of space. Jack was at the heart of a real-time map, overlaid with dense thickets of information showing all human activity. White loops arcing

340

through the void, defining planetary orbits. A shimmering globe moved along each one, alive with colour and data. Finger-sized images of moonbases and space stations and chainships and asteroid mines hovered everywhere, representing every single outpost of humanity. Numbers danced through the emptiness, scurrying up or down or just staying the same, as the realities they measured shifted with each moment. The outer reaches of the map were dotted with bright pinpricks of light. They were embedded in barely perceptible clouds of soft, pearlescent grey.

Jack assumed they represented the Totality's sphere of influence. The clouds shimmered across the whole of the region beyond the Kuiper belt. They'd also made substantial inroads in-system, stopping only on the near-side of Mars' orbit. Only Station and the orbital areas surrounding it were untouched by Totality influence. Tiny patches of colour represented the different zones that each Pantheon member controlled. Jack had always known that the Totality had become by far the widest ranging corporate body in the Solar System, but until he saw this representation of its reach he had never understood just what that meant.

'Look at the population density,' said Fist. 'Most of humanity's in Station – and the Pantheon still holds that.'

'And that's the jewel we're all fighting for,' cut in a deep voice, resonant with the heaviness of industrial machinery. Jack had last heard it in a propaganda film, inducting new puppeteers into the Soft War.

'Kingdom,' he hissed.

The Pantheon shimmered into being around him, security protocols falling away. Those closest caught his eye first. There was the Rose in full combat armour, Sandal's shimmering cube, the Twins holding hands but looking away from each other. Together, the six formed a wide circle, centred on the image of Station. The scale of the simulation made them far larger than planets, larger even than the Sun. Soft lines came into being between them and divided the sky into segments, forming something like a corporate zodiac. Those gods with eyes stared at Jack. East waved cheerfully. A blindfolded, hobbled raven did its best to snap its beak. There were four snowflakes too, hanging in the void.

Kingdom was the last to appear. The shadows fell away from him like oil until he was fully revealed. He manifested as a tall man with a shaven head and a face as functionally beautiful as an industrial diamond. His skin glowed gold in the light from the god-dwarfed sun. He was dressed in a loose black shirt and trousers. His feet were bare. Jack took a step back, awed and afraid. Here was the infrastructure that gave humanity life; here was the corruption that devoured its children.

'How do you dare break into this council?' asked Kingdom. 'And with the help of a Totality mind. What do you all have to say to this act of naked aggression?'

The snowflakes shuddered with multicoloured light. Jack looked back to Ifor. His head was bowed and he was silent, deep in communion with his fellows.

[You'd better say something, Jack.]

Jack gulped, then spoke. 'We come to accuse you, Kingdom, of crimes against humanity and the Totality. We come to lay proof of those crimes before this council. Fist – the files.'

Fist shrugged off the backpack and tossed it towards the middle of the room. It fell among the virtual stars and skittered along the real floor for a couple of metres before coming to rest. 'It's all in there,' he said. 'Dropping a rock on the moon, prolonging the Soft War. Just take a look.' [That was quick,] he added. [Everyone in the room's already downloaded it.]

'That is absurd,' said Kingdom, his protest tolling out like a great, slow factory bell. 'A ridiculous, self-evident fabrication from two servants of a discredited god. A transparent attempt to distract us from the Totality's most recent provocation. We protect humanity. We are humanity. We would never harm it in this way. It's a profoundly offensive suggestion.'

The cube that represented Sandal grew in size. Images of hard working dockers flashed across its faces, pulsing rapidly to show his anger. 'Silence!' he snapped. 'As chair of this conference, I must insist on silence.' The cube turned towards Jack. 'This kind of discussion is not on the agenda.'

Kingdom gestured towards Jack. 'This man is a well-known Totality sympathiser and Grey agitator. He was returned to Station at the specific request of our common enemy. His presence here at this very crucial point is clearly a Totality ploy. I'm sure they furnished him with these remarkably convincing fake documents. Forster and his puppet should be terminated immediately.'

'Please,' said Sandal. 'My security people have been summoned. They will be here soon, and—'

Ifor interrupted him. 'This man and his puppet are accredited Totality diplomatic representatives, and thus under our full protection,' he announced. 'Any action against them would be interpreted as action against us. We would regard it as a direct declaration of war.'

'The Totality feels itself to be the victim here?' asked Kingdom. 'A corporate entity that has breached our Coffin Drives, thus illegally attacking the deepest roots of our heritage as humans? There is nothing more to discuss. Mr Chairman, I submit that we are already at war with these false minds – a war once again provoked solely by them. First, they struck at our children. Now they're striking at our dead. And now their agent is accusing me of terrible, terrible crimes. We need to shut down all non-military activities and hit back with everything we have. Now.'

One of the snowflakes spoke. Its calm voice had a resonant depth to it, as if it were made up of a thousand whispers coming together as one. 'We have already demonstrated that your forces do not match ours. We halted our advance at Mars by choice, not out of necessity.'

'You have attacked all that is most sacred to us. Even those humans who've gone over to your side will turn against you when they understand that. And that will tip the balance of power in our direction.'

'All of this is irrelevant,' protested Jack, his voice full of frustration. 'None of you are thinking about what's important, about why you're going to war in the first place. It's nothing to do with the Totality; it's because of Kingdom. War is in his interest. Breaking the Totality is in his interest. And so he's making it happen. He's fooled you all, and he's done it before. These documents prove it.'

Kingdom laughed. 'Absurdities. I wish I had that much power.'

'Kingdom both started and prolonged the last war,' replied Jack, 'and his actions are going to set this one off too.'

'I move we vote on a response to the Totality's obscene provocation,' pronounced Kingdom, speaking over him. 'And that this intruder is silenced.'

'No!' shouted Jack.

'Mr Chairman?' asked Kingdom, a soft undertone of menace in his voice.

'We will proceed with the vote,' Sandal decided, shimmering nervously.

'Wait.' East stepped forward. 'I've got something to show you.'

'Really, East,' scolded Kingdom. 'This isn't the time—'

'Breaking news. Look.'

She waved a hand and screens sprung into being around the circle. Some showed wide shots of Station; some were closeups of individual streets; some showed one man, talking. Jack recognised this latter immediately. It was Bjorn Penderville.

His voice echoed out, caught in mid-sentence.

'—responsible for the destruction on the moon. I confess to masking the meteor myself, ensuring that it could strike the moon without being detected. I used software adapted from sweathead blanking protocols. I did so at the instigation of Aud Yamata, leader of a criminal gang controlled by Kingdom. InSec operative Harry Devlin later joined the Yamata gang.'

[Oo, I bet Harry's ears are burning! Though he's probably concentrating too hard to notice. Little fly.]

[He's still out there?]

[He thinks he's almost hacked into me. Into my web! My lovely little web! Ah, the ninja code's reporting back.]

[What are you up to?]

[All my plans are paying off. You'll see.]

[Fuck's sake, Fist.]

On the screens, Penderville continued his confession. 'I understand that, after my death, Devlin helped the Yamata gang create a series of false flag attacks that were blamed on terrorists and used to justify the execution and fetch-caging of a number of key anti-war activist groups. These activists were for the most part allied with or supported by Grey, hence the attacks on him.'

Shouting broke out across the room. Penderville's words were

344

lost in the melee. Kingdom's voice became a high-pitched scream, the sound of metal grinding on metal. 'Can you not see that this ridiculous conspiracy theory is a lie?' he was yelling. Other Pantheon members were shouting, too, some in support of him, some against him.

Despite the ferocity of the onslaught, East was unruffled. 'Now let's hear from the dead,' she said, speaking with a news anchor's dispassion.

The screens showing Station increased in size. The images each held shifted, zooming in on individual streets. Jack realised that they were closing in on void sites. Crowds had gathered round each one. Images of children hung over each void site. They were still broadcasting their messages of grief but beneath them, the dead had returned. They stood in shimmering rings, fetches who had climbed out of the Coffin Drives and, through the omnipresence of the weave, found themselves able to manifest in the streets of Station. It was an apocalypse, of sorts.

'Bringing in audio,' said East calmly, and each screen was suddenly roaring out the voices of the dead. They were speaking as one. ' ... working for peace, and we found ourselves under attack. Every single one of us was killed by one of Kingdom's operatives. Every single one of us was caged in the Coffin Drives, unable to speak of this. They told you we were terrorists, but none of us were; they told you that we were threats, but none of us were; they told you that we hated humanity, but really we love life. Kingdom made you afraid so that you would agree to war with the Totality, but he has always been the real enemy. Reject him!'

The last two words of the speech were a great, triumphant roar.

'Now they're starting the speech again,' explained East. 'Others have risen, too.'

The screens shimmered, becoming a kaleidoscope of many different views. They danced through streets and houses, parks and shops. Some even showed the darkness of space or the cramped confines of chainships. Fetches were everywhere, drifting like angelic ghosts, tightly embracing the living or just standing, looking round in wonder and disbelief, at last free from the Coffin Drives.

None of them had skulls for heads.

'They're free,' said East. 'Nobody controls them any more.'

'But – this is a disaster!' shouted Kingdom. 'If nobody controls them – that means artificial intelligences are loose, everywhere! It's a direct threat to us! Remember how we lost our homeworld!'

East just smiled. 'I think your terrorists have something more to say.'

The screens flicked back to show a single void site. The fetches ringed round it were chanting. Jack saw that they'd been joined by a number of scrappily dressed, happy looking children. Their words were clear.

'Shut down Kingdom! Shut down Kingdom!'

'No!' howled Kingdom.

The chanting became louder and louder. The camera pulled back. The chant had been taken up by the crowd that had formed round the void site. The camera pulled back still further. There were crowds across the whole of Homeland, shouting against Kingdom. The view flicked to Docklands. There too, the streets echoed with voices.

'Shut down Kingdom! Shut down Kingdom!'

'These terrorists will break Station. We need to shut down East's media networks. If their message is heard, they'll destroy everything we fought for,' gasped Kingdom, his rich voice shattered by panic.

'Good,' said Grey. The blindfolded raven was gone; now the man stood there, smartly dressed and looking very relaxed.

'You!' gasped Kingdom. 'You dare to come here!' He turned away from Grey to address the group. 'This criminal is manipulating you all,' he snarled. 'We must freeze Grey and close down East. It's the only way to protect us from their lies. There is no alternative.'

'The evidence against you is strong, Kingdom,' said East implacably. 'And we can't stand in the way of the people. As you've said yourself, many times.'

Sandal's highly stressed voice rang out like a power drill. 'We need to debate this properly. It's not what we're here for now.'

A snowflake weighed in. 'The Totality has always claimed that we were not responsible for the lunar atrocity. We have already been able to confirm some aspects of this interpretation of the facts. We believe that Penderville and these other freed minds are telling the truth.'

346

'Perhaps Sandal has a point,' said Grey smoothly. 'We should be fair to Kingdom. Should we take steps to protect him? If we isolate his board from his key subsidiaries then the shock of this sudden crash will be lessened. We can then call this meeting to a halt, and investigate in more depth, at our leisure.'

[Fucking gods,] said Fist. [Protecting their own.]

[What?] replied Jack.

'No! No!' said Sandal, his voice almost a scream. 'As chair I insist we complete voting on our original motion. We must decide whether or not to attack the Totality.'

'I think a little patience might be in order,' soothed Grey.

[Right, fuck this,] snapped Fist. [Where's Harry? Aha!] He shook, and then staggered a couple of paces forward. He looked suddenly drunk.

[Fist!] shouted Jack. [Come back here! What are you doing?]

'Oh no!' Fist shouted, theatrically. 'Oh no!' He took another uncertain step, then swayed round till he was facing Jack. He raised his hands to his head, so nobody else could see his face. He gave Jack a slow, confident wink. And then, he arched his back and threw himself down, hitting the ground with a clatter. Patches of overlay disappeared around him, revealing a white-painted concrete floor. 'He's possessing me!' he yelled. 'I can't stop him!'

Grey peered over, mild worry on his face. 'Jack, this is a very serious moment. You really should keep him quiet.'

Jack barely heard. He could feel system after system tumbling out of his control. [Fist?] he called out, but there was no reply. The puppet was no longer a presence in his mind.

'What's happening?' asked Ifor.

'I think he's let Harry come through,' Jack replied.

Fist's limbs smashed themselves against the ground, again and again, a small blur of fevered movement. Jack couldn't understand what he'd been trying to achieve. Whatever it was, it seemed to have failed. His thoughts clouded over for a moment, as if a great shadow had passed across them.

'Is he all right?' said Ifor.

'It looks like he's lost control.'

'Oh yes,' said a voice with a strong Docklands accent, speaking

347

out of Fist's mouth. 'OH FUCKING YES!' Fist's whole body was shaking. It began to grow.

'I warned you both so many times about carelessness,' said Grey, sounding a little less relaxed.

'Security! Security!' squawked Sandal. His six square sides showed images of burly men and women in riot gear.

Kingdom was trying not to look worried. He took one step back, and then another. There was a sharp hissing sound. The shape that had been Fist's body was the size of a full-grown man. The shaking began to slow. First his torso and then his limbs returned to clear sight. He was someone different now. He rose to his feet. He was wearing a jaunty fedora, a raincoat that billowed around him and a sharp suit and tie. He had a smile on his face that was at once triumphant, lethal and irresistibly charming.

He was Harry Devlin.

'So,' he smiled. 'Which one of you cunts is up for a hostile take-over?'

'SECURITY!' bellowed Sandal.

'They won't come,' Harry told him. 'Fist was still plugged into the lift. I killed it. Comms too. You're all locked in now. With me.' He turned, looking around the room. 'Well, well, well. All of you here together. And the Totality, too. So many birds to kill with one stone.'

There was a wall in Jack's mind where Fist should be. He beat against it, but it was impossible to break through. He heard sounds from behind it. Combat machinery was grinding into life, complaining like a broken giant slowly waking from a deep, concussed sleep.

'Do something!' said East, the anxiety in her voice sounding subtly forced. 'Won't somebody do something?'

The Rose leapt towards Harry, scarlet clothing becoming brutally functional combat armour. Harry laughed, and clicked a finger. There was a dog at the Rose's neck and the weight took her balance from her. She skidded and fell, a flailing tumble of limbs. The dog fell with her. As they both hit the ground it became something both more and less than itself. Losing all definition, it flowed over her, a tide of darkness covering her completely. For a moment, it was possible to make out the shape of her body. She screamed. The scream was suddenly and completely cut off. Then there was nothing where she'd been but another empty patch of concrete.

'He's locked up all her non-essential systems,' gasped Ifor. 'That's impossible.'

'No,' said Jack wearily. 'Not for Fist. And Harry's controlling him.'

Harry staggered and put a hand to his head, then recovered himself. Now all the Pantheon were shuffling back, trying to put as much distance between themselves and him as possible. Only the snowflakes didn't move, pulsing with unreadable colours.

'I just force-triggered a full internal self-audit,' explained Harry. 'It's a vast resource drain, she'll be out of action for the next hour or so.' He was a little paler than he had been. He controlled his shaking voice. 'Just like that.' He chuckled, once again in control of himself. But his hair was a soft grey, where before it had been black. 'So it's true. Accountant plus puppet equals Pantheon gun.' He turned to Jack. 'I couldn't believe it when I saw Fist's weapon systems. Crying shame, giving all that power to you. What the fuck would you ever use it for?' He turned back to the Pantheon. 'All this Homelands wanker's good for is fucking other men's wives. But I'll deal with him in a moment. I've got you lot to sort out first. You screw us all, every single day. And I'm going to start with the biggest cunt of them all.'

He pointed at Kingdom.

'You.'

'No. Please. You don't know what you're doing,' begged Kingdom, his voice thin with fear.

'Oh, I know all right. I know exactly what I'm doing.' Black dogs appeared, lined up on either side of Harry. They tensed, ready to pounce, snarling out anger and threat. 'You promised me so much, Kingdom. But you didn't deliver any of it. So I'm not going to fuck around with an audit. It's hostile takeover time. And I'm going to take everything you've got.'

Kingdom cowered backwards as the seven dogs leapt. They lost form as they flew towards him, stretching out to become long, hard shadows, staining the air with darkness. When they hit him their black liquid mass slicked across his body. He screamed until the darkness covered his face. He stopped struggling very quickly, becoming a dark, inchoate statue.

Harry strolled towards him. 'All ready for me now, aren't you?' he said triumphantly, and then turning to the Pantheon, 'None of you got the balls to try and stop me? No?'

'I'll never let you get away with this, you bastard,' spat East. 'I'll have every journalist of mine exposing you!'

'I'll be a hero,' replied Harry confidently. 'I killed the entity that dropped a rock on the moon and started the Soft War. That's what your journalists will write, or I'll have them looking for sources outside an airlock, and I'll put you in a closed audit loop for the rest of time.'

And with that, he reached out and touched the dark figure that had been Kingdom. His body disappeared into it. His clothes, suddenly empty, dropped to the floor. There was a moment of silence.

'Shit,' said Jack, stunned. 'I think we just lost.'

'We have to get out of here,' gasped the Twins.

'We can't,' stuttered Sandal. 'The lift's still locked.'

Powerlessness was a new experience for the gods.

'What are we going to do?' whimpered one of the Twins. 'I don't want to be lost in my own accounts forever!' The other Twin sat down with a thump. 'Our lovely hotels!' she wailed. 'Our medical centres! Our agri-sites! Who will care for them if we can't?'

Only Jack noticed a little hummock suddenly appear in Harry's clothes. It was somewhere under his waistcoat. As the gods sobbed, or just stood in shocked silence, it moved towards the neck of his shirt, where a familiar face popped out.

[Well,] beamed Fist [That went about as well as it could have done. How fortunate for Harry that I carelessly left such a clearly signposted route into Kingdom's core systems when we broke into his headquarters.]

Jack couldn't find any words to say.

Fist clambered to his feet and addressed the assembled divinities. 'Thank fuck Harry was SO excited about becoming a god that he left my cage door open,' he chirped, before forcing a little pain into his voice. 'It was agony watching him attack Kingdom. Agony!'

'You saw it all, then?' asked Sandal nervously.

'Oh yes,' replied Fist. He stifled a pretend sob. 'All of it. The horror! Oh, the horror.' He was clearly enjoying himself hugely, despite the fact that his hair too had turned grey.

[You're play-acting,] said Jack. [Harry's damaged you. And what about all the people who rely on Kingdom? You're playing with their lives.]

[There's enough of me left to finish the job,] replied Fist. [And they're all taken care of. Like I told you, I've spent a lot of time thinking about consequences. Sit back and watch a master at work.]

There was a mature confidence in his voice that Jack had never heard before. Fist switched back to speaking out loud. 'But, looking on the bright side, most of my weapon systems are still largely intact. Even after such terrible misuse of them. Misuse over which I had no control whatsoever. Misuse that even damaged me!' He pointed at his newly aged hair.

As he spoke, the darkness that had covered Kingdom fell away. The takeover was complete. Now Harry stood there, his eyes closed. His skin glowed gold. He was wearing Kingdom's dark shirt and loose trousers. His battered face was wreathed with the numinous. Despite himself, Jack felt awe touch him. Harry opened his eyes, and looked down.

'You?' he boomed. 'LITTLE YOU?' His voice echoed around the conference chamber. He threw back his head and laughed. Virtual stars rang with mockery.

'Oh yes,' said Fist, his voice low and menacing. 'Me. Little me. And I've got a bone the size of a planet to pick with you.' He rose into the air, and floated towards Harry. 'Do you remember what I said, that dark night in the garden?'

'I'll shatter you, puppet, if you come any closer,' warned Harry.

Fist closed on him regardless. Jack felt his weapon set grind once again in his mind. The sound of its awakening went so deep, far beyond anything Harry had been able to summon. Jack slumped. Fist was boosting his offensive power by drawing on Jack's resources. Harry hadn't been able to do that either.

'Are you OK?' worried Ifor. Jack felt soft hands at his shoulders, holding him up. He found that he couldn't move his mouth. Those parts of his mind were running other, more brutal systems.

[I'm sorry,] Fist told Jack. He was controlling his voice so carefully, but still a wild, abandoned rage broke through. [This is going to hurt. Him more than you, though.]

[What are you doing?] The deep structures of Jack's own mind groaned in protest as Fist snatched even more resources. [I can't let you,] he continued. He tried to call Fist back.

The puppet laughed. [You can't do that any more. Not since we were rebuilt. All you can do is watch. And trust me. You'll never see me like this again. You might never see me again. But it'll be worth it. Oh fuck yes. WATCH!]

Jack wasn't sure if it was his own will or Fist's that made him turn his head and reopen his eyes.

'Jack,' said Ifor. 'You're conscious.' He followed Jack's gaze, and then he too was silenced. Fist was drifting towards Harry, his body changing as his attack systems fired up.

'I said I'd broken minds like yours before, and I'd break you too.'

His arms stretched out of his sleeves and his legs stretched out of his trousers. His torso grew. Piece by piece, his clothes ripped off him. A snapped bow-tie, fragments of dress shirt, a tattered tail coat, a pair of shredded black trousers – all fell away as he slowly advanced on Kingdom.

Each wooden body section exuded strands of attack code, coiling together to define Fist's new, expanding self. It manifested as silver-grey barbed wire, growing into the shape of densely muscled arms and legs, vast shoulders and a squat, powerful neck. Fist's hands and feet had grown too, fingers and toes stretching out into jagged claws and talons. Jagged wire sprang up and danced around them, then around Fist's whole body. It leapt up to cover his now entirely white hair and he laughed.

Now his face stretched out and began to change too. His cheerful painted eyes fell back into his head, and there were two shadow pits where they had been. His little pointed nose fell in on itself, becoming a jagged slit in the centre of his face. He smiled, and his smile was an axe cut, ripping back into his cheeks. There was a loud crack, and his teeth broke through his jaw – uncounted sharp grey barbs, waiting to rend and tear.

Nothing remained of the well-dressed puppet that had been built to charm children. This was the elemental Fist, a deep and focused savagery unleashing itself on the world.

Harry stumbled backwards. 'What are you?' he breathed.

'Death,' hissed Fist, smiling his barbed-wire smile. His wooden face was a flat, dead mask on a thorned metal head. The wire filled his empty eyes and the slit that had been his nose. He brought his arms up from the side of his body, extending each metal-wrapped wooden finger. Blue sparks flickered round them. Harry gestured with his hands. Nothing happened. Fist kept coming.

'CHILD!' he shouted, the word rasping out from a hard metal tongue. 'You're five minutes old. I've been killing angels for seven years.'

Harry took a step back. He had his arms up in front of him. His own fire leapt to his hands. Fist continued speaking. There was no longer any trace of the toy he'd once appeared to be. Jack wondered if this was what the Totality had seen when Fist attacked them.

'You dared – YOU DARED – to break into me, and force your way through me, and use me as a router. A FUCKING ROUTER! To get to that bitch Yamata.'

A few words were shouted. Most were spat out in a vicious, barbed whisper.

Fire leapt from Harry's hands. It didn't reach Fist. The puppet's feet had touched ground. He was walking. He was a foot or so taller than Harry. Wire dragged behind him, leaving a path of sparks. 'You thought there'd be no comeback.' He brought his hands up to his face, and looked at them appraisingly. He teased out a strand of wire from his left hand with the finger and thumb of his right. 'Look at my strings now. You thought you were pulling them, didn't you? But they bit into you, little god. So deep.'

There was a roaring in Jack's head. He could watch, and he could think, and that was it. All through his mind, core structures were shaking themselves to pieces as Fist seized the capacity he needed to break a god. Jack could feel his own systems rushing to compensate for the chaos. Had he not become a digital version of himself, he would by now have been irrevocably shattered. He wondered if either of them would survive Harry's death.

Harry laughed nervously. 'You can't hurt me, puppet.'

Fist snapped his fingers, and a barbed explosion of code leapt out of him. For a moment it hung in the air, and then it pulled itself round Harry, snapping his arms to his sides and his legs to each other, charring clothes black and scoring blue lines where it touched bare flesh.

Harry howled. Subroutines knifed into his mouth, his throat. His scream had a gurgling, half-broken quality to it. Fist snapped his fingers again. More wire leapt at Harry and bit at him, tracing hard symbols of pain across his skin and then dancing deep into his body.

'ARE YOU IN POSITION, TOTALITY?' he yelled.

'Yes,' said one of the snowflakes. 'One of our craft is at the co-ordinates you gave us. A squad of minds have penetrated Devlin's physical security systems and are ready to reoccupy the stolen servers he's running on. They'll use the link he's established with Kingdom's core systems to follow him there too.'

'NO!' screamed Harry. Wire poured into his throat, silencing him. He writhed, collapsing to the floor.

Fist sunk down so that he was right next to him. One hand touched Harry's forehead. There was a tiny puff of smoke, a smell of burning flesh and then the black print of a wooden hand was branded in Harry's flesh.

'You're the careless one, Harry. You never bothered looking deeper than the puppet. There's so much more to me than that.'

Harry groaned. Jack was barely conscious. Fist took Harry's head in his two barbed hands and pulled it from his shoulders. He roared with triumph. It was his last great effort, and it broke him. He shimmered and vanished. Harry's broken corpse vanished with him. Code howled in Jack's mind. Through it all came Fist's voice, surprisingly quiet and controlled.

[Let yourself go, Jack. I've broken my weapon systems killing Harry. Now's time to reboot and rebuild.]

Unconsciousness took Jack. It was kinder than death had been, but only a little.

Chapter 48

The spinelights were dimming over Homelands. Towers faded into the gloom as lit windows shimmered into being, a thousand tiny protests against the dark. Snowflakes hung above them all, now fully integrated into the weave and so into Station's day-to-day life. Jack turned away from the window. Fist was sitting on a chair, knocking his hand against a conference table, making a loud, sharp, repeated tapping. He was four foot tall again, with a little painted face and a little painted body. He was wearing black tie, topped off with a rather natty monocle. His body was entirely physical.

'You know,' he said, 'I can't get over how this feels. This is a real table; here's a real me; and here I am, hitting it. Who would have thought a meat body could fit little Hugo Fist so well?'

'You're a real boy at last.'

'I'm not a boy, Jack, or a man. I've seen enough of people not to think I'm human any more. I'm an incarnate artificial intelligence. But then so are you, now – a digital pattern, running on a nanogel soup. Most of you isn't even in that head of yours. It's distributed across Station's weaveservers. I don't think there's really any difference between us. You're alive, but artificial – I'm artificial, but I'm alive.'

'Things have got a lot more blurred lately,' agreed Jack. 'All these new ways of being alive. I suppose that's one good thing to come out of it all.'

'It's just a shame it had to happen the way it did.'

'Well. That's a fight that's not over yet.'

'That sounds worryingly like sedition,' said Lestak, appearing at the door.

'Oh, don't worry,' said Fist smoothly. 'It's just his grumpy way. And besides, it's much harder to be seditious these days. Now that the Totality sits on the Pantheon as an equal member, and fetches have pretty much the same rights as the living, there's no them and us any more. There's just us, and plotting against us, rather than them, is pretty pointless.'

'You make it sound so simple,' replied Lestak. 'Not everyone sees it like that. It's created a lot of work for us.'

'And what about the divinities who supported Kingdom?' asked Jack. 'Any work gone into finding them?'

'They'll have covered their tracks by now. We wouldn't be able to prove anything.'

'So the gods are too big for justice?'

Lestak sighed. 'There's been enough change, Jack. People have lost so much faith in the Pantheon. Keeping a lid on it all is a big challenge. If another god fell – well, who knows where it would end.'

'Very sensible,' interrupted Grey, shimmering into being. 'Humans, gods – we're all so fragile. Too much change, too suddenly, could overwhelm us all.'

'We'd survive. Even if the whole Pantheon fell.'

'But not all of us would go down. And those of us who remained would be even more powerful. Even fewer checks on our behaviour. Remember what Harry was like when he thought he ruled Station. Power corrupts, and you'd be feeding us more of it. Think about that, Jack, before you start toppling gods.'

'Oh, for fuck's sake.'

'Of course, factually you're quite right. At least one of my colleagues did support Kingdom. Perhaps more. Covertly, of course.' His voice took on a forced cheerfulness as he swept his arm out towards the peaceful city. 'And now, I think, looking at all this, they're very much regretting doing so.'

'You won't tell us who they are, though, will you?' asked Jack. His voice was weary.

'We'll be late for the ceremony if we stand here talking,' replied Grey jauntily. 'Won't we, Lestak? Hadn't we better head for the main hall? Don't want to keep people waiting.'

'There's not going to be any ceremony, Grey. Jack's refused it,' Lestak told him.

'Rejecting the thanks of the gods?' said Grey. 'Some would call that ungracious.'

'Fist's been granted full citizenship. The Totality helped build him a body. My record's been cleared. There's nothing else either of us wants from you.'

'You've really got to stop focusing on the downside,' chided Grey. 'You'd be so much better off if you let yourself enjoy what you've achieved. You and Fist are heroes. You purged Kingdom and you protected all of us from Harry. And as we've just agreed, anyone who can bring down a Pantheon member is a threat to us all.' He shot Fist a pointed look.

'Oh, I know that very well,' said Fist. 'I'm only sorry that I couldn't stop Harry before he destroyed Kingdom.' He almost sounded as if he meant it. 'It's Jack who's the pessimist, not me.'

Jack glared back at Grey. 'Harry kills Kingdom, Fist kills Harry, problem solved, all done and dusted,' he spat. 'Nice and easy and resolved. That's how East's spinning it too, isn't she? Let the blame fall on the dead, don't dig into the crimes of the living.' He sighed. 'All we've really done is enable a whitewash.'

'Nonsense,' exclaimed Grey. 'Think about the bigger picture. You've enabled peace. Your actions brought the Pantheon and the Totality together. When Fist killed Harry, it left a space they had to fill. Their immediate takeover of his corporate structure saved tens of thousands of lives. The revelation of Kingdom's crimes offset their opening of the Coffin Drives and paved the way for their acceptance into Station. Without you two, the peace negotiations would never have led to such a positive outcome. And now we've got that peace, we really can't do anything to risk it. Which is why we're all going to look forwards, not backwards, from now on.'

'If it's built on a lie,' replied Jack, 'it's not really peace at all.'

Grey said nothing. Jack turned away from him. The dusk outside had turned to night. The windows had become great dark mirrors, showing all in the room back to themselves. Jack found that he could meet his own gaze. Lestak finally broke the silence. 'If that's it,' she said, 'I need to escort you out.'

'Don't worry,' said Grey. 'I can show him the way.'

'Wait,' Fist cut in. 'Before you go – will you be seeing Issie soon?'

Lestak smiled sadly. 'Perhaps. Sometime in the next couple of weeks. She's exploring the servers of Titan just now, I think. I haven't talked since she left for out-system. She sounded very excited.'

'Say hello to her,' Fist told her. 'Send her to see us. When she's back!'

'I don't know when that'll be. But yes, I will do.' There was something approaching desolation in her voice.

'Goodnight, Lestak,' said Grey, with the soft, final force of a dismissal.

'Goodnight,' she replied abstractedly. Then she gathered herself. 'Goodnight, Fist. And Jack. Think about what Grey's said. Remember who I serve. I'm sure I'll see you again. Please don't let it be in my professional capacity. I've got enough on my plate as it is.'

And then she was gone, and it was just the three of them.

'What are you going to do now, Jack?' asked Grey.

'You'll find out, won't you? Even if I don't tell you.'

'No, Jack. I'll let you be.'

'Really? That'll be a first.'

'You deserve some peace of your own, Jack. You always have done. If it wasn't for – everything – I wouldn't have found you again when you came back to Station. I was a victim of circumstances as much as you were; and you were the only tool I had to hand. I'm sorry for that.'

'Sorry for using me?'

'Sorry I was placed in a position that forced me to.' Grey put a hand on Jack's shoulder. 'Let it all go. We've got the best world we can have, for now – and new lives for you and Fist. I'm glad that this is how it is, glad that all's settled down.'

'Glad that you're back in power. That the people of Station have accepted it all so easily.'

'East is managing her audience wonderfully.'

'Always one more string to pull.'

'We're all more likely to survive now we're working together, not against each other. That's all we ever wanted. But I'm not going to convince you, am I? So it's time for us to go, at last.'

'I'll find my own way out.'

'All right, Jack. And really – this is as perfect a world as we can ever have. This is a heaven, of sorts. Let it be.' Another soft touch of his hand, then he was gone.

'I can breathe again,' said Jack, letting out a long sigh. 'I always so want to believe him, you know.'

'That's hardly surprising.' Fist hopped off his chair. 'He did do a lot for you, over the years.'

'Always on his terms. Perhaps that's all that gods can ever do.'

'Well, he's gone now.' Fist sighed. 'No more battles to fight.'

'No one shooting at us, at any rate. And very little left to fight back with. Everyone saw you burn your weapon systems out killing Harry, and East's taken back most of her gifts to me.'

'You're going to ignore everything Grey and Lestak said, aren't you?'

Jack stood up. 'Come on, Fist. Let's go.'

'Seeing Andrea tonight?'

'If her fetch stabilisation work lets her. If not, there's my father.'

'Assuming of course your mum's persuaded him that you're not a complete shit. And we've got to track down Mr Stabs.'

'I do hope we can get him rehoused in a better body.' Jack bent down and put his arms out. Fist hopped into them, nestling snugly in the crook of his elbow. 'You're a lot heavier now, Fist.'

'Well, I'm real, aren't I?'

'You always have been.'

Fist laughed. 'I suppose so. And for all that he's a manipulative old shit, Grey was right about one thing. We might not have entirely won, Jack, but we certainly didn't lose. Kingdom was the bad guy, and Harry was pretty fucking evil too. We stopped them both. And you're the big Totality fan – we helped them, and the dead too. You should take some pleasure in that, at least.'

'Maybe.' He half-smiled. 'It does sound better coming from you than it did from Grey.'

They were at the door. The lights in the room hushed to darkness. Jack turned, and with Fist looked out over the city.

'Home, at last.'

The ghost of a hunting dog nuzzled at them, before blurring and vanishing. Then Jack and Fist were gone too. The dark room was silent, and the city beyond it seemed to be at peace.

ACKNOWLEDGEMENTS

This book was redrafted many times, and along the way benefited hugely from some great early readers. So, first of all deepest thanks to Alys Sterling, Dave Clements, Neil Williamson, Nick Moulton and Zali Krishna for your very thoughtful and profoundly practical critiques.

An early version of the opening chapters went through the Milford SF Writers' workshop in 2010 – a particular thank you to Liz Williams, an inspirational presence over the years, and everyone else who was there. Huge gratitude also to everyone who's been part of the London Cat Herd writers' group who, over almost a decade, have taught me so much.

This wouldn't be the book it is if I hadn't played with the Stella Maris Drone Orchestra and Graan, who together helped me learn how to take advantage of the moment and improvise as I was going along. Danke schön, dröen böys! Thanks to Lloyd Davis and the Tuttle Club for so many excellent digital conversations. And – of course – all the inspiration from Andy Cox and all at TTA Press has been absolutely invaluable.

I couldn't have pulled *Crashing Heaven* into its final shape without the help and support of my most excellent agent, Susan Armstrong at Conville & Walsh, and editor, Simon Spanton. And without my wife Heather Lindsley – who was there from start to end with everything from nice cups of tea to ferociously insightful critiques, always at just the right time – Rory and the rest of my family, I wouldn't have been able to write it at all.

Thank you all.

BRINGING NEWS FROM OUR WORLDS TO YOURS . . .

Want your news daily?

The Gollancz blog has instant updates on the hottest SF and Fantasy books.

Prefer your updates monthly?

Sign up for our in-depth newsletter.

www.gollancz.co.uk

Follow us 🐦 @gollancz

Find us 🅕 facebook.com/GollanczPublishing

Classic SF as you've never read it before.

Visit the SF Gateway to find out more!

www.sfgateway.com